'The entire ho...
am your mistre...

'There is a solution to your unfortunate situation,' Gabriel said blandly.

'What?'

'You could become my mistress in fact as well as reputation.'

She stared at him, her lips parted in shock. Then the colour drained out of her face. Her mouth worked for a few seconds before she managed to utter a word.

'How could you?' she whispered. 'I was good enough to be your wife. But now… No! *Never!*' She sprang to her feet, knocking over the stool. 'Is this your idea of revenge? Because I will *never* let you humiliate me like that!'

'It's my price for providing you with safe passage back to England,' he said. 'That *is* what you want from me, isn't it?'

Dear Reader

The stories in the **City of Flames** trilogy take place during the reign of Charles II. This was an era of great colour, drama and variety. The King scandalised some of his subjects with his many mistresses, but his reign also saw the emergence of modern banking among the London goldsmiths. Actresses appeared for the first time in London theatres, while members of the Royal Society met every week to witness scientific experiments.

Athena Fairchild, Colonel Jakob Balston and the Duke of Kilverdale are cousins, but they've led very different lives. Athena grew up in England, Jakob in Sweden, and Kilverdale spent his childhood exiled in France as a result of the war between Charles I and Parliament.

The cousins' romances take place in various locations, but London is at the heart of the **City of Flames** trilogy. The cousins all meet the one they love in the city—although Athena's happiness is destroyed almost before it begins.

Athena's story, *The Defiant Mistress,* begins in May 1666 in Venice, and the events span the rest of the summer. Jakob's story, *The Abducted Heiress,* and Kilverdale's story, *The Vagabond Duchess,* both begin in London at the start of September 1666. In the early hours of the morning of 2nd September a fire in Pudding Lane will burn out of control...

While I was writing these books I fell in love with the characters and their world. I hope you enjoy reading their stories as much as I enjoyed writing them.

Claire

THE DEFIANT MISTRESS

Claire Thornton

MILLS & BOON®

All the characters in this book have no existence outside the imagination of the author, and have no relation whatsoever to anyone bearing the same name or names. They are not even distantly inspired by any individual known or unknown to the author, and all the incidents are pure invention.

First published in Great Britain 2005
Harlequin Mills & Boon Limited,
Eton House, 18-24 Paradise Road, Richmond, Surrey TW9 1SR

© Claire Thornton 2005

ISBN 0 263 84376 9

Set in Times Roman 10½ on 12 pt.
04-0705-89313

Printed and bound in Spain
by Litografia Rosés S.A., Barcelona

Claire Thornton grew up in Sussex. It is a family legend that her ancestors in the county were involved in smuggling. She was a shy little girl, and she was fascinated by the idea that she might be distantly related to bold and daring adventurers of the past—who were probably not shy! When she grew up she studied history at York University, and discovered that smugglers were often brutal men whose main ambition was to make money. This was disappointing, but she still feels justified in believing in—and writing about—the romantic and noble heroes of earlier ages. Claire has also written under the name of Alice Thornton.

Previous novels by Claire Thornton:

RAVEN'S HONOUR
GIFFORD'S LADY

Look for Jakob's story in
THE ABDUCTED HEIRESS
Coming in September 2005,
in Historical Romance

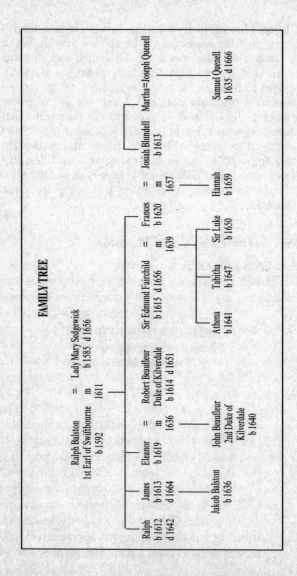

FAMILY TREE

Ralph Balston
1st Earl of Swiftbourne
b 1592
= m 1611
Lady Mary Sedgewick
b 1585 d 1656

Ralph
b 1612
d 1642

James
b 1613
d 1664

Eleanor
b 1619
= m 1636
Robert Beaufleur
Duke of Kilverdale
b 1614 d 1651

Sir Edmund Fairchild
b 1615 d 1656
= m 1639
Frances
b 1620
= m 1657
Josiah Blundell
b 1613

Martha = Joseph Quenell

Jakob Balston
b 1636

John Beaufleur
2nd Duke of
Kilverdale
b 1640

Athena
b 1641

Tabitha
b 1647

Sir Luke
b 1650

Hannah
b 1659

Samuel Quenell
b 1635 d 1666

Prologue

London, June 1658

Tonight a maid…tomorrow a bride.

Athena's heart sang with expectation. Her mood was as sunny as the afternoon as she stepped lightly along Cheapside, slipping with practised ease through the crowds that thronged one of London's grandest thoroughfares. Her route took her past some of the City's most renowned silk mercers' and goldsmiths' shops, but she didn't spare them a second glance. She had finished her own less exalted shopping and she was on her way home.

Tomorrow she would be Gabriel's wife.

She experienced a brief *frisson* of tension as she contemplated her wedding night—she could not help but feel a little nervous at what some of her wifely duties would entail—but she loved and trusted Gabriel. Whenever he held her in his arms or kissed her he always tempered his male passion with exquisite tenderness for her innocence. In fact—she skipped out of the path of a sedan chair carried by two sweating porters—in fact, sometimes Gabriel was a little *too* tender. One of the chairmen turned his head to look appreciatively after her, but she was used to men's admiring glances and she didn't pay any attention. Her thoughts were too full of her coming wedding night. A quiver of illicit anticipation stirred deep inside her as she imagined how much more passionately Gabriel would kiss her when he no longer had to keep such a tight rein upon his desire. Tomorrow night she would find out.

She turned off the broad expanse of Cheapside into a narrower side street. Here, even in the summer, the houses with their projecting upper floors were too close together to allow the mid-afternoon sun to penetrate all the way to the ground. The shade provided a respite from the glare of bright sunlight, but only an illusion of coolness. The air was hot and still. Athena's skin felt gritty with the grime of the city.

She pushed a strand of damp blonde hair away from her face and turned her thoughts to the supper she meant to prepare for her aunt. It was the last night she would spend under Aunt Kitty's roof and Athena wanted to show her appreciation for the older woman's generosity and kindness. She had already bought most of the ingredients she needed early that morning. This second shopping trip had been to fetch the few items she'd originally forgotten because her mind had been too full of Gabriel.

Well, for the rest of the afternoon and evening she would not let so much as one stray thought of Gabriel cross her mind. She would concentrate only on preparing the most splendid supper imaginable for Aunt Kitty—and her reward…her reward would be to lie in bed and think of Gabriel all night! Athena couldn't suppress the saucy smile that tugged at her lips at the prospect. Her whole body hummed with happiness as she stepped into the passage that led to the small courtyard in front of her aunt's lodgings.

'Hello, Athena.' A man's voice spoke suddenly from the shadows.

She jumped, her stomach lurching with surprise, but at first she was startled rather than afraid.

'You naughty girl,' he said, chiding her in a repellently indulgent tone. 'What a tease you are.'

Samuel?

Horrified disbelief held Athena immobile for several seconds. She recognised that hateful voice, but she'd hoped never to hear it again. Samuel didn't belong in London. He had no place in her new life. How had he found her?

He moved into the light, his glittering eyes roaming greedily over her body. Her skin crawled at his lascivious interest.

'Such a tease,' he said thickly. 'Have you been getting impatient for me to find you, sweetling?'

He reached towards her.

She jerked backwards, bumping her basket against the wall. The impact jolted her into action. She spun around, driven by a panic-stricken need to run as far and as fast as possible.

Samuel lunged forward. He grabbed her wrist and pulled her close to him.

'Don't run,' he said, his breath scalding her cheek. 'I've been patient, but now it's time you came to heel.'

'No!' Athena desperately tried to break free. 'Let me go! I won't marry you!'

'Yes, you will.' He twisted her arm painfully, punishing her for her resistance. 'It's arranged. Your father approves. Your mother—'

'Josiah Blundell is *not* my father.' Athena continued to struggle. 'He's my *step*father. My *real* father would never force me to marry *you*.' Her voice shook with scorn and contempt. 'He would have protected me from you.'

Samuel hissed angrily. 'Your fine father is dead. He was nothing. *I* am Cromwell's friend,' he boasted.

'I doubt he even knows your name!' Athena mocked him, too angry to be cautious.

Samuel's uncle, and her stepfather, Josiah Blundell, was indeed Cromwell's friend. She knew that Josiah did have

some influence with Cromwell. But she was sure the same
could not be said for the twenty-three-year-old Samuel. He
was an indulged only son, and Josiah Blundell's favoured
only nephew, but he could not lay claim to any great achievement in his own right.

'He does, you bitch!' Samuel's grip tightened cruelly. 'And
if you don't mind your manners, you'll find out how much.'

'Leave me alone.' She flailed wildly at him with her basket, ignoring the pain in the arm he held as she tried to kick
her heels against his shins.

'A woman should show more respect for her husband.'

'I'll *never* marry you,' Athena panted. 'I'm going to marry
someone else.'

Samuel swore vilely and forced her along the passage and
across the courtyard into her aunt's lodgings. 'Be quiet, or the
old woman will pay,' he threatened her.

Athena stopped struggling, appalled at the possibility Samuel might take his spite out on Aunt Kitty. He shoved her
across the threshold and into her aunt's parlour. Then he released her.

Athena stumbled forward, nearly tripping over her skirts.
She righted herself and whirled around, frantically searching
the room for her aunt.

'She's not here,' said Samuel. 'A little precaution I'm sure
won't be necessary. She's come to no harm. As long as you
behave yourself, she'll be back here soon enough.'

Athena stared at Samuel. He had wanted her from the first
moment he'd seen her, and all his life he'd been given what
he wanted. Fright and anger jangled through her. She had
done everything in her power to escape him. It seemed mon-
strous that he should have found her now, on the very eve of
her wedding.

Most of Athena's life had been lived in the shadow of the
war between King and Parliament but, though she had heard

dreadful stories of battles and sieges elsewhere, the conflict had not directly impinged on her childhood. That had changed in 1656 when she was fifteen. Her father had died and she'd discovered that her family's situation was more precarious than she'd realised. Sir Edmund Fairchild had secretly sympathised with the royalist cause, but he'd trod a skilful path through the volatile rivalries of his predominantly parliamentarian neighbours. On Sir Edmund's death, the Fairchild estate had passed to Athena's younger brother, Luke, but the new baronet was only six years old. The Parliamentarian leaders of the county looked covetously upon Fairchild Manor.

To safeguard her family and preserve her son's inheritance, Athena's mother had remarried eight months after Sir Edmund's death. She had chosen as her second husband one of their closest neighbours, Josiah Blundell. Josiah was a man of stern, puritan feeling—but there was no doubt he held Athena's mother in stiff-backed affection. Upon their marriage he had promised to preserve the young baronet's inheritance and protect the rest of the Fairchild family. So far he had been as good as his word—except in one respect. From the first he had been in favour of a match between his nephew, Samuel, and Athena.

Athena had done everything she could to change her stepfather's mind. But Samuel only ever revealed his most charming face to his uncle, and Josiah could not understand Athena's objections to the marriage. At last, in desperation, she had fled from her home in Kent to the bustling anonymity of London. She'd taken refuge with the widowed sister of her father's brother-in-law, a distant family connection she was sure was unknown to Josiah and Samuel. To make it even harder to track her down, she had altered her name from Athena Frances Fairchild to the less memorable Frances Child and pretended she had no family apart from Kitty.

But now it seemed all her efforts to make a new life had been in vain. Samuel had found her.

She stepped back, moving her basket instinctively in front of her. It was a flimsy shield and an inadequate weapon, but it was all she had. She lifted her chin and forced words through her fear-tightened throat.

'You can't make me marry you,' she said. 'You can drag me to the altar, but you can't make me say the words.'

'Yes, I can.' There was an expression of gloating self-satisfaction in Samuel's eyes. 'You will say the words willingly.'

'Never.' Fear chilled her. He was so horribly confident. She had to get away from him.

Athena backed up another step. Samuel stood in front of her. From the corner of her eye she could see the doorway on her left. She didn't dare look in that direction in case she signalled her intentions to him. She took another hesitant step backwards, looking down at the basket she held in front of her. Suddenly she hurled it at Samuel and made a dash for the door.

She saw Moses Spink, Samuel's friend, too late to avoid capture. She struggled wildly in Spink's arms, hardly aware that Samuel was speaking to her. At last his words penetrated her angry, panic-clouded mind.

'…unless you want to see Vaughan hanged for treason.'

'What?' she gasped, lifting her head to stare at him through a veil of untidy blonde hair. 'What sick nonsense are you talking?'

'Your noble bridegroom is a spy for Charles Stuart,' Samuel informed her triumphantly. 'I have one of his letters to prove it. He is a traitor—and here is the evidence that will hang him.'

'You're lying.' But despite her bold denial, doubt crept into Athena's heart. Gabriel Vaughan was the third son of the Marquis of Halross. As the youngest son he had to make his own way in life and he'd chosen to apprentice himself to a City merchant. But he'd once mentioned to Athena that, during the Wars, his father had fought for the King. A picture of

Gabriel rose powerfully in Athena's mind. He was so full of glorious male vigour, so high-couraged and honourable. Had he decided to follow in his father's tradition and take up the cause of the exiled King?

'See for yourself,' said Samuel, as if reading her thoughts.

Spink released her. She stepped out of his reach with a proud toss of her head, but she couldn't prevent her hands from trembling when she took the tattered fragment of letter Samuel held out. She knew Gabriel's writing. He had composed a sonnet for her a month ago. He had presented it to her with a flush of hopeful male awkwardness, not quite at ease with the romantic gesture; but Athena had been so enchanted with him that soon he had puffed out his chest with pride in his lover's skill.

Now she recognised his confident initials signing the letter and the sentences above that clearly proved his involvement in a plot to kill Cromwell and restore Charles II to the throne.

'Your choice is simple.' Samuel's voice came to her from a distance, as if her head was underwater. She felt as if she was drowning. 'Marry me tomorrow in place of your traitorous bridegroom—or Vaughan will hang.'

Athena looked into his eyes and knew it was not an idle threat. If Samuel showed this evidence to Josiah, her stepfather would go straight to Cromwell—and then Gabriel would die. One of Athena's uncles had been hanged by the parliamentarians after the Battle of Worcester—simply because he had fought at the King's side. If an officer in the King's army could be treated so dishonourably, then a King's spy would receive even less quarter if he fell into his enemies' hands. Athena could not bear Gabriel to suffer a traitor's death.

'If I marry you, will you promise that no harm will come to Gabriel?' she asked in an unsteady voice.

'You used Vaughan to make me jealous, you minx.' Samuel stroked her cheek in a gesture that was an obscene mock-ery of true tenderness. 'A lively spirit is attractive in a woman. But you must know when to put an end to the teasing games. Vaughan is a fool twice over. For plotting against Cromwell and for not realising you only flirted with him to provoke me. But I'm the one you really want. If you come willingly to my bed tomorrow, I won't accuse Vaughan of treason. Crom-well's too well protected for the plot to succeed, and there's no need to punish Vaughan for being vain enough to think he caught your heart.'

It was not the wedding day of Athena's dreams. She'd left home to avoid marriage to Samuel. She had never once con-sidered the possibility that there would come a time when she would willingly take vows with him.

She wasn't willing now, but the image of Gabriel hang-ing limp in the hangman's noose tormented her. No matter what the cost to herself, she couldn't let such a fate over-take him.

After the brief ceremony was completed, Samuel took her to what she assumed was an inn. Athena hadn't thought this far ahead. Samuel had made a pretence that there was noth-ing unusual about the marriage. Athena had slept in her own bed the previous night—though Spink had guarded the door. She hadn't been able to sleep from fear and worry. She'd wondered where Gabriel was and what he was doing. She'd longed to send him a message to warn him, but with Spink on guard there was no chance of doing so. Besides, she was terrified that, if she made any attempt to contact Gabriel, Samuel would take cruel revenge.

In all her pacing and fretting she hadn't allowed herself to think about what would happen after the wedding. It had been too dreadful to contemplate. And perhaps she'd hoped that by some miracle she would still be rescued at the last minute from her nightmare. But as Samuel led her upstairs her fears changed focus and became more acute. It was no longer Gabriel's uncertain future that was at the forefront of her mind, but her own present predicament. The harsh reality of her situation threatened to overwhelm her. Did she truly have the courage to keep her end of the bargain with Samuel? What would happen to Gabriel if she failed?

She tried to speak, but her throat was so tight with fear she could barely force words past her cold lips.

'Where are you taking me?' she whispered.

'In here.' Samuel opened a door and pushed her inside.

Athena's gaze locked on the large bed. Horror congealed in the pit of her stomach. This was what Samuel wanted. What he had wanted since he had first laid eyes upon her. This was why he had married her.

'Remember,' he said in her ear. 'A willing wife in my bed or Vaughan dies a traitor's death.'

The church had been stripped of all its ornaments. Even its name had been changed to satisfy the puritan dislike of idolatry. No longer St Mary's, it had become simply a public meeting-place—but it still *felt* like a church. Whispers echoed beneath the high, vaulted ceiling.

Gabriel's stomach clenched with tension. It was cool inside the building, but his palms were damp with perspiration. He laid his hands against his thighs and tried to ignore the increasing restlessness of his companions. He could hear the questions they asked one another, the growing doubt and disapproval in the softly muttered comments.

'I *said* she was no good match for him!' Lucy's voice rose clear above the rest.

'Hush!' Lady Parfitt reprimanded her daughter.

Gabriel gritted his teeth. Where was Frances? Where was his bride?

The minister caught his eye and Gabriel forced his lips into a confident smile while his mind seethed with questions.

What could have delayed her? Was she hurt? His chest expanded as he dragged in a deep, anxious breath. He wanted to rush out of the church in search of her. It required all his self-control to remain still.

The church door banged open. Everyone turned to look. It wasn't Frances. The new arrival was a nondescript stranger. He obviously had nothing to do with the wedding. The guests lost interest in him. They all focused their attention on Gabriel. He saw the curiosity, worry and, in some cases, morbid satisfaction in their faces.

Everyone in the church was there on his behalf. Only one member of Gabriel's real family was present, but that didn't matter. Gabriel had spent seven years apprenticed to the wealthy City merchant, Sir Thomas Parfitt. During the first two years of his apprenticeship Gabriel had lived in Sir Thomas's household, treated almost as an additional member of the family. Then Sir Thomas had sent him to the Tuscan port of Livorno. For the next five years Gabriel had been trained to look after Sir Thomas's trading interests in Italy. Now Gabriel was back in London, his apprenticeship complete. He was twenty-two years old, a member of both the Levant Company and the Mercers' Company, and a freeman of the City of London. And he was getting married. Sir Thomas had made no secret of his disapproval of this improvident match, but he had not withheld his support from his young friend.

And now the bride was late. Very late.

Gabriel decided to send a messenger to her lodgings. Unlike him, Frances had no close friends or relatives in the city except for the aunt with whom she lived. If Frances was ill, her aunt would not be able to leave her. In her distress, perhaps the woman had not thought to send a message to the church.

Gabriel caught the eye of one of Sir Thomas's younger apprentices, intending to ask him—

'I have a message for Gabriel Vaughan!' The stranger's voice rang mockingly from the back of the church, startling everyone.

'I'm Vaughan.' Gabriel faced the man, his heart thudding with anxiety. 'Have you come from Miss Child? Is she ill?'

'Aye, my message is from the lady herself,' the stranger confirmed.

Gabriel had no idea who the man was, but he expected the fellow would approach him to deliver the message. Instead, the stranger kept his station at the back of the church, grinning at the curious wedding guests. Gabriel started to walk down the aisle towards him.

'Miss Frances begs your indulgence—but it's not convenient for her to wed today,' announced the stranger. 'Just yesterday she had a better offer from a gentleman with a bigger purse and a bigger…'

The crude words rolled over Gabriel. He didn't hear the gasps of shock and outrage from his friends. His confident stride faltered. For a few moments he was aware only that Frances had deliberately not come to the church. Frances didn't want to marry him.

Stunned disbelief filled him. How could this be? Frances loved him. He knew she did. His unfocused gaze sharpened. He moved forward, intent on asking Frances's messenger where she was. If he spoke to her, he was sure he could sort out the confusion. Frances was only seventeen. If she wasn't ready for the serious commitment of marriage he would wait for her. He'd clearly been over hasty in his plans.

Then he saw that the stranger was backing towards the door, his lips still stretched into that same, unpleasant grin. Gabriel suddenly remembered and understood the full import of the message he'd been given.

Savage fury surged through him. 'You're lying!' he roared and leapt for the stranger.

The fellow had anticipated Gabriel's rage and fled through the church doors. Gabriel raced after him into the glaring sunlight. He seized the stranger just before he escaped into a narrow alley and slammed the man against the wall, his hands locked about a grimy throat.

'Careful, lordling!' the stranger croaked. 'Squeeze harder an' I'll *gut* you!'

Gabriel felt the prod of a dagger against his belly. The blade pierced his clothes and cut his skin. He ignored it.

'You're lying,' he said through clenched jaw. 'Frances didn't send that message. Where is she? What have you done to her?'

'I haven't done anything to her,' the stranger replied. 'My purse isn't deep enough for the likes of her. But she's found herself a nice rich protector now. He's wealthy beyond her dreams—' The man gasped as Gabriel's grip on his throat tightened. He retaliated by pressing his knife harder against Gabriel's stomach. 'Not so tight, coxcomb. Your guts'll make a nasty mess o' those fine clothes of yours.'

Gabriel relaxed his grasp and shifted his weight as if he intended to step away. The stranger reduced the pressure on the blade. The next second Gabriel seized his wrist and spun him around in a shoulder-wrenching hold. He forced the man's arm up behind his back and thrust him against the wall, grinding his face against the plaster.

'Where's Frances?' he demanded harshly.

'I'll show you,' the man choked. 'No need to break my arm. I'll show you.'

'What is this place?' Gabriel balked, looking around in displeasure.

From the outside he'd assumed he'd been led to an alehouse. From the inside it was clear that the building was both more sumptuous and a lot less respectable than he'd anticipated. He heard laughter and raucous voices behind one half-open door. Another door crashed open and a woman emerged, her head turned as she giggled teasingly at the occupant of the room. She was barely wearing her shift. The garment had slid down both shoulders, only her hands clutched to her breasts prevented it from falling off completely.

'Frances isn't here.' Gabriel turned to leave. 'You've brought me on a fool's errand.'

His guide blocked his way, grinning with disagreeable self-assurance. Gabriel felt a stab of fear, not for himself, but for Frances. He'd been unwise to follow a stranger into an unfamiliar part of the City, but he was confident of his ability to extricate himself from trouble. Frances had grown up in the country. By her own account she had come to London less than a year ago to live with her aunt after the death of her father. She was still unversed in the many hazards of the sinful capital.

'What have you done to her?' Fear roughened his voice.

He made an involuntary movement towards the man and saw, just in time, the dull glint of the knife.

'Upstairs, lordling.'

Gabriel's heart thumped with apprehension as he mounted the narrow stairs.

'In here.' A thump between his shoulder blades directed him into a small chamber. 'Now look here,' said his guide in a low voice. 'And keep quiet if you want to know the truth about your virtuous Frances.'

A spyhole!

Gabriel bit back a curse. What kind of fool was he being played for? He took a step backwards and felt a dagger against his side. He'd half-turned towards the man, intending to deal with his impertinence once and for all, when he heard a muffled voice he thought he recognised.

Shocked and disbelieving, he put his eye to the spyhole. Frances? Dear God, it *was* Frances!

Gabriel pressed his hand flat against the wall as he watched her accept a wine posset from a man he'd never seen before. Frances drank and handed the vessel back to her companion. The man made a show of turning the cup so he could drink from the very place her lips had touched. He spoke, complimenting her on her beauty and Frances smiled at him!

Gabriel's hand closed into a fist, his knuckles pressing into the plaster as he saw Frances lift her face to be kissed. The man's lips touched her cheek and then her mouth. Frances laid her hands on his shoulders, inviting his liberties.

A few moments later the man turned Frances and began to unlace her bodice. She allowed him to remove it and made no protest when he fumbled at the neckline of her chemise. The man exposed her breast and bent his head to lay his mouth against the soft flesh.

Gabriel broke free from his horrified paralysis. He reared up and around, nearly blind with outrage and the pain of betrayed love. So intent was he on confronting his traitorous bride and her lover that he'd forgotten his companion.

The man hit Gabriel neatly on the back of the head with the hilt of his dagger.

Gabriel's awareness clouded. He struggled to remain conscious, but his knees sagged and he slid painfully into darkness. The last thing he heard was a woman's mocking laughter.

Athena sat on a straight-backed chair in the dark, waiting with sick dread for Samuel to come to bed. Her cold fingers twisted and curled ceaselessly around each other as she thought of all that Samuel had done to her in the two weeks since their wedding day. Soon he would join her again. Waves of revulsion surged through her. She twisted her fingers against each other until her hands hurt.

When she had fled from Samuel ten months earlier, it had never occurred to her that her flight would eventually end with her back in Kent and married to him. But at least Gabriel and Aunt Kitty were safe. To Athena's huge relief, Aunt Kitty had been restored unharmed to her home a couple of days after the wedding. Athena didn't place much faith in Samuel's integrity, but he had kept his promise where Aunt Kitty was concerned. She had to believe that he would also keep his word not to inform on Gabriel.

Samuel veered wildly in the things he said about Gabriel. Sometimes he claimed Athena had only allowed Gabriel to court her to provoke his—Samuel's—jealousy. At other times he said things that indicated he did know that Athena really loved Gabriel. On those occasions it was easy to believe that Samuel had married her primarily to punish her for rejecting him, rather than because he wanted her.

Athena found a certain, terrible, comfort in her conviction that Samuel had married her to punish her. It meant that Gabriel was relatively safe from arrest. After all, if Gabriel *was* seized and executed, Samuel would no longer have any power over her. Athena had repeated that simple fact to herself over and over again during the past fourteen days. She was keeping Gabriel safe. It was the only thing that had enabled her to endure her new life. Her head jerked up, her breath catching in her throat, as she heard footsteps outside the door. She squeezed her fingers cruelly together in anticipation of Samuel's entrance, then realised what she was doing and forced herself to fold her hands quietly in a semblance of serenity. She would not give Samuel the satisfaction of knowing how much she feared him.

The room was suddenly illuminated by the flickering light of a single candle. Samuel walked across the room to stand over her.

'Sitting in the dark? I've married an economical wench,' he said sarcastically.

'The light strains my eyes,' she replied in a low voice.

'You were thinking about your lover!' he accused her. 'Dreaming that he might come and claim you!'

'No.' Late at night, when Samuel slept, Athena yearned for such a miraculous rescue. But she'd already discovered how angry Samuel became when he thought of her with Gabriel. His charade that she'd only trifled with Gabriel to incite his jealousy had worn very thin.

'You're lying, you whore. You look so sweet and innocent, but beneath that beautiful face you have the heart of a harlot.'

Athena gazed slightly to one side of his face, trying to let his tirade wash over her. She was starting to learn how to survive his verbal abuse. Let him rant and rage and do as he pleased. Eventually he would go away, lose interest, or simply fall asleep. She could survive.

He hated it when she didn't respond to him. What he had always craved most from the moment he'd first laid eyes on her was her attention—her smiles and favour for preference, but at the very least her attention.

'He's gone to Turkey!' he jeered.

'What?' Athena's eyes jerked to Samuel's face.

'Your faithless former bridegroom. He never turned up for the wedding, you know. I had him watched. If you'd failed to keep our little bargain, I would have had him arrested. But he doesn't even know you jilted him because he never went to the church! He never meant to marry you!'

'I don't believe you!' Athena could not—would not—believe Samuel's cruel claim. Gabriel loved her. She knew he did.

Samuel laughed. 'Did you really think you meant more to him than a pleasant interlude? He sailed in one of Parfitt's ships for Turkey two days ago.'

'Turkey?' Athena whispered. She knew that Sir Thomas Parfitt's trading interests extended to the Turkish empire and perhaps beyond. Gabriel had often talked about how much he'd enjoyed his years in Italy. Could it be true…?

'You said he was plotting against Cromwell.' She tried to make sense of how the letter incriminating Gabriel in the plot against the parliamentarian leader fitted with the news that he had sailed for Turkey.

'Fickle noblemen. They treat everything as a game.' Samuel dismissed Athena's comment with a disdainful gesture. 'You're lucky I found you in time. Otherwise you'd have been left standing alone at the church. The whole world would have known you for a foolish maid, easily duped by a faithless cavalier. Come to bed, wife.'

Athena did not protest. Since their wedding day Samuel had required no more from her in bed than her passive acceptance of him, and it was over quicker that way.

Later she lay on her side, listening to him snore behind her, silent tears running down her cheeks. Until tonight she had still preserved a glimmer of hope that Gabriel might be looking for her. That somehow there was a way out of the nightmare her life had become. Of course such hopes were not logical. If Gabriel found her, it would put him at risk and her sacrifice on his behalf might end up being for nothing. But still she'd hoped for a miracle: that her love for Gabriel and his for her would triumph over Samuel's obsessive desire to possess her.

But Gabriel had gone to Turkey. Despite her longing to believe otherwise, she was already half-certain Samuel's story was true. She knew Sir Thomas Parfitt traded there. Gabriel was adventurous and ambitious. He would surely see this new venture as an exciting opportunity to improve his fortune. Besides, it had been Gabriel's presence in England, his vulnerability to arrest by Cromwell's agents, that had given Samuel his hold over her. Why would Samuel tell her Gabriel had left, and thus willingly relinquish his power over her if it wasn't true?

Athena swallowed an anguished sob. All her efforts to protect Gabriel had been meaningless. By now he must be beyond Cromwell's retribution. And he hadn't even gone to the church to marry her. She had pictured him so many times waiting for her, worrying about her, trying to find her—and now it seemed he didn't even know or care that she hadn't turned up.

Her throat burned with stifled grief. It had all been for nothing. And now she no longer had the thought of Gabriel's safety to sustain her in her nightmarish marriage. She had nothing at all. She opened her eyes and stared into the darkness at the bleak future ahead of her. Soon Samuel would destroy her spirit. She could already feel her self-confidence seeping away day by day. Soon she would be so browbeaten she would no longer have the will to resist.

She could not let that happen. Slowly her despair hardened into cold determination. Gabriel had left England. It made no difference to his safety whether she stayed with Samuel or not. She had run away before, she could do it again. And this time she would make sure Samuel never found her.

But…but…

A small doubt slipped into her mind. What if Gabriel came back to England after she'd left? Would Samuel inform on him just for spite? She bit her lip—no matter how inconstant Gabriel had proved, she couldn't bear the thought he might hang. Before she left she would find and destroy the fragment of letter Samuel had shown her that proved Gabriel's complicity in the plot against Cromwell. Then she would disappear.

And she would never again be any man's dupe.

Chapter One

English Convent, Bruges, April 1666

'What do you mean—she's not here?' the Duke of Kilverdale's voice rose in angry disbelief.

'Exactly what I said, your Grace,' the Abbess replied. 'I am afraid your cousin is no longer here at the convent.'

The Duke's black eyebrows snapped together. 'For the past seven years my mother has made generous contributions to your order,' he said. 'With the clear understanding that Athena would be free to live here peacefully under your protection. Why did you send her away?'

'I did not send her away,' the Abbess replied. 'She chose to leave on an errand of mercy.'

'To go where?'

'Venice—'

'What!' Kilverdale leapt to his feet. At six feet tall he towered over the seated Abbess. He was dressed in the height of fashion in silk brocade and a magnificent black periwig, but his costly garments could not disguise the underlying power in his lean body. Nor could the profusion of black curls, which framed his face and tumbled about his shoulders, soften the

somewhat predatory appearance of his hawkish features. The Abbess considered him a dangerous man and a far from suitable visitor to her convent, but in the circumstances she could hardly refuse to speak with him.

The Duke's mother and Athena's mother were sisters. Seven years ago the widowed Duchess of Kilverdale and her son had been living in exile in France. When Athena ran away from Samuel, she had made the perilous journey to France to beg for her aunt's protection. In early 1659 the Duchess had brought her niece to Bruges, to live as a guest within the English convent. A year later Charles II regained his throne. The Kilverdales had returned to England, but the Duchess had continued to give generous donations to the convent and the Duke had come to Bruges at irregular intervals to meet with his cousin.

'Kindly allow me to finish,' the Abbess said, before Kilverdale could say any more. She disliked his obvious intention to intimidate her in her own quarters. 'Mrs Quenell left here of her own free will as, indeed, she first arrived here.'

Kilverdale raised a sardonic eyebrow, clearly unimpressed.

The Abbess strove for patience and continued. 'Several weeks ago the wife of one of the undersecretaries to the English Ambassador in Venice arrived in Bruges. The young woman was brought to us in great distress. We discovered she was urgently seeking to join her husband in Venice—apparently she had not been kindly treated by her husband's kinfolk in his absence. Mrs Quenell was much moved by her plight and offered to accompany her to Venice as her companion and guide—'

'*Guide?*' Kilverdale exploded. 'You allowed my cousin, who has not been outside the security of these walls for seven years, to go gallivanting across Europe with only a foolish wench for company—and you say she's a *guide!* Where were your wits, madam?'

'They are accompanied by the manservant the young

woman brought with her from England and Mrs Quenell's own maid. In addition, they are being escorted by a local gentleman of good family who is on his way to study at the university of Padua,' the Abbess snapped, out of all patience with her noble visitor.

The Duke's muttered response was barely audible, but supremely uncomplimentary.

'Your cousin is a woman of great resource and common sense and I have every confidence she will reach her destination unharmed and without difficulty,' the Abbess retorted. 'Don't forget she managed to make her way safely all the way from England to find your mother in France when she was only seventeen.'

'She cut off her hair, dyed it brown, and pretended to be a boy!'

'A sensible precaution for a woman travelling alone. She came to no harm. She has often entertained me with the story of her journey.'

'Entertaining!' Kilverdale snorted scathingly. 'Yes, and it is very entertaining for me to come to Flanders to tell her that her husband is dead and it's now possible for me to escort her back to England—only to find she isn't here!'

'She knows her husband is dead. She received a letter from your mother just before she left for Venice.'

'She knows? Well, why the devil didn't she wait for me to come and fetch her back?'

'It is weeks since she heard the news,' the Abbess said drily.

Kilverdale scowled. 'I was preoccupied with other business,' he said. 'I'm here now.'

'So you are.' The Abbess watched as he took a couple of glowering circuits around the room.

He stopped and drew in a deep, annoyed breath. 'I'll just have to follow her to Venice and fetch her back from there,' he announced. 'Damned troublesome females!'

He strode over to the door and left without a backward glance. The Abbess allowed herself to relax a little. The mercurial Duke could be a most unsettling visitor. Less than thirty seconds later she heard his decisive footsteps once more approaching her room.

He stepped over the threshold and looked straight at the Abbess. For a few moments his penetrating gaze focused entirely upon her with disconcerting intensity.

'It seems this is the last time we shall meet, madam,' he said. 'I thank you for offering your protection and hospitality to my cousin these past seven years.'

He swept her a deep bow, his every movement filled with proud masculine grace. Then he turned once more on his heel and departed without waiting for her to respond.

Venice, May 1666

'Our bargain is complete, *illustrissimo.*' Filippo Correr sat back and smiled with satisfaction. 'The glass will look beautiful in your new house.'

Gabriel smiled at Correr, just as pleased as the Venetian merchant with the outcome of their bargaining. The two men had first met twelve years ago when they were apprentices in Livorno. They'd both worked hard to learn their respective trades, but they'd enjoyed themselves as well. Gabriel had many happy memories of his youthful exploits in Filippo's company—but neither man had allowed sentiment to interfere with their afternoon of hard bargaining over Gabriel's purchase of Murano glass.

'I am sure it will,' he said. 'When you next visit London you must be my guest so that you can see it in place.'

'I will be honoured,' said Correr. 'Is the house finished?'

'The construction work should be completed by the time I return home,' said Gabriel, stretching out his legs. Now that the business part of the meeting had been concluded, he relaxed as he discussed his newest project with his old friend. 'The interior will still need furnishing and decorating. I have some ideas in mind, but I decided not to make any final decisions until I could walk through the rooms.'

'Ah.' Correr nodded, and then gave a sly smile. 'You need a wife,' he said. 'Women enjoy that kind of thing.'

Gabriel laughed. 'I don't think so,' he replied easily. 'If I need assistance—which, after fifteen years in the silk trade, I don't believe I do—I'll consult an expert.'

'But your "expert" won't give you sons,' Correr gestured expansively. 'Children are a joy—'

'Your children are,' said Gabriel. 'Not all men are so blessed.'

'If you raise them right…they are like little seedlings,' said Correr. 'They lift their heads to the sun and grow straight and strong.'

Gabriel grinned. Filippo's children were the only chink in the hard-headed merchant's armour.

'You think I am foolish and sentimental,' said Correr cheerfully. 'Just wait, my friend. The first time you hold your son in your arms you will feel exactly the same.'

'Perhaps,' said Gabriel, cautiously conceding the point. To his knowledge, he had no children, but he was certainly fond of his various nieces and nephews.

'But first you need a wife,' said Correr. 'I know a sweet and modest maid—'

Gabriel threw up a hand. 'I don't need you to act as my marriage broker,' he said. 'And I've no wish to marry a Venetian.'

'This lady is Florentine,' said Correr, unperturbed by Gabriel's objection. 'The gracious sister-in-law of my cousin Marco Grimani. Very quiet. Very gentle and modest. Most skilled at housekeeping.'

'No dowry?' Gabriel raised an eyebrow as he noted his friend's emphasis on the lady's personal qualities.

Correr shrugged. 'You do not need a wealthy woman,' he pointed out. 'You need a wife to make you a comfortable home and give you heirs. Giulietta Orio could do that.'

'I certainly need heirs,' said Gabriel, 'but, with all due respect to the gracious sister-in-law of your cousin Marco, I'll marry an Englishwoman.'

'I tried,' said Correr philosophically. 'I will tell Marco I tried. Giulietta Orio is a charming lady but, on reflection, she might be a little too timid to begin a new life in London. We will have to look elsewhere for her husband.' He glanced out of the window.

Gabriel followed the direction of Correr's gaze. He saw that twilight was falling on the city, cloaking the canals and buildings in mystery.

'It's getting late,' said Correr. 'Let's go and find my wife and the children. Will you eat with us?'

'It will be my pleasure,' Gabriel replied, and meant it. Gabriel had always appreciated Filippo's friendship, even though he was less appreciative of the Venetian's matchmaking tendencies. Gabriel knew he needed a wife, especially in view of the unexpected course his life had taken. He'd been very busy since the death of his brother, but when he returned to England this time he would seek out a suitable bride. A modest, well-bred lady who would understand the duties expected of his wife. He certainly wouldn't repeat his youthful mistake of thinking himself in love with the woman. He would treat the marriage contract as he would any other business contract, and make sure his prospective wife understood the terms of their union.

'Oh God, I hope he's pleased to see me!' Rachel Beresford muttered. She stared straight ahead, showing no interest in the extraordinary city that rose around her from the waters of the lagoon.

'Of course he will be,' Athena said reassuringly. She took one of Rachel's cold hands between both of hers. 'He may be a little surprised at first, but I'm sure he will be pleased to have you with him,' she said.

'I don't know how I would have managed without you,' Rachel said jerkily. 'I am so grateful… Oh God! I'm so nervous!' She pressed her free hand to her mouth.

'It won't be long now. Soon you'll be safely together again.' Athena devoutly hoped Edward Beresford *would* be pleased to see his young wife. If he wasn't, she might find herself in the middle of a very difficult situation, but she didn't regret her decision to travel with Rachel.

As soon as she'd heard the young woman's story, Athena's compassion had been stirred. She remembered all too clearly what it was like to be alone, far from home, and unsure of receiving a warm welcome. She'd offered to accompany Rachel for the rest of the journey because she understood and sympathised with Rachel's obvious anxiety. But Athena was honest enough to admit to herself that she'd been growing restless within the confines of the convent—especially after she'd received the news of Samuel's death. Rachel's need for support had given her a legitimate excuse to leave. Unlike her companion, Athena had enjoyed their trip across Europe.

They had arrived in Venice just as twilight was falling. Despite her concerns on Rachel's behalf, Athena was enthralled by her first glimpse of the city. She turned her head left and right in an effort not to miss anything as the gondola slid through the waters of the grand canal. She was almost sorry when they came to rest at the watergate of the Ambassador's palazzo.

Rachel didn't share her companion's curiosity about their surroundings. Her hands felt icy cold as Athena helped her climb out of the gondola. It was clear she was thinking only of her imminent reunion with her husband.

A member of the Ambassador's staff appeared before them on the steps. Pieter Breydel, the gentleman who had escorted them from Bruges, spoke to the servant, explaining who Rachel was and that she had come to join her husband. Athena checked that the rest of her little party was complete, and that their luggage was being attended to. Then she took Rachel's hand. They followed Pieter Breydel and the embassy servant into the palazzo. Her maid and Rachel's manservant trailed behind them.

They entered a large hall, which appeared to stretch all the way from the front to the back of the building. It was paved with alternating squares of diagonally laid white and red stone. It was a dark and forbidding place, especially since the lanterns had not yet been lit. There were doors on either side, but the page ignored them. He led the party straight through the palazzo and out into the courtyard behind the building.

Athena looked around, fascinated by her introduction to Venetian architecture. She was even more intrigued when she realised that to reach the Ambassador's quarters on the first floor, they must climb an external staircase located in the courtyard itself.

They were ushered into a grand chamber which stretched the full length of the palazzo from the courtyard at the back to the grand canal at the front. Large windows overlooking the canal admitted what little daylight remained. Several men were present, standing with their backs to the windows, their faces in shadow.

Athena saw one shadowy man step apart from the others, heard his sudden, disbelieving, but welcoming cry of, 'Rachel!'

Rachel released her convulsive grip on Athena's hand and rushed forward to throw herself into her husband's arms.

Athena didn't need to see Edward Beresford's face to know that he was overjoyed at his wife's arrival. The way his arms closed around her as if he never intended to let her go, the way his head bent over hers, and his husky, urgent questions all told their own story.

Athena's eyes unexpectedly filled with tears. She tried not to dwell on her broken dreams, but this was what she had once yearned for so desperately. She had longed to find Gabriel and fling herself into his arms. Have him tell her that everything would be fine. Everything would be just the way they'd planned it—but he'd left London without a backward glance…

She gave her head a small shake, annoyed with herself for indulging in such romantic nonsense, and gave her full attention to her immediate surroundings.

Pieter Breydel was introducing her to the Ambassador. She curtsied and smiled. It was her plan to return to England from Venice, but she knew she would need the Ambassador's help in making her arrangements.

'Since you have now arrived safely, I will take my leave,' said Pieter in correct, but heavily accented English.

'Surely you'll stay tonight, at least,' the Ambassador protested. 'I must insist.'

'I am expected in Padua,' Pieter demurred.

'You can leave first thing in the morning,' the Ambassador assured him. 'We would not want to keep you from your studies. But for tonight, please enjoy the hospitality of the embassy.'

Pieter hesitated. 'Thank you,' he said at last, bowing. 'You are very kind. As you say, I can leave first thing in the morning.'

Athena bit back a smile. Pieter was a grave and studious young man. He'd taken his responsibilities to his travelling companions very seriously, but she suspected he was eager to get back to his normal routine. She held out her hand to him.

'You made our journey very comfortable,' she said. 'I know Mrs Beresford is as grateful as I am.' She glanced to where Rachel was still wrapped in conversation with her husband. 'Thank you.'

He flushed and nodded. 'It has been my pleasure,' he said stiffly.

At that moment a member of the embassy household came to stand beside them. 'My secretary, Mr Roger Minshull,' the Ambassador introduced him to Athena.

She saw an uncomfortable warmth in the secretary's eyes as he looked at her, and greeted him with reserved courtesy. She wanted to remain on good terms with everyone she met, but she did not need the complications of an admirer in the embassy.

The pre-dawn light was a blend of cool greys, blues and dark shadows. There was a chill in the air and a slight mist that would only burn away after the sun rose. When Gabriel touched the balcony balustrade the stones felt cold and damp beneath his hand.

Below him the early morning market was in full swing on the grand canal. The surface of the water was crowded with rafts and barges piled high with fruit and vegetables. The vessels jostled constantly for position as the vendors cried their wares.

The busy scene was familiar to Gabriel. He watched absently, his thoughts elsewhere. By all accounts there had been quite a stir at the Embassy the previous day. He'd returned late in the evening from Filippo Correr's to find the entire household abuzz with excitement. Everyone he had encountered from the Ambassador's chaplain to the most junior page had been determined to tell him the romantic story of the under-secretary and the devoted new wife who had followed him all the way from England.

Correr's matchmaking attempt had already put the unsettling idea of marriage into Gabriel's mind, and the story of Rachel Beresford's loyalty made a painful contrast to Frances's treacherous behaviour. By the time Gabriel had reached his temporary quarters in the Embassy, his patience had been in shreds. When his own valet had started to repeat the tale Gabriel had dismissed the fellow with a couple of curt words—but he couldn't so easily dismiss the story from his mind. Dreams of Frances and the foolish hopes he'd had for their future had disturbed his sleep, until at last he'd risen from his bed to watch the market from the shadows of the balcony.

He tried to focus on the tasks that lay ahead of him later in the day, but his thoughts kept returning to the journey the undersecretary's wife had made to reach her husband. The presence of a nun in the story puzzled him. Why in the name of all that was holy would a nun leave her cloisters to accompany a stranger halfway across Europe? Perhaps she was on a pilgrimage to Rome?

Annoyed with himself for wasting so much thought on the incident, Gabriel made a final decision to banish the whole matter from his mind. There had been a time when he'd been an idealistic fool who believed in love and fidelity, but now he prided himself on being a man who dealt in the here-and-now of solid reality, not romantic fantasies. And in the here-and-now he was hungry. He leant over the balcony and studied the produce on offer in the nearest barge. His choice made, he called down in Italian to the vendor. After a brief exchange they settled on a price, Gabriel threw down a coin and a loaf of cake-bread was tossed up to him in return.

By now all the nearby traders had noticed the well-dressed man on the balcony and they began to vie eagerly for his custom. Gabriel grinned at their efforts, but refused to purchase anything else. Eventually they gave up and turned their attention elsewhere.

He ripped off a piece of cake-bread and chewed thoughtfully as he planned the day's business. When he'd eaten his fill he tossed the crumbs on to the balcony for the pigeons and turned to go inside.

Most Venetian palazzi had been built to a standard pattern,

even though some dated back two or three hundred years and others were of more recent origin. The Ambassador's residence was no exception. The first floor, known to the Venetians as the *piano nobile* consisted of a great chamber that stretched the full length of the palazzo with a series of smaller chambers opening off from it on either side. The large hall, which could be utilised for many purposes, was called the *portego*. The balcony overlooking the grand canal on which Gabriel currently stood was reached from the *portego*.

The Ambassador, Sir Walter Cracknell, had his own quarters on the *piano nobile*. Gabriel, as the Ambassador's honoured guest, also had his quarters on the same floor. The second floor followed a similar layout and here less important guests and the Ambassador's gentlemen staff were housed.

Just as Gabriel was about to re-enter the *portego*, the Ambassador joined him on the balcony. Gabriel was mildly surprised, Sir Walter was not known for being an early riser.

'Morning, your lordship!' the Ambassador greeted him. 'Looks like it's going to be a fine day, doesn't it?' He peered hopefully at the sky.

'I believe so.' Gabriel glanced over the balustrade. The floating market had dispersed until the following morning. The first rays of sunlight were beginning to give a hint of warmth to the air.

'You missed a deal of excitement last night!' the Ambassador exclaimed.

'So I heard,' Gabriel said.

'Of course. Of course.' Sir Walter nodded vigorously. 'No need to tell you old news. But I wonder if I might ask a favour of your lordship—on behalf of young Beresford and myself?'

'A favour?' Gabriel raised his eyebrows in surprise. 'For your…undersecretary, is he not? Of course, if it is within my power—but what is your request?'

'Shouldn't cause you any inconvenience,' the Ambassador

assured him. 'You'll be returning to England in a week or so, will you not? I believe you told me you'd travel to Livorno and then take one of your own ships back to London?'

'Yes.'

'Excellent. Then I wonder if you would be kind enough to provide safe passage back to England for Mrs Quenell and her maid?'

'Mrs Quenell?' The name was completely unknown to Gabriel.

'The gentlewoman who was kind enough to act as Mrs Beresford's companion between Bruges and Venice,' Sir Walter explained. 'Mrs Beresford is full of praise for Mrs Quenell. She is sure she would not have managed the journey without her help. Mrs Quenell's only request is that I might find her a safe escort back to England. It seems the least I can do. Young Beresford is almost beside himself with joy at having his wife with him once more. So, what do you say, your lordship? Mrs Quenell is a very quiet, modest woman. I'll warrant she'll be no inconvenience to you at all.'

'Why does a Flanders nun want to go to England?' Gabriel asked, puzzled by the request.

Sir Walter stared at him in surprise. 'She's not a nun,' he replied. 'She was a guest at the convent….'

Gabriel heard a soft rustle of skirts. He turned his head to see a woman being shown on to the balcony by a page. For a moment her face was hidden in shadows, then she stepped into the light.

Gabriel was standing still, but the shock of what he saw had the same impact as slamming into a stone wall. His lungs froze. He couldn't breathe. Disbelief rang in his ears, blocking out all other sounds. His vision narrowed until he saw nothing and no one but the woman in front of him.

Frances?

It couldn't be Frances, here in Venice. Surely the resemblance was just a trick of the morning light. Talk of Beresford's devoted young wife had raised the ghost of another, less than devoted bride in his mind. Memories he'd tried to forget had disturbed his sleep. Somehow he'd now superimposed Frances's face on to that of another blonde woman.

He deliberately closed his eyes for a few seconds. Remembered to breathe. Rubbed his temple. Opened his eyes. Stared at the woman.

She stared back, shock in her blue eyes. Her lips slightly parted. Colour drained from her face. There was recognition in her stunned expression.

It *was* Frances.

His blood began to pound sluggishly through his veins once more. The tempo of his heartbeat began to increase. He didn't hear a word of Sir Walter's introduction or explanation. He forgot the Ambassador was even on the balcony. His attention was locked on the woman who had betrayed him so badly.

She'd changed her hairstyle, but a single blonde curl had escaped to lie against her cheek, just as he remembered it. Her skin was soft and smooth, unlined by the passing of time. Her eyes were still an entrancing blue. The colour of cornflowers, he'd once claimed in a foolish poem. Her lips were full, her mouth a little wider than true beauty required. But there had been a time when he's sworn her lips had been created for laughter—and for his worshipful kisses.

His gaze was drawn irresistibly lower. He'd once thought she was the most beautiful woman he'd ever seen. Her waist was still as trim as he recalled. How he'd longed for the moment when he would remove her boned bodice and touch her warm, yielding flesh. Today she wore a simple blue gown with an elegance few other women could match. The full silk sleeves of her bodice ended at her elbows, but the soft white cambric sleeves of her chemise extended an inch or two further and were trimmed with a graceful fall of lace that reached almost to her wrists. Matching lace decorated the neckline of her bodice and the hem of her skirt.

He could see the merest hint of the soft swell of her creamy breasts above her bodice. His eyes locked on to that small part of her anatomy. The place he had seen another man kiss her on the very day planned for their own wedding.

For a few seconds he was back in the bawdy house, watching in agonised disbelief as she turned willingly into her lover's arms. His hands clenched into fists at his sides. He heard again her mocking laughter as he sank into the painful oblivion of unconsciousness.

The slow chug of shock exploded into boiling rage. His lip curled into a snarl. Every muscle in his body tensed. Coiled to spring.

'…and please allow me to introduce you to Lord Halross.' Gabriel heard the Ambassador's voice as if it came from a great distance. 'As I mentioned to you last night, he intends to return to England in one of his own ships. I'm sure he can provide you with a safe passage home.'

Frances opened her mouth, but no words emerged. It was clear she had not expected to see him. Her lips were pinched and pale. Gabriel wondered if she was about to faint and thought savagely that it would be poor justice compared to his own humiliating fate eight years ago. He'd woken in darkness to find he'd been left lying in a stinking ditch outside the City walls. It was only by luck and God's good grace he hadn't been stripped of his clothes, and perhaps even his life, while he was unconscious.

And Frances had given the order for his degradation. She had *laughed* at the prospect of it.

His muscles twitched. Power surged through his body, but he didn't move an inch. He had made a fool of himself once over this woman. He would not do so again. He drew in a deep breath. His lungs burned. It felt like the first breath he'd ever taken. He took another breath. Air seared through his throat like fire, but when he spoke his voice was harsh and cold as hoar frost. 'Is it my *protection* you crave, madam? Or my indulgence? I—'

'*Neither!*' Frances's chin snapped up. Hot colour suddenly burned in her pale cheeks. 'I ask nothing of you, my lord. I am sorry to have intruded upon you.'

She whirled about in an angry swish of skirts, clearly intending to leave the balcony.

Fury speared through Gabriel when he saw the disdainful way in which she turned her back upon him. He would not allow her to dismiss him so lightly a second time. He took two long strides towards her, then reached out to seize her arm—

But he was thwarted in his intentions by the sudden appearance on the balcony of the Ambassador's secretary. Roger Minshull stepped between Gabriel and Frances. He uttered appropriate greetings to Gabriel and Sir Walter but, to Gabriel's disgust, it was Frances who occupied his attention.

'Mrs Quenell, if you have rested sufficiently from your journey, I would be honoured to show you the sights of Venice,' Minshull said, bowing ingratiatingly.

Athena hardly noticed when the secretary took her hand. She saw only Gabriel. Heard only Gabriel. Even when she turned her back on him, every fibre of her body was attuned to every movement he made.

Gabriel.

Lord Halross, the Ambassador had told her yesterday. She'd been prepared to encounter Gabriel's brother this morning. She'd fretted over it all night. She didn't want to meet any member of Gabriel's family. But she'd calmed herself with the thought that she'd never met either of his older brothers.

There was no reason for Lord Halross to know that she'd ever had an association with his younger brother.

But it was Gabriel who turned his head to look at her when she walked out on to the balcony. Shock seized her, paralysing her mind and body. But she'd been thinking about Gabriel all night. Wondering how to present herself to one of his brothers. It was a devastating but short step to understand that it was Gabriel himself who stood before her. In some distant corner of her mind she realised his brothers must be dead. There was no other way he could have inherited his father's title. But that wasn't important now. The only thing that mattered was that Gabriel was here—standing only a few feet away from her. She stared at him, hungry to look at the man for whom she had sacrificed so much.

He was as tall as she remembered. Perhaps even taller. She did not remember him as this grand, imposing figure. Eight years ago he had dressed soberly, as befitted his status and the austerity of Cromwell's London. And in her memories he was much younger. A man certainly, but flushed with the fresh enthusiasm of youth.

The Gabriel who confronted her today was a male in the prime of his power. Sure of his authority and his strength. Arrayed in all the magnificence of a wealthy nobleman. His coat of burgundy velvet was edged with gold lace at the cuffs and on the front facings. His coat sleeves ended at the elbow to reveal a contrasting cascade of white lace that extended almost to his wrists. His cravat was edged in a deep band of heavy Venetian lace. His dark brown hair fell in rippling waves around his shoulders. The early morning sunlight gilded a few shining strands with an aura of gold, so that he seemed to be clad from head to toe in extravagant riches.

But the fine clothes could not conceal his raw masculine power. The man who wore the soft velvet was lean and hard-muscled. The fine lace beneath his chin emphasised the unyielding line of his square jaw. Hatred and fury burned in his amber eyes.

His hostile gaze sliced through her, deadly as a sword to the heart. Her very soul reeled beneath his silent assault upon her. She couldn't move. Couldn't speak. She saw his body coil with furious intent and still she was held prisoner by the scalding fire in his eyes.

When he spoke, his voice was so laden with contempt she hardly recognised it.

She didn't understand his anger or the significance of his question—he'd not cared enough to turn up at the church, so why was he angry now? Her first shock receded. Pride came to her rescue. She lifted her chin, found the words to answer him, and turned to leave.

She felt Gabriel's sudden movement towards her, but then the Ambassador's secretary stepped between them. She barely noticed the secretary take her hand. All her senses were attuned to Gabriel behind her.

'Mrs Quenell?'

She jumped and looked at the secretary in confusion, then realised he had asked her a question and was waiting for her answer. She replayed his last few words in her mind.

'I would be honoured to show you the sights of Venice.'

'Oh. That is very kind of you…' She couldn't remember his name. Somehow she managed a semblance of a smile instead. 'Sir, but I…if you don't mind, I think I may…'

'I'll show you.' Gabriel's hand closed around her arm, just above her elbow.

Her heart jolted at the sudden contact. The anger thrumming through his powerful body almost overwhelmed her senses, splintering her thoughts. It was quite beyond her to frame a coherent response to the secretary or to Gabriel.

She saw the secretary's eyes widen in surprise. Heard the Ambassador say something but didn't catch his words. Then

Gabriel compelled her to leave the balcony. He strode the length of the *portego,* his hold on her arm unrelenting.

Athena had no choice but to go with him. Her legs were unsteady with shock and she nearly stumbled. Gabriel hauled her mercilessly upright. He didn't slow his pace and she was forced into a scrambling run to keep up with his long stride.

He propelled her out of the *portego* and onto the outside staircase. She tripped. If not for his iron grip on her elbow, she would have pitched headlong down the flight of stone steps.

Muttering furiously under his breath he clamped his arm around her waist and carried her unceremoniously down to the courtyard. Her heart hammered in her chest, but she was too confused and shaken to be angry at his astounding behaviour.

She could feel the barely controlled rage within him. This was not the Gabriel who had courted her so tenderly eight years ago. She didn't know this man who threatened to erupt with fury at any moment.

He set her on her feet and hauled her through the ground floor hall.

Athena dug her heels in, her feet slipping on the smooth stone paving. 'Let me go!' She tried to wrench her arm out of his hold.

Without a word he picked her up and carried her through the watergate. 'Get in,' he ordered.

There were several gondolas floating in front of the palazzo. The one he directed her into was painted the customary black, but seemed far more luxurious than the vessel Pieter Breydel had hired yesterday to bring the small party to the Embassy. It possessed a cabin-like structure, which could be enclosed to protect the occupants from the weather—or to provide them with privacy. When she stepped into the cabin she saw it was furnished with a fine carpet and curtains. And the reclining seats were covered with black velvet.

She stopped short at the sight of those couch-like seats, her overstretched nerves jangling at the prospect of almost lying beside Gabriel in his present mood.

'Sit down,' he said in her ear.

She trembled at his proximity and did as he commanded, perching upright on the very front of the velvet cushion. The gondola rocked gently as Gabriel stepped into it.

'Where are you taking me?' She watched nervously as he sat down beside her.

'To see Venice.' His smile was all predator.

'Halross? What are you about, man?' Sir Walter shouted.

The Ambassador's voice seemed to come from above. Startled, Athena looked up. The roof of the cabin hindered her view, but after a moment's confusion she realised Sir Walter must have seen Gabriel's gondola from the balcony.

Gabriel leant out of the cabin to reply. 'Showing your guest the sights of the city. You will allow I am better qualified than any member of your household to do so.'

'Humph. Oh. Yes. Your advice has been invaluable,' Sir Walter acknowledged, disgruntled. 'But is Mrs Quenell warm enough? Surely a moment to prepare herself before you carry her—'

'She will be warm enough.' Gabriel settled back on to his seat, clearly considering the exchange at an end. Already the swift-moving gondola was beyond comfortable shouting distance from the palazzo.

There was a gondolier standing at the back of the gondola and another one in front of the cabin, but Athena knew she could expect no help from the two men. She'd heard Gabriel give them curt orders in Italian. They were in his pay, they would do whatever he said.

He leant back in the seat, stretching out his legs in a semblance of relaxation. Athena sat upright, staring straight ahead, her hands gripped together on her knees. Gabriel's casual posture didn't fool her. She could feel the fierce emotion vibrating through his body, sense his angry gaze burning the back of her neck. She didn't turn her head to look at him. Instead she glanced down and a little sideways. She saw his hand lying on his thigh. It was a large hand, with long, strong fingers. The last time she'd seen Gabriel's hand he had stroked a finger tenderly across her cheek. As she watched, it clenched into a fist.

In the years since she'd discovered he hadn't turned up at the church for their wedding she'd taught herself to accept he hadn't loved her as she'd loved him. She'd forced herself to face the fact that, if they ever met again, he would treat her with indifference. Perhaps wouldn't even remember her.

She'd never anticipated this hostility.

She waited for him to speak. He didn't say anything. She took a breath. Her ribs felt as if an iron band had been placed around them and she had to force her chest to expand when she inhaled.

When she heard him take a harsh breath, she wondered dizzily if he had the same problem with his ribs.

She stared at his hand on his leg. Gabriel's hand. Gabriel's leg. The fine cloth of his breeches touched her petticoats. He was only inches away from her. And more distant than she'd ever imagined.

She knew he was watching her. She could feel the intensity of his gaze. Like a deer caged with a hunting lion she felt compelled to look at him. His eyes burned into hers. His visual assault was so devastating her body went slack with shock.

Athena swayed. The world swirled about her.

He caught her arm and pulled her back on to the seat beside him. A second later he loomed over her, his large body half-covering hers, pinning her in place.

'Gabriel,' she whispered. She lifted a trembling hand to touch his cheek.

He was real. The weight of his body on hers was real. The slight rasp of stubble on his smooth-shaven jaw was real.

'Gabriel.' Her eyes filled suddenly with tears. She touched his face with quick, fluttering gestures, hungry for more assurance of his reality. Stroked his hair, traced his dark eyebrow. 'I wanted you so much.' Her voice caught on a sob and she flung her arms around his neck, clinging desperately to him.

She buried her face in his shoulder, momentarily forgetting his hostility in the miracle of being once more able to touch him. But his hard body was unyielding as oak in her embrace.

She became aware of his silent rejection and began to pull away, shaken anew by his inexplicable anger.

He growled low in his chest, moving suddenly, forcing her back against the velvet upholstery. His action triggered memories of another man who'd used force against her.

'No!' Panic shot through her. She struggled wildly, pounding at Gabriel's shoulders with her fists. Water slapped against the sides of the rocking gondola.

'My God!' He lifted his head a few inches.

'No!' she panted, twisting her face away from him, thrusting at his chest in an unavailing effort to shove him away from her.

His curse emerged as little more than a snarl.

'How much will it cost to make you say yes?' he demanded. *'What?'*

'You thought you could play your tricks on some poor bastard who'd be fooled by your innocent face,' he said savagely. 'It must have been a shock to discover this particular pigeon has already been plucked.'

Athena stared up at him, bewildered by his accusation. 'What? What pigeon?'

He laughed harshly and lifted himself away from her. 'Save your breath, madam. I've seen you unmasked. I'll not be duped again.' He flung a curt order at the gondoliers. 'I might have guessed you'd one day find your way to Venice,' he said bitterly. 'A whore belongs in the city of whores. You'll fit in very well.'

The gondola stopped at a landing stage. In one lithe movement Gabriel sprang out. He issued another incomprehensible order to the gondoliers and turned to stride away across a large square.

'Wait…' Athena's voice faded. Gabriel had already disappeared into the crowds. The gondola was once more gliding through the waters of the grand canal. Life continued all around her as if nothing of moment had happened.

She swallowed and pushed a strand of hair behind her ear with shaking fingers. Emotion suddenly threatened to overcome her. She propped her elbows on her knees and buried her face in her trembling hands.

Chapter Two

'My lord, the banquet is about to start!' The young page bounced on his toes as he waited for Gabriel to pay off the hired gondola.

'Banquet?' Gabriel frowned. This was the first he'd heard of any banquet.

'In honour of Mrs Beresford and Mrs Quenell,' the page explained eagerly. 'Come, my lord. Sir Walter sent me down to wait for your return. You are the most important guest!'

Gabriel bit off a curse. He had no desire to raise a glass in honour of Frances—but the meal would be over soon enough.

'I'm likely the only guest,' he said drily, striding beside the page through the *andron,* the ground-floor hallway that corresponded to the *portego* on the floor above.

Venetian citizens such as Filippo Correr were permitted to deal directly with foreigners, but the nobility refused to mingle with visitors to their city. The Ambassador was only able to meet with the Doge and other important patricians in the most restricted and formal of circumstances. Usually the embassy household had to rely on each other for companionship—though not necessarily for entertainment. Venice had many attractions for men in search of diversion. But it wasn't surprising Sir Walter had seized on this excuse for a grand dinner.

'Yes, my lord. But you are a *very* important guest,' said the page.

True to his usual habit, Gabriel took the steps two at a time, arriving in the *portego* before the breathless servant. He paused just inside the door. The long chamber was crowded with members of the Ambassador's staff. Roger Minshull, the Ambassador's chief secretary, the two undersecretaries, one of whom was Edward Beresford, the chaplain, various young gentlemen who were supposedly being trained in the art of diplomacy…

Frances.

Gabriel's eyes locked on to her immediately. But that meant nothing. She was one of only two women present. Naturally she drew his attention.

'Halross! Splendid!' Sir Walter spotted him. 'In good time! We are having a banquet in honour of our gallant new arrivals.'

'So I see.' In Gabriel's absence the *portego* had been transformed into a dining chamber with the addition of a large, magnificently laid table and finely carved chairs. 'Most impressive.'

'Yes. Yes. Come, my lord. You must sit on my right. Mrs Beresford on my left…' The Ambassador immediately began to arrange his most important guests.

Gabriel saw that he was to sit almost opposite to Frances. He would be able to see her every move throughout the meal. She glanced at him, then looked quickly away. Her fingers fidgeted briefly with her closed fan, then her grip on the ivory sticks relaxed. She turned to smile at Roger Minshull who was sitting on her left. Minshull spoke to her and she replied in a light, untroubled tone. Gabriel saw that the ferret-faced secretary was already halfway to being besotted by his beautiful companion.

Frances's composure grated on Gabriel's temper. If she had any shame or conscience she would be begging him not to disclose her treacherous behaviour eight years ago. She must know it would take only one word from him to destroy her credibility with the Ambassador. For a few seconds Gabriel almost felt a grudging admiration for her obvious determination to brazen out the situation. There must be a backbone of steel concealed within her graceful feminine curves. Then his painfully acquired cynicism reasserted itself. In truth, it required no great courage for Frances to continue her masquerade. She was undoubtedly relying on his reluctance to reveal his youthful folly to the world. And she was right. He had no intention of providing any further entertainment for the embassy household. From now on he would treat her with the indifference she deserved.

'It is a testament to the power of love,' said the chaplain.

'What?' Gabriel's head snapped around.

'Mrs Beresford's epic journey to rejoin her husband, my lord,' the chaplain replied. 'I have never seen two young people more truly matched. True love can overcome the greatest obstacles.' He looked at Rachel Beresford with sentimental admiration. Gabriel followed the direction of the chaplain's gaze.

Rachel noticed their attention was fixed upon her and blushed. 'I could never have managed without Mrs Quenell's help,' she said. 'I was so overset by the time I reached Bruges that I don't know what I would have done if the innkeeper hadn't taken me to the convent. After that Mrs Quenell took care of everything. I will never be able to repay her for what she has done for me.'

'Nor I,' Edward Beresford interjected. 'I will always be in your debt, madam. It gives me nightmares, imagining what could have happened to my poor Rachel without your protection. And that of Mr Breydel as well, of course,' he added. 'I am sorry he was not able to attend this banquet.'

Gabriel hid his opinion beneath an impassive expression. The others might believe Frances's story that she'd been a guest at the convent for a considerable time, but Gabriel knew better. She'd lied to him eight years ago, and it seemed she hadn't lost her talent for telling plausible untruths. Frances had certainly been serving her own ends when she adopted the role of guardian angel to Rachel Beresford. No doubt she was between patrons and, just like Rachel, had taken temporary refuge in the convent. Now she was on the lookout for a new protector. The Ambassador must have told her he had a noble guest without mentioning Gabriel's name. What a shock Frances must have had when she discovered the wealthy man she'd selected as her next victim was someone she'd duped already. Gabriel had no intention of playing her fool again.

Frances acknowledged Edward Beresford's gratitude with a modest smile and a quiet word of thanks, but she continued her conversation with Minshull. She had changed her gown since that morning. The blue dress had been very becoming to her fair beauty, but the primrose silk taffeta revealed even more of her charms. The wide neckline showed off to perfection the graceful curve of her shoulders. It was trimmed all about with a broad lace collar more than six inches deep. A length of such fine, wide lace would have been expensive. Who was the man who had paid for the silk gown and costly lace she wore with such self-assurance? And why was she no longer with him?

'Amazing coincidence, meeting Mrs Quenell again in Venice,' the Ambassador remarked cheerfully.

'*What?*' Gabriel stared at the Ambassador. 'You knew her before?'

'Who? What?' Sir Walter looked confused by Gabriel's sharp question. 'Not me!' he exclaimed, his expression clearing. 'I meant you, my lord.' He laughed. 'Must have been quite a surprise for both of you. Mrs Quenell was telling me.'

'Telling you?' Gabriel looked at Frances through narrowed eyes. She was even more brazen than he'd supposed. Perhaps it was time to call her bluff. 'Indeed, yes. We were acquainted

years ago,' he said coldly. 'But so long ago I confess I've forgotten the details. Perhaps you would be kind enough to remind me...*Mrs Quenell.*'

Her naturally fair skin grew even paler as he watched. He
saw her swallow, then she looked directly at him. In that instant her eyes were the eyes of the girl he'd loved eight years
ago—filled with hurt and confusion. Her unguarded blue gaze
found an unexpected chink in his armour-plating of cold disdain. He looked away first, shaken by memories he'd tried so
hard to destroy.

'Of course. Your reunion this morning was cut short when
you met one of your merchant acquaintances,' said the Ambassador. 'A very inopportune interruption.'

Gabriel realised the whole table had fallen silent. A quick
sideways glance informed him that everyone was waiting
more or less openly to hear about his previous friendship with
Frances. He should have known his behaviour that morning
would arouse curiosity.

'Mrs Quenell,' he challenged her, his voice deadly soft.
'Your memory is obviously so much clearer than mine. Please.
Remind me of our last meeting.'

The occasion when she'd laughed and consigned him to a
ditch. He stared at her, daring her to admit her perfidious behaviour. As he watched, she summoned a smile to her lips that
didn't reach her eyes.

'I fear I don't remember our *last* meeting, my lord,' she replied lightly. 'But I do recall our first.'

'Really? I made more impression on you at the beginning
of our acquaintance than I did at the end? What a damning
indictment of my address.' He paused briefly. 'But I believe
I am harder to overlook now,' he concluded, a diamond-hard
edge to his voice.

'You certainly appear *grander* than you did when serving
behind the counter in the silk mercer's,' Frances snapped. 'I

vow, when I first saw you this morning decked out in velvet and lace, I scarcely recognised you.'

Further down the table Gabriel heard a gasp. Behind his back he was known as the Merchant Marquis, but very few men had the gall to call him that to his face.

Frances's sharp response brought a feral smile to his lips—while at the same moment he felt the barest lessening of tension in his muscles. He remembered her occasional hot temper. So that at least had been real—even if everything else had been an act.

He recalled their first meeting in Sir Thomas Parfitt's mercer's shop. It was pure accident Gabriel had been present when Frances came in to make a purchase. Even as a young apprentice he had been employed in Parfitt's warehouses, not in the shop on Cheapside. But as soon as he'd seen Frances he'd stepped forward to serve her—much to the amusement of Lady Parfitt, who kept the shop for her husband. And then he'd followed Frances home, just so he could arrange another, accidental meeting with her. God, what a young fool he'd been.

'We both seem to have improved our condition in life,' he said, his eyes on the wide fall of expensive lace about her shoulders.

'You have certainly *changed,*' she retorted. 'Whether it is an improvement remains to be seen.'

The chaplain gasped. Someone lower down the table laughed and quickly converted it to a cough. A gleam of satisfaction suddenly appeared in Roger Minshull's eyes. He moved so that he presented a subtle, but unmistakable shoulder to Gabriel and engaged Frances once more in conversation.

Athena barely heard a word Minshull said to her. She had forgotten her resolution to keep the uncomfortably attentive secretary at a distance because all her attention was focused on Gabriel. Her face ached with the effort of preserving an untroubled expression. She could feel Gabriel's hard gaze upon her. He'd left her in no doubt of his contempt. His silent hostility threatened to suffocate her. They were separated by the width of the table, but every tiny movement of his powerful body flicked across her raw nerves. She forced herself to smile at Minshull while her thoughts whirled frantically this way and that. Why had Gabriel turned against her?

She forced herself to eat a little of the feast laid on partly in her honour, but the last mouthful stuck in her throat. She struggled to swallow. A wild image of choking to death at the Ambassador's table danced in her mind. Her fingers closed desperately around her goblet. The wine helped. She took several sips, then set the goblet down. She dare not cloud her wits with the heady liquid.

She risked a fleeting glance at Gabriel. His amber eyes widened briefly when they encountered hers, then narrowed warningly. Athena felt the jolt of a sizzling connection between them. Her breath caught in her throat. Shaken, she ripped her eyes away from him, picked up her goblet with trembling fingers and put it to her lips. She closed her eyes as she drank, taking temporary refuge in the illusion that she could hide behind the goblet.

But there was no escape. Minshull was already asking her a question about the convent at Bruges. She composed herself to reply, astonished that her voice sounded so calm.

What had happened to Gabriel? She remembered so clearly the day they'd met. He had not been hard and angry then. He'd been tall and handsome and full of open-hearted vigour. From the second she'd entered the mercer's shop her eyes had been drawn to him. When he'd stepped forward to serve her she'd been so overwhelmed that at first she'd forgotten what she wanted to buy. At last she remembered and stammered out her request, feeling foolish and embarrassed. But by then she'd seen the admiration and interest in his eyes. She was used to men looking at her with lust-filled intent—she'd fled from her childhood home to escape just such a man—but Gabriel's male admiration didn't repulse her. The fluttering of nervous excitement he aroused within her had been entirely pleasurable.

He still drew all her attention. He was more handsome and compelling than ever. She wished she could look at him to her heart's content. Trace every change time had wrought upon him. From the corner of her eye she could see his hand lying upon the table. It was the same hand that had touched her so long ago. Yet it seemed somehow different. It was familiar in all its lineaments, but it almost seemed like the hand of a stranger.

'What a lucky circumstance that you already know his lordship, Mrs Quenell,' said the Ambassador suddenly. 'It is so much more comfortable to travel with an old friend rather than a stranger,' he continued.

His comment nearly destroyed the remnants of Athena's composure. She'd been so overwhelmed by the shock of seeing Gabriel again she had forgotten he was to escort her back to England. She instinctively shied away from the prospect.

'As to that, we have not yet discussed arrangements,' she hurried into speech. 'As I mentioned, his lordship met an acquaintance before we had a chance to do so. It may not be convenient—'

'I am sure we can come to an arrangement that will be mutually satisfactory,' Gabriel interrupted, a dark, enigmatic note in his voice.

Athena's eyes snapped to his face. He tilted his head to look directly into hers. For several seconds she forgot to breathe.

'If the arrangement is not to your liking we can make alternative travel plans for you, Mrs Quenell,' said Minshull. 'I will deal with it first thing in the morning.'

Gabriel turned almost lazily to look at the secretary. 'Don't trouble yourself,' he said, his words a devastating command, not an assurance.

It seemed to Athena that she was not the only person holding her breath as she waited for Minshull to respond. There was no other conversation at the table. Gabriel held everyone's attention.

'I…I… Mrs Quenell?' The red-faced secretary turned towards her.

'Thank you for your kindness, Mr Minshull,' she said, trying to give him a dignified way to back away from the confrontation. 'But I have barely been in Venice a day. I'm not yet sure myself what arrangements I wish to make. You may be sure I'll call upon you for help if I need to do so.'

'Yes. Yes. Of course. At any time,' he said.

A brief, cold smile curved Gabriel's lips at the secretary's words. Then he turned to say something to the Ambassador, quite clearly dismissing Minshull from his attention.

The meal continued. Athena longed to escape to the privacy of her chamber, but she knew that if she did so it would arouse even more curiosity among the Ambassador's household. So she smiled and nodded and exchanged inconsequential remarks until Sir Walter suddenly declared a desire to dance.

The table was moved, chairs placed against the walls of the *portego* and a trio of musicians struck up a lively tune. As the only two women present, Athena and Rachel Beresford were obliged to dance every measure. Athena guessed from the fixed smile on the younger woman's face that she was as uncomfortable with the situation as Athena. Rachel wanted to be alone with her husband. Failing that, she wanted to dance with her husband. But since Edward Beresford's career depended on the Ambassador's goodwill, neither he nor his wife had any choice but to acquiesce to Sir Walter's pleasure.

Athena had never in her life danced in public. She had never had occasion to do so. She gritted her teeth, tried to watch Rachel whenever she could, and did her best to move through the steps without making a total fool of herself.

Gabriel didn't invite either woman to dance. At first he leant against the wall and watched, his gaze inscrutable. Athena took care not to glance in his direction, though her consciousness of his scrutiny made her feel flustered and clumsy. After half an hour she became aware of a sudden absence. She looked around and discovered that Gabriel had disappeared.

His departure left her with a sense of an anticlimax. It also seemed to lead to an increased exuberance in the mood of everyone else. The impromptu ball became more boisterous. At last Edward Beresford pleaded weariness on behalf of his wife after her long journey and they left the chamber.

Athena found herself alone among a crowd of increasingly inebriated gentlemen. Without Gabriel's brooding presence several of them, most notably Roger Minshull, became more familiar in their advances. Gabriel's treatment of her had undermined her status in the men's eyes. The previous day they had been inclined to treat her as if her years in the convent had given her the untouchable sanctity of a nun. This evening they were more prone to cross those invisible boundaries.

Athena knew she couldn't afford to linger. Even though she might have to endure no more than a lewd question or two about her past friendship with Gabriel, and perhaps an inappropriately intimate caress, any sign that she was complacent about such treatment would quickly undermine her reputation and her status.

She paid the Ambassador several graceful compliments about the dinner and the subsequent entertainment he had arranged and left the *portego* as speedily as good manners would allow. After the last exchange of courtesies with a persistent Minshull, she escaped on to the external staircase.

The cool night air felt like balm on her overheated face. The friendly darkness was a relief after the strain of maintaining her public composure for so long. She paused for a moment to enjoy the pleasure of being alone. A burst of laughter from the *portego* prompted her to climb a few steps to avoid any possibility of one of the revellers noticing her and perhaps deciding to join her on the privacy of the stairs.

She walked up another few steps.

Suddenly all her senses screamed a warning. She hadn't seen or heard anything, but a dark shape swooped on her from the shadows. Strong arms wrapped around her in an unbreakable hold. Her heart thudded so loudly she hardly heard his soft-voiced command to be quiet, but she didn't need to hear his voice to know it was Gabriel. Even in the darkness she recognised his familiar, once-beloved scent, and the feel of his hard body close to hers.

He swept her off her feet and carried her down the stairs. Athena thought of struggling, but their discovery was more likely to cause her embarrassment than result in her rescue. Besides, despite his undisguised hostility towards her, she knew Gabriel would never hurt her. And she had questions for him. As soon as they were alone she wanted some answers.

A few moments later she found herself once more seated in Gabriel's gondola. This time the curtains were drawn, enclosing her in a black velvet cocoon lit only by a single lantern. Gabriel swiftly joined her. His tall, broad-shouldered frame made the small cabin seem even smaller.

'Why are you so angry?' Athena demanded, before he'd even had a chance to lean back in the reclining seat beside her.

'What?'

'You didn't even turn up at the church!' Furious indignation vibrated in her voice. 'You sailed off to Aleppo two weeks later without a backward glance! How *dare* you treat me with such contempt!'

'How dare *I*…?' Gabriel half-turned on to his side so that he could stare directly into her face. His blazing eyes were only inches from hers. 'Harlot! I *saw* you with your lover. Did it amuse you to know I watched? You *laughed* when that bastard knocked me cold! But I'm not the callow boy I was then. You won't fool me again with your lies.'

His accusation was so unexpected that, for a few seconds, Athena could hardly think straight.

'What lover? I *never* had a lover!' She found her voice. 'You're the one who's lying! If you never meant to marry me—'

'In the bawdy house!' In an instant Gabriel was stretched half on top of her, the tip of his nose almost touching hers. 'I saw him drink from the very spot your lips had touched. I saw you smile at him and lift your mouth for his kiss. I saw—'

'Samuel?' Athena gasped. For a moment she was back in that hateful room, afraid and longing for Gabriel to rescue her. 'You saw?' Her memories disintegrated beneath a mist of red-hot fury. 'You saw and you didn't *help* me! How could you? *How could you?*' She pounded her fists at him, hitting wildly at his shoulders and chest, catching him a blow on his cheek, fighting him as she'd never fought Samuel. Blind to everything but memories of the nightmare she'd endured for Gabriel's sake and her sense of bitter betrayal that he'd seen and done nothing to help her. She didn't hear the shouts and curses of the gondoliers as they tried to prevent the gondola from overturning.

Gabriel swore. He pinned down her flailing legs with the weight of his own body and seized her forearms in his hands. He pressed her wrists against the black velvet behind her head.

Athena glared up at him through the untidy mess of her hair. 'You monster!' she panted. 'How could you be so cruel? How could I have been so *stupid* as to love *you!*'

Gabriel laughed savagely. 'Love had nothing to do with it! You saw a likely pigeon and played me along until a richer prize came your way.'

'Richer…?' Athena stared at him. The pressure of his body

forcing her against the reclining seat meant that at least one of the bones in her tightly laced bodice pressed painfully into her side, restricting her breathing. He held her arms prisoner above her head. But he hadn't hurt her.

His hair was dishevelled. The lace at his throat was torn and she saw scratches on his chin where her nails must have caught him. There was a mark on his left cheek from the blows she had rained about his shoulders and head. But he hadn't hurt her.

She'd never fought Samuel. She'd known instinctively that if she did he would beat her so badly she might not survive. Tonight, driven by long-held feelings of pain and betrayal, she'd struck out wildly at Gabriel—but he'd not made any attempt to retaliate. She must have known—even after everything that had happened—she must have known on some deep, instinctive level she was safe with Gabriel.

'He told me you didn't go to the church,' she whispered. 'He told me you didn't even know I hadn't gone.'

'Who told you?'

'Samuel. Samuel Quenell. My…' She hesitated, hating even now to refer to Samuel in such terms. 'My husband.'

'Your *husband?*'

'How could you have seen us? How did you know where we were?' She searched Gabriel's face for an answer. 'Why didn't you *help* me?'

'*Help* you?' he jeered. 'You seemed more than satisfied with your lot.'

'You *did* go to the church,' Athena breathed. 'He lied to me.'

'Don't think you'll cozen me with your fairy tales,' Gabriel said. 'I have seen the evidence of your true character with my own eyes.'

'Your eyes are blind if you think I was happy to be with Samuel!' she flung at him, hurt and insulted anew by his scepticism. 'How did you know where to find us?'

'I'm getting tired of your evasions, Frances,' Gabriel said harshly. 'You know damn well you sent a messenger to find me in the church.'

'A messenger? Who?'

'You know, what with having his knife pressed against my belly and then grinding his face into the plaster to teach him respect, we never did take the time for polite introductions,' Gabriel said sarcastically. 'He had the last laugh however. He caught me unawares when…' he paused and gritted his teeth '…when I saw *you* and your pimp.'

Athena gazed at him. The Gabriel she'd nearly married eight years ago had been honourable, occasionally hot-headed and always direct. The Gabriel holding her captive had not changed so very much in essentials. He had no reason to lie about what had happened. The truth was too damaging to his pride and self-esteem.

'Samuel lied to both of us,' she said bleakly.

'I am impressed by your resourcefulness, madam. Not to mention your tenacity in holding to a story in the face of all the evidence against you.'

'There was supposed to be evidence against me.' Athena suddenly felt tired. Had *everything* Samuel had told her been a lie? She remembered the scrap of letter implicating Gabriel in a plot to kill Cromwell. That at least must have been real. She'd recognised Gabriel's writing immediately. As it had turned out, there had been no need to kill Cromwell because he'd died of natural causes a few months later. After Gabriel had written the letter the plotters must have come to the conclusion that time would complete their task for them. That there were other, better ways to further the King's cause.

'The greatest evidence of all is your willing compliance in your pimp's arms.' Gabriel's gritty voice cut across her reflections.

'I had no choice—'

'No *choice?* No choice but to offer your lips to him, allow him to mumble at your breast with his mouth like—'

'Do you think I *liked* that? I wanted to rip his guts out!'

'Words! Words!'

'He told me if I didn't marry him—' She broke off staring at Gabriel's flinty, cynical expression. The bitter sense of betrayal that he'd seen her with Samuel but hadn't helped her still gnawed at her soul. His disbelief in her explanations wounded her deeply. She could not bear to admit she'd married Samuel to save Gabriel himself. Couldn't make herself so vulnerable to him when he treated her with such disdain.

'He caught me on the eve of our wedding,' she said. 'I was so sure I'd escaped him—but he was hiding in the shadows by the courtyard. He dragged me into the parlour and told me...' she swallowed, remembering the sickening horror she'd experienced then '...told me he'd taken Aunt Kitty. She was...she was the guarantee that I'd marry him willingly. He wouldn't hurt her if I did.'

'And you just gave yourself up without protest. Without even trying to send for help?' Gabriel said scornfully. 'Do you think I'd have let him hurt Kitty if I'd known? Or you? How could you be so feckless?'

'*Feckless!*' To hear her sacrifice described in such contemptuous terms infuriated Athena. Even though she'd decided not to tell Gabriel that her primary motive had been to save *his* life, it still hurt that he dismissed her plight so lightly.

'Get off me!' She jerked her body in an effort to throw him off. The gondola rocked, but her efforts made no impression on Gabriel. She winced and caught her breath in sudden pain.

'Why do you flinch? I'm not hurting you at all.' He frowned at her.

'A bone in my bodice has broken, you great lummocking bully!' She glared at him. 'It wasn't intended for this kind of treatment.'

'Hmm.' He adjusted his position on top of her carefully. Athena didn't realise until he released her hands and flipped her over beneath him that he'd been taking care he wasn't kneeling on her petticoats. She found her cheek pressed down on the velvet upholstery.

'What are you doing?' Alarm skittered through her as she felt his hands at her back.

'Relieving you of pain, madam harlot.'

'What?' An instant later she knew exactly what he was doing. *'No!'* She braced her hands against the seat and tried to push upwards.

Gabriel held her still with his thighs around her hips and one firm hand between her shoulder blades. With his other he unfastened the bodice her maid had so diligently laced her into before dinner.

'No. Please!' she begged desperately, as the tight-fitting bodice fell away from her body. 'Please God, *don't!'*

Chapter Three

'**D**on't what?' he purred. 'Touch you?'

His free hand slipped inside the open edges of her bodice. Only her thin chemise prevented him from touching her naked skin. He stroked his fingers delicately from her waist to the nape of her neck.

She gasped and trembled. His caress aroused so many conflicting emotions within her she scarcely knew what she felt.

'Please,' she whispered.

'Please more?' he taunted her. His hand roamed freely over her back. Trapped beneath him as she was, she could do nothing to prevent his caresses. The rich velvet beneath her cheek was smooth yet slightly abrasive when she moved her head against the grain of the fabric.

'No.' She closed her eyes. She'd longed so many nights for Gabriel's touch. But she'd never expected he would be holding her captive when he did so.

'No?' He put one hand on the seat beside her and carefully repositioned himself over her. He pushed her long curls aside, his fingers lingering on the smooth skin of her shoulder, then she felt him lower his upper body until his weight lightly pressed against her. For a few tantalising seconds his breath heated her skin, then he kissed her shoulder.

He took his time, tasting her with his tongue, teasing her with his lips. She quivered, unexpected pleasure shimmering through her body. During their betrothal he had kissed her chastely upon her hand and occasionally on her cheek. Once or twice he had stolen a kiss from her lips—but never with such unfettered sensuality.

For a few moments she lost herself in the illicit delight he gave her. She forgot her undignified position face down in the gondola. She forgot Gabriel's hostility towards her and her own sense of betrayal that he had seen but not protected her from Samuel. She was acutely aware of the contained strength in his hard body as he hovered just above her. The lace of his cravat trailed teasingly across her bare shoulder almost as tantalisingly as his lips.

His powerful thighs gripped her hips, holding her prisoner. She was completely at his mercy. And at the mercy of the desire he aroused in her. She whimpered softly.

She heard a low growl in his throat. His teeth closed on the curve between her shoulder and her neck. He didn't bite hard enough to hurt her, but he growled again, the sound vibrating through her body. Through her arousal-dazed senses she became aware of the change in his mood from passion to anger.

'Do you take pleasure where you can find it, like any bitch in heat?' he said against her neck. 'Little harlot.'

'I am *not* a harlot!' Her denial emerged as a sob of frustration and self-disgust. 'Get *off* me!'

'That's not what you want.' His words burned against her ear. 'You want me to haul up your petticoats and—'

'*No!*' The velvet upholstery swallowed her gasping scream, but she began to struggle in earnest beneath him. Jabbing backwards and upwards with her elbows, she heard him grunt as one sharp elbow connected with his ribs.

He cursed and rolled off her. As soon as she was relieved of his weight she scrabbled around to face him, clutching her bodice against her breasts and drawing her knees up in an instinctive attempt to protect herself from further assaults.

The gondola rocked beneath their shifting weights, and she heard the canal water slap against the sides of the elegant craft. The lantern swung from side to side before once more coming to rest.

Gabriel stared at Athena in the shifting light. 'That's twice you've inflicted injury upon me,' he said, his eyes narrowing. 'Your pimp did not treat you well.'

'I never had a pimp! I had a husband. And, no, he didn't treat me well!' Athena panted with overwrought emotion.

'Where is he?'

'He's dead.'

'How convenient.'

'He died a few months ago.'

'And now you're looking for a new patron. Did he pay for your silk and lace, or did you bewitch some other poor fool into giving it to you?' Gabriel's long fingers flicked scornfully at the broad lace collar around Athena's neckline.

'No one gave it to me!' Athena spat. 'I made it! I'm not looking for a man. I survived eight years without Samuel. Why should I put myself at any man's mercy ever again? You only cause pain and misery.'

'*I* caused you pain and misery? I think not, Frances—'

'That's not my name,' she interrupted, without considering her words.

'Not your name?' He stared at her, then threw himself back on to the seat beside her with a crack of scornful laughter. 'You tell a series of fairy tales, expect me to believe them— then tell me I don't even know your *name?* Well, what could I expect from a born harlot? You never intended to marry me, so what did it matter what name you used?'

'It *is* my name,' Athena corrected, flushing angrily.

'First it isn't, then it is—'

'I was christened Athena Frances. Before God I am both Athena and Frances. I was *not* marrying you under a false name because you knew me by my second Christian name, not my first. I would have made my vows before God in good faith, knowing that He knows who I am.'

'God knows, but not your future husband.' Gabriel stared at her. The hard light in his eyes softened by a few degrees as he studied her face, dwelling on each feature in turn. 'Athena,' he repeated under his breath. 'Perhaps. But you will always be Frances to me.'

A sob rose unexpectedly in Athena's throat. 'Frances died when Samuel found me,' she said.

'Who the hell is Samuel? Why was he looking for you?' Renewed suspicion appeared in Gabriel's eyes.

'Was. He's dead,' Athena reminded him. 'He was my stepfather's nephew.'

'Your *stepfather?* You told me you went to live with your aunt in London after you were orphaned.'

'My father died,' said Athena. 'My brother was only six. Several of our neighbours wanted to seize our house and estates. My brother was too young to defend his inheritance, so my mother remarried to protect us. My stepfather was—is—a good, upright man. But he favoured a match between me and his nephew. Samuel. When I could see no other way to avoid the marriage I ran away to London where I altered my name. I thought Samuel would never find me. He did. He found me the day before our wedding was meant to take place.'

For several long moments there was silence in the gondola.

'Why the hell didn't you tell me that story before—when I asked you to marry me?' Gabriel growled at last. 'Did you plan to leave me forever in ignorance of your family?'

'No. I was so happy. I didn't want anything to spoil·it…'

'If what you claim is true, you were a stupid, heedless wench,' Gabriel said brutally. 'You deserved your fate.'

'Never!' Athena thought of all she'd endured to keep Gabriel safe from Cromwell's executioner. 'How dare you judge me so harshly. You know nothing. *Nothing.'*

'If you're telling the truth, I know more now than I did then. You *lied* to me in London. From beginning to end—you *lied* to me. You were even going to marry me without telling me your real name. How the devil did you expect me to protect you if I didn't know you were in danger?' he exploded.

'Protect me? You watched and did nothing to stop Samuel—'

'Before!' Gabriel roared. 'If I'd known before, do you think I'd have left you under the protection of one elderly widow woman? You could have had a place in Sir Thomas Parfitt's household until the wedding. You didn't *think,* Frances. You just danced through your days, expecting life to fall into your pretty lap.'

'I didn't dance,' Athena whispered, hating the way he made her sound so heedless.

'Yes, you did,' he said flatly. 'You danced and left the practical business of life to others.'

'I don't even know *how* to dance,' she protested, remembering her awkwardness earlier that evening.

'Your spirit danced.' He stared up at the roof of the gondola, then laid his forearm across his eyes.

'Oh.' Tears trembled in Athena's own eyes. 'I was a foolish virgin,' she whispered. They had gone on a picnic once, and she'd been so lost in thoughts of Gabriel she'd forgotten to pack the bread. He had teased her about the parable of the wise virgins who had filled their lamps with oil in preparation for the coming of the bridegroom, and the foolish virgins who hadn't been so well prepared.

'It would appear so,' he said.

'Well, I'm not—' she began without thinking, then bit her lip to stop herself crying.

'No.'

'Foolish now!' she snapped, lifting her chin defiantly, although he wasn't looking at her and would not therefore be impressed by the gesture. 'I may have been foolish once, but I am not foolish now.'

'You arrived in Venice with no idea how you were going to continue your journey and had to beg the Ambassador to arrange your transport home! How much more damned foolish can one woman get!'

'I was not foolish!' Athena fired up. 'Rachel needed my support. She was in such distress. Only someone with a heart of stone would have refused to help her.'

'Another foolish wench. Has she any idea how much her presence here may hinder her husband's career?' Gabriel said derisively.

'She didn't come to hinder his career, she came to save herself from her lech of a brother-in-law! If her husband had left her better provided for, she wouldn't have needed to come to Venice. Men always think they know best. They don't know anything.'

'What were you doing in the convent?' Gabriel asked.

'That's where I ended up after I ran away from Samuel the second time,' said Athena.

'You ran away? When?'

'Three weeks after the wedding.'

'Three weeks!' Gabriel swore. 'If you had the resolution to run away then, why not earlier?'

'Because earlier I didn't know—' Athena caught herself up before she revealed that it was only after Gabriel had set off for Turkey that she'd run from Samuel. 'Circumstances changed,' she said instead. 'There was no longer any risk involved if I left him. My mother's sister lived in exile in France. Her husband was a royalist who fought for Charles at Worcester. He was hanged when the Roundheads captured him after the battle. I went to her.'

'To France? All on your own?' Gabriel's voice was redolent with scepticism.

'Yes! I cut off my hair, dyed it brown and pretended to be a youth,' Athena declared proudly. 'I got all the way to my aunt's without anyone seeing through my disguise.'

Gabriel looked at her in disbelief, his eyes resting on the womanly curve of her breasts.

'I bound them and wore baggy clothes,' Athena said impatiently. 'And I practised walking like a cocky youth. I based my impersonation on you. People only see what they expect to see.'

Gabriel raised his eyebrows. 'In my experience cocky youths usually walk straight into trouble in unfamiliar surroundings,' he said drily.

'Hmm. Well,' Athena muttered, discomfited. 'After certain incidents I concluded, upon reflection, that a more modest bearing might be advisable. But I reached my destination quite safely. I am not the only woman who has chosen the protection of male clothing when travelling,' she pointed out.

'And what happened when you reached your aunt?'

'We decided, Aunt Eleanor and I, that the English Convent in Bruges would be the safest place for me to hide. One of her childhood friends is the Abbess there. She took me to the convent early in 1659 and I stayed until Rachel needed a companion on her journey here.'

'Seven years in a convent,' Gabriel mused, his expression unreadable as he looked her up and down. 'You are certainly not *dressed* like a nun.'

'I wasn't a nun, I was a guest of the convent.'

'Hardly a charitable case, by the look of you.'

'My aunt made donations to the convent. But I also worked for them in the infirmary and sometimes the gardens,' Athena said. 'And I made my lace.' She touched her bodice. 'It fetches a good price, you know.'

'Yes.' His eyes raked her face. 'It is a very plausible story,' he said.

'Don't you believe me?'

'I reserve judgement.'

'You have no right to judge me!' Athena fumed.

'It was judgement that separated the wise from the foolish virgins.'

'It was common sense and foresight,' Athena shot back.

'Both of which you completely lack if this latest exploit is any indication.'

'And you've lost your compassion. And your gallantry,' she added, as an afterthought. 'How *could* you treat me so rudely at dinner?'

'Very easily.' He moved suddenly, startling her into huddling back into her seat, but all he did was twitch apart the curtains a couple of inches to speak to the gondolier standing in front of the small cabin.

'Oh, my God, they heard us?' she whispered in horror, as Gabriel sat back again.

'They don't speak English,' he replied indifferently.

'What did you say to him?' Athena still kept her voice lowered.

'I ordered them to take us back to the embassy.'

'Oh.' Athena experienced a strange sense of anticlimax. 'Then what?'

'You may retire to your quarters and I will retire to mine.'

'That's it?'

'What else would you prefer to do?' His eyes glittered in the lantern light.

Athena clutched defensively at her bodice and realised she

was still unlaced. 'I can't walk into the embassy like this!' she gasped.

'I could carry you in,' he offered.

'Certainly not!' She bit her lip as she considered her options. 'You may do me up,' she decided, 'but mind you touch nothing but the points and my bodice!'

'You want me to do the work of a lady's maid?' he said. 'For what hire?'

'Nothing. You shouldn't have undone me in the first place.'

'Turn around,' he commanded.

She did so, looking warily over her shoulder to see what he would do.

'So suspicious,' he mocked her.

'No more than you.' She held her breath as he pulled on the laces. 'Not too tight. The bone is broken,' she reminded him.

She wasn't sure whether she was relieved or disappointed that he did exactly as she'd asked. Despite everything, some small part of her still yearned for his caresses.

'There. You may return to the embassy as respectably dressed as you left it,' he said.

'What did he do to you?' Athena's maid demanded the instant she entered her room.

'Nothing.' Athena had known there was little chance her interlude with Gabriel would go unnoticed, at least by Martha. Her maid had been given a pallet bed in Athena's chamber.

Martha sniffed disbelievingly. 'Richard saw him carry you off the steps. He said you didn't even struggle.'

Richard was the manservant Rachel Beresford had brought with her from England. Martha hadn't wanted to come to Venice, but she'd been partially consoled for the inconvenience of the trip by the friendship she'd struck up with Richard.

'Did he?' Athena sat down on a stool and brushed her hair wearily back from her face. It was hard to dredge up answers to satisfy Martha when she had so many unanswered questions of her own whirling in her mind.

'I didn't struggle because there was no point,' she said. 'Do you suppose anyone in this place would gainsay Lord Halross?'

'No,' Martha admitted grudgingly. 'He has them all in thrall. And he's in better standing with the Venetians than the Ambassador, by what I hear. Why did he take you? What did he do to you? Did he hurt you?'

'To talk. No, he didn't hurt me.'

'*Talk!*' Martha snorted in disbelief. 'How do you know him? You never mentioned him before.'

The stool was close to the wall. Athena leant back gratefully. 'I knew him before I was married,' she said.

'Were you his *mistress?*' Martha sounded shocked.

'*No!*' Athena lifted her head in indignation. 'I was to *marry* him.'

'Marry him?' Martha's mouth fell open. 'Why didn't you?'

'We had a small misunderstanding several years ago. Lord Halross wanted to clear it up this evening, that's all,' said Athena, trying to conclude the conversation.

'It's not all, by a long shot,' Martha said grimly. 'Richard wasn't the only one who saw the Marquis carry you off. Sir Walter's valet also saw you. By tomorrow morning everyone in the embassy will be sure Lord Halross has set you up as his mistress.'

An inn, Brussels

'There is one other matter, your Grace,' said Philpott, Gentleman of the Privy Purse to the Duke of Kilverdale.

'What is it?' Kilverdale sat back and looked at his servant.

Philpott had just finished presenting a detailed account of the expenses the Duke had so far incurred on his unexpected trip to Venice. As ever, the Gentleman of the Privy

Purse had carried out his duties with efficiency and discretion, but Kilverdale knew something was troubling the man. An agitated Philpott was such an unusual sight that Kilverdale waited with interest to discover what had disturbed him.

'Your Grace may not be aware that Brown's wife is expecting their first child in a few weeks,' said Philpott. Brown was the groom who had come to Flanders in the Duke's retinue.

'The fact had slipped my memory,' Kilverdale acknowledged, guessing where the conversation was leading. Brown's devotion to the chambermaid he had married the previous autumn was well known in the Duke's household.

'He didn't realise when we first came to Flanders that we would be away from home so long,' said Philpott, approaching the problem with less than his usual directness.

'I didn't know either,' said Kilverdale, losing patience with Philpott's long-winded explanation. 'By all means tell him he may return to his wife. I am sure you will be able to find a local man to replace him.'

'Thank you, your Grace. You are very generous.' Philpott hesitated; clearly there was something more.

'What? Spit it out, man! How the devil can I deal with the problem if I don't know what it is?'

'Yes, your Grace. I beg your pardon. Unfortunately, Brown is a nervous traveller. He speaks no other language but English and is ill at ease with foreigners. I am not entirely sure he will be able to get safely back to England on his own.'

'Then Leith had better go with him to hold his hand!' Kilverdale said impatiently. 'Does that satisfy your concerns?'

'Thank you, your Grace,' said Philpott looking sheepish. 'I am sorry for troubling you with this matter. If I'd had more forethought, I wouldn't have brought Brown. I'll see you are not inconvenienced.'

'Very well,' said Kilverdale. 'Make sure they have adequate

funds and directions for the journey. Then you'd better set about finding replacements.'

Philpott bowed out of the Duke's presence. Left alone to entertain himself for the rest of the evening, Kilverdale picked up his lute and checked the tuning. He smiled at the harmonious ripple of notes and began to play a jaunty galliard.

It was already mid-morning and the day promised to be warm and fair when Athena took a small table and the stool from her bedchamber on to the second-floor balcony. She was tired and a little headachy from her restless night, but the early summer sunshine felt like a soothing balm for her troubled mood. She paused to look over the balcony at the glittering water below. Gondolas passed by in either direction. She wished she could explore more of Venice, but now that everyone in the embassy apparently believed she was Gabriel's mistress she needed to be more careful than ever. She wanted a period of quiet reflection before she decided what to do next.

She rested her elbows on the stone balustrade and watched the canal for a while. The waterborne traffic fascinated her. Painted poles rose from the canal in front of every palazzo. Many of them had gondolas tied to them. When she leant right over the balcony she could see several gondolas outside the embassy. One of them belonged to Gabriel.

He'd waited at the church! He'd really meant to marry her!

She was sure he'd told the truth. There was no other reason why he should be so angry with her. No other way he could have seen her with Samuel unless he'd cared enough to look for her when she didn't arrive at the church.

Many confused and often painful thoughts jostled for attention in Athena's mind, but the simple fact that Gabriel had truly meant to marry her was the most important. She hugged the knowledge to her heart. All these years she had half-believed Samuel's lie that Gabriel had only been amusing himself with her. Now she knew better. No matter what had happened afterwards, Gabriel had waited at the church for her. He hadn't rescued her from Samuel. His faith in her hadn't been that strong. But he *had* meant to marry her.

Tears misted her view of the canal. She swallowed a sob of gladness and smiled a little at her mixed-up response to everything she'd just discovered. She brushed away her tears, then went back into her chamber and fetched out her lace pillow.

She had finished her last piece of lace just before she'd left Bruges. She'd wound several bobbins with flax thread on the journey to Venice, but she hadn't begun her next piece. She put the wedge-shaped pillow on the small table, with the narrow edge towards her. From the drawer on the right side of the pillow she took a parchment pricking. The pre-pricked holes in the parchment showed her the positions for the pins in the design she intended to work. She attached the parchment to the pillow and covered the lower portion of both with a protective cover cloth. Then she inserted the first pins and hung the bobbins in pairs from them. She was ready to start.

She'd chosen a pricking for a simple edging lace. It was one she had worked many times and required no special concentration on her part. She'd set up the pillow mainly to find solace in a familiar activity, but it pleased her that the lace she was making would have many uses. It was pleasant sitting in the shade on the balcony, and she worked for a couple of hours, barely aware of the passage of time.

By almost imperceptible degrees, a new awareness crept over her. It was hardly noticeable at first until she suddenly experienced an absolute conviction she wasn't alone. She lifted her head to discover Gabriel standing a few feet away. Her heart skipped into her throat—then continued beating at a faster pace. She hadn't heard him come on to the balcony and had no idea how long he had been silently watching her.

She gazed at him, the bobbins forgotten in her hands. He

wore a blue brocade coat with silver buttons. The midday sun picked out shining highlights in his long, dark brown hair. The overhead light cast his deep-set eyes into shadow, hiding his expression, but she sensed no simmering hostility in his powerful body. His mood appeared quiet and watchful.

She couldn't tear her eyes away from him. He was so close to her and yet still so far away. There were tiny creases at the corner of his eyes that hadn't been there eight years ago. He had crossed thousands of miles since she'd last met him, across the seas and continents of the world. And perhaps the journey from the young man who'd believed he would have to make his own way in the world to his present position as the Marquis of Halross had been one of the longest.

She wondered suddenly what had happened to his older brothers. His current status meant that they were dead. She couldn't remember if he had any other family. Did he find his grand inheritance a lonely burden?

A wife?

Did he have a wife? Until that second Athena hadn't even considered the possibility. Her stomach turned over with sudden dread. 'Are you married?' she burst out.

His eyes widened momentarily. 'No.'

'Oh.' She ducked her head, staring at the pillow with unfocussed eyes. Relief cascaded through her body, robbing her limbs of all strength. She couldn't think of another thing to say.

He cleared his throat. 'I've been busy,' he said. 'With the ships, and then sorting out the mess Edmund made of the estate before he died. Now that everything is in order I plan to take a wife this summer.'

'Oh.' Athena's tiny bud of hope withered. He hadn't remained unwed because of his memories of her. He'd just been too busy to get round to marriage.

'Ashworth has been pressing the virtues of his eldest daughter,' said Gabriel. 'I think she may do very well.'

'That is…very good.' Athena did her best to keep her expression impassive. She straightened her back and began to ply the bobbins once more, following the pattern by instinct.

'A wife appears to be a necessary inconvenience to a man in my position,' said Gabriel.

Athena blinked and flicked the bobbins across each other even more quickly. She'd never cried before Samuel and she was damned if she'd cry in front of Gabriel.

'Did you have something you wished to say, my lord?' she asked. 'As you can see, I am somewhat busy myself.'

'Most industrious,' said Gabriel, watching her push a pin into the pillow.

Flick, flick, pin, flick, flick. Flick, flick, pin, flick, flick.

Frances was angry with him, he thought, judging by the jerky movements of her hands. Once he had been confident he could tell her moods, but now he was no longer sure. If she was angry, he couldn't entirely blame her—it had been an unkind comment. And untrue. He had no plans to marry Elizabeth Ashworth, even though the last time he'd visited London Lord Ashworth had hinted that his daughter would be a good match for Gabriel. Elizabeth Ashworth was virtuous and well bred, exactly the kind of wife Gabriel was seeking; but Gabriel had smiled and politely evaded the subject with Charles Ashworth just as he'd fobbed off Filippo Correr's matchmaking attempts two nights' ago.

Frances's head was bent over her work. He couldn't see her face, but her hair shone like spun gold in the sunlight. This morning she had dressed for comfort in an unadorned brown skirt and a loose-fitting jacket. They were probably the clothes in which she'd travelled. Even the most fashionable of ladies did not wear their boned bodices when they relaxed in private.

Her choice of attire hinted that she'd regarded the balcony as a safe refuge. Gabriel smiled faintly at the foolish idea. If he decided to seek her out, she would not find it easy to hide from him. He was not in the habit of being thwarted in the achievement of his goals.

He watched her, remembering the past. For eight years he'd been convinced she had deliberately humiliated him. The evidence against her had been so damningly conclusive. He'd hated himself for the way she'd continued to plague his memory, even after knowing the worst of her. He'd gone to Aleppo in the Turkish empire, hoping the change of location would rip all thought of her from his mind. Instead her image had accompanied him along every road he'd walked and into every room he'd entered for over a year. Though Frances had never been to Aleppo she was inextricably bound with his memories of the place.

Now she was back in his life again. Invading every corner of it, just as she had before. Since he'd first set eyes on her yesterday she'd filled his mind, throwing his usually well-ordered emotions into turmoil. It was impossible to ignore her. He could not even *pretend* indifference to her presence in the embassy. He'd spent the morning on his business affairs, but every restless instinct in his body had urged him to seek her out. Now that he'd found her his restless urgency dissipated. For a few minutes he was content simply to look at her, forgetting she'd asked him a question.

He'd always enjoyed looking at her. Her beauty aroused his desire, but her womanly grace soothed him. He watched her slim hands manipulating the bobbins. Once he had pressed chaste kisses against her fingers and fantasised of the time when he could kiss her with all his passion unleashed—and she would touch him intimately with those beautiful hands.

She still stirred his lust. She was twenty-five now, but she was as beautiful and desirable as she had been at seventeen. Even without the aid of tight lacing he could see the pert swell of her breasts beneath her demure jacket and a hint of her slim waist. When he remembered the feel of her legs trapped between his thighs in the gondola his body began to harden with arousal. His hands flexed as he recalled the feel of her soft, warm skin beneath his fingertips and the taste of her shoulder against his tongue. Eight years ago he'd wanted her with the eager urgency of youth, now he wanted her with the fierce, unrelenting intensity of a man.

He willed his body into quiescence. Lust was simple, but the emotions Frances aroused in him were far from simple. He'd loved her and hated her. Now he didn't know what to believe about her. He didn't even know what to call her. Frances or Athena? There was no evidence to prove she was telling the truth about what had happened on their intended wedding day. Or even that she'd finally given him her true name. By her own admission, she had not told him the truth eight years about who she was and why she was in London. Was this new story just another one of her deceptions?

He stared at her, trying to see through the plain brown jacket to the heart that lay beneath. Eight years ago he'd believed her soul was as beautiful and angelic as her appearance. Before their wedding day he would never have believed she was capable of lying to him. After years of believing the worst about her, he was slowly coming to accept she wasn't the harlot he'd believed her to be. But nor was she the innocent girl he'd put on a pedestal during their courtship. Had she ever loved him? Or had she only wanted to marry him because, as his wife, she would have been protected from Samuel Quenell's unwanted attentions? Gabriel's eyes narrowed as he tried to see through her composure to the answers hidden in her heart.

The wooden bobbins suddenly rattled against each other. She stopped flicking them back and forth, lifted her head and glared at him.

'Are you planning to stand there staring all day?' she demanded.

'If it pleases me.' Her show of temper entertained him. It was only fair that she should be as conscious of him as he was of her.

'Well, it doesn't please *me*.' She straightened her back and squared her shoulders in a way that pushed her breasts forward.

Gabriel was sure she was unaware of the effect of her action, but he was *very* aware of it.

'Do you realise the entire household believes I am your mistress?' she demanded. 'The situation is unendurable.'

'I don't find it so.' He suppressed a smile at the sparking anger in her blue eyes.

'Not to you. To *me*! And it's your fault! What are you going to do about it?'

'What do you want me to do? Tell them that it turns out you aren't to my taste after all?' he said carelessly. 'I'm sure there are several members of the Ambassador's household who'd be only to glad to take my leftovers.'

'I am not your leftover!' Frances gasped with outrage. 'I am a respectable woman. I have *always* been considered a respectable woman until I came to Venice.'

'Hmm. I'm afraid those days are over, sweetheart. At least as far as the residents of this palazzo are concerned.'

'That's scandalous.' She jabbed a pin at random into the pillow.

'Yes, we are.' He strolled over to lean on the balustrade.

'I have done *nothing* to deserve this,' she raged, paying no heed to his comment. 'I came to Venice in good faith because Rachel needed my help and now look what has happened! I'm stuck in this prison palace surrounded by a lot of lechers who think I'm a loose woman! I hardly dare leave my room in case I give them false notions.'

'Perhaps not the best tactic,' Gabriel observed. 'You could be getting up to all manner of scandalous activities in your room, but if you're in full public view—'

'I don't care to be in full public view,' she replied through gritted teeth. 'I wish I'd never come to Venice.'

'So do I.' Gabriel straightened up and moved away from the balustrade. He'd wished more than once that he hadn't been in Venice when she'd arrived, but it caused him a pang of some unrecognisable but unpleasant emotion when she voiced the same wish.

Her gaze flew to his face. For a few seconds he thought he saw hurt in her eyes before she guarded her expression.

'There is a solution to your unfortunate situation,' he said blandly.

'What?'

'You could become my mistress in fact as well as reputation.'

She stared at him, her lips parted in shock. Then the colour drained out of her face.

Her mouth worked for a few seconds before she managed to utter a word. 'How could you?' she whispered. 'I was good enough to be your wife. But now… No! *Never!*' She sprang to her feet, knocking over the stool. 'Is this your idea of revenge? Because I will *never* let you humiliate me like that!'

'It's my price for providing you with safe passage back to England,' he said. 'That *is* what you want from me, isn't it?'

Chapter Four

'Sir Walter, may I speak with you a moment?' Athena intercepted the Ambassador in the *portego*.

'Surely, Mrs Quenell. What may I do for you?' His eyes were bright with curiosity. So far no one in the embassy had alluded directly to her supposed status as Gabriel's mistress, but she knew from Martha that speculation was rife.

'I wonder if you could assist me with a business transaction?' she asked. She hated the need to ask for his aid but, since she spoke no Italian, she could see no alternative.

'Of course. Why don't you come into my rooms? I'm sure you'd prefer to discuss the arrangements in private.'

Athena took a step in the direction he indicated before it suddenly occurred to her that Sir Walter might think she wanted him to act as her broker in making her terms with Gabriel.

'Oh, no!' She stopped dead. 'That is, my business is not of a private nature,' she said, embarrassed by what she was afraid the Ambassador might be thinking. 'I wish to sell a piece of lace.'

'Lace?' Sir Walter gaped at her.

'I finished it just before I left Bruges,' she hurried on. 'I'd like to find a buyer here in Venice, but I don't speak Italian. I wondered if there might be someone in your household who could…'

'Ah, I see,' said Sir Walter. 'Is that the lace?' He nodded to the rolled linen bundle under her arm.

'Yes. Would you like to see it?' Athena crossed to a table against the wall of the *portego*. She unrolled the linen and laid out the large piece of lace on the dark polished surface. 'Venetian lace is needle-made,' she explained to the Ambassador. 'You are wearing some yourself, in fact.' She indicated Sir Walter's cravat. 'My lace was made with the very finest Flanders thread with bobbins. As you can see, it is much more delicate than Venetian lace. I know that Venetian lace is very fashionable at present, but I believe my lace may be something of a novelty here, and therefore fetch a good price.'

'It is exquisite,' said Sir Walter. 'I compliment you on your skill, madam.'

'Thank you,' said Athena. 'I was well taught by Sister Theresa. Her lace was truly exceptional. Do you suppose you will be able to help me find a purchaser, sir? I would like it to fetch as good a price as possible?'

'Well…' the Ambassador hesitated, looking uncomfortable. 'There is a difficulty in dealing with the Venetians,' he confessed. 'I have not been here so very many months and I'm still trying to find my way around their customs. You may be better advised to sell to an English visitor if—'

Footsteps echoed behind them on the *terrazzo* floor.

All Athena's senses sharpened as she focused on the man who approached. Every muscle tensed. She didn't need to look around to know it was Gabriel. A complicated mixture of emotions washed over her. Indignation, mortification, and a small *frisson* of nervous anticipation. She had hoped she would be able to complete her plans to sell the lace before she encountered Gabriel again. Now she would have to make the best of a very awkward situation. She summoned an air of calm indifference and turned to face him.

Sir Walter also turned, and his expression cleared as he recognised Gabriel. 'Lord Halross!' he exclaimed. 'I'm sure you will be able to help us, my lord.'

'Help? In what way?' Gabriel's appraising gaze flickered from Sir Walter to Athena, then moved beyond them to the lace lying on the table. He scrutinised it through narrowed eyes.

Athena held her breath, wondering what he would say. She despised herself for wanting his praise, but she couldn't pretend his opinion didn't matter. Perhaps that was why his offer to make her his mistress hurt so badly. There had been a time he had thought so much more highly of her.

'A fine piece,' he said at last. He didn't touch it, but rested the fingertips of his arched hand on the table beside it. 'Did it take you long to make?' he asked; his assessing gaze was as impersonal as any merchant's when he looked at Athena.

'More than two years,' she replied, disappointed despite herself by his brief comment and curt question. 'It is slow work, lace-making.'

'Yes, I know. In what way do you believe I can help, Cracknell?' Gabriel asked the Ambassador.

'Mrs Quenell wishes to sell her lace here in Venice,' Sir Walter explained. 'I thought one of your merchant friends might be able to help her. Get the best price for her.'

'I see.' Gabriel threw another piercing glance at Athena. Her stomach fluttered with apprehension as she saw the slow, unsettling smile that curved his lips. She knew he had guessed her purpose for selling the lace. She wanted the funds to arrange an independent passage back to England.

She reached for the lace, suddenly suspicious of his intentions, but he was before her. With a deft flick of his wrists he laid it flat on the linen and re-rolled the bundle before she could intervene.

'I will be honoured to take care of this transaction for you, Mrs Quenell,' he said, a mildly mocking note in his voice as he strode towards his own quarters. 'Good afternoon, Crack-

nell,' he added over his shoulder. 'You no longer need to concern yourself with this matter. I will see to everything.'

Athena followed her disappearing lace, which meant she
had no choice but to follow Gabriel as he disappeared into his
own private guest quarters in the embassy.

'Give it back!' she ordered as soon as they were beyond
the Ambassador's hearing. 'Right now!' She made a grab for
it, but he easily held it out of her reach. Belatedly she realised one of his servants was present, observing their interaction with a carefully blank face.

She stepped back, biting her lip with irritation and
embarrassment.

'May I offer you refreshment, Mrs Quenell?' Gabriel asked.

'No, thank you. Please give me my lace.'

Gabriel smiled and dismissed his servant. 'All in good
time,' he said.

Before Athena had fully divined his intention he unlocked
a chest and placed the lace inside it.

'*No!*' Too late she dived across the room to save it.

Gabriel closed the lid, locked it and put the key in his
pocket.

Athena fell on her knees before the chest and tugged use-
lessly at the lid. It wouldn't budge. She twisted on her knees
to face Gabriel.

'You've stolen my lace!' Her voice throbbed with furious
indignation. She couldn't believe he'd done something so
despicable.

'Not at all.' There was a rigid set to his jaw, but his voice
was blandly polite. 'It is a valuable item and I doubt if you
have such a secure place to keep it. Shall we discuss the terms
of its sale? Why don't you sit down?' He gestured to a chair
opposite his. The furnishings in his quarters were far more elegant than those in the room allotted to her.

Athena ignored his invitation as she sat on the floor by the chest in a heap of disordered petticoats. Her anger slowly dissipated, to be replaced by the chilling realisation that she had lost her only means to preserve her independence. She still had a little money left, but she had always intended to sell the lace when she reached Venice. It had been her guarantee that she would not be stranded far from home. Now Gabriel had taken it, and she knew what terms he would impose upon its sale or return.

'You've become cruel, Gabriel Vaughan,' she whispered. She leant against the chest and covered her face with her hands.

'You haven't heard my terms for its return yet,' he replied coldly.

'I don't need to. How could you stoop so low? To blackmail me into your bed?'

'It's the usual way a man gets you into his bed, isn't it?'

'Not for a piece of lace.' She felt close to despair. She'd married Samuel to protect Aunt Kitty and Gabriel, but she knew most men judged a woman on *what* she'd done, not on *why* she'd done it.

'No?' said Gabriel. 'I thought perhaps you preferred being given an excuse to discard your tiresome virtue.' The taunting note in his voice wounded Athena even more than his words.

She rested her elbow on the top of the chest, rubbed her palm across her forehead, then turned her head to look at him.

'How can you say this is not revenge?' she asked. 'If you hate me so much—'

'I have not said I hate you,' he interrupted roughly.

'Then God help anyone you do hate,' she said. 'I would not want to be your enemy.'

She stood up stiffly and shook out her skirts. There seemed to be nothing left to say so she walked towards the door. She didn't look at Gabriel. She couldn't bear to do so.

He caught her upper arm when she was still only halfway across the room. His touch burned through her sleeve, si-

lently communicating to her the fiercely controlled passions
in his powerful body. She looked up, helpless to resist his will.
His amber eyes blazed with unreadable emotions.

'We haven't discussed our terms yet,' he reminded her, a
silky, dangerous note in his voice.

'Terms?' She raised her eyebrows. 'I didn't think you'd left
me any choices,' she said ironically.

'I will return the lace to you when we reach England,' he
said. 'And in addition I will give you…five times…its value
in gold. If you share my bed until we reach London.'

'Five times… How long will the journey take?' Athena
asked, a numb sense of unreality creeping over her.

'From now until we arrive? Perhaps three months. It de-
pends how long I delay here. If there is any business I need
to attend to in Livorno before we leave, it could take longer.'
Gabriel shrugged, dismissing the importance of the question.
'Allowing for possible delays, I imagine we'll arrive in London some time in late August,' he concluded.

'They say a labourer is worthy of his hire,' said Athena bitterly. 'It seems I am worth six times the value of my lace to
you in total. I don't think much of your terms, my lord.'

She wrenched her arm from Gabriel's grip and walked out
of his quarters. She didn't look back.

Gabriel stood still for several minutes after Frances left. He
closed his eyes and allowed the tension to seep from his muscles. As soon as he'd seen the lace and Sir Walter had asked
for his assistance he'd known what Frances intended. If she
sold the lace she would have the funds to disappear without
warning. She had already successfully travelled halfway
across Europe. Gabriel had no doubt that she would be bold
enough to continue her journey alone. He had almost lost her
a second time. He could not allow that to happen. Pure instinct
had prompted him to take the lace and lock it in his chest. Now

she couldn't run. For good or ill they would play out their reunion to its conclusion.

He took several deep, steadying breaths and opened his
eyes. Then he unlocked the chest and lifted out the lace. He
unrolled it and sat down, draping the fine, cobwebby cloth
across his knees. The delicate design featured birds and flowers, quite different from the bold patterns of Venetian lace.
Frances had made it. He touched it gently between his thumb
and forefinger, marvelling at her patient skill. He had bought
and sold many pieces of lace, but he knew at once that this
was one of the finest he'd ever seen. He thought of her sitting
at her pillow, as he had seen her that morning, in a place he
had never known her. The English Convent in Bruges. It was
indirect evidence that she had indeed lived at the Convent for
several years. That's where she had met Rachel Beresford, and
it would have taken years to acquire the skill to make the lace
he held.

He lifted it to his lips. It still retained a hint of her familiar scent. The elusive fragrance he associated only with Frances. He pressed the lace against his mouth and knew that, no
matter what happened, he would never sell it to another buyer.

'Richard has promised to keep his lordship's valet talking,
and Hobb has gone with Lord Halross,' Martha said. Hobb
was Gabriel's Gentleman of the Privy Purse.

'Good. You'd best come with me.' Athena stood up, feeling sick with nervousness.

Martha looked a little sour at Athena's words.

'You won't have to come into Lord Halross's rooms with
me,' Athena said, wishing Martha was a little more sympa-
thetic to her plight. 'But I may need you to distract attention
while *I* go in.'

Martha's expression didn't show much improvement.

'If I don't get my lace back we will both be stranded in Venice—and I won't have enough money to pay your wages,' Athena said, driven in desperation to state the exact truth.

'If he makes you his mistress, you'll be able to pay me,' Martha muttered, but she followed Athena out of the door.

By good fortune they didn't encounter anyone as they left the second floor but, to Athena's dismay, there was a footman lounging in the *portego*. She ducked back on to the external staircase.

'I was right,' she said in a low voice. 'He'll see immediately where I'm going if I walk past him. Could you, do you suppose, tempt him away?'

Martha pressed her lips together. 'What will Richard say if he knows I've been bandying words with a good-for-nothing fellow like that?' she demanded.

'You could ask him for advice on where to buy…where to buy *chocolate* for me?' Athena said, suddenly inspired. 'Men like being asked for advice. See if you can get him on to the balcony, to point out the route.'

'You spent too long in that convent!' Martha muttered but, despite her obvious reluctance, she did as Athena requested.

Athena hovered on tenterhooks as Martha spoke to the footman. It suddenly occurred to her that he might hear her footsteps so she slipped off her shoes, just as Martha enticed him on to the balcony. She clutched a shoe in each hand and ran in her stockinged feet across the empty *portego*. Her heart thudding with alarm, she slipped into the relative safety of Gabriel's quarters.

She paused in the middle of the room, allowing her heart-rate to return to normal. Her nerves still tingled with unfamiliar tension, but now the only risk was that she would be found by one of his servants—or by Gabriel himself. If his servants found her it would be mortifying. If Gabriel found her…

She refused to think about it. Every time she allowed thoughts of Gabriel into her mind she nearly drowned in a flood of chaotic emotion. She had to rescue her lace and leave. That's all there was to it.

She looked around the room, feeling Gabriel's presence even though he wasn't there. He had been staying at the embassy for several weeks before her arrival and his quarters had taken on the unmistakable imprint of his strong personality.

Then her gaze fell on the chest. Once again she was engulfed by a tidal wave of disbelief and indignation that Gabriel had taken her lace. He had no *right* to steal the product of two years' hard work from her.

She rushed across the room and fell on her knees in front of the chest. She reached into her pocket for the various implements she had brought to help her pick the lock. Then it occurred to her that perhaps, by some miracle, it was open. She tugged hopefully at the lid. No, it was locked.

She settled down to experiment with her various improvised tools. She *had* successfully picked one lock before. Surely this one wouldn't be more difficult?

Forty-five minutes later she was hot and frustrated and no closer to her goal than when she started. She sat back on her heels and glared at the chest. She'd broken into Samuel's locked box quite easily before she'd run away. She'd hoped that this lock would prove equally amenable. She scowled. How typical that Samuel should have had a useless lock while Gabriel's seemed impervious to all her efforts.

She brushed the back of her hand over her hot, damp forehead and decided to make another attempt with the piece of wire.

'You stupid chest! Why won't you open?' she exclaimed aloud, kneeling back on her heels and thumping it with the heel of her hand.

'Have you tried saying "please"?' Gabriel asked.

Athena jumped several inches at the sound of his voice. She

threw herself around to face him, clouting her elbow on the chest in the process. Her heart pounding, she stared up at him, shocked and aggrieved by his sudden appearance.

'What are you doing here?' she demanded, leaning against the chest and rubbing her aching elbow.

'I live here…temporarily,' he replied. His expression seemed perfectly serious, but Athena saw a well-remembered gleam in his eyes. He thought her predicament was funny.

Her sense of aggrievement increased. First he'd stolen her lace. Now he was laughing at her. She glared at him, opened her mouth to tell him exactly what she thought of his infamous behaviour—and realised he wasn't alone.

Hobb, Gabriel's Gentleman of the Privy Purse, stood slightly behind him. Athena closed her mouth, mortified at being discovered in such an undignified position by Gabriel's servant. Now the whole embassy would hear and no doubt embroider the tale with all kinds of insulting speculations.

'Mrs Quenell appears somewhat…warm,' said Gabriel, only a small twitch of his lips hinting at his amusement. 'Lemonade would be more refreshing than wine. See to it, Hobb.'

'Yes, my lord.'

Athena straightened her petticoats with as much dignity as she could muster and gathered herself to stand.

Gabriel bent and took her hand. She froze, staring up at him. The last time he'd touched her he had not been courteous.

'Allow me.'

'I want my lace back,' she said flatly, resisting his effort to draw her to her feet.

'I know.' He smiled slightly, but she couldn't read the expression in his eyes. 'By all means let us negotiate.'

'There is nothing to negotiate. You stole it. I want it back.'

'But I have possession.' His thumb stroked the back of her hand. 'Thus you have no choice. Unless you can hire a more efficient thief to act as your proxy.'

Athena snatched her hand away from him and stood without assistance.

'How can you be so dishonourable? So ruthless?'

The smile faded from his eyes. 'Sweetheart, I learnt that from you,' he said, a cold note beneath the aristocratic languor in his voice.

His words chilled Athena and she moved away from him. It was hard to come to terms with the changes in Gabriel. Harder still to think that what had happened on the day of their intended wedding might have caused the cold cynicism he now displayed.

'I was expecting to meet your brother yesterday,' she said, choosing a less disturbing subject. 'One of them. I did not realise they were both dead.'

There was a bookcase on the other side of the room, inset into an alcove and surrounded by ornate carvings. It caught her attention and she walked over to it.

'I'm sorry I disappointed you,' Gabriel replied.

'That's not what I meant. I was surprised to see you.'

'No more surprised than I was to see you,' Gabriel replied drily. 'Thank you,' he added.

Athena looked over her shoulder at his surprising gratitude and saw his remark had not been directed at her. The lemonade and other refreshments he had requested had arrived. She turned back to the bookcase, unwilling to show her face to the curious servant. She reached out to pick up a leather-bound volume and banged her hand against the wall instead. She gasped, rubbed her fingertips, which had made unexpectedly sudden contact with the hard surface, then stared more closely at the bookshelf.

'*Trompe l'oeil,*' said Gabriel, at her side. 'The Venetians are fond of such conceits. It must have been done before Cracknell rented the palazzo from its owner.'

'This side of the room is not so well lit,' Athena replied, feeling foolish at her mistake. 'And my attention was distracted.'

'Many people have been fooled by such illusions,' said Gabriel. 'That is their purpose.'

Athena turned to find he was offering her lemonade. She took the glass, fascinated by the exquisite workmanship. Even at the ambassador's banquet she had not seen anything so fine.

'From Murano,' said Gabriel, answering her unspoken question.

'Murano? Isn't it Venetian glass?' Athena turned it slowly in her hands, admiring the delicate, translucent crystal.

'Yes. But the glassworkers live and work on Murano—another island in the lagoon—to protect Venice itself from the risk of fire,' Gabriel replied. 'If you like, I can take you to see the glass works there—although they are uncomfortably hot.'

'Why do you want to take me anywhere?' Athena put the glass to her lips. The lemonade was sweet yet refreshingly tart upon her tongue.

'The negotiations,' Gabriel reminded her.

'Oh.' Athena had hoped he simply wanted to spend time with her. 'If you take me to Murano, what must I do in exchange?' she asked.

'Nothing. Such a trip would provide an extended opportunity for us to conduct our negotiations,' he said.

Athena looked at him over the glass, wary of what such negotiations might entail. His gaze was upon her lips. There was a heat in his eyes that stirred an immediate response within her. She saw that he'd watched her taste the lemonade and it had aroused him. Whenever she was with Gabriel, she was aware of a strong sensual attraction between them. Now that attraction overwhelmed every other emotion. She couldn't look away.

She lifted her glass and took another sip, watching Gabriel watch her. The hot glow in his eyes burned to a darker intensity. Her pulse rate increased and her gaze locked with Gabriel's. She flicked the tip of her tongue over her lips, tasting lemonade and the piquant tang of danger. Gabriel stood so close. His large, powerful body dominated her senses.

She licked her lips again, this time from nervousness rather than with any intention of teasing him. It wasn't wise to play with fire.

'You have learned much since we last met,' Gabriel said coldly. 'A practised temptress indeed.'

'What? No!' Shocked at his accusation, Athena stumbled away from him.

'Our bargaining promises to be amusing,' said Gabriel. 'What other whore's tricks will you display to raise your price?'

Athena threw the lemonade in his face. The valuable glass slipped from her fingers and shattered on the floor.

'How many diamonds will purchase an amiable temper?' Gabriel asked. He pulled a lace-edged handkerchief from his pocket and wiped the lemonade from his face.

'Courtesy.' Athena's whole body shook with anger. 'Respect. Not diamonds. You cannot buy me with gold.'

'But you *can* be bought.' Gabriel seized on her words. 'Was the protection of my name the purchase price of your devotion to me eight years ago?'

Athena turned away, too hurt by his suspicion to think of a quick retort. She supposed he might have some grounds for his cynicism. After all, she'd already admitted she'd been planning to marry him under, if not a false name, certainly a name she'd used to hide her true identity from Samuel. If the marriage had gone ahead and she'd told Gabriel the truth afterwards, her deception might still have been a source of conflict, but it would have been resolved much more easily. Now it was just another one of many complications in their relationship.

She headed for the door. It was hard to part from Gabriel with such bad feeling between them. Especially when, deep down, she still felt such a powerful connection to him. But she'd hurt and angered him, he'd hurt and offended her, and she didn't know what else to say.

'Wait.'

'You can take the cost of the glass from the lace,' she said over her shoulder.

'It's not important. Sit. Are you hungry?'

'Hungry?' she turned to look at him in disbelief. 'Are we to exchange pleasantries about the weather—or the state of the roads?'

'Canals,' he corrected her, a rough edge to his voice. She'd thought he was angry, but when she risked a glance into his eyes she changed her mind. He was in the grip of some fierce emotion, but she wasn't sure it was anger. *She* was angry. Even though she knew he had grounds to be suspicious of her, she was furious at his continued insults to her honour and virtue. She might have misled him about her full name but she was not, and never had been, a whore.

'You have stolen from me and insulted me,' she said, lifting her chin. 'I would like to see you whipped at the cart tail but I don't want to talk to you.' She tried to push past him, but he moved to block her way.

'Not many carts in Venice,' Gabriel observed. 'Haven't you noticed? There aren't any horses in the streets.'

'How could I notice?' Athena remembered a fresh grievance. 'Apart from when you abducted me, I haven't been outside the embassy door. And it was dark the second time. I wanted to explore Venice. But thanks to you I've had to hide in my room like a prisoner.'

'Prisoners don't hide. Penitents hide.'

'Penitent! You're the one who should be doing penance.' Athena prodded his chest for emphasis. 'Not me. You're a thief and a defamer. What?'

She couldn't read the expression in Gabriel's eyes, but she

sensed yet another change in his mood. He didn't say anything for several moments, just continued to look at her. Almost as if he couldn't quite believe she was standing before him, berating him in such a familiar way.

Once again the intervening years faded away. Athena was back in London, talking to the man she had loved and trusted and with whom she'd meant to spend the rest of her life. Trusted?

'I should have told you,' she whispered, voicing a very old regret.

'Told me?' His gaze sharpened.

'About Samuel.' She averted her face and took a few restless steps away from Gabriel.

'Why didn't you?'

'I thought I'd never see him again. I thought I was safe.' She threw a quick glance at Gabriel. He was watching her with his dark brows drawn together in a frown of concentration.

'It was such a special time,' she said. 'Magical even. I was so happy. I didn't want to spoil it talking about ugly things.'

'How could you be so irresponsible?'

'If I was, I paid,' Athena flung at him, stung by the condemnation in his tone.

'So did I. What amends do you propose to make to me for the damage you did?'

'Make amends?' His comment infuriated Athena. 'You deserve none. You have abused me and stolen my lace.'

'Do not keep harping on your imagined wrongs. You gave yourself to another man on our wedding day.'

'And you did nothing to save me. You saw, but you didn't help me. You should hang your head in shame for what you let him do to me!'

Gabriel's jaw clenched.

She blinked and pushed her hair out of her face, regretting her angry words. She didn't want to think about her wedding day. From his expression, Gabriel didn't either.

'Perhaps, madam, we could move this conversation forward,' he said grittily. 'More particularly, our negotiations. You want your lace back. You also want to see Venice.'

'Not for the price you're asking!'

His eyes narrowed. 'You do not know my price for escorting you on a tour of the city.'

'Isn't it the same as for the lace?'

'No.'

'Oh.' She looked at him, nonplussed. 'What then?' she asked cautiously.

'A civil conversation,' he growled.

'A civil conversation? You mean I am to suffer your insults and false assumptions in silence without defending myself?'

'I mean that we will disport ourselves like civilised individuals,' he said coldly. 'You will refrain from insulting me at every opportunity—'

'*I* will?' Athena's mouth fell open at this outrageous comment. 'What about *you?* You have been mistreating me, manhandling me and abusing me since you first laid eyes on me. Am I not allowed to defend myself?'

'We will *both* refrain from insults,' he said, through very stiff lips. 'That is the nature of civilised conversation.'

'What recourse do I have if you break the bargain?' Athena demanded.

'You will be relieved of the necessity to be polite to me.'

Despite herself, Athena uttered a short laugh. 'Hardly a substantial compensation,' she retorted. 'No, I think…' She paused, considering. 'I think that, every time you insult me during our tour of Venice, you must give me one gold piece.'

'You intend to provoke me to insults to pay for your journey home?' A dangerous light gleamed in Gabriel's eyes.

'Since you stole the means by which I intended to finance the journey, it seems a legitimate bargain,' said Athena, pleased that she'd turned the tables on him. 'Do you accept these terms?'

'Hmm.' He gazed at her. 'Do not forget that I too must claim recompense for every occasion you insult me.'

'Oh.' Athena looked at him warily. She was not entirely comfortable with this aspect of their bargain.

As she watched, Gabriel smiled slowly.

'I have it,' he said, his voice the purr of a satisfied lion. 'For every time you call me a thief or heap other such terms of abuse upon me, you must kiss me.'

'*Kiss?*' Athena's gaze instinctively settled on his mouth. She swallowed. 'I do not like your terms,' she protested.

His smile broadened. 'I do not care for yours,' he pointed out. 'It seems we shall both have good reason to ensure our conversation remains courteous. On these terms, will you permit me to show you Venice?'

Chapter Five

'How do the buildings stay up?' Athena asked. 'Why don't they sink into the water?'

It was mid-morning and they were sitting in Gabriel's gondola, travelling along the grand canal. Athena's intense interest in her surroundings was obvious. Unlike Gabriel, who leant back at his ease, she sat upright, gazing all around her with undisguised excitement and curiosity.

Gabriel watched Athena. He was as fascinated by her every gesture and change of expression as she was with Venice. When he didn't answer her question, she turned to look over her shoulder at him. He was lying back in the shade of the small cabin, but her face was illuminated by a bright shaft of sunlight. Her hair shimmered like gold. Her cheeks and lips were flushed with excitement. His body quickened with desire. She said something else, but he was too intrigued by the seductive movement of her mouth to pay attention to her words. His fingers flexed with the half-formed intention of pulling her back onto the seat beside him and tasting her lips.

A spark of annoyance flashed in her fine eyes. She frowned at him. It occurred to him that he might be entitled to a kiss sooner than he'd expected if he didn't soon reply to her. The notion had a certain appeal, but as a seductive technique lacked subtlety.

'Timber piles,' he said, remembering her original question. 'The buildings are supported by timber pilings.'

Athena frowned at a gothic palazzo they were passing. 'How?' she persisted.

Gabriel felt a stir of amusement, coupled with something akin to pain. He had forgotten her unfailing, bright-eyed curiosity. During their courtship she had questioned him about everything. He had spent hours describing his travels, his duties as Sir Thomas Parfitt's agent in Livorno, his dreams for the future. Later, when he'd decided that her interest had been a cynical ploy to attract him, he had felt like a fool for revealing so much of himself. He had hated himself and her for the way he had allowed her to lead him so shamefully by the nose. Or perhaps by other parts of his anatomy. It was not his nose that ached to be closer to her now. Even her familiar, never quite forgotten, scent aroused him.

'How do they build the houses on the pilings?' she said impatiently.

A crooked smile twitched Gabriel's lips. It seemed that though his mind was full of amorous fantasies, the lady wanted to discuss construction methods.

'Sit back comfortably and I'll tell you,' he said.

She looked from him to the space on the velvet upholstery beside him. He saw awareness, scepticism and amusement flicker in her eyes. And another emotion he had no time to recognise before she turned her head away.

'I think not,' she said. 'Oh! Why is that woman on stilts?' She twisted her head to keep the strange sight in view as their gondola glided past the entrance steps of a large palazzo.

Gabriel turned to look in the same direction and saw a patrician's wife being helped from her gondola by two female servants.

'She's not on stilts. They're shoes called *zoccoli*—the Venetian equivalent of pattens. They can be well over a foot in height, as you can see. It's a sign of rank. Only the patricians may wear them.' Gabriel saw the high-ranking woman put her hands on the heads of her attendants as she strove to keep her balance in the awkward footwear. It was a common sight in Venice. He looked back at Athena and saw she was watching with frank astonishment.

'Her skirts are so long. She looks so peculiar. And if she takes them off indoors she'll fall over her petticoats. It doesn't seem very practical!'

'A lady of such high status has little need to worry about practicality,' said Gabriel, amused by Athena's reaction. 'Though I believe originally the intention was to keep the feet clear of dirty streets.'

'Well, that is sensible,' Athena conceded. 'Though surely they never needed to be so high. Did they wade through the canals?'

'You'll see players on far taller stilts at the fair,' said Gabriel.

'What fair?' Athena's eyes widened with anticipation.

'In two days' time it will be Ascension Day,' said Gabriel. 'The Doge will marry the sea and then there will be—'

'The Doge will marry the sea?' Athena looked at him suspiciously. 'I think you are teasing me.'

'I'll take you to see the ceremony. We can watch from the gondola.' Gabriel was undisturbed by her scepticism. 'After that, there is a fair that lasts for two weeks. It promises to be most entertaining this year.'

Athena could almost feel the way his eyes caressed her lips when he spoke. She wondered what entertainments the fair had to offer, and what exactly Gabriel was thinking when he looked at her with such an intensely speculative expression in his eyes.

All morning her senses had been acutely tuned to Gabriel.

Though she looked around with genuine wonder, nothing completely distracted her from her heightened awareness of his proximity. He hadn't touched her since sitting beside her, but his thigh was inches from hers. When she turned to look sideways her skirt fell over his leg. He made no effort to move it. All the time she asked him about Venetian building techniques most of her attention was focused on that innocent, unintentional intimacy. Perhaps she should straighten her skirts. But, if she did, she might accidentally touch his leg. The thought brought heat to her face. She knew that if she settled back on the seat beside him it would be only moments before she was in his arms. Would he close the curtains before he kissed her?

Of course, he wouldn't kiss her unless she insulted him. She resolved, once again, as she had done many times before, not to say anything that could be construed as an insult. She was here only because there was no other way to get her lace back. And without her lace she would not be able to travel independently to England.

But when Gabriel answered her questions, just the way he used to, it was hard to remember everything that had happened since they'd last met face to face in London.

'You are lucky to have seen so much of the world,' she said.

He raised his eyebrows. 'You have travelled further than the average Englishwoman—or man,' he pointed out.

'Yes, I know. But I spent most of my time in the convent.' Despite her gratitude to the sisters, she couldn't help a small, wry grimace. 'The Abbess and the nuns were very kind to me, but it was a little…that is…there was not much variety,' she said.

'I didn't know you're Catholic,' said Gabriel.

'I'm not,' Athena responded, surprised. They had naturally discussed religion at the time they'd planned their marriage. They had both been raised as Protestants, though neither were comfortable with the extreme Puritanism of Cromwell's regime.

'But surely the convent…?' Gabriel said, surprised in turn. She wondered if he thought she'd lied about that as well.

'Oh, yes,' she said. 'The Abbess made several attempts to convert me to Roman Catholicism, but when she saw I would not she did not press it. That is to say, she did continue *trying* to persuade me of the rightness of her form of worship,' Athena added scrupulously, 'but not in a way that made it impossible to remain as her guest. We learnt to respect each other.'

'Then your aunt who took you there is Catholic?' Gabriel persisted.

Athena wasn't surprised by his assumption. There were deep divisions between Protestants and Catholics throughout Europe. In England such religious differences had contributed to the causes of the Civil War and, in turn, been made worse by the conflict. *No king, no bishops,* had been the cry of many staunch republicans.

'No,' said Athena. 'Aunt Eleanor was a childhood friend of the Abbess, but she herself adheres to the Church of England. But when I threw myself on her mercy it was difficult to know where to put me so that I would be safe from Samuel. And it wasn't comfortable in my aunt's household. I…attracted attention.'

'You will always attract attention,' said Gabriel. 'Men used to look at you with desire and me with envy whenever we walked down a street in London. Every man in the embassy would like to be beside you now. Men will always want you.'

Athena shivered. His words sounded less like a compliment and more like a condemnation. She felt a mixture of anger and discomfort. She'd had experience of the lengths one man at least had been prepared to go to have her. She'd hated the experience.

'I am not to blame for some men's shameful behaviour.' She straightened her back and held her chin up. 'I will not be blamed.'

'Are you claiming you do nothing to heat men's blood?' he challenged her.

'Men are fools. They lust without reason.'

'Did you give me no reason to lust yesterday when you tasted the lemonade?'

'I did not—that was *you*. No other man—'

'Are you claiming you didn't try to seduce me into returning your lace yesterday?'

'Of course not! I would not so demean myself. You are—' Athena snapped her mouth shut, remembering just in time the consequences of an angry accusation.

'Am I, indeed? And what are you for tempting thus?'

Athena turned her head away from the suspicion in Gabriel's eyes. Her throat thickened with tears she refused to shed. She remembered once again that Gabriel had seen her with Samuel. She had been driven only by a desperate need to protect Gabriel himself, but it was not surprising he doubted her virtue or her motives.

'Why didn't you scream?' Gabriel demanded, and it was clear his thoughts had paralleled hers. 'If you didn't want him to touch you, why didn't you fight?'

'*Fight?*' She turned on him furiously. 'I wanted to fight! I wanted to rip him to pieces. To hurt him the way he hurt me. But it is a wife's *duty* to submit.' She stopped, panting for breath, and then uttered the words that rose from deep in her heart. 'It was *your* duty to protect me. And you didn't.' She blinked and immediately turned her head away. She would not let Gabriel see her cry.

They sat in silence as the gondola continued along the canal. Athena knew that her accusation was not truly reasonable. Gabriel had seen his intended bride willingly submit to another man. The evidence of her infidelity was unequivocal. Any reasonable man would have believed the worst of her in that London bawdy house. But there was a small, unreasonable voice deep inside Athena crying that surely, if Gabriel had truly loved her, he would have *known* she was only with Samuel under duress. That he would have moved heaven and earth to find her and rescue her. But such unquestioning love only existed in fairy tales.

'Well, it is done,' she said at last, her voice sounding curiously flat in her own ears. 'Words will not change it. Is there more of Venice you wish to show me, my lord? Or shall we now return?'

'There is more,' Gabriel said coolly.

The gondola stopped near a bridge on the grand canal. Gabriel stepped out and turned to offer her his hand. She would have preferred to refuse assistance, but that would reveal how much his touch disturbed her. She let him take her hand, but she didn't look at him. His fingers tightened on hers and he steadied her as she climbed out of the bobbing gondola. She'd meant to avoid his eyes, but she couldn't help looking up at him. Immediately she was snared by the expression in his eyes. She couldn't interpret the stormy emotions she saw— but she knew he was no more indifferent to her than she was to him. Of course not. His fury had erupted when she'd mentioned Samuel.

What a fool she was!

She stared at him, her lips half-parted with surprise at her sudden revelation. Gabriel was jealous of Samuel. If he was jealous, then perhaps he still felt more for her than he'd been willing to admit. Perhaps he hadn't only been motivated by revenge when he'd stolen her lace. Perhaps his affection for her wasn't completely dead. She knew they could never wipe out the past, but she would give almost anything to establish peace and a renewed friendship between them.

Gabriel's eyes narrowed. He frowned and she realised she'd been staring at him for several moments. She looked away before he could demand an explanation.

'Come.' He drew her hand through his arm. 'I'll show you the Rialto.'

Athena followed him, her mind still full of increasingly hopeful speculations, but the famous bridge soon captured her attention. The Rialto spanned the grand canal with a single arch. There were two rows of shops on the top, separated by a wide passage through the middle. There were two narrower paths on either side of the bridge between the shops and the balustrades.

Gabriel took her into a couple of shops and she listened as he bargained in Italian with the shopkeepers.

'It is very fine,' she said, when at last they continued their tour. 'But I do not think it is as fine as London Bridge,' she added loyally, though it was years since she'd seen the many-arched bridge that was crowded with shops and houses.

Gabriel laughed. 'Let me see what I can find in the Merceria to impress you,' he said.

His mood seemed to have lightened since that disturbing interlude in the gondola. His arm beneath Athena's hand felt relaxed. She resolved to take care not to spoil his temper again. She looked about at the busy streets and saw two young men in the shadow of a doorway, watching her. From their dress and manner they were of high rank, amusing themselves by observing the crowd.

One of the young men was looking at her with a lustful gleam in his eye. She immediately turned her head away, disconcerted by what she'd seen. She was well aware that men liked to look at her. She'd learnt that to her embarrassment when she was still not much more than a child. But most of the time she'd lived in London she'd been too wrapped up in Gabriel to notice any other man, and since then she'd spent most of her adult life in the convent. It would be terrible if now, when she could least afford such attention, Gabriel noticed the young man and accused her of deliberately trying to attract admirers. For the next few paces she kept her eyes rigidly fixed on the ground in front of her.

'You will not see much if you keep your eyes in the gutter,' he said drily.

Startled, she looked up at him.

'Men will always look at you,' he said. 'Even if we covered you head to toe in a white veil like the citizens' daughters, men would still look.'

'That's not what I want,' she said, wondering if Gabriel had seen the brazen-eyed young man. She was annoyed by his comment. 'Men are knaves and then they blame women for their bad behaviour,' she said tartly. 'I have no patience with it.'

'It is very fashionable to be blonde in Venice,' said Gabriel. 'The Venetian ladies go to great lengths to bleach and colour their hair. You have the advantage of them.'

'What's that got to do with anything?' Athena had expected a more direct response to her implicit challenge.

'It means I know you cannot help it when men look at you. They did so when you were seventeen. They will still do so when you're seventy. In London I was proud when I saw their envious glances.'

'Oh.' Athena instantly wondered if he still felt proud. Probably. Men like owning pretty things.

She didn't realise she'd muttered the words aloud until he laughed.

'You've made it plain I don't own you,' he pointed out. 'Our negotiations are not yet concluded. There is everything to play for.'

'My honour and self-respect?' she said, offended by his tone. 'I don't consider their loss a trivial matter.'

'Did—?' He broke off and took a deep breath. They walked in silence for several minutes. Athena wondered what he'd intended to say. If he insulted her, he would have to pay a forfeit in gold. She deliberately replayed their recent argument, wondering if he had said anything that could enable her to make a claim upon him.

'It is ridiculous!' she said suddenly.

'What is?'

'You have behaved abominably—but I'm still fool enough to believe that if you offer me another insult you'll abide by our agreement to give me a gold coin. How can I be so naive?' She was absolutely disgusted with herself.

'Or so unwary?' Gabriel responded. 'If a man called me a liar and doubted my integrity as you have just done, I would demand more than the satisfaction of a kiss, madam.'

'What? *Oh!*' Athena stopped walking and scowled at him. 'You are—!' She clamped her lips together before she made things worse.

He smiled. 'I will claim the forfeit later,' he promised.

He touched the side of her face with his fingertips, gently pushing back a wayward curl as people thronged all around them. They were in one of the busiest parts of Venice, but Athena was aware only of Gabriel.

For a few seconds his eyes gleamed with satisfied amusement at the advantage he had just gained. As she looked up at him she saw his expression change. The humour slowly faded, to be replaced by a much more intense emotion. He rubbed his thumb over her lower lip and she caught her breath, captivated by his magical touch.

He smiled faintly. 'A prize worth savouring,' he said softly. 'I trust you will anticipate with pleasure your reward at the end of our tour?'

'You are—'

His eyes gleamed.

'A man of unusual capacity,' she said, glaring at him. 'I do not think I have ever met another man so well endowed with all the qualities necessary to achieve renown.'

He laughed softly. 'What kind of renown?' he asked.

Athena did not dignify his question with a reply and they began to stroll along the street once more. A few minutes later she forgot all about Gabriel's devious behaviour and the forthcoming kiss in her amazement at the splendid display around her.

She stood on one spot in the narrow street and turned in a circle, marvelling at the rich fabrics hanging from the first floor of every shop she could see. Cloth-of-gold, damasks and silks of every colour glowed in the shafts of midday sunlight that penetrated between the buildings. Tantalising aromas drifted from the shops, and birdsong filled the air.

'Nightingales!' she exclaimed, seeing the cages hung up in many of the shops.

'We're in the Merceria,' said Gabriel. 'Does it please you?'

'It's beautiful!' Athena hurried on a few paces, then stopped again to look around at the colour and wealth so extravagantly displayed in every shop. 'I have never seen anything like it,' she breathed.

'Come.' After a little while Gabriel took her hand and led her into a shop.

'Oh, why?' Athena didn't want to go into the shadows of the apothecary shop. She wanted to stay outside and feast her eyes on the rich colour.

'I am performing an errand for you,' Gabriel said.

'An errand for me? What do you mean?' Athena looked around suspiciously. She could smell many intriguing scents, some were pleasant, others less so—but she couldn't imagine what might have brought Gabriel there.

She listened as he spoke to the apothecary in Italian, understanding nothing of what they said. But then as the man started to prepare Gabriel's purchase she caught the scent of a favourite, but seldom enjoyed treat. One word among the Italian suddenly made delicious sense.

Cioccolata.

'Chocolate!' she exclaimed. 'You're buying chocolate!'

'That was what your maid was enquiring about, wasn't it?' Gabriel said.

'Is it for me?' Athena couldn't quite help licking her lips in anticipation.

'I hope you'll share it with me,' Gabriel said. 'My valet is particularly good at its preparation.'

'You mean I can only have some if I drink it with you?' Athena slipped her hand through Gabriel's arm as they walked back into the street.

'Is the allure of chocolate strong enough to overcome your reservations?' he asked, looking down at her from the corner of his eye.

'It would be discourteous to refuse such a treat,' she said sedately.

'In other words, you will condescend to accept my offer.'

'In the matter of chocolate,' said Athena, suddenly wary.

They continued to wander through the brick-paved streets. The shopkeepers were keen to attract their attention but, since Athena didn't understand anything they said, she simply smiled and left Gabriel to respond as he saw fit.

He seemed quite relaxed now. In her excitement at the fascinating sights around her, Athena forgot to be self-conscious. She asked him questions about everything. He showed his local knowledge with familiar good humour. By the time they reached St Mark's Square they were chatting as comfortably as if they'd never been parted. Gabriel pointed out the Doge's Palace to her.

'He is to marry the sea on Ascension Day?' she said, remembering Gabriel's earlier comment and looking at him with her head on one side.

'They renew their vows every year,' said Gabriel. 'That is, the Doge does. The Adriatic's response is somewhat more inscrutable. But, according to tradition, the *Serenissima* has already lasted for hundreds of years.'

'*Serenissima?*'

'The Serene Republic of Venice.'

Athena nodded, her attention distracted by all the people thronging the square. She asked more questions. Gabriel identified the patricians in their traditional robes. There were visitors from many nations—Persians, Turks, Moors, Greeks—and all dressed in the fashion of their own countries.

'People are so interesting.' Athena allowed Gabriel to help her into the gondola that had been waiting for them by the Piazzetta next to the Doge's Palace.

'You must have found life in the convent very restricting,' said Gabriel, sitting down beside her.

'A little,' she admitted, sufficiently relaxed in his company to lie back against the seat. 'But the nuns were interesting too. It is not always as peaceful as you might think inside a nunnery. But in any case I had some dealings with the outside world. The nuns needed friends to act on their behalf in various necessary transactions. I often oversaw purchases from the market for them.'

'I am sure you are a crafty shopper,' said Gabriel languidly.

'I believe I was not often cheated,' Athena replied. 'The King visited once soon after I first arrived.'

'The King? Old Rowley in a convent?' Gabriel turned his head sharply to look at her. 'Talk about putting the fox in the henhouse.' His eyes narrowed. 'What did he ask of you?'

'Of me he asked nothing,' Athena replied, refusing to reveal her irritation at Gabriel's quickly aroused suspicion. The King's reputation as a womaniser was well known. 'It was while he was still in exile. I saw him only from a distance when he visited the Abbess. The English nuns in Flanders did much to support his cause. Much of the correspondence between his supporters in England and those in exile passed safely through their hands, avoiding the attention of Cromwell's spies. I think they expected a better reward when he was restored to the throne.'

'A wise man—or woman—never expects a prince to keep his promise,' said Gabriel cynically.

He closed the curtains on his side of the gondola, then reached over Athena to close those on her side. Her heart-rate accelerated as she realised where his preparations were leading. In a few moments they were enclosed in shadowy intimacy. Gabriel left a small gap in the black velvet to admit a narrow band of sunlight, but it was not wide enough for anyone to look into the small cabin.

Athena bit her lip. 'I was provoked,' she protested, filled with not entirely unpleasant nervousness.

'So have I been these past two hours,' he retorted.

He settled back beside her. His nearness agitated her. She immediately tried to sit up and he laid one hand on her waist. He stroked it up a little so that it rested on her ribs, just below her waist, and exerted a steady, firm pressure, compelling her to lie back beside him.

She obeyed his silent command, too disturbed and excited by the commanding familiarity of his touch to resist. She could feel the heat of his palm through her bodice and her heart started to beat double time. His fingers were tantalisingly close to her breast. She held her breath, wondering if he would slide his hand a little higher. He leant over her, and his dark hair fell forward, brushing her cheek.

'Only a kiss,' she whispered. 'That was the bargain.'

'Hmm.' He bent his head a little lower until his mouth hovered just above hers.

'One kiss,' he murmured, 'for one insult. Or would you say your remark counted as two separate insults?'

'One. Only one.' She couldn't help herself, she lifted a hand to touch his hair.

'Then we must make the most of it.' As he spoke he

brushed his lips gently against the corner of her mouth. 'Derive the maximum pleasure from the moment.' His lips touched her eyebrow, then her forehead in feathery caresses.

Athena lay half-beneath him. Every inch of her body responded to him. There was a sweet, insistent ache deep inside her. She threaded her fingers through his hair, moved restlessly beneath his hand.

He growled deep in his chest, then his mouth collided with hers. Passion exploded between them. Her hands locked in his hair as he claimed her with a searing kiss, his mouth hot and demanding on hers. His tongue probed past her lips, asserting his right to possess her in the most intimate way possible. She put her arms around his neck and pulled him closer. She had waited so many years for this moment, and now she kissed him as wildly as he kissed her.

He moved over her, pushing her back against the velvet-covered seats. She welcomed the demanding weight of his body. Opened her legs wider beneath her skirts so that he could settle between them. He kissed her beneath her ear. Trailed his hot lips over the sensitive skin of her throat. She slipped her hands inside his coat, frantic in her need to touch more of him. She tugged at his waistcoat, found and pulled at his fine cambric shirt. A second later she touched the naked skin of his back. His muscles were taut with passion. She could feel the urgent power coursing through his body. She stroked upwards as far as she could beneath the restricting bunching of his garments.

He swore softly and jerked against her. She felt his hand at her thigh. He half-lifted himself to tug up her skirts. But even then he didn't stop kissing her. She kissed him back, just as frantic with suddenly unleashed desire. He kissed her cheek, her neck. Pushed down the neckline of her bodice to kiss her breast.

She felt his lips against her warm skin and sighed with

pleasure. She lifted herself against him, eager for more of the exquisite sensation.

His body suddenly went rigid. Beneath her hands his back became as unyielding as iron. He lifted his head and swore again. Not the hoarse, eager imprecation of a heavily aroused man, but with bitter self-disgust.

Athena was too dazed by arousal to understand his sudden, unfathomable change of mood. But his anger shocked her into full awareness of her loss of control.

She disentangled her hands from his clothing just as he rolled away from her. She stared up at the roof of the gondola, listening to his harsh breathing, horrified at her own reckless response to him.

'You are a *witch!*' His voice shook with rage. 'I should drown you in the canal.'

'*No.* It was you. *You...*' Her own voice was so unsteady she couldn't complete her furious, deeply wounded response to his accusation.

She lay her forearm across her eyes, hating herself and Gabriel. He should not have treated her so disrespectfully. But she should not have permitted him to do so. When she remembered how she'd frantically pulled at his shirt she nearly moaned aloud with mortification.

'Even in the shadows you weave your spells. Does it give you pleasure to destroy a man's self-control?'

'You kissed me! It was your stupid bargain—not mine!'

'It is so dark in here I can barely see you. But I can still see *him. His mouth on your breast!*'

Gabriel's fierce, roiling emotions filled the small, shadowed cabin. Athena was acutely conscious of the rigid tension in the powerful body beside her. She heard the lap of water against the side of the gondola. Voices and even laughter from beyond the black velvet curtains that separated them from the rest of the world—but all her senses were attuned to Gabriel.

'What did you see?' she said at last.

'What?'

'You said you can still see him. Samuel. What is it you saw?'

'What I told you! His lips on yours. You kissed him. He kissed your breast—' Gabriel broke off, his words lost in a savage curse.

'And then what?'

'The bastard hit me. I don't remember any more until I woke up in a ditch. You laughed.'

'I didn't laugh. I didn't know you were there.' Athena closed her eyes. She could hear the pain as well as the fury in Gabriel's voice.

'What difference does that make? It was our wedding day, but you gave yourself to another man.'

'And you'll never forgive me.' Cold misery washed over Athena. 'All you want is revenge.'

'No! Not revenge. I want—'

'What? We can't go back.'

'You know what I want,' he said harshly.

'To take me as your mistress. To make me the whore you claim I am. Is that not revenge?'

'You will be well rewarded.'

'Rewarded and discarded when we reach London. I'll find another way home,' she said, steeling herself against the thought of parting from him again. 'You owe me a gold piece,' she added, vaguely proud that she could still think so clearly.

'What?'

'You called me a witch,' she reminded him. 'That is certainly an insult, my lord.'

Without speaking, he delved into his pocket and tossed a coin into her lap.

Chapter Six

Athena took the coin and slipped her hand through the slit in the side of her skirt to put the money safely in the pocket she wore underneath.

They completed the rest of the journey in silence. Gabriel made no attempt to stop her when she opened the curtains. He moved once, adjusting the set of his coat. He did nothing about the shirt she had pulled from his breeches. He didn't need to. His elegant brocade coat reached almost to his knees and hid the disorder beneath. Just as her petticoats hid the pocket in which she carried her diminishing resources.

Athena sat forward on her seat and pretended to study her surroundings. Early afternoon sunlight turned the surface of the water into a glittering path of silver, broken by the passage of shiny black gondolas and other water craft. Athena narrowed her eyes against the glare. When she looked away she discovered the brilliant reflections on the water had clouded her vision. For a few moments she could not see the details of the buildings they passed. She blinked, and briefly closed her eyes to rest them.

Her spirit felt bruised. She was hurt and tired from the day's excursion. She thought wistfully of the regularity of her life in the convent. She had spent years holding boredom at bay.

Now she would have appreciated a little comfortably secure tedium.

Her anger had receded. She felt sad and empty, drained of all hopefulness by their last exchange. Gabriel had been shamefully treated. She wished she had found a better way to deal with Samuel's threats. But she'd learned long ago there was no profit in regretting the past. To survive—and perhaps even to prosper—one must deal with what is, not with what might have been.

She gripped her hands together in her lap as she remembered what Gabriel had seen. At least he'd witnessed no more than a couple of kisses and Samuel's lips on her breast. It was clear the image was indelibly stamped on his memory. But when he forgot what he'd seen he was very much the Gabriel she had first loved. He was not exactly the same. He had gained experience and an additional worldly sophistication with the years. He was a man in the prime of his ability and power, but patient and good-humoured with her endless questions. For the most part he had enjoyed showing her Venice. She was sure that sometimes she had seen warmth, even affection, in his eyes when he looked at her, when he forgot what he'd seen in that London brothel and talked to her as he had when they'd first known each other.

She felt a renewed flicker of the optimism she'd felt earlier on the Rialto. Gabriel *had* loved her once. Perhaps he could learn to love her again. But first he would have to forget. He had not moved for several minutes, but she didn't believe he had gone to sleep. She was too aware of his silent attention. When she glanced over her shoulder she saw he was watching her with half-closed eyes from the shadows of the cabin.

'You are a difficult companion,' she said. 'One minute charming, the next…'

He smiled, showing his teeth but no warmth. 'Your charms are far greater than mine. By now you should be able to wind a man around your little finger. Avoid such difficulties.'

'I'm not in the habit of doing anything with men,' Athena

said grittily. 'When I did deal with men while I lived with the nuns it was entirely for business purposes.'

'How apt. The arrangement I am suggesting will be very businesslike.'

Athena bit back a sharp retort. 'You said I could have chocolate,' she reminded him.

'Chocolate?' His eyes widened. She had surprised him. He gave a disbelieving laugh. 'You want to come to my quarters to drink chocolate with me? To discuss the terms on which you'll share my bed?'

'No! Not that. But you said I could have chocolate,' she repeated stubbornly. She knew she risked provoking Gabriel's scorn with her request, but the only way to change his opinion of her was to spend more time with him.

'And your desire for it is so strong you will risk entering the lion's den?' he said sardonically.

'Chocolate is a rare treat for me,' she said. 'One of my cousins brought it to the convent once or twice, but I haven't tasted it often. The nuns used it sometimes in the infirmary. It is very healthful.'

Gabriel's smile was predatory. 'And your good health must be my first concern,' he said. 'By all means let us take chocolate together.'

Athena glanced in the small mirror and patted one unruly blonde curl back into place. She had been waiting on tenterhooks all afternoon for her next meeting with Gabriel. Now the appointed time was almost upon her she felt a little sick with nervousness.

She smoothed the slate-grey cloth of her petticoats. This evening she was dressed with such sober restraint that even the severest puritan would be unable to cavil at her appearance. The blue and yellow silk gowns that she'd worn earlier in the embassy had been gifts from her aunt, the Duchess of

Kilverdale. She'd had few opportunities to wear them before her arrival in Venice, but now she wondered if she'd made a mistake in doing so. She balked at the notion of wearing her shabby travelling clothes to visit Gabriel, so she'd selected the restrained but formal costume she'd worn to dine with the Abbess. She didn't want to give Gabriel a false impression of her reason for visiting him this evening.

After one last check in the mirror she drew in a deep, steadying breath and went out in the second-floor *portego*. From here she could descend the external staircase to Gabriel's quarters. She hoped she wouldn't meet any of the embassy staff on the way, but knew she was unlikely to be so lucky. Perhaps it didn't really matter. No doubt they all already believed she was Gabriel's mistress.

She was halfway to the stairs when Roger Minshull emerged suddenly from one of the side chambers. Her heart sank, even as she summoned a polite smile of greeting.

'Mrs Quenell.' He bowed before her. 'I am glad to see you.'

His eyes proved his words as his gaze roved over her conservative gown before coming to rest once more on her face.

'Thank you, sir,' she said, taking care not to offer her hand. 'Please don't think me rude if I don't linger, but I have an appointment.'

She disliked revealing her private business even by implication, but if Minshull believed she had an assignation with Gabriel it might deflect his attention.

'I know,' he said, speaking rapidly. 'That is why I accosted you tonight. I can help you. Please step into my quarters so we can talk more privately.'

'Oh, no!' Athena moved back, narrowly avoiding his reaching hand. 'Thank you for your kind intentions, sir, but I am not in need of any help,' she said emphatically.

'It is well known that Lord Halross has confiscated your property. That he holds you to ransom. I could help you.'

Athena had suspected that the embassy household knew more about her business than she was comfortable with, but she was horrified to receive a counter-offer.

'You are mistaken, sir,' she said, backing further away. 'No one is holding me to ransom. Lord Halross has already found a purchaser for my lace. I go to discuss terms with him now. Good evening, sir.' She turned, whipped through the door and ran down the steps to the first floor.

'Please, please, please,' she whispered under her breath. Don't let anyone have overheard her shocking encounter with the Ambassador's secretary. And please God don't let Gabriel discover what had just happened.

'Mrs Quenell, my lord.'

The servant's formal announcement startled Athena. The contrast between Minshull's almost furtive attempt to speak to her and the grandeur of her introduction into Gabriel's presence disorientated her.

She stared at him, dressed now in indigo brocade and silver lace, and remembered again what she so easily forgot. He was no longer Sir Thomas Parfitt's young agent, recently returned from Livorno, but the Marquis of Halross. Still flustered by her unwelcome encounter with Minshull and overwhelmed by her sudden recollection of the change in Gabriel's circumstances, she curtsied.

A sardonic gleam appeared in Gabriel's eyes. He strolled forward, dismissing the servant with a few brief words.

'You present yourself in an entirely new guise, I perceive,' he drawled. 'The obsequious nun, perhaps.' His gaze flicked over her severe grey gown. 'Have you also taken a vow of silence? That would seem the only way you'll be able to maintain such doe-eyed deference for any length of time.'

Athena straightened up and glared at him. 'You are…' She hastily amended the rest of her sentence. 'One gold piece,' she finished, and brazenly held out her hand for payment.

Gabriel's eyebrows shot up. 'For calling you a nun?'

'For calling me obsequious. Also doe-eyed. I was taken by surprise, that's all.'

'Surprised at what? You invited yourself to take chocolate with me. You can hardly be surprised to find me here when you arrive.'

'Of course not. I suddenly remembered you are now a marquis.'

'I see. When I was a humble apprentice I merited only a saucy glance. Now I'm a marquis I rate a curtsy and down-cast eyes…'

'You were not an apprentice when we met,' she corrected him. 'And you were never humble.'

'Nor were you. Why have you insulted *me* by wearing that ugly garment?'

'It is not ugly. It is simple but elegant. I wore it when I dined with the Abbess.'

'I am not a nun and I do not expect my mistress to dress like one when she entertains me.'

'I am not your mistress and I will dress how I like.'

'Have your other patrons allowed you such licence?'

'I've had no other patrons!' Athena took a deep breath and resisted the urge to throw something at Gabriel.

It was easy to see that he was spoiling for an argument. She'd never seen him in this mood in London. But in those days he'd not had the memory of her surrendering in another man's arms as a constant goad to his temper. She wondered if he would ever be able to forget. She had wounded his pride and his dignity as well as his heart. And if he knew she'd done it to save his life he might still not forgive. At seventeen it had not occurred to her that a man might prefer to risk the gal-lows than be saved by the self-sacrifice of another. When she'd surrendered her virtue and honour to Samuel, she had not appreciated that she was also surrendering Gabriel's pride and honour—and without his permission or knowledge. If she told him now, she would only add another load of recrimination and guilt to the mountain they already had to traverse.

'We have to carry on from here,' she said, speaking her thoughts aloud.

'I beg your pardon?' Gabriel turned to keep her in view as she walked over to the large window overlooking the balcony.

'What is done is done,' she said, gazing out at the twilight as she picked her words with care. 'We cannot go back and change the past. I admit I made a mistake. I was very young and frightened. I never expected to see Samuel again. I did what I thought I had to do. I'm sorry everything turned out so badly. But it's all in the past now. Over. Samuel is dead. We have to put it all behind us and go on with our lives.'

She turned to face Gabriel, gripping her hands tightly at her side as she waited for his response.

He stared at her, his expression unreadable. 'You always did have a talent for closing your eyes to things you didn't want to see,' he said.

'That's not true!' Athena bit her lip, realising there was some truth in his observation. When she'd been happy in London she'd pushed her problems with her family and Samuel to the back of her mind. In the convent she'd tried to focus on the small pleasures of her daily life, rather than dwelling on her underlying sadness.

'Perhaps you're right,' she acknowledged. 'But I consider it a gift—not a fault,' she continued boldly. 'I'd much rather think about happy things than fret about things I can't alter. You should cultivate the same skill. I'm sure your temper would benefit. And your digestion.'

'That's the difference between us,' said Gabriel. 'If I consider something is unsatisfactory I change it—I don't learn to live with it. My digestion, by the way, is excellent.'

'Because you're always in command,' said Athena. 'Every-one answers to you, and you make all the decisions,' she con-tinued, half-speaking to herself as she realised the truth of what she was saying. 'You wouldn't like it if someone acted without your approval—even if they were doing it on your behalf.'

At that moment a servant arrived with their chocolate. The rich scent filled the room.

'Sit.' Gabriel waved Athena to a chair.

She noted wryly that the single word was an order, not an invitation. It was yet another reminder of the high status and power he now enjoyed. Sir Thomas Parfitt's former appren-tice had indeed risen high in the world.

Gabriel watched as Athena took a sip of chocolate. She looked graceful and composed. She had no money and her sit-uation in Venice was precarious, yet she seemed completely at ease. He couldn't help admiring her sang-froid. In her po-sition he didn't think he would be so relaxed. She was right, he hated being at the mercy of the whims of others. He'd al-ways preferred to be in control of events, and that tendency had grown stronger over the years. And after his experience in the bawdy house, when he'd been hit from behind while his attention was distracted, he'd made it a point never to let his guard drop.

He couldn't decide if Athena's serenity was because she didn't fully understand the hazards of her position, or whether she believed she could manipulate him into returning her lace without conditions. If it was the latter, she was going to be disappointed.

'Why did you come here this evening?' he asked.

'You offered me chocolate,' she said.

He raised his eyebrows sceptically. He knew perfectly well she'd had an ulterior motivation for holding him to his invitation.

'You may be able to indulge in such luxuries whenever you want, but I can't,' she said tartly.

'As my mistress you could have chocolate every day,' he pointed out.

She put the cup down with a sharp click. He saw a flash of indignation in her eyes. 'You are offensive, my lord.'

'Generous,' he corrected. 'Many women would sell their souls to receive such an offer from me.'

She stared at him so intently he began to feel a twinge of discomfort beneath her scrutiny.

'From the Marquis of Halross,' she said at last. 'It wouldn't matter if you were old, ugly and as sinful as the Devil. The Marquis of Halross will always be able to buy a woman to share his bed.'

Her words stung. Gabriel was proud of all he'd achieved before he'd inherited his title. More wounding still was her dismissal of his personal appeal as a man. He was still angry with himself for allowing passion to overwhelm him in the gondola, and now his determination not to allow himself to be manipulated intensified.

'So you're holding out for a higher price,' he said coldly. 'What are your terms for enduring my embrace? You weren't so reluctant this morning—or were you just allowing me to sample the goods before I bought?'

Her face paled, but she held her head erect and met his eyes without flinching. 'I want my lace back,' she said. 'Then neither of us will have to endure the other any more.'

A knife twisted inside Gabriel. He wanted Athena on his terms, but he did want her. The idea that she was simply enduring his company cut deeper than he could bear to acknowledge, even to himself.

'Ah, yes, your lace,' he said. 'Our conversation appears to have come full circle.'

'It was shameful of you to take it! If you were a man of honour, you would return it at once.'

'But I'm not a man,' said Gabriel. 'I'm a Marquis. And by your own admission, I will always be able to buy a woman to share my bed. You know very well the only terms on which I shall return your lace.'

Time, Athena thought. Time was what they needed and didn't have.

She sat at her lace in her own room, by the window that overlooked a narrow side canal. She'd wanted to sit on the balcony as she had the first morning, but Martha reported that Roger Minshull was hovering in the vicinity.

'Buzzing about where he's not supposed to be like a nasty wasp.' As Martha had put it.

The last thing Athena needed was another encounter with the secretary, so she stayed in her own room. The bobbins were familiar old friends beneath her hands. She made the simple lace by instinct. The repetitive task soothed her, yet allowed her thoughts to roam freely.

It was time that allowed wounds to heal. Time that provided the perspective necessary to become reconciled to change. Athena had had too much time in the convent. Now she didn't have enough. She had only as long as Gabriel stayed at the embassy. She knew his business in Venice would soon be completed. The Ambassador had told her so the very first evening.

When Gabriel left, would he give back her lace, or would he really force her to choose between destitution and travelling with him as his mistress? In one respect the outcome for her would be little different. Without the financial independence provided by the sale of the lace, if she wanted to survive she might have no choice but take up an offer much like Gabriel's from another man. Roger Minshull sprang instantly to mind. The prospect chilled her. If Gabriel forced her hand, she already knew she would go with him. She had loved him once. Years ago she had dreamed of her wedding night to him. If only they could get past this first shock of meeting so unexpectedly and reconcile themselves to what had happened, perhaps they could at least part as friends.

Athena was under no illusions about her suitability to marry the Marquis. Her father had been a baronet, and on her mother's side she was related to both an earl and a duke, but her own status as a poor widow estranged from most of her family meant that she had little chance of making a good second marriage.

But they didn't have time…

Her hands paused on the bobbins. She stared at the lace without seeing it.

…unless she became his mistress.

If she agreed to the bargain, they would have the entire journey to adjust to the changes in each other. But she would also have destroyed any remote possibility of one day becoming Gabriel's wife. He would not marry the woman who had been his mistress. He would be generous to her when they parted. She'd known that even before he'd taunted her with the fact. Most likely he would give her more than he had offered in his original bargain—but if she agreed to become his mistress she would fatally devalue her own worth.

The bobbins clicked together as she resumed her work. She would not give in to Gabriel's blackmail until she had no other choice. Perhaps in the meantime she could encourage him to see her in a more favourable light.

It was essential that she did not surrender to his love-making so completely and passionately in future. Her wild response to Gabriel when he'd kissed her yesterday in the gondola had shocked her, though it didn't, on reflection, entirely surprise her. Her inner smile was a rueful acknowledgement of her own weakness. Eight years is a long time to wait for your wedding night, and she'd always known Gabriel aroused her senses and her passions more powerfully than any other man. But self-restraint must now be her watchword.

Perhaps Gabriel was right, she was feckless. Impetuous, certainly. Her stepfather had always disapproved of that aspect of her character. She had come to Venice with the confident assumption that she could sell her lace to provide for her homeward journey, but if it had been stolen by a real thief her plight would be far worse than it was now.

On the other hand, if she'd been less impetuous she'd not have fled Samuel only three weeks after their marriage. By now she might have borne six or more of his brats. Athena liked children. She had dreamed of bearing Gabriel's sons and daughters, but the idea of having Samuel's baby had always made her shudder. She stabbed a pin into the pillow with more energy than necessary. Thank God that possibility no longer existed.

A knock at the door brought her head around. Her first anxious thought was that Minshull had grown tired of loitering. She glanced at Martha. The maid put down her mending and went to open the door. She knew well enough not to allow the secretary admittance.

From her position by the window Athena couldn't see who was at the door, but she saw from Martha's jerky reaction that the maid was startled and a little disconcerted by the visitor. Athena laid the bobbins down, wondering who it was. Rachel had visited her several times, but she wouldn't discomfit Martha. Which of the embassy staff—?

'I wish to see Mrs Quenell,' said Gabriel.

Athena's breath caught. For some reason it had not occurred to her that Gabriel would come to her door. A man of

such consequence was more likely to send his servants to
summon others to an audience with him—as he had done yesterday when he'd sent his footman to inform her of the time
she was to visit his rooms to take chocolate.

Martha looked at Athena, clearly seeking guidance on this
unprecedented situation.

Athena stood up, her heart thumping loudly in her chest,
her mouth suddenly dry. 'Come in, my lord,' she said to her
as yet unseen visitor.

Martha opened the door wider and Gabriel stepped over the
threshold. The maid looked another question at Athena.

'Thank you, Martha,' she said, surprised her voice sounded
so steady when her whole body was in the grip of nervous tension. 'You may go. Unless…' She suddenly remembered her
duties as a hostess. 'Would you care for some refreshment,
my lord? I am afraid I cannot offer you chocolate, but…'

'No, thank you,' he replied, just as formally.

'Thank you, Martha.' Athena waited until the door closed
behind her maid.

Why had Gabriel come to her room now? She glanced
around, looking for a suitable seat to offer him, and her eye
caught the bed. Her stomach flipped over. They'd reached no
agreement yesterday—surely he hadn't come to consummate
their bargain?

Chapter Seven

Athena was suddenly desperate to make Gabriel sit down. Standing, he was too tall and dominated the space around him. If he sat down, she'd feel more in control. But there was only the backless bench on which Martha had been sitting and the stool on which she'd been working at her lace. The bench was too close to the bed for comfort.

Athena picked up the stool, planted it in the middle of the room and pointed at it.

Gabriel looked at the stool, at her pointing finger and then at her face. To her utter mortification he started to laugh.

She pressed her hands against her burning cheeks, appalled by her lack of finesse. She had been more adept at such social niceties when she was seventeen.

'If you'd only put the stool in the corner, the schoolboy humiliation for my transgressions would be complete,' said Gabriel. 'I see I remain in disgrace.'

'My room is not as well appointed as yours.' Athena tried to cover her embarrassment with a show of dignified practicality.

'No, it isn't. But it has all the essentials.' His gaze lingered for a moment on the bed.

Athena's embarrassment faded as she realised Gabriel had

laughed with natural good humour. They had laughed a lot during their first courtship. If she could still make him laugh with genuine amusement, however unintentionally, surely that was a hopeful sign?

'I thought I would find you on the balcony,' he said, sitting down on the stool.

'It… I thought it would be more convenient to stay in my room today,' Athena said, covering her confusion by straightening her skirts as she sat on the bench.

'Really?' He glanced around again, his gaze resting a moment on her lace pillow. 'There would be more light on the balcony, and it is a pleasant morning.'

'I was seeking privacy,' she said. 'I didn't think anyone would bother me in my room.'

'Including me?'

She looked at him, her attention captured as much by the tone of his voice as his question.

'You are right,' he said quietly. 'We must go on from where we are now.'

His words took Athena by surprise. She gazed at him, hopeful, but a little wary of his unexpected change of heart.

He smiled slightly, not in amusement, but in acknowledgement of her cautious response.

'You were always more practical than me,' he said. 'I was so full of grand dreams and plans and then, with one common sense remark, you'd bring me straight down to earth.'

Athena's lips parted slightly in surprise. That was not how she had seen their earlier relationship.

'I thought you thought I was feckless,' she said, finding her voice. 'The foolish virgin…'

'Sometimes.' A shadow flickered in his eyes. 'But mostly you were just young and inexperienced. I was the one with my head in the clouds, daydreaming about the grand merchant fleet that I meant to build. You were the one who asked the awkward, pertinent questions that reminded me ambition is not enough.'

'I did? I must have been very annoying,' said Athena, disconcerted by his unexpected revelation. 'I'm sorry. Anyway, from what the Ambassador told me, you did build your merchant fleet.'

'Yes,' said Gabriel. 'I remembered all those questions you'd asked, tried to answer them in the appropriate order, and gradually increased the number of ships I owned.'

'But you hated me then.' He was full of astonishing revelations this morning.

'True. But you'd asked the right questions. I'd have been a fool to ignore them. More of a fool than I already was.'

Athena stared at him, remembering all those conversations they'd had in the weeks before their intended marriage. She'd asked questions because she'd wanted to understand Gabriel's business. Because he was the man she loved and it was so important to him. She'd often felt awkward at exposing her ignorance, and worried that Gabriel might think her too young and foolish to be his bride. But then she'd continued because the only way she could stop being so ignorant was to keep asking questions.

'How amazing,' she murmured. 'I had no idea. Does this all seem as odd to you as it does to me?' she burst out suddenly.

'Odd?' He looked at her, a guarded expression in his eyes.

'To be here like this with you. You look the same. Very much the same, only grander than you were before. You sound the same. Sometimes yesterday, when we were walking through Venice, I even forgot we'd ever been apart. Then, other times, I look at you, and I can hardly believe you're there in front of me. Talking to me. And you're real. But there is a such a strange distance between us, as if I hardly know you at all. And then I don't know what to say to you. Does it seem as odd to you as it is does to me?'

He didn't immediately reply, just looked at her with that same guarded expression. Then he half-closed his eyes in an almost imperceptible agreement.

He gave no other indication that he had found their unexpected meeting in Venice as disturbing as she did, but for the first time she realised that beneath his arrogant manner he might be just as confused as she. To a man who liked to be in control, the current situation must be unsettling at the very least.

She looked down to hide the sudden shine of tears in her eyes. She realised they were both vulnerable and afraid of being hurt again, no matter how hard they tried to hide behind past grievances.

'There is a great deal of Venice left to see,' said Gabriel. 'Shall we continue our tour?'

He stood up and held out his hand to her. After a moment's hesitation she laid her hand in his. His fingers tightened on hers in a firm clasp for several seconds in an unspoken, hard-to-decipher message. She smiled up at him with misty hopefulness. Then she allowed him to pull her to her feet and escort her from the chamber.

Basel, Switzerland

'*Sacré bleu!*' The valet made a grab for the bottle of orange water he'd just knocked over. 'Excuse me, your Grace,' he continued in French, clearly mortified by his clumsiness. 'I am very sorry.'

Kilverdale pushed himself away from the dressing table just in time to avoid the rivulet of water dripping on to his blue brocade-covered knee. He rescued a pair of fine chamois gloves, already scented with jasmine and not in need of any further perfume, and watched while Jean-Pierre tried to clear up the mess.

'Stop!' he said, in the same language the valet had spoken.

Kilverdale had lived in France from the age of three until he was twenty. His French was as fluent as his English.

'Your Grace?' Jean-Pierre looked up in alarm.

'Stop fidgeting and tell me why you've been acting like a jittery maid on her wedding night these past few days,' Kilverdale ordered.

Jean-Pierre stared at his master. He'd been appointed the Duke's valet when Kilverdale was seventeen years old. Kilverdale thought it was ridiculous that the man should display such nervousness in his presence.

'Have I ever beaten you?' he demanded. 'Have I inflicted unnatural punishment on you for laying out my blue brocade suit when I distinctly remember telling you I'd wear the red today?'

'Your Grace…' Jean-Pierre's face contorted into an expression of distress, anxiety and abject apology.

'Tell me what is wrong,' said Kilverdale. '*Diable!* I know what is wrong. We are not so very far from Dijon. You want to go and see your mother.'

Jean-Pierre stared at him in mute appeal. In his efforts to tidy the dressing table he had picked up one of the sarcenet bags filled with scented powder which had been lying in the path of the orange water. In his agitation he squeezed the bag so tightly it dripped on to his shoe.

Kilverdale sighed. 'England is at war with France,' he pointed out.

'*I* am not at war with anyone,' Jean-Pierre replied quickly, a hint of indignation in his voice.

'No. But even if I were not in a hurry to reach Venice, it wouldn't be wise for me to cross the border,' said Kilverdale.

'But I am not important,' said Jean-Pierre. 'I have not seen my mother for three years. She is getting old…'

'As I recall, her hair is as black as mine and she is the terror of all her neighbours,' Kilverdale said drily.

'But that was three years ago. I would make only a short visit. I will be back before your Grace even notices I've gone,' Jean-Pierre said optimistically.

'Hmm. I suggest you make a long visit—'

'Your Grace, don't dismiss me!' Jean-Pierre fell on his knees. 'I will not visit my mother. Please forget I ever mentioned it.'

'I suggest you make a long visit to your mother,' Kilverdale said, as if he hadn't heard the valet's interruption. 'Perhaps a month? And then return directly to England. It will probably be best for you to travel back through Ostend, the way we came.'

Jean-Pierre's face broke into a brilliant smile. 'Thank you, your Grace. Thank you,' he said fervently, bowing and smiling and bowing. Since he was still on his knees his head practically touched the floor.

'Don't be so theatrical. You knew perfectly well what I would say. Get up and clear up this mess. I will give you letters explaining you are my servant and what you are about. Philpott can make enquiries to see if there are any particular arrangements we should make for you.'

'So,' Kilverdale said to Philpott half an hour later. 'I left England with a retinue of four men. Now you are the only one left. Do you have any pregnant wives or ageing mothers secreted somewhere I should know about?'

'No, your Grace. I will be with you to the end of the journey.'

'Good,' Kilverdale said. 'Then let us see if we can travel somewhat faster in future. There is not much chance we can catch up with my cousin on the road, but I don't want her to be left alone and friendless in Venice for longer than necessary.'

'She is going to the English Embassy,' Philpott reminded him. 'Surely the Ambassador will treat her kindly.'

'Fetch me a pen, ink and some paper,' said Kilverdale. 'I

will write a letter to her. And another one to the Ambassador—to make sure he treats her with proper respect until I arrive. You'd better find a messenger to carry them. Also an honest man to take care of my gear. Honest, mind! I don't want to wake up one morning and find all my clothes have been stolen.'

'Yes, your Grace.'

Flowers covered the surface of the sea. A continuous peal of bells drifted across the water from Venice. The repeated thunder of cannon fire added to the grandeur of the ceremony and emphasised Venetian power to all who watched.

Athena sat beside Gabriel in his gondola, enthralled by the spectacle all around her. The *Bucintoro,* the Doge's galley, had been rowed out beyond the port of San Nicolò di Lido. It was the most splendidly ornate vessel Athena had ever seen. On the prow crouched the winged lion of St Mark, the emblem of Venice, fabulously covered with gold leaf and glittering in the sunlight. A little behind the lion stood an effigy of justice in the form of a woman, also extravagantly covered in gold leaf. The Doge himself was dressed in ermine and gold and wore his *corno* hat, made of cloth of silver and gold and covered in precious stones.

The *Bucintoro* was surrounded by a cortège of smaller but unquestionably splendid vessels belonging to prominent Venetians. It was an astonishing display of the wealth of the city.

Athena shaded her hand against the glare of sunlight on the sea and tried to make out what the Doge was doing in the stern of the *Bucintoro*.

'He's throwing the nuptial ring into the sea,' Gabriel explained. 'As he does he will reaffirm his vows: "We marry you, oh sea, in token of our true and perpetual possession".'

'Possession?' Athena threw him a quick glance before returning her attention to the drama before.

'The Venetians like to believe they rule the seas,' said Gabriel, somewhat drily.

'Don't they? Of course not.' Athena remembered Gabriel's own small fleet of merchant ships.

'Their empire was very powerful, but their influence is beginning to wane,' he replied. 'Their garrison on Crete has been continuously under siege by the Turks for more than twenty years. The Venetians have fought bravely, but the war is draining their resources and they are losing trade to others.'

'Is that why your ships go to Livorno, rather than come here?' Athena asked.

'Livorno is a free port.' Gabriel showed his teeth in a smile that reminded Athena he was, first and foremost, a hard-headed merchant. 'It is cheaper to unload goods bound for the Veneto at Livorno and transport them the rest of the distance over land than it is to bring them directly into Venice.'

Athena watched the Doge's cortège prepare for the procession back to Venice, and wondered if she would be with Gabriel when he returned to Livorno. There had been a subtle change in their relationship since Gabriel sought her out in her room. Both of them avoided referring to their shared past, and their conversation had become more formal, as if they really had only just met. Athena was careful not to touch Gabriel except when he assisted her in or out of the gondola or offered her his arm when they strolled through the streets. She noticed that he was equally careful in this respect. His hand no longer strayed of its own volition to caress her cheek. He no longer teased or taunted her with reference to forfeit kisses. They were both maintaining a safe distance.

But the past still lay unspoken between them. They were not strangers. And Gabriel could still fill her mind and overwhelm her senses in a way no other man had ever done. Sometimes she saw his guard lower for a few moments. Saw the latent heat in his eyes as he gazed at her lips or held her hand a fraction too long as he steadied her descent into the gently rocking gondola. He was keeping his emotions on just as tight a rein as she was, but the fire had only been contained, not extinguished.

In the meantime, Athena saw no reason why she couldn't take advantage of their mutual courtesy to find out more about Gabriel's life over the past few years.

'You have still not told me about your brothers,' she said, as their gondola joined the flotilla of vessels returning to Venice. 'I don't know exactly how and when you came to inherit.'

'Harry died in 1661 of smallpox,' said Gabriel. 'My father was still alive then. I was in Aleppo. Father died eight months later and Edmund inherited the title. He was well on the way to bankrupting the estates when he was killed two years ago in a drunken brawl over some allegedly loaded dice.' Gabriel's tone was dry.

Athena remembered that he'd had very little contact with his family after he'd been sent away to make his own way in the world. In the circumstances she wasn't quite sure what response was appropriate.

'How very uncomfortable for you,' she said carefully. 'That his death was surrounded by…controversy.'

'Scandal, you mean,' Gabriel corrected her, sounding surprisingly sanguine about it. 'Edmund was the accuser, not the cheat. There was no loss of Halross honour.'

'It was foolish,' said Athena. 'Men should not die over a pair of dice.' She bit her lip at her unfortunate choice of words, hoping Gabriel didn't think she'd made a deliberate pun on his brother's death.

'No, they shouldn't,' he agreed quietly. 'I barely knew Harry. I only became acquainted with Edmund after I returned to England at the end of 1661. He was a charming, good-humoured fellow. But improvident as the devil. Too busy enjoying himself at Court and drinking with his cronies to take care of his estates.'

Athena heard Gabriel's mixed emotions in his voice. She suspected he had grown fond of the brother who had been a stranger to him for so many years, while at the same time becoming increasingly frustrated by his lack of care for the Halross inheritance.

'I was not even surprised when they brought me the news,' said Gabriel, and she knew from the tone of his voice that he had grieved for his older brother.

'Did neither of your brothers marry?' she asked. She knew Gabriel was thirty, but as a younger son he'd had no need to marry to produce heirs. It seemed strange that his two older brothers had left no sons to claim their inheritance.

'They both married,' said Gabriel. 'Harry died before he had any children. His widow married again a year after his death—for which I am everlastingly grateful. Edmund's wife, Sarah, bore two living daughters and one son who died a month after he was born. She was pregnant again at the time Edmund died. The babe eventually proved to be a girl.'

'Oh, dear,' said Athena, imagining the complications the pregnancy must have created for the smooth succession of the title and estates.

Gabriel smiled sardonically. 'My older sister Mary left her husband and family and went to live with Edmund's widow for the last three months before the child was due.'

'That was very generous of her,' said Athena, wondering why Gabriel seemed to be amused by his sister's act of kindness.

He laughed aloud. 'Kind, nothing!' he said. 'Mary was convinced that if Sarah had the misfortune to deliver another girl she was going to switch it for a newborn boy. Mary watched Sarah like a hawk up until and throughout the birth to prevent such a perfidious usurpation of my inheritance.'

Athena stared at Gabriel. 'Do you think that was likely?' she asked.

Gabriel grinned. 'A little melodramatic, but it's not impossible,' he conceded, 'since Sarah insisted on retiring to the most distant of the Halross estates and took an impoverished but pregnant kinswoman with her—she claimed for support and to be *her* child's wet nurse. It's possible she had some such substitution in mind, though I doubt she has the wit to be a successful conspirator.'

'But your sister Mary did not give her a chance to dispossess you,' said Athena, immediately warming to Mary, even though she'd never met her and seldom heard about her in the past.

'I had no idea she would be so partisan,' Gabriel admitted, a little wryly. 'She is the oldest child. I am the youngest. I was barely six years old when she left home to marry Chantler. For years after that I rarely saw her. She told me recently she doted on me when I was a baby. I have a few fragmented memories of her playing with me when I was very young. But her memories are much clearer. She has been a staunch ally these past few years.'

'I'm glad,' said Athena. She felt a pang of regret at the un-complicated affection in Gabriel's voice when he spoke of his sister. She wondered if he would ever again trust her enough to think of her as an ally as well as a potential lover.

'What happened to Sarah?' she asked.

'Nothing. She had another daughter. All four of them—Sarah and her three daughters—now live very comfortably at Halross Court in Suffolk. I usually live in London. I've just built a new house in Fleet Street,' he added, on a note of pride.

Athena burst out laughing, then tried to turn her amuse-ment into an unconvincing cough when he turned a baleful glance upon her.

'You built a new house to escape from your sister-in-law?' she couldn't help teasing him.

'Certainly not,' he said coldly. 'My business is in London. It is appropriate I live there. Father preferred to spend most of his time in Suffolk and rented a house when he came to

London. Edmund did not choose to alter those arrangements. I decided it was time the family had a permanent house in the capital.'

'To reflect the growing Halross consequence,' Athena murmured.

Gabriel narrowed his eyes, obviously not appreciating this interpretation of his motives.

'What about Sir Thomas and Lady Parfitt?' Athena asked hastily. 'They were your second family.'

'They were both well when I was last in London. It was partly on Sir Thomas's behalf that I made this trip to Italy.'

'How so?'

'Sir Thomas has a young nephew he wanted to send out to Livorno. The boy has potential, but little experience of the world. I brought him out with me and introduced him to various friends I have in Livorno. I left him to find his feet while I came on to do some business in Venice. We will go home via Livorno, on one of my ships. I'll spend a day or two with him to make sure he has settled in well.'

'You are very considerate,' said Athena, most of her attention focused on Gabriel's use of the word 'we'. Was he including her in that easily spoken 'we' or simply referring to his small retinue of servants?

If he *was* taking her presence on the trip for granted, she wasn't quite sure how she felt about it. Once she would have found it flattering and reassuring. Now perhaps he rated her along with his servants and chattels.

'Mary has been trying to find a new husband for Sarah,' said Gabriel, his words indicating his thoughts had been running on quite different lines to Athena's.

'*Mary* has?' Athena blinked, then she thought she understood what motivated Gabriel's sister. 'You mean she wants to marry her off to someone else so you can go and live in your own home again!' she exclaimed.

Gabriel grinned rather reluctantly. 'Something like that,' he admitted. 'You and Mary share some alarming similarities. Sarah was Edmund's wife for seven years and I will always honour my obligations to provide for her and her daughters—but I would not object if she decided to live elsewhere.'

'But you can't get a man to offer for her?'

'I am not involved in matchmaking for my sister-in-law,' said Gabriel haughtily. He relaxed a little. 'That's Mary's task. Unfortunately, Sarah seems to be so attached to being the Marchioness of Halross that, unless a duke can be persuaded to come up to scratch, I doubt she'll trade her existing title for a lesser one.'

'So she's going to be your pensioner for the rest of her life?'

'Probably. But it may be a small price to pay. Edmund was on his way to bankruptcy. Sarah has no taste for gambling. None that I can discover, at any rate. And her daughters are pretty little things. It's not their fault they had a wastrel for a father.'

'You are a generous, kind-hearted man,' said Athena warmly, and had the pleasure of seeing Gabriel flush with embarrassment at her praise.

He looked towards the head of the stately procession they were following.

'There,' he said, obviously determined to change the subject, 'the Doge and his entourage are on their way to a grand feast in the Banqueting Hall and *we* can go to the fair.'

St Mark's Square was always full of colourful activity, but now it had been transformed. There were stalls and booths selling goods of every description. The heavy, elaborate Venetian gros point lace. Glass from Murano. Silks and spices.

The thronging crowds were composed of every nationality. Athena saw patrician ladies, mounted on their tall shoes, towering above lower-ranking visitors to the fair. Everyone wore their finest clothes. Costly brocades, silks and velvets glistened in the sunshine. Athena held firmly to Gabriel's arm as he guided her through the crowds, fascinated by all that she could see. A small crowd had drawn around a man juggling with fire. Elsewhere stages had been set up upon which mountebanks performed little playlets. Athena's attention was caught by a stall selling Venetian lace.

'Look.' She stopped to study a particularly fine piece. 'It is rather like the stump work I used to do. Do you remember? The way they build up the contours of the design with stitches reminds me of it. It is very interesting.'

She bent closer to examine the lace more minutely. Unseen by her, the lace vendor's eyes sharpened with interest at a potential sale.

Gabriel had not come to the fair intending to make purchases. He wore a piece of Venetian lace just as fine at his throat, but he could not resist the impulse to buy it for Athena. She looked up, surprised, when he spoke to the stall holder. He knew that she didn't understand what he said, but she clearly understood the nature of their transaction.

A myriad emotions flickered in her eyes—surprise, pleasure, uncertainty—followed by wariness and unmistakable suspicion. Gabriel had been motivated, as he so often had in the past, by the simple desire to please her. Now his hasty action discomfited him. He was no longer her indulgent suitor, and not yet her indulgent patron. He took the carefully wrapped lace, but didn't offer it to her.

'I will keep it safe for you so that you may study it later at your leisure,' he said gruffly.

'It would make you a fine cravat,' she replied swiftly, apparently just as disconcerted as he was by the incident. 'I thought so as soon as I saw it.'

'Perhaps,' he said, and steered away from the booth of lace to a group of silk merchants. Here he felt no impulse to buy.

He had already nearly completed a transaction to buy silk from two Venetian merchants. In any case, he had a warehouse of fabrics just as fine should he ever decide to deck Athena in gauzy silk or cloth of gold.

The thought of Athena in transparent silk gauze had an inevitable effect upon his libido. With an effort of will he banished the siren vision. It was becoming ever easier to think of Athena as his Frances. As a younger man he had been obsessed by her. As preoccupied by her physical allure as by her friendly, innocent charm. His desire to possess her body had not lessened, but there had been many interludes during the past couple of days when he had delighted simply in the pleasure of her company. In the lengthening intervals when he forgot what he'd seen in that London brothel he felt happier than he had done for years. But his happiness was built on fragile foundations, and was far more liable to collapse than the city, which apparently floated on water.

'It's a play!' Athena exclaimed, startling him out of his introspection. 'On a little stage. Let's go and see.' She tugged on his sleeve. 'What are they saying?'

Gabriel allowed her to lead him over to watch the mountebanks' performance.

'They are selling an elixir which…' he paused to listen to the many virtues the mountebank extolled '…will restore lost youth, cure impotence and…' he paused again while the small group of players on the stage acted out a little vignette depicting the experience of a previously satisfied customer '…make a man irresistible to every woman he meets.'

Athena frowned. 'Let's move on,' she said, pulling him firmly in a new direction. 'Look at the birds. Don't they sing sweetly?' She pointed out some caged song birds.

Her lack of amusement at the mountebanks' overblown claims for their elixir surprised Gabriel. For the first time it occurred to him to wonder if she'd ever been jealous of him?

He glanced down at her face as she determinedly enjoyed the music of a canary. It was not a question he cared to ask at this time, but he found the picture of her lying in her convent bed, torturing herself with images of him in another woman's arms, surprisingly pleasing.

'I'm hungry,' he said. 'Would you like some fritters?'

There was no one in the *portego* when Athena crossed it to reach Gabriel's quarters. The footmen who should have been on duty were on the balcony watching the festivities on the canal below. Most of the rest of the household had either not returned from the afternoon's entertainments or had already departed to enjoy an evening of celebrations. Even Martha had been in a hurry to finish dressing Athena so she could go out with Richard.

Athena smoothed her taffeta silk petticoats and wondered, with a mixture of excitement and nervousness, what Gabriel had in store for her tonight. She was not sure of the wisdom of going out with him after dark. She was even less sure how long their fragile truce would last, but she had agreed as soon as he'd invited her to accompany him this evening—even though she had no idea of their destination.

As always, her first sight of him made her heart beat faster. It had been like this when she was seventeen. She would be simultaneously thrilled and tongue-tied in his presence for several moments before her initial nervousness gave way to the heady excitement of simply being with him. Some things, it seemed, had not changed. A single glimpse of his tall, broad-shouldered frame set her pulse racing and her blood tingling.

He looked up as she entered the room. An involuntary smile lit up his eyes as he saw her. He was *pleased* to see her. The unexpected revelation took her breath away. For several moments she simply smiled back, unable to say a word because she was overcome by happiness.

Eventually Gabriel cleared his throat and looked away.

'Here, these are for you,' he said, picking up a domino and a full-face white mask from a small table.

'Are we going to a masquerade?' Athena asked, curiously turning over the smooth, cool mask in her hand.

'No, but masks are part of the Venetian tradition. During Carnival—between St Stephen's Day and Shrove Tuesday—everyone wears them. And they are often worn at other times as well. They are certainly appropriate for our destination tonight.'

'Is it…illicit?' she asked, wondering uneasily exactly what Gabriel had in store for her. Perhaps it was foolish of her to go with him without question.

Unexpectedly he grinned. 'Possibly,' he conceded. 'But only if we want it to be. I'm actually going out on business tonight, but I thought you might enjoy the novelty.'

'Venetians do business in masks?' Athena asked dubiously.

Gabriel laughed. 'An understatement if ever I heard one,' he said. 'But, yes, they do. It is very difficult for foreigners to have informal contact with high-ranking Venetians. Any nobleman discovered in such conversation is liable to be suspected of treason.'

'Treason?' Athena stared at Gabriel in disbelief.

'It is only thirty years since Antonio Foscarini was executed because an informer claimed he'd been having secret meetings with Lady Arundel and others in her palazzo,' Gabriel replied.

Athena gasped. 'Simply for *talking* to her ladyship?' she said, appalled.

'For selling state secrets. Except he wasn't. The Great Council later admitted he was completely innocent and ordered that he be dug up and reburied with full honours.'

'*That* must have made him feel a lot better!'

Gabriel smiled in acknowledgement of her interjection and continued. 'But it can make doing business a little complicated. However, the Venetian empire was built by merchants, and it is still possible to do business even with the most exalted individuals—if you know how.'

'And you do?' Athena looked at him with admiration mingled with uneasiness. 'They won't execute you for treason if something goes wrong, will they?' she asked.

'No, I'm not buying state secrets, I'm concluding a transaction to buy silk. I've already carried out most of the negotiations with the citizen who is the nobleman's business partner on this venture—citizens *are* allowed to deal directly with foreigners. I am also going to gamble in the *casino*. If there is one kind of foreigner Venetians really appreciate, it's the kind who loses money to them.'

'*Casino?*' said Athena, rather reluctantly putting on her domino. 'I thought you didn't approve of gambling.'

'All life is a gamble. In this case I'm only going to grease the wheel of negotiation. In fact, our terms have almost been agreed—for the purchase of the silk,' he added, and Athena remembered that other unfinished transaction involving her lace that had still not been concluded.

'*Casino?*' she prompted, unwilling to think about that now.

'*Casa* is house in Italian,' he explained. '*Casino* means little house. Many Venetians have pavilions in their gardens for informal entertaining. We are going to one tonight.'

'To gamble?' said Athena.

'To gamble,' Gabriel agreed.

Chapter Eight

I t was early evening. The grand canal was crowded with revellers. Music, laughter and the sound of people enjoying themselves filled the air. Coloured lantern light was reflected on
the dark waters of the canal. Venice had become a rippling se-
quence of ever-changing images. Between the shadows and
the lights and the shimmering water Athena could no longer
be sure what was real and what was an illusion.

She glanced at Gabriel. The mask he wore unsettled her far
more than she would have supposed. Its smooth, black surface
revealed no expression. In the shadows of the small cabin she
couldn't see his eyes. Her only clue to his mood was his voice
when he spoke, and the subtle signs he might reveal when he
moved. At the moment he was as still and inscrutable as a statue.

She touched her fingertips to her own mask. It was not uncomfortable to wear, but she was sensitive to the way it cut off
the outer edges of her vision. She slowly adjusted to the idea that,
behind her mask, she was anonymous. Perhaps even invisible.
An observer who could not be observed. If only she'd had such
a device on her second evening in Venice, when she'd had to endure the torment of the Ambassador's grand banquet, knowing
that she and Gabriel were the focus of everyone's attention.

The *casino* was indeed set in a garden, the first Athena had seen since her arrival in Venice. She paused, looking across the shadowy parterres and the dark spears of cypress trees towards the palazzo. Under other circumstances she would have liked to stroll along the fragrantly scented paths beneath the moonlight, but she was still feeling mildly alarmed by Gabriel's description of aloof Venetians. She didn't want to do anything that might offend their host or result in either Gabriel or an unknown Venetian being accused of treason. She intended to be on her best behaviour this evening.

She had formed no clear expectation of what the *casino* would be like, but, even so, the room into which Gabriel guided her took her by surprise. She associated gambling with drunkenness and quarrels. Even the good-humoured card games between her parents and their friends had often become quite noisy affairs, though they had been characterised by laughter—not accusations of cheating.

It appeared that the Venetians, by contrast, gambled in a chilly, forbidding silence. The only sounds were the soft clink of coins and the occasional shuffling of cards. Athena hardly dared breathe in case she disturbed the solemn atmosphere. She kept as close to Gabriel as she could, terrified at the possibility of losing him among the masked, silently forbidding crowd.

Gabriel led the way to a table presided over by a man who wore crimson velvet robes and diamonds in his hat. The man was not wearing a mask. He didn't need one, Athena decided. His aristocratic face was as expressionless and unrevealing as any creation of papier mâché or silk.

Athena watched, her heart in her mouth, as Gabriel joined in the gambling. She was torn between fascination and revulsion. She trusted Gabriel to know what he was doing, but she couldn't help disliking the man with the disturbingly benign expression.

She glanced around and noticed that not all the gamblers were men. There were women here too, risking everything on the turn of a card. She suppressed a shiver. She had taken many risks in her life, but she could not contemplate trusting her entire future to fate. She had made every difficult decision knowing the odds against her and determined to do everything to improve upon them. But no one could improve the odds here. Everything depended entirely on the fall of the cards—and on the honesty of the man who dealt them.

As the minutes passed she started to feel a sense of unreality. The eerie silence and the expressionless masks made those around her seem less than human. She was seized by the irrational fear that it wasn't Gabriel standing beside her. That somehow he had been replaced by a stranger. She gripped her hands together to stop herself ripping off his mask. Bit her lip to save herself from shattering the ghastly silence with a cry of horror.

Surely Gabriel didn't intend to stay here gambling all night? How could he bear it?

But then she saw that he was leaving the table. Relief overwhelmed her. Although he'd come here with the avowed intention of losing, she thought he might actually have won a little. She wasn't sure and she didn't care. She just wanted to escape the oppressive atmosphere. She was glad when he took her into another room where people talked and laughed in normal voices and some had even removed their masks.

'Are you sure people do this for fun?' she whispered.

She heard him laugh behind his mask. 'I believe it may be more of a compulsion than a pleasure for many,' he replied.

'I cannot imagine why,' she said. 'To rest your entire fortune on a randomly shuffled pack of cards. It's absurd!'

'No doubt in a similar situation you'd try to pick the lock with a piece of wire beforehand so you could stack the deck in your favour,' Gabriel teased her.

'That would be cheating,' said Athena indignantly, then realised he was referring to her attempt to steal back her lace.

'It was an entirely different situation,' she said coolly. 'I was trying to retrieve what is rightfully mine. I would never cheat. I would simply decide not to play a game that leaves everything to chance.'

'Some games of chance involve skill,' said Gabriel. 'Though I grant you precious little was involved in the game I just played.'

Before Athena could reply they were approached by a man who greeted Gabriel with formal politeness in Italian. She noticed that he called Gabriel *illustrissimo,* which she had discovered was a term of courteous deference often used in Venice. It pleased her that this stranger called Gabriel illustrious and, though she did not understand Gabriel's introduction, she curtsied gracefully to the Venetian. This might well be one of the men from whom Gabriel was buying the silk.

She stood quietly while the two men talked, wishing she knew some Italian, although Gabriel had told her the Venetian dialect was somewhat different from the Tuscan Italian he had originally learned in Livorno. She noticed that several ladies had removed their masks and wondered if she should do the same. Then she decided that in this strange environment she preferred to remain completely anonymous.

One of the ladies nearby had allowed her domino to fall open. Athena was studying with a professional eye the lace revealed by the parted domino when she realised that the conversation between her companions was coming to an end. She glanced at them in time to see something small exchange hands. It wasn't a coin. She'd seen a flash of brass and thought it might be some kind of token. She resolved to ask Gabriel more about Venetian business customs when she had an opportunity.

'I am sorry you've been so neglected,' he murmured in her ear. 'But you have been very patient. For the rest of the night my attention is all yours.'

'What do you mean?' Athena asked, as he once more led

her through the *casino*. Although she felt quite disorientated by the time they arrived at a lamp-lit door, Gabriel seemed to know exactly where he was going. He produced a key with a disconcerting sleight of hand, unlocked the door and ushered Athena into a small chamber. She took two or three steps inside, bewildered by their strange destination, and heard the soft click as he turned the key again. He had locked them in together.

She whirled to face him, her heart racing in sudden alarm. The room was illuminated only by moonlight shimmering on the lagoon beyond the window, and the pale light reflected on the shiny black surface of Gabriel's mask made him seem a stranger. A stranger whose mood could not be guessed at, except for the occasional glitter of his eyes behind the mask as he moved into a band moonlight. His body, swathed in the black silk domino, remained shadowy, but large and forbidding in the small, locked room.

'Gabriel?' Panic clawed at Athena's throat. She backed away towards the window. For an instant she was afraid he really was a stranger. That he'd changed places with one of those faceless men downstairs.

'Take off your mask!' she ordered, fear making her voice strident in her ears.

He removed it without hesitation, tossing his hat, mask and domino on to a chair as if he was glad to be rid of the encumbrances. Then he looked at Athena, still standing pressed against the window and smiled, a wicked gleam in his eyes.

'What? Am I to stand exposed while you hide behind your mask with your back to the light?' he teased her.

'I…you didn't look like yourself.' She took off her mask with fingers that shook despite her best efforts not to reveal her sudden alarm. He took it from her and tossed it aside with his own. Then he took her hands in his.

'I frightened you,' he said.

'Of course not.' She tried to brazen it out.

'Frances?' His thumbs stroked the back of her hands, both soothing and coaxing her to answer his question.

'You didn't look like yourself,' she mumbled. 'In the mask. For a moment I thought…'

'I was someone else? Or a monster in human form?' He smiled as he spoke, but he turned them both so they stood side on to the window and the light fell on her face as well as his.

She looked up at him, searching his face for answers to questions that neither of them had spoken aloud. Why had he called her Frances? Was it a good sign? She knew he'd loved her as Frances until the devastating events of their wedding day. Did it mean he was beginning to love her again?

He released one of her hands and gently traced her eyebrow with the side of his thumb. Then he touched his fingertips to her cheek as his thumb stroked her mouth.

Athena lifted her hand to grasp his wrist. His tenderness released a flood of warmth within her, disrupting her ability to speak—or even to think. She responded instinctively, turning her cheek into his hand and pressing her lips against his palm in an unmistakable kiss.

He murmured wordlessly. His hand slid lower to cup the side of her neck. He slipped his fingers beneath her hair to stroke the nape of her neck. The simple caress was both innocent, yet charged with erotic promise.

Athena's breath quickened. Beneath Gabriel's fingertips her skin tingled with pleasure. Deep inside her anticipation began to build. His grip tightened on the hand he still held. He drew her slowly towards him. Just as slowly he lowered his head.

Athena lifted her face. In the moonlight she saw his dark lashes lower. She held her breath as his lips brushed hers. He raised his head a little and she reached up to grip the front of his coat. Stood on tiptoe to bring her mouth back to his.

Against her lips he gave a laugh that became a groan—or was it a groan that became a laugh? He let go of her hand and put his arm around her, pulling her hard against him. How quickly the kiss had gone from gentle and teasing to hot and potently erotic.

Athena could feel the power in the hard muscles that surrounded her. Gabriel's body was taut with virile energy. His splayed hand in the small of her back pressed her against him. His other hand cupped her head, allowing her no escape from the kiss.

Athena closed her eyes, swept on the tide of their mutual passion. She was aware only of glorious, irresistible sensations. Gabriel's mouth, hot and compelling on hers. His tongue, one minute gently stroking her lips, the next urgently demanding her complete surrender. Her knees weakened. She clung to him, not even aware he supported much of her weight as she returned his kisses as passionately as he gave them.

He moved his hand from the back of her head to the curve of her hips. Even through her petticoats and domino she felt the heat of his touch against her bottom, crushing the silk as he pulled her closer. She pressed her hips against him, frustrated by the layers of fabric between them.

He bent lower to kiss her throat. She let her head fall back, revelling in the delight he gave her. She'd dreamed of this pleasure in his arms, though for so long she'd given up hope of ever experiencing it.

But now she was passively enjoying his love-making, rather than kissing him back as ardently as he kissed her, a tiny sliver of awareness entered her mind. Slowly she remembered her determination that she would not allow herself to surrender to the passion that flowed so easily between them. Not while so much was unsettled between them. Gabriel had been very courteous over the past few days, but she hadn't forgotten how he'd put the worst interpretation on her susceptibility to him the last time he'd held her in his arms.

He was kissing her earlobe. She felt him tug it between his lips, then explore it delicately with the tip of his tongue. His breathing was as ragged as hers, and her sigh became almost a moan of pleasure, mixed with frustration. She had never felt so aroused. Never been so aware of every hot, aching part of her body, which longed for his touch.

It took all her self-discipline to push herself away from Gabriel. He didn't make it easy for her. At first he didn't even notice, caught up as he was in his own passion.

'Stop!' she gasped.

He went quite still. 'Stop?' he muttered disbelievingly in her ear.

'Stop,' she repeated, putting as much conviction as she could muster into her voice. She was afraid it wasn't very convincing. She sounded as husky and reluctant to stop as he clearly was.

He muttered something under his breath, which sounded like 'contrary woman!'

'I am not.' She pressed her fingers to her swollen lips.

'You're the one who kissed me,' he pointed out. 'And you are holding on to my coat like a limpet.'

She released him immediately and sagged a bit at the knees. She stumbled away and sat down on the first available chair. Something cracked. She blinked, realised the cracking sound directly related to her last action and moved cautiously to discover what she'd just sat on. A second later she held up her mask. Even in the moonlight she was chagrined to notice a large crack halfway across it.

Gabriel started to laugh.

'Stop that! You brought me to a…a room of *assignation*. You locked me in. You tried to seduce me. And now you've made me break my mask! These are not laughing matters.'

'I did not *try* to seduce you,' he retorted. 'You ignite like dry tinder whenever I get close to you.' He sounded very smug about it, and perhaps a little rueful, but Athena instantly tensed at his comment.

'This is a room of assignation, isn't it?' she said, looking around and noticing for the first time the couch, illuminated by a band of moonlight. Apart from a table and several upright chairs, the couch was the only other piece of furniture in the room.

'It can be,' said Gabriel.

'Have you brought other women here?' Athena couldn't prevent the question from slipping out.

'No,' he said.

'But you have been in this room before?'

'Once. It has a beautiful view of the lagoon.'

'Let me see.'

Gabriel moved away from the window so that Athena could look out without coming too close to him. The speed with which he withdrew made her wonder if he too was not quite comfortable with his loss of control a few minutes earlier. He had been quick to blame her for what had happened, and during the past couple of days he had tacitly conspired with her to avoid such incidents. But if he didn't want to make love to her, why had he brought her to this locked room?

The window panes allowed in the moonlight, but distorted the image of the lagoon into peculiar patterns. Athena leant closer in an attempt to make sense of the view. Her body still thrummed with arousal. She was very conscious of Gabriel only a few inches away. She could see him from the corner of her eye. Every time she moved it seemed he moved in counterpoint. When she stepped closer to the window he stepped back the same distance. When her skirts swayed towards him he made a quickly arrested gesture towards her. They even seemed to be breathing in perfect time. She closed her eyes. She didn't need to look at Gabriel. She could *feel* every tiny movement he made.

His breathing quickened again. Her pulse rate increased in response. Her body felt like an over-tightened lute string, and she gripped the window casement in desperate fingers. She fought the impulse to fling herself from the room, to escape the ever-intensifying awareness coiling between them. But her impulse to throw herself back into Gabriel's arms was even stronger.

She heard the soft rasp of brocade as Gabriel moved and she uttered a tiny, wordless murmur of protest that emerged as little more than a whimper. She swallowed. Tried to think of something to say. Anything to break the tension that had stretched so taut between them.

Gabriel cleared his throat. 'Let me unlatch the window for you.'

Athena opened her eyes. That wasn't what she'd expected him to say and she had no reply. She watched, dazed, as he suited his actions to his words. Only minutes ago his hands had been touching her. Now they seemed not quite steady as he unfastened the window. He was just as much in thrall to his passions as she was, and struggling just as hard to maintain his composure.

The night air was cool and damp. It soothed the heat in Athena's face. Gabriel stepped away from her once more. She tried to concentrate on the view she could now see without impediment. The palazzo was on the edge of Venice. Its garden and the *casino* looked directly over the lagoon. Stars glittered in the clear sky and the moon was nearly full, a large luminous pearl in the black velvet heavens. Its cool light created a gently rippling path on the dark water. The darker shadow of an island rose mysteriously from the lagoon some distance away.

'The city really is built in the sea,' she murmured, struck by the thought and grateful for the distraction it provided.

'The lagoon has always been Venice's greatest protection,'

Gabriel said. 'And her isolation no doubt contributes to some of the idiosyncrasies of her subjects.'

'Masks and *zoccoli*,' said Athena, remembering the high shoes on which the noblewomen perched so precariously.

Her own position felt equally insecure. A balancing act in which her own unruly emotions were just as likely to prove her downfall as anything Gabriel said or did.

'Did you manage to discuss your business?' she asked. 'About buying the silk, I mean? I wish I spoke Italian. It is very frustrating not knowing what's going on.'

'Especially for an endlessly curious and interfering female,' Gabriel said. He seemed to have his voice well under control now. He sounded almost his usual self.

'I am not interfering.' Athena rose to the bait, then bit her lip, wondering when she would ever learn to be less impulsive.

'You travelled all the way from Bruges to Venice on a whim with a woman who was little more than a stranger to you. And without her husband's knowledge or approval. That sounds damned interfering to me,' he said.

'It was an act of charity.' Athena forgot about her plan to display cool restraint for the rest of the evening. 'And it would have been truly interfering—unforgivably so—if I'd sent a message to her husband before I deigned to help her. It was up to her whether she chose to send him a message or not. Rachel didn't tell him she was on her way because she was afraid he'd worry about her.'

'One hopes he would have done something a little more useful than simply worrying,' Gabriel said drily. 'But I will concede that my few conversations with her suggest she's not as lacking in sense as I first supposed.'

'You've spoken to Rachel?' Athena was surprised. 'I didn't know. When?'

'On a couple of occasions when she was visiting with

the Ambassador,' said Gabriel. 'You have kept so cloistered in your room that you have missed our occasional soirées.'

'Oh.' Athena wasn't sure whether she felt glad or sorry at this unexpected discovery.

'Mrs Beresford has nothing but praise for you,' Gabriel said. 'She has told me about meeting you in the convent, and of the great respect and affection in which the nuns held you.'

'I see.' Athena realised he had questioned Rachel about her. Of course he had. He'd wanted to find out if she was telling the truth. She was glad that Rachel spoke well of her, but it hurt that Gabriel had so obviously sought confirmation for her word. Even though he had agreed they must put the past behind them, he obviously still didn't trust her.

'At least you've been spared the trouble of sending a messenger or going to question the Abbess yourself,' she said, a little bitterly.

'I didn't ask,' said Gabriel. 'Mrs Beresford volunteered the information most eagerly. She appears to be somewhat nervous of me. I'm not sure why. It took courage for her to speak so boldly on your behalf. She stammered so much that at first she couldn't get the words out.'

'Oh, poor Rachel!' Athena exclaimed, tears starting to her eyes at the girl's generosity. 'She is so kind.'

'Loyal,' said Gabriel. 'But you brought her halfway across Europe. She has reason to be grateful. She says she can never repay her debt to you. I believe this was her way of trying. Of course, it should be Beresford who takes responsibility for their obligation to you but, unlike his wife, he seemed less able to overcome his awe of me.' Gabriel's tone was so dry that Athena was torn between reluctant amusement and disapproval.

'You frightened him on purpose,' she said.

'No, not deliberately. But he had the look of a man who meant to call me to account. I didn't care for it.'

'I don't suppose you did.' Athena could imagine how easily Gabriel had overawed the younger man.

She knew Edward Beresford considered himself to be under obligation to her, but she'd realised almost immediately that he lacked both the resources and the determination to be of much help. No one in the embassy, including the Ambassador himself, was likely to risk running foul of Gabriel. But Rachel had spoken up for her. Athena hugged the knowledge to her.

'It is not fair for you to frighten Rachel,' she said.

'I didn't,' said Gabriel. 'I admit I may have become a trifle...austere...when speaking to Beresford, but I did nothing to alarm his wife. We did better when Beresford was called out to run an errand for the Ambassador. Perhaps it is her husband who makes her nervous.'

'More likely the discomfort of seeing you intimidate him,' Athena retorted.

'I have never intimidated you,' said Gabriel. 'Ever.'

'Do you consider that to my credit?' Athena asked, deciding not to reveal that, since meeting him again in Venice, she had sometimes found him extremely intimidating. The open-hearted youth she had known had become a man with the ruthless authority to match his higher rank.

'Yes,' said Gabriel. 'Most of the time,' he added. 'I didn't ask Mrs Beresford about you,' he continued, going back a stage in the conversation. 'When she spoke first, yes, I questioned her further. I did not set out to verify your story.'

'But you were glad to have the opportunity?' Athena whispered. Gabriel was a proud man. She could believe he had not deliberately set out to question Rachel, but he'd obviously been glad of the chance to double-check her story.

He moved restlessly, walking away from her towards the table.

'I meant to light some candles when we first came in,' he

said. 'Our host has a fear of fire. He won't allow them to be left burning in an empty room.'

'We don't need them,' said Athena. 'The moonlight is restful. Or would I be more trustworthy by candlelight?'

'I saw what I saw,' said Gabriel. 'You in another man's arms. For eight years I believed you were a clever strumpet who'd set out to entrap me—only to discover I did not have as many prospects as you'd hoped.'

'You thought I was stupid, as well as wanton,' said Athena. 'It was obvious you would be a success, even if you'd never inherited. By now you would probably have been knighted at the very least.'

'But I wasn't a success then,' said Gabriel. 'Just the third son trying to make an independent way in the world. I was told at the church you'd found another patron with a bigger purse than mine.'

'In the church?' Athena was confused.

'The villain stood at the back of the church and announced to the wedding guests that you'd found another man whose assets outstripped mine in every respect,' said Gabriel, his jaw rigid.

Athena pressed her hands to her cheeks, horrified at the image he'd conjured up. His public humiliation had been greater than she'd fully understood.

'I did look for your aunt after I staggered out of that ditch,' he said. 'I couldn't find her. I decided you'd been in league together. She'd played her part to provide a veneer of respectability to your deception.'

'Samuel held her hostage for my good behaviour,' Athena whispered. 'I am sorry—'

Gabriel moved his hand in a quick, angry gesture. 'Don't. Your regrets—or mine—are futile. But you said I don't trust you. It is hard to change everything I believed about you for so many years on the turn of one conversation. When trust has been so utterly destroyed it is hard to regain.' He suddenly sounded as bleak as Athena felt.

She turned towards the window, not to look at the view, but to hide the tears which filled her eyes.

'I already believed you were a guest at the convent,' said Gabriel. 'You told me the first night and I believed you. And I believed what you told me—that Samuel was already your husband when I saw you together.'

'That's not what you said!'

'Until a few days ago I always believed it was impossible to believe two conflicting things at the same time. Now I've learned different.'

'Sometimes you believe I'm a strumpet? Sometimes you believe everything I've said.' Athena hugged her arms around herself.

'Sometimes I believe both at the very same instant.' There was no humour in his voice.

'I believed you hadn't even gone to the church and went off to Aleppo without ever knowing I'd not turned up for the wedding. But when you told me otherwise I stopped believing that,' she said over her shoulder. She felt the pain of his continued distrust as acutely as a fresh wound.

'I *said* you were the practical one,' he replied. 'The one who sees things as they are and deals with what is—not what you'd like it to be.'

'I can't change what happened.' She struck the heel of her hand against the windowsill. She knew he was right; of the two of them he had always been the romantic one. He'd even written a poem for her. It was one of the qualities she'd loved about him, but perhaps that trait made it harder for him to come to terms with what they'd lost. His vision of perfect first love had been destroyed forever and she couldn't mend it for him.

'We can't make things the way we wanted them to be,' she said. 'There's no use wishing for it.'

'But we can wish for something. What should we wish for?' He came up behind her.

'I don't know. Peace? An end to the torment?' she said wildly.

His rough laugh seemed to indicate he felt just as confused and tormented as she did.

'For you or me?' he asked. He put his arms around her from behind.

She tried to step out of his grasp, angry that he should act the lover after what he'd just said.

'Shush.' His arms tightened around her. 'Peace you wanted? Just…stand quietly for a while. Let us look at the lagoon together.'

She held herself rigid in his embrace, but he made no effort to caress her into a more amorous mood. She wanted to lean against him. Once she had been confident she could always do so, now she was no longer sure.

'I will take you back to England,' he said.

'I have not yet agreed to your terms,' she replied stiffly.

'There are no terms,' he said. 'Only those on which the Ambassador first tried to engage my help.'

'Not as your mistress?' She tried to turn in his arms, but he wouldn't let her.

'No.' He hesitated. 'We may renegotiate again later, if we both choose,' he said. 'But it is not on that condition that I will take you home.'

'Will you give me back my lace?'

He was silent for a few seconds. 'I will keep it safe for you until we are on board the ship,' he said at last. 'You do not have the means to keep such a valuable item safe—not now that its existence is known.'

Athena thought the same could be said of her two silk dresses with their extravagant lace trimmings, but she didn't say so. The large piece of lace she had made was indeed exceptional, fit even for presentation to the King if its purchaser so desired.

She stared at the dark lagoon. The moon had moved across the sky and no longer created a silver path over the water to the window. The night air had turned chilly, but Gabriel was warm and solid at her back.

He found her hand in the darkness. She let him take it. He'd reached for her hand many times over the past few days. Every time the clasp of his fingers had conveyed a message of warmth and reassurance at odds with the angry words he'd often uttered. She felt that same unspoken communication now as his hand closed over hers. She returned his grip, feeling the flex of his strong sinews beneath her fingers.

She thought she heard him sigh, and the arms around her suddenly seemed a little less tense. She realised he had been waiting for her answer, and that he had interpreted the clasp of her hand as a positive response. Whatever he did or didn't say, he wanted her to travel with him. He was keeping her lace so she had no choice but to agree. And she was almost sure that he was not motivated by a lust for revenge.

She allowed herself to relax back against him, her head resting on his shoulder. He immediately enfolded her more closely in his embrace. His breath gently stirred the curls on top of her head.

'You may keep the lace,' she said quietly. 'I always intended it to pay for my journey home.'

'Mmm.' His breath warmed her skin, then his lips brushed her temple in a delicate kiss.

'Don't.' Their awareness of each other always simmered just below the surface, but she was grateful for the moment of relative tranquillity.

'If you don't turn around.' His hand tightened commandingly on hers. 'And you don't kiss me and incite me beyond endurance, I believe we are safe enough.' He sounded amused.

Athena was indignant. 'I do not incite—'

'Shush. Of course you do. And it seems to me I have a similar effect upon you.'

'A gentleman wouldn't boast about such matters,' she said, disgruntled.

'Do I?' he persisted. His lips tracking a seductive path over her cheek to the corner of her mouth. 'Has any other man provoked you to tear his shirt from his back at your very first kiss?' His tone was superficially teasing, but she heard the sharper note beneath the lightness.

'I have only kissed two men,' she said steadily. 'And when Samuel touched me all I wanted to do was kill him.'

Gabriel's entire body tensed, his arms like steel bars around her. She closed her eyes and waited for his outburst of rage. His breath rasped in his throat for several long minutes but he didn't say anything. Then, to Athena's surprise, he pressed his cheek against her temple.

His silent inner battle and then apparent acceptance of what she'd said touched her deeply. She lifted her free hand to stroke his other cheek and he turned his head beneath her hand to kiss her palm.

Love welled up inside her. She wanted to turn and fling her arms around him. Hug him tightly to her heart. But she didn't. She knew how quickly such an innocent gesture would be overtaken by the physical desire they restrained but could never ignore.

'Why did you bring me to this room?' she asked.

'It wasn't my idea.' The undercurrent of humour had returned to his voice. 'Our host was most insistent I enjoy his hospitality to the full. I felt I could hardly refuse.'

'He sent you up here to seduce me!'

'I imagine he assumes I've already done that. But once would never be enough.'

'You have ruined my reputation.' Athena did not allow herself to speculate how many times *would* be enough.

'Not with our host,' said Gabriel, abruptly releasing her and moving away a few paces. 'He doesn't know your name.'

'It must be beyond salvage at the embassy,' said Athena, thinking of Roger Minshull's disquieting offer. She had taken care to avoid him ever since.

'My business in Venice is finished,' said Gabriel. 'And I had word yesterday that the ship we will be sailing in has already left Messina. We can leave tomorrow if you wish. Or would you like another day at the fair?'

Chapter Nine

'Richard has asked me to marry him,' Martha announced, looking almost defiantly at her mistress.

It was first thing in the morning. Athena had been preparing for their departure, her thoughts preoccupied by the coming journey. She laid the blue silk gown on the bed and looked at the maid.

'Did you say yes?' she asked, not certain from Martha's expression whether she should congratulate her or commiserate with her. She knew from experience that not all proposals were flattering to receive—though she had believed Martha liked the Beresfords' manservant.

Martha nodded firmly. 'The Ambassador's chaplain is to marry us,' she said.

Athena smiled. 'I am happy for you,' she said.

'I am not coming back to England with you,' said Martha. 'I am to stay here with Richard. Mrs Beresford needs a maid. I can work for her, just like I did on the way here.'

'She will be fortunate to have you,' said Athena.

'You won't be needing me now!' Martha burst out. 'He'll hire you a much fancier maid.'

'No, he won't,' said Athena quietly knowing, without needing to hear his name, which 'he' Martha meant. 'He is only going to escort me to England, just as the Ambassador first asked him to do.'

She saw the scorn in Martha's eyes and knew the maid, just like everyone else in the embassy, believed she was already Gabriel's mistress.

Athena made no effort to explain or justify herself. Martha had served her well in Bruges, though she had not been an easy travelling companion. She also felt a small flicker of relief that she wouldn't have to travel with Gabriel under Martha's critical eye. She would manage without a maid for a while, and when she arrived in England there would be one less witness to spread gossip about her.

She slipped her hand through the slit in her skirts to her pocket and extracted the remains of her diminishing funds. She counted out the wages owing to Martha, and added the two gold coins she had won from Gabriel as a parting gift. She had barely enough left to pay for a meal. Her throat tightened with anxiety. If Gabriel failed her, she was destitute. She would have to throw herself on the Ambassador's mercy. Hope he would believe her when she claimed kinship with her more illustrious relatives, and be more inclined to help her as a consequence. It would be embarrassing and awkward, and she didn't want to do it, so she swallowed her worries and handed the coins to Martha.

'You have served me well,' she said. 'I know you will serve Mrs Beresford just as loyally.'

'Your lordship.' Minshull bent in a deferential bow.

'Yes?' Accosted just as he was entering his quarters, Gabriel curtly acknowledged the Ambassador's secretary.

'I wonder if I might beg a favour of your lordship,' said Minshull.

'What is it?' Gabriel paused with barely concealed impatience. He was in the best mood he had enjoyed for days, but he'd never liked Minshull, and even less after the fellow had fawned over Athena at the Ambassador's banquet, so Gabriel didn't feel inclined to do him any favours.

'I have a letter for Mrs Quenell—'

'You're sending her letters?' Gabriel's eyes narrowed.

'Your lordship mistakes,' Minshull said hastily, backing up a pace. 'That is, I beg your pardon, my lord. The error was mine. I was not clear in my statement. The letter is not from me.'

'What the devil are you talking about?' Gabriel's good mood had completely evaporated. 'Speak up, man!'

'Yes, sir…my lord.' Minshull visibly collected himself. 'A letter has been delivered by messenger for Mrs Quenell,' he said. 'I am sure she would like to receive it as soon as possible. But her maid is off preparing for her own wedding, and Mrs Quenell hardly ventures outside her room. Many of us have not spoken to her for days. I wondered if I might prevail upon your lordship to give it to her?'

The news of a letter for Athena was an unwelcome surprise. To Gabriel's knowledge she knew no one in Venice. If she was receiving letters it was from an acquaintance she had kept secret. Did a secret letter signify a secret admirer?

'Give it to me.' He held out an imperative hand. 'I'll see she gets it.'

'Thank you, my lord.' Minshull bowed again as he passed it over. 'I am most obliged.'

Gabriel took it and strode off without a backward glance, his mind seething with questions. Had Athena deceived him again? Aware of Minshull's continued scrutiny, he didn't look at the letter in his hand until he was alone in his chamber. In the few strides it took him to obtain privacy, two unexceptional possibilities occurred to him. Perhaps the Abbess had written to Athena? Gabriel had no objection to such a correspondence. Or perhaps the young gentleman from Bruges who had escorted Athena and Rachel to Venice had written to her. Breydel was a student at Padua University. If the letter wasn't from the Abbess, it must surely be from Breydel.

The tension in Gabriel's shoulders eased a little. He did not approve of another man writing to Athena, but this would be no more than a letter of courtesy from a former travelling companion. Rachel Beresford had been impressed by Pieter Breydel's obvious scholarship and his grave, respectful demeanour.

Gabriel looked down at the letter, prepared to give it to Athena with a suggestion they send a small gift to Padua in thanks for Breydel's respectful protection on her journey to Venice. The direction on the letter was written in a flowing hand that was legible, but hardly that of a careful scholar. Rather it gave the impression of an arrogant, impatient personality.

Gabriel turned the letter over and looked at the seal. The flamboyant K surrounded by a ducal coat of arms had nothing to do with any Paduan scholar.

Kilverdale?

Gabriel stared at the seal—momentarily too startled by what he saw to either believe it or to be angry. Gabriel had met the Duke once or twice. He recognised him on sight, but they did not move in the same circles. Gabriel still devoted most of his days to business. Kilverdale, by all accounts, devoted all his time to pleasure. He was a favourite of the King. A pampered nobleman. And a rake.

A furious tattoo began to beat through Gabriel's veins. Kilverdale had already openly acknowledged two bastards. He had an eye for feminine beauty to rival the King's. And now he'd written to Athena.

Never in his life had Gabriel read another person's private correspondence, but the compulsion to do so now was beyond his control. He broke the seal with unsteady hands and read the letter.

Athena, you are enough to try the patience of a saint—and

God knows I am no saint. Why the devil did you leave the convent? Never mind, the Abbess told me. I will arrive in Venice soon. I've written to the Ambassador. If he kicks up a fuss about your expenses tell him I am on my way and I will cover any costs you have incurred. Women are a sore trial. Don't fret, sweetheart. I will be there soon, and then I will take you home. Jack.

Gabriel crushed the letter between his hands. Athena had lied to him.

Only two men had kissed her. That's what she'd said the previous evening—and she'd hated the other man. But Kilverdale had not written to a stranger. It was clear he was already on terms of intimacy with Athena.

Sweetheart.

A growl of murderous fury shook Gabriel's body. Kilverdale had even signed the note with his Christian name. A indication of familiarity and condescension from the Duke that suggested great indulgence, despite the exasperated tone of his letter.

There could be no innocent explanation for this letter. A man might occasionally write to his sister with such affection, but Athena was not Kilverdale's sister. She was a beautiful, penniless woman with no means to support herself unless she sold her lace. Gabriel thought of the black-haired Duke as he had last seen him, dressed in crimson velvet and gold lace. Entertaining the party with a witty but salacious story. A sophisticated, worldly courtier. There was only one reason why a man of Kilverdale's ilk would pursue a woman across Europe. The Duke lusted after pretty women, and Athena's beauty was so great it would tempt the most jaded palette.

Gabriel imagined Frances just as charmed by Kilverdale's superficial glamour as the audience of courtiers the Duke had entertained. He saw again the scene he'd witnessed on his intended wedding day, but this time it was Kilverdale who put his lips to Frances's breast, his hair as black as the Devil's against her fair skin.

The image tormented Gabriel. Sent his anger soaring out of control. Twisted deep, knife-cutting pain in his gut. His hands clenched. He took two strides towards the door and stopped short. He refused to let Frances see how obsessed he had become with her. He fought for control, his muscles jumping with the compelling need to vent his boiling rage. He stared about the room as if it were a prison cell, but even in his darkest rage he knew the prison was in his own mind. He would take it with him wherever he went until he could finally eradicate Frances from his blood.

His eyes fell on the locked chest. The chest that contained her lace. He dropped to his knees before it, fumbled with the key and dragged out the lace. He clenched his fists in the delicate fabric. The first few, fragile threads tore—

He froze. His muscles trembling with ruthlessly imposed self-control. A few seconds later he dropped the lace and gripped the side of the chest, his knuckles white and his head bowed as he struggled to gain mastery over himself. Gradually his rage chilled to an emotion akin to despair. After all these years he was still in thrall to Frances. Still as much at the mercy of his passion for her as he had been so long ago in London.

He pushed himself to his feet, his limbs as stiff as an old man's. He picked up the lace and sat down in a high-backed chair. He stared at the delicate fabric. It held so much significance in his conversations with Athena, but this was only the second time he had looked at it. The fine lace was creased, and pulled a little out of shape, but the tear on one side was barely half an inch long. He smoothed it across his knees, carefully lining up the edges of the small tear.

His eyes burned. The design of birds and flowers reminded him so much of the Frances he'd thought he was to marry. The innocent young girl who had delighted in throwing crumbs to the sparrows while she teased him about his ambitious plans for their future. The lace was so perfect that the idea that he could have destroyed it in his rage was almost unbearable.

He pinched the bridge of his nose between his fingers and thumb, trying to force his emotions into abeyance. He'd believed Frances was perfect, but she hadn't been. She'd planned to marry him under a false name. He understood and even accepted her motives for hiding from Samuel in London, but it was much harder to forgive the fact she'd meant to marry him without revealing the truth. She'd made it so difficult for him to unquestioningly trust her again. He pulled in a ragged breath and his ribs creaked beneath his cramped muscles.

He knew Athena had been a guest at the convent. Rachel Beresford had told him, and this lace was testimony to the skills she had learnt in Bruges. He traced the pattern of a flower with one finger. The design of the lace had captured so much of the carefree, exuberant girl he remembered. He touched the shape of a bird that, even in an inevitably stylised silhouette, looked remarkably like a sparrow…

It had taken years to make this lace, and she was prepared to sell it to survive. If she sold her body to a wealthy, indulgent patron she would not need to sell the product of so much painstaking craftsmanship. Instead she would be swathed in silk and jewels—at least for as long as the passion lasted. But she had tried to sell her lace with the Ambassador's help. Surely that was a sign that she hadn't been expecting—or perhaps even wanting—Kilverdale's arrival?

Gabriel retrieved the letter, now a crumpled ball on the floor. He smoothed it out and re-read it, searching for some evidence that it was a mistake. A young woman should not be receiving letters from any man outside her family—let alone from a rake of Kilverdale's reputation. Perhaps the Duke had intended it for another lady? But, no, he mentioned the convent and the Abbess. He had even *spoken* to the Abbess. Why had a nun been willing to talk to the Duke?

Gabriel focused on the intellectual puzzle before him in an effort to keep his churning emotions under control. If Athena truly had been safely cloistered in the convent for so long, how had she ever met the libidinous Duke?

Athena was preparing her lace pillow for travel when she heard the knock at the door. This time she recognised the decisive rap. Her pulse skittered with nervous anticipation. She glanced around to check the room was tidy, then went to the door.

He knocked again—an imperative demand for admittance—a second before she opened it. She felt a brief flicker of amusement. Gabriel was not a naturally patient man. But as soon as she saw him her amusement died. She knew something was wrong. His lips were pressed together in a hard line. There was a stormy, yet disturbingly remote expression in his eyes.

'What's the matter?' she asked.

'Nothing.' He stepped past her without waiting for an invitation.

Athena closed the door and turned to look at him. She wondered why he had come. She had been feeling reasonably hopeful about the future, but his appearance filled her with foreboding. Something had happened since last night. Her throat was suddenly dry. She swallowed, gripped her hands together and waited for him to speak.

He prowled around the room, paused to stare out of the window, then to study the lace pillow. She'd already secured most of the bobbins, but he flicked one of the loose ones with an irritable finger.

'If you'd found a rich lover, you wouldn't have to spend hours at such tedious work,' he said.

'I like making lace,' Athena replied. 'If I had a rich lover,

I would have to waste tedious hours pleasing him. I prefer to please myself.'

Gabriel glanced up at the tart note in her voice. 'You never considered such an option?' he said. Even with his back to the window she could see the hard gleam in his eyes.

'No.' She bit down on the angry response which rose to her lips. Something had happened, she was sure of it—or did Gabriel simply regret his offer to escort her without recompense?

'What is wrong, my lord?' she asked again. It was important she remain calm, but her mind was already full of increasingly distressing speculation.

'Are you expecting to receive a visitor?' he said.

'A visitor? Who?' She stared at him in bewilderment.

Gabriel hesitated for a moment. 'The fellow from Bruges who brought you to Venice,' he said. 'Don't you think it odd he hasn't called to pay his compliments?'

Athena blinked, nonplussed by Gabriel's unexpected question. 'Hardly,' she said. 'He only brought us at the request of his father who wished to be in good standing with the Abbess. I am sure he felt his duty was well and truly done when he delivered us into the Ambassador's care. Why should he trouble himself to come to Venice from Padua?'

Gabriel grunted. 'It's not far.' He prowled to the bed, then back to the window again.

'For heaven's sake!' Athena exclaimed. 'You're worse than a caged lion. Why don't you sit down?'

'On a stool only fit for a milkmaid?' He glanced down scornfully.

'Don't be pompous. You were an apprentice once yourself. You told me how bare your room was.'

'I'm not an apprentice now.'

'You seem to have turned into an addle-witted, temperamental Marquis! What is wrong?'

He stopped his restless pacing and glowered at her.

Strangely, beneath his bad-tempered glare his expression seemed to lighten a little—as if being forthrightly insulted had improved his mood.

'Are you ready to leave?' he asked.

'Martha's getting married.'

'Martha?' He frowned at her *non sequitur.*

'My maid. She's to marry the Beresfords' manservant. The one who came from England with Rachel,' Athena explained.

'So you are now without a maid.' The news apparently added to Gabriel's discontent. 'I doubt we'll easily find another English maid in Venice. It will mean a delay.'

'It doesn't mean anything of the kind,' said Athena with asperity. 'I've managed without a maid before. In any case, having paid Martha off, I can no longer afford such luxuries. Unless you offer me some more insults and gold coins as a forfeits,' she added, in a mild attempt to lighten the mood.

'You have no money at all?' Gabriel scowled at her.

Since she saw no reason to pretend, Athena reached into her pocket and pulled out her few remaining coins.

'My entire capital,' she said. 'Unless I try to sell my clothes, I suppose. But that would be a very desperate course of action to take.'

'Good God!' Gabriel looked appalled. He thrust his hand into his own pocket and dropped a small pile of gold on to Athena's palm.

'I don't want your money!' she exclaimed, trying to return it to him. 'If you take me safely back to England, that will be enough.'

'With only two silk dresses and a piece of lace to your name? When you get there where will you go? What will you do?'

'I would like to visit my mother. See my brother and sisters again. I have a new half-sister who was born after I left I've never seen.' Since Gabriel refused to take back the coins she squirreled them beneath her skirts. 'My brother was eight when I last saw him, just before I ran away from Samuel. Perhaps it will be for us the way it was with your sister.' She smiled sadly. 'I have such fond memories of him, but he probably doesn't even remember me. He will be sixteen now. Perhaps they will all be ashamed of me.'

She sat down on the bench at the foot of the bed. She longed to see her family again, but she had brought scandal upon them all. She was afraid she would never be welcome under her stepfather's roof.

'Then why did you leave the convent? Why not got back there if there is no welcome for you in England?' Gabriel demanded. 'The nuns would have you back. Rachel Beresford was clear about that.'

'Aunt Eleanor will receive me,' said Athena. 'She has told me so many times. Perhaps she will accept me as her companion.'

'She sent you to the convent last time you went to her for help,' said Gabriel. 'What makes you think she'll be more welcoming this time?'

'I was hiding from Samuel then,' said Athena. 'I don't need to hide from him now. I will go to Aunt Eleanor.'

Gabriel sat down beside her and took her hand, holding it between both of his.

'Is Samuel the only man you have ever had to hide from?' he asked.

Athena immediately thought of Minshull. He seemed to have abandoned his efforts to speak to her privately, but she still took care to avoid him. She was terrified there would be trouble if Gabriel found out about the secretary's attentions to her.

'I will be glad to leave Venice,' she said, her words echoing her thoughts.

Gabriel clasped her hand more tightly. 'We will leave today,' he said, his voice sounded more as if he was offering her an assurance rather than simply announcing their travel arrangements.

Athena glanced sideways at him, wondering if he did know about Minshull's importunities. She decided not to ask. If he didn't know, she might just put unnecessary suspicions into his head.

He began to play with her fingers, distracting her from other matters. It reminded her of when they'd courted in London. He'd played with her hands then, caressing her fingers and measuring her smaller span against his larger one, as if it was the only liberty he would allow himself to take with her innocence. She glanced at him, wondering if he remembered too. She had time only to see the dark intensity of his eyes before he put one hand behind her head and kissed her.

This time there was no pretence that the kiss was only a token gesture. From the moment his lips touched hers he ravished her mouth mercilessly. The kiss was urgent, hungry and deeply possessive. There had been no warning of his intentions. Athena was first dazed, then aroused by his fierce, demanding passion.

She put her arms around his neck, kissing him as desperately as he kissed her. Somehow she ended up sprawled half on the bench and half across the foot of the bed. Gabriel's weight pressed her into the mattress. Her position was awkward and uncomfortable, but she didn't notice.

His hand slid down to her waist, then slipped up beneath her loose-fitting jacket. His palm touched her breast through her chemise and she gasped against his lips, arching towards him. His fingers found her nipple and began to circle it through the soft linen. Insistently teasing it to a hard, sensitive peak. Athena's body hummed with urgent need, and there was a swelling ache between her legs. Her knees were hooked awkwardly over the edge of the bench. One leg was trapped beneath Gabriel's hard thigh, but she drew up her other knee. Her foot caught in her petticoats but she hardly noticed. She simply wanted to touch Gabriel in every way that she could.

She pressed her bent leg against him, glorying in the feel of his taut muscles.

He reached down and dragged up her skirts and she felt cool air on her exposed skin, then his hand on her thigh. His groan of pleasure mingled with hers. Then he raised his head and stared into her eyes as his hand stroked boldly up her outer thigh. She held her breath, snared as much by the fire in his eyes as by his devastating caress. Cupping her hip in his palm, he moved his splayed hand across the lower part of her stomach in a possessively seductive caress. His thumb stroked lightly across the soft skin just beneath her navel, but he exerted more pressure with his fingers as they moved over the hidden blonde curls.

Athena released her pent-up breath in a shaky gasp.

'Gabriel?' She wriggled beneath him, not sure if she was trying to evade his commanding touch or invite more of the delicious quaking he created deep within her.

He held her still with a firm hand and the heat that blazed in his eyes. He moved slightly so that his thigh no longer lay across her leg. Then he replaced the touch of his leg with the far more intimate caress of his hand. He stroked over the jut of her hip, down the front of her leg, curving his fingers to tease the soft, sensitive skin of her inner thigh. Eyes still locked with hers, he reversed the direction of his caress. This time his hand slid up the inside of her leg. Her inner muscles clenched with anticipation as his fingers brushed her soft curls—but then he stroked across her stomach again. He repeated the caress again until tension built inside Athena to such a pitch she could hardly bear it. She had no thought for anything but Gabriel and his glorious, maddening touch. She lost all consciousness of modesty. Her breath came in short pants. She lifted her hips insistently beneath his hand. He rewarded her immediately, his strong fingers slipping over the damp curls and delving deeper. The sensation was so intense she turned her head away and closed her thighs on his hand.

'Open your eyes,' he ordered, his voice harsh with his own arousal. 'Look at me! Look at me,' he said again, softly this time.

As soon as she obeyed he began to stroke her intimately. Her breath caught in her throat as she was lost in the exquisite, overpowering sensations his touch excited. Her muscles relaxed, her legs fell apart, allowing him easier access. Gabriel stroked her slick, swollen flesh, flicked his finger back and forth in a quick, subtle caress that made her cry out. He pressed a long finger deep inside her and she moaned. Her hands locked in the bed cover as she lifted her hips against his hand. The coil of need tightened and grew inside her until it *had* to be satisfied. She bucked against him. Clever fingers continued to tease and stroke until her whole body shuddered with uncontrollable pleasure. Tight waves of ecstasy pulsed out from her centre until even her toes curled with the intensity of her release.

Gabriel kept on stroking her, playing her tautly strung body like a lute string until he'd compelled her to feel every last tingling, soul-shaking ripple of delight. Until she lay beside him, limp and dazed and satiated. He moved his hand to rest undemandingly upon her thigh in an oddly reassuring gesture.

It took several minutes for Athena's breathing to return to normal and her dazed thoughts to clear. For her to realise the shocking immodesty of what she'd just allowed Gabriel to do—and the fact that he had not obtained his own release.

He lay beside her, his hand still on her thigh beneath her petticoats. His features were tight with arousal and the self-restraint he imposed upon himself. Now she wasn't in the grip of all-encompassing sensations she noticed the hard tension in his body, but her thoughts were confused and uncertain. She wasn't sure whether she should pull down her skirts and berate him for taking scandalous advantage of her—or pull them higher and beg him to find the same exquisite pleasure he'd just given her.

She lifted a hand to his hair and smiled tentatively at him. A small answering smile curved his lips, but the predominant expression in his eyes was one of fierce satisfaction, which, in the circumstances, Athena couldn't understand.

'Did that please you?' he said.

'Ah…' Athena didn't very well see how she could deny it. Her gaze slid away from his. The embarrassment flushing her already overheated cheeks was his only answer.

'Am I the only one?' He resisted her fumbling efforts to push down her skirt.

'To do this to me?' Hot indignation filled her. 'Of course.' She grabbed his wrist and made him move his hand. This time he allowed her to restore a semblance of modesty to her appearance.

'Has any other man ever given you that pleasure?' he demanded.

Athena sat up. There was a slight ache in the small of her back from the awkward position in which she'd just been lying. She flexed her shoulders and tried to ignore Gabriel's unmannerly question. Somehow she had to regain a modicum of dignity. Suddenly it occurred to her why he might be asking.

'I suppose patrons require a lot of praise for their prowess,' she said. She was quite proud of the way her voice remained steady, when inside she didn't feel steady at all. 'I'm afraid I'm not acquainted with the etiquette of these situations, my lord. What is it you want me to tell you? Beyond the fact that you took ruthless and ungentlemanly advantage of me.'

She stood up and shook out her skirts, wishing her legs felt less inclined to tremble. She could hardly believe she was trying to make polite conversation with Gabriel after what just happened.

'Praise for my prowess?' Gabriel propped himself up on one elbow so that he could look at her. His position made his own state of unfulfilled arousal very evident when Athena took the risk of glancing at him. She looked hastily away. She'd always suspected that, sooner or later, their passion would get the better of them, but she'd never imagined it would be like this. There was an undercurrent she didn't understand.

'No other man has, has he?' He stood up.

Athena lifted her head to look at him. She saw that he needed her to answer the question. That beneath his arrogance and male triumph at forcing her to surrender to him so completely he needed not praise, but reassurance. She wondered what had disturbed him before he visited her, and why it had driven him to prove his power over her when he had imposed such restraint upon himself until now. She couldn't ask. She knew he wouldn't tell her or even admit to such a motivation.

'No other man has made me feel like that,' she said. 'I do not believe any other man could.' She laid her hand on his arm. 'And you are the only man I would ever willingly allow to take such a liberty,' she added, although she was already resolving not to allow him to do so again.

He breathed in, breathed out, his gaze searching her face. At last the hard glitter left his eyes.

'Are you ready?' he said. 'I'll give the orders for our departure.'

Chapter Ten

They left the embassy so quickly that Athena found herself taking leave of the Ambassador with her body still glowing from Gabriel's love-making. She did not understand what prompted Gabriel's haste any more than she understood exactly what had driven his behaviour barely an hour ago in her room. The strength of their mutual attraction had always had the potential to leap beyond their control, but she didn't believe Gabriel had been overcome by simple lust. He had not sought release for his own unfulfilled desire, only forced pleasure on to her.

She resisted the urge to fidget with her skirts, as if by smoothing them she could hide or deny what had so recently happened. She felt disorientated and confused, in some ways more than she had in the immediate aftermath of Gabriel's devastating caresses. She did not look at Gabriel, though every particle of her body was aware of him standing only inches away from her.

She curtsied sedately to the Ambassador, mortifyingly afraid he would notice and guess the cause of her agitation. Then she remembered that everyone in the embassy believed she and Gabriel had been lovers ever since her arrival in Venice. She bit back a gasp of slightly hysterical laughter.

'Thank you for your hospitality, Sir Walter,' she said, hearing the tremble in her voice and hoping nobody else noticed it. 'And for your great kindness during my stay in Venice.'

'You have been a charming guest. A charming guest,' the Ambassador replied. 'I am sure Lord Halross will escort you back to England in perfect comfort and safety.'

Athena bit the inside of her cheek as another burst of unseemly laughter threatened.

'I am grateful for his lordship's assistance,' she said, trying to sound as formal as possible. Then she thought of how Gabriel had assisted her such a short time ago and had to resist the urge to dive into the concealing shadows of the waiting gondola.

Fortunately Sir Walter returned his attention to Gabriel. The Ambassador, as ever, was most punctilious in his final conversation with his important guest. Athena listened, glad that now she need do nothing but maintain an appearance of serenity.

But when she found herself side by side with Gabriel in the gondola her composure nearly deserted her. Embarrassment flushed her cheeks. She couldn't bring herself to look at him. Couldn't think of a single thing to say to ease the mutual awareness that hummed between them in the small cabin.

From the corner of her eye she could see that Gabriel was leaning back in a superficially relaxed posture. She wasn't fooled. She could feel tightly wound tension in his powerful body. Heat flooded her at the memory of how he had wreaked havoc with her senses, filling her with quivering, boneless ecstasy. Why had she allowed him to take such liberties with her? She was humiliatingly aware that, if he'd wanted more, she would have given it to him. But he hadn't taken more. He had chosen to destroy her self-discipline while ruthlessly preserving his own. It was that, more than any other aspect of the strange interlude, which disturbed Athena most. She sensed that Gabriel had been making a point to her—and perhaps to himself. Her first instinct had been to soothe the turmoil she'd seen in his eyes. Now resentment began to stir at his arrogant behaviour. It was only last night he'd promised to take her back to England *without* making her his mistress. He might not have broken the letter of his promise, but he'd certainly undermined the spirit of it.

Gabriel forced himself to lounge in the seat beside Athena, the very image of a bored and idle nobleman. He'd ruthlessly set aside all thought of passion while he gave the final orders for their hasty departure, but now he had nothing to distract him from the arousal pulsing through his body. He was aware of every tiny movement Athena made, every breath she took. She had arched and writhed in pleasure at his touch, forgetting all decorum in the intensity of her response to him. But it wasn't enough.

He was hard with the need to thrust into her and finish what he had started. He was grateful for the long skirts of his coat, which he had pulled forward across his thighs as he sat down. The folds of fabric hid the insistent evidence of how very far he was from being either relaxed or in control of his own responses.

Kilverdale's letter burned in his pocket. At first he'd meant to confront Athena with it. Then he'd decided to withhold the letter while he questioned her in the hope of eliciting a voluntary admission that she knew the Duke. He had done neither of those things. Instead he had only succeeded in tormenting himself even further. Athena hadn't confessed to knowing Kilverdale. Gabriel still didn't know why the Duke was following her. But he could not forget the feel and sound of her glorious in passion. His craving for her had multiplied a hundredfold at the very moment he had strengthened his resolve never to let his lust for her overwhelm his judgement.

He put his hand in his pocket, feeling the seal on Kilverdale's letter. His hand clenched on the paper. He saw Athena glance towards him, clearly puzzled by the muffled crackle that seemed to originate within the gondola. He almost dragged it out and thrust it under her nose. Explain this!

But he didn't. He wanted Athena to tell him about her connection with Kilverdale of her own free will. She'd kept important information from him before and it had resulted in disaster. If Gabriel had known Samuel was a threat to her, he would never have left her unprotected. This time he wanted her to trust him completely—and demonstrate her trust in him. If he demanded an explanation immediately, she would never have a chance to confide in him voluntarily.

He would wait—keep Athena safe from all external threats—and hope to God it wouldn't be long before she mentioned Kilverdale. She talked about everyone else she knew, from the Abbess to her Aunt Eleanor and the various tradesmen she'd made purchases from in Bruges. If her acquaintance with the flamboyant and memorable Duke was innocent, surely it wouldn't be long before his name fell from her lips?

They travelled to Livorno via Bologna and Florence. The journey over the Apennines, which in poor weather could become impossible, was remarkably comfortable. Athena had expected nothing less. The carriages were of the first quality, and Gabriel's servants were as efficient and well travelled as their master.

But though the journey was not physically demanding, it took a high toll on Athena's inner reserves. Gabriel's behaviour just before they left Venice had heightened Athena's sensual awareness of him to such a level that she found it impossible to act normally in his presence. Sometimes she was overwhelmed with mortification at how easily she'd surrendered to him, at other times her mind filled with erotic memories and speculations. What would it be like when Gabriel made love to her properly? She no longer wondered if it would happen. It was just a question of when.

The tension between them stretched her nerves to screaming point. Every time she found herself alone with Gabriel she half-expected him to pull her into his arms, but instead he asked her questions about her life in Bruges. She couldn't imagine what he found so fascinating about the routine of the convent. Every night she lay in bed, her breath fluttering in her throat, wondering if this would be the night he came to her room. And every night she slept alone. Gabriel was in a strange, unreadable mood. Occasionally she glimpsed strong emotions burning in his eyes, but every time it happened he quickly masked his feelings behind an impassive expression. It gradually dawned on her that he seemed to be waiting for her to do or say something, but she had no notion what he wanted. She even asked him once if there was something wrong, but he pressed his lips together and denied it.

In self-defence she adopted an air of cool detachment whenever he spoke to her. He was the one who had breached the terms of their agreement. It was up to him to explain why. In the meantime, she was determined not to let him put her at any more of a disadvantage than he already had.

By the time they reached Florence, Gabriel's patience was in shreds. He'd given Athena every opportunity to tell him about Kilverdale, even occupied the wearisome carriage rides by asking her leading questions about her life in Bruges. But instead of explaining how she knew the Duke, she'd become increasingly remote from him until their conversation had dried up completely. Without even thinking about it, he had assumed she would ask him about the sights they encountered on their journey much as she had done in Venice. It was that lively, endlessly curious aspect of her character which he was

most familiar with, and found most reassuring. It was an indication that she really was the same girl he'd known in London. The girl he'd meant to marry. But, apart from asking him
if anything was wrong, she'd asked hardly any questions since
leaving the embassy.

Gabriel sat outside the Florentine inn, contemplating the
unsatisfactory situation. On the table in front of him there was
a broad earthenware bowl of water in which several little
glasses of wine floated to keep cool. He lifted one of the
glasses and drank it down, water dripping from his fingers as
he did so. He drank another glassful, his temper growing at
the thought of how Athena continued to play games with him.
He had given her every opportunity to confess her…friend-
ship…with Kilverdale. She had not once innocently allowed
the Duke's name to fall from her lips. And she should have
done. If Kilverdale meant nothing to her, she should not have
concealed that she knew him. If she was fleeing from the
Duke's unwelcome advances, she should have mentioned it.
She knew as well as Gabriel the disaster that had resulted
from her concealment of Samuel's pursuit. It was easy to believe the only thing she wanted from Gabriel was free passage
back to England. Now she'd won his agreement to that, it
seemed she no longer saw the need to waste any further charm
upon him.

Gabriel thrust away from the table and lunged to his feet.
He had been led by the nose long enough. He strode into the
inn, heading straight for Athena's room.

Athena sat by her window, making lace and wishing she
could explore Florence. She had no idea how long Gabriel
meant to remain in the city, and if he had any intention of inviting her to stroll through the streets with him as they had
done in Venice.

She frowned, her movements irritable as she threw the

bobbins. Gabriel's mood since they left Venice had been inexplicable and, during the past few days, increasingly cold. As if she had seriously displeased him. Was he treating her with such disdain because he now had proof of how easily he could reduce her to incoherent pleasure at his touch? The thought chilled her. But almost instantly her doubts were replaced with white-hot fury. How *dare* he condemn her when he was the one at fault.

She threw down the bobbins, intending to find and confront Gabriel. If he had a complaint about her, let him make it openly so she had a chance to answer his charges.

She'd half-risen from her seat when she heard hasty footsteps outside her room. The door crashed open and then slammed shut. Gabriel stood in front of it. She hardly had time to notice the stormy expression in his eyes before he advanced on her. With one sweep of his hand he sent the lace pillow flying. Bobbins clicked together in a high-pitched wooden jangle as the pillow hit the floor.

'I'm sick of your games!' he growled.

Athena's heart thudded with shock. She was too stunned by his accusation to reply.

His hands clamped around her upper arms and he hauled her to her feet. She saw the anger and torment in his eyes, smelt the wine on his breath, a moment before he crushed her mouth beneath his. This kiss was neither erotic nor coaxing. It was intended to punish.

Athena's surprise turned to fear-laced fury. She'd been taken against her will before. Then she'd had no choice but submit—but now she was free to fight. She struggled against the vice-like grip on her arms, kicked his shins, but he hardly seemed to notice. In blind rage she slammed her knee up into his groin with all her strength.

His reflexes were not as hazed by wine as she'd expected. He reared back just in time. Her knee barely grazed his thigh, but she was off balance. When he thrust her away from him, she fell in a heap on the floor.

'*Don't touch me!*' Fury throbbed in her voice, and seared through her body like scalding lava.

'Don't touch you?' His eyes narrowed. 'I pleased you well enough in Venice. Now you hardly bother to reply when I speak to you. You treat me like a damned lackey.'

Athena stood up. She beat her skirts smooth as she very much wished she could beat Gabriel.

'It is you who doesn't speak,' she said furiously. 'You glare and glower, but you won't say what's wrong.'

'Nothing is wrong. Only that I have allowed you to play your games too long. Are you laughing at the way you tricked me into offering you free passage back to England?'

'*Tricked* you? What are you talking about?'

'But you made a mistake.' He cut across her question as if she hadn't spoken. 'You believed I would keep my word because I'm an honourable man.'

'You *are* an honourable man.' Athena watched him warily.

'That's your mistake, sweetheart—and very nearly mine.' His voice lowered to a panther's terrifying purr. 'For just as you once broke your sacred promise to me, I do not consider myself bound by my promise to you.'

He made a sudden movement towards her and Athena tried to dart way. He seized her arm, swung her around and flung her on the bed. A second later he followed her down, pinning her to the mattress. She struggled, fighting him with all her strength. He smiled down at her, a feral expression that showed his teeth.

For the first time Athena felt genuinely afraid of him. Then the nature of her fear changed. She stopped being afraid of what he might do to her in the next few minutes. She was far more terrified of the damage he might to do his self-esteem and their future together if he continued along this path. Gabriel really was an honourable man. How would he live with himself afterwards if he allowed rage to master him? And would she ever be able to forgive him if he sank to such depths?

Instead of trying to wrench her wrists out of his clasp she forced herself to relax beneath him. Saw the pain as well as the anger in his eyes. He was in torment and she didn't know why.

'Gabriel?' she whispered.

He growled wordlessly in response.

Tears filled her eyes. How had they come to this? He had loved her once. Even if he didn't love her now, he still had powerful feelings for her. And she loved him as much as she had ever done. She wanted to put her arms around him, lay his head on her breast and soothe away his torment. But he did not look like a man who would willingly accept such comfort.

He swore suddenly and coherently. 'Dammit, don't cry.'

He released her wrists and rolled away from her, lying on his back with his forearm across his eyes.

'Gabriel?' Athena propped herself up on one elbow and looked at him. His chest rose and fell as if he'd just run a race. She half-reached out to lay a hand on his arm, then thought better of it.

'Please tell me what's the matter,' she said quietly.

He laughed harshly. 'If you don't think there's anything wrong, who am I to say otherwise?' he said. 'Examine your conscience, madam. Is there any final secret you have neglected to tell me?'

'Secret?' Athena gnawed at her lower lip. 'Nothing important,' she prevaricated.

'Nothing *important?*' Gabriel stared at her from beneath his raised arm. His expression was so coldly scornful she flushed.

'You may consider Mr Minshull's advances important, but I don't,' she flared. 'I found him a nuisance, nothing more.'

'Minshull?' Gabriel's voice rose in astonishment. 'What the devil are you talking about?'

Athena frowned. 'If you're not talking about Minshull, what *is* the problem?' she demanded.

'Tell me about Minshull,' Gabriel ordered.

'There's nothing to tell,' she said impatiently. 'He was a little more attentive than I found comfortable. He offered to make alternative arrangements if I didn't want to travel with you. That's all. I didn't like him so I avoided him. You *know* that. You even commented on me staying in my room instead of sitting on the balcony.'

'Alternative arrangements?' Gabriel's expression darkened.

'Oh, for God's sake!' Athena exploded. 'I dare say the man was just as eager to make me his mistress as you. But I didn't like him and I took good care to stay out of his way. You should be pleased at my common sense—not throwing a tantrum because I rejected an unwanted suitor.'

'If you'd told me, I'd have made sure he didn't bother you,' Gabriel said.

'It wasn't necessary,' said Athena, climbing off the bed and going to pick up the lace pillow. 'I was afraid he might make trouble. Spiteful because I refused him. Was he the one who told you whatever has been eating you since the morning we left Venice?' She turned suddenly on Gabriel.

'No,' he said, but his eyes shifted a fraction beneath her gaze.

'He *was!*' She left the pillow where it lay and marched back to the bed. 'What did he tell you?' she demanded. 'I have a right to know so that I can answer the accusations.'

'He accused you of nothing,' said Gabriel coldly.

He swung his legs off the bed and stood. They stared at each other across the width of the mattress.

Athena put her hands on her hips. 'So are you now going

to hold it against me that I had to put up with an unwanted admirer at the embassy? Why must I be punished for the stupidity of a man I couldn't abide?'

Gabriel shook his head very slightly, as if denying he had any suspicions about her dealings with Minshull. There was a distracted expression in his eyes, as if he'd just been presented with a new idea that he had not yet had time to fully consider.

'And another thing!' Athena's temper was well and truly riled. 'How dare you keep questioning my past for non-existent lovers. Have I questioned you about your lovers?' She strode around the bed so she could confront him directly. 'Have I interrogated you about the number of women you've taken to bed these past eight years? Have I impertinently insisted on knowing if they pleased you?'

She prodded him furiously in the chest. 'Why should there be one rule for you and another for me?'

'The situation is entirely different.' He seized her hand. 'What is acceptable for a man—'

'Should be acceptable for a mistress,' Athena snapped. 'You judge me by the same standards of virtue you would judge a future wife—yet all you've asked is that I share your bed till we reach England. Do you impose such exacting standards upon all your mistresses?'

'You refused to be my mistress.'

'I still have some self-respect.'

They stared at each other, their eyes locked together in anger and frustration.

'You will share my bed,' Gabriel said, his voice inflexible. 'If not now, then when we are aboard ship. You will share my cabin and my berth. You'd best prepare yourself.'

He stepped around Athena and strode out of the room before she could summon a reply. She glared at the back of the door for several minutes. Then she picked up the lace pillow and tried to untangle the threads. But her hands shook too much, and her mind was so agitated she only made the muddle worse.

Venice

'Your Grace, we are honoured to receive you.' The Ambassador himself waited on the steps of the embassy to greet the Duke.

As soon as Kilverdale had reached the environs of Venice he'd sent another message to the embassy. He himself had been delayed a further hour while he waited to be granted a Bill of Health and permission to continue into the city—but that was an inconvenience every visitor suffered. The interval had given the Ambassador the opportunity to make hasty preparations for his noble guest.

'Thank you.' Kilverdale alighted from the gondola without assistance. It was not his first trip visit to Venice. Philpott needed the steadying hand of the gondolier. 'I am glad to arrive at last.'

'Please come this way.' Sir Walter bowed the Duke in through the watergate. 'I have had a suite of rooms prepared for your grace.'

'Excellent. Is Mrs Quenell waiting there?'

'Mrs Quenell?' The Ambassador faltered.

'My cousin,' said Kilverdale impatiently. 'I sent a letter about her to you.'

'Your *cousin?*' Sir Walter's expression shifted from confused to alarmed. 'I beg your pardon, your Grace, but I received no letter from you. Do you mean to say that Mrs Quenell is *related* to you?'

'Her mother and mine are sisters. Do you interrogate all your guests about every branch of their family tree? Where is my cousin? I hope you have provided every comfort for her while she awaited my arrival.'

Since the Ambassador and the other members of his staff who were present all seemed incapable of responding, Kilverdale strode ahead of them into the Embassy. He was familiar with the typical layout of a Venetian palazzo and easily found the stairs leading to the *portego*.

'Your Grace!' The Ambassador broke into an undignified trot to catch up. 'Let me show you to your quarters.'

'Very good.' Kilverdale gave a cursory glance around the chamber. He noted in passing the trompe l'oeil bookcase on one wall and that the room overlooked the grand canal, but he was far more interested in seeing Athena than admiring his surroundings.

'Send for Mrs Quenell,' he ordered.

'Your Grace, I regret to tell you that Mrs Quenell is not here,' Sir Walter said.

'Not here?' Kilverdale spun around to stare at the Ambassador.

Sir Walter took a step backwards. 'We had no idea she was your cousin,' he said.

'Where is she?' Kilverdale felt sharp anxiety, combined with rising anger that Athena had been turned out of the Embassy.

'On her way to Livorno,' said Sir Walter.

'Livorno? Why? I sent her a letter telling her to wait for me. And you a letter to tell you to take care of her.' Kilverdale couldn't believe what he was hearing.

'I…don't think she knew that,' said Sir Walter. 'That you were on your way. And I assure your Grace that I have never received a letter from you.' He was nearly twice Kilverdale's age, but he gave the impression that he might start shuffling like a schoolboy caught in a misdemeanour.

'Diable! I've followed her from Bruges. Why can't she stay in one place for thirty seconds?'

Sir Walter didn't even try to answer Kilverdale's exasperated exclamation.

'Why did she leave? Did you make her unwelcome?' Kilverdale frowned at Sir Walter.

'No indeed!' the Ambassador replied. 'Mrs Quenell is charming. A delightful guest. She left with the Marquis.'

'What Marquis?' Kilverdale's voice dropped to a lower, much more dangerous note.

'Halross. He has ships,' Sir Walter said jerkily. 'Your Grace may be aware that the Marquis has many trading links with Italy. When Mrs Quenell arrived here she asked me if I could help her arrange her journey back to England. I immediately thought of Lord Halross. He was shortly to return home in one of his own ships. From Livorno.'

'I see.' Kilverdale looked at the Ambassador through half-closed eyes.

There was a lot more going on here than Sir Walter had yet revealed. Not least of which was why neither Athena nor the Ambassador had, apparently, received his letters. He knew Athena too well to believe that, if she'd known he was following her, she would have left without a backward glance.

'Where is the woman she travelled with? Mrs Beresford?' he said abruptly. 'Let me speak to her.'

Two irritating hours later, after speaking to both Rachel Beresford and Martha, and then questioning several other members of the Embassy household, Kilverdale had pieced together a fair picture of what had happened. It was clear to the Duke that Roger Minshull had taken advantage of his position of trust to take spiteful revenge on Athena for rejecting his advances.

Kilverdale immediately demanded that Minshull be dismissed; but the Duke was also determined to exact retribution on Halross, who had taken dishonourable advantage of Athena's impoverished situation.

'I'll have his liver!' he swore.

'She said that once they were to have married,' said Martha, keeping a wary distance from her interrogator.

'Married?' Kilverdale threw a sharp glance at Athena's former maid.

'Yes, your Grace.' She dropped him a nervous curtsy.

'Very good, you may go—with your lady's permission,' he added, belatedly remembering that Martha was Rachel's servant, not his.

If Martha was right, he had just discovered the identity of the man for whom Athena had sacrificed herself eight years ago. She had told Kilverdale and his mother only the barest outline of what had happened in London, and never revealed the name of the man she had meant to marry. The man who was implicated in a plot to kill Cromwell.

If Halross *was* Athena's former bridegroom, the situation required careful consideration, though the new information did nothing to reduce Kilverdale's determination to catch up with the couple before they left Italy. There was still a chance he could overtake them before they reached Livorno.

'Your Grace,' Rachel said, and paused.

He looked at her, gentling his gaze because he knew he made her nervous and he wished her no ill.

'I believe, from the way he spoke, that Lord Halross holds Mrs Quenell in…affection,' she said carefully.

'Affection?' Kilverdale kept his voice mild. 'And what of my cousin? Does she reciprocate that affection?'

Rachel looked at him with a troubled expression in her eyes. Clearly she was afraid to say anything that might do a disservice to Athena.

Kilverdale took pity upon her and smiled. 'You have been very helpful,' he said, standing up. 'And now it seems I must set off for Livorno.'

'Surely tomorrow morning will be soon enough,' she exclaimed, glancing at the window. It was already nearly twilight. 'I'm sure the Ambassador will give a banquet in your honour. He did when Mrs Quenell and I arrived, and you're far more important.'

Kilverdale blinked at this unsophisticated reference to his consequence and then smiled at Rachel with genuine amusement. There were a number of replies he could have made, but he chose not to embarrass her.

'I wouldn't want to disappoint the Ambassador,' he said.

'I wish to see something of Florence,' Athena announced.

Gabriel raised his eyebrows. 'I had intended to make an early start this morning,' he said.

'Can you not spare one day for me to see the city?' Athena asked. She still didn't know what had prompted Gabriel's outburst the previous evening but, as far as she could tell, his temper had somewhat improved this morning. It was as if their argument had released some of the tension growing between them. She decided to make the most of his good mood. She wasn't likely to get another chance to visit Florence.

Gabriel frowned as he considered her request. 'One day,' he said abruptly. 'We can spend one extra day here.' He stood up and held out his hand to her. 'Come, then. There's no sense in wasting the time we have.'

Athena took his hand and followed him out into the sunlit streets, her heart lifting at his gruff acquiescence to her request.

'Tell me about your family,' Gabriel said, as they strolled beside the River Arno.

'My family?' Athena's thoughts immediately flew to the last time she'd seen her mother so many years ago. Her hand tightened unconsciously on Gabriel's arm.

'What's wrong?' he asked quickly.

'Nothing.' She shook her head. 'I will be able to see them soon. I hope…I hope they will be pleased to see me.'

'Are you afraid they won't welcome you?'

Athena hesitated over her reply. 'I believe my mother will be pleased to see me,' she said at last. 'But I don't know if her husband will allow her to receive me,' she confessed in a rush.

'Why?' Gabriel's voice sharpened.

'Because I ran away from his nephew!' Athena said with a flash of temper. 'He thought I would make Samuel a fine wife.'

'I'd forgotten,' said Gabriel. 'So your stepfather thought you would be a good match for his nephew?'

Athena looked at him suspiciously. 'Why are you suddenly so interested in these details?' she asked.

Gabriel gazed out across the river for a few seconds, then brought his gaze back to Athena's face. 'I just wondered why there was such haste to marry you off,' he said. 'Whether, perhaps, you were…?' He paused, clearly seeking the precise words he needed.

'A shame on my family?' Athena pulled her hand away from his arm. 'I was a modest maid! No shame to anyone! I was only just seventeen when I met you, and you were the first—' She looked away, pressing her lips together as she felt tears pricking her eyes.

'That's not what I meant,' said Gabriel. 'I was the first what?'

'What does it matter now?' Athena turned away from the river to plunge deeper into Florence.

'I was the first what?' Gabriel caught her arm.

'Man to kiss me.' She glared at him. 'Why are you asking these questions? What do you care what kind of family your mistress comes from?'

'You're not my mistress.'

Athena's breath caught at his flat statement. Just last night he had told her she was to share his berth on the ship. What exactly did he want from her? 'If I'm just your travelling companion, then my past matters even less,' she said, recovering her composure.

'I was making polite conversation. I told you all about my

family,' Gabriel reminded her. 'Tell me about your father. What was his name?'

'Edmund. Sir Edmund Fairchild of Kent.' Athena lifted her chin proudly. 'He was a good, honourable man.'

'Yes, you told me your real name was Fairchild,' Gabriel said softly. 'Athena Frances Fairchild. I suppose it is not such a great leap from that to Frances Child.'

'Not far enough,' said Athena, with a touch of bitterness. 'If I'd changed it more completely, perhaps Samuel wouldn't have found me.'

'I imagine he found you through your aunt. How is Kitty, by the way?'

'She died a few years ago.'

'I'm sorry.'

Athena nodded. She'd been sad when her aunt had died. But she'd been comforted by the fact that Kilverdale had, in his usual high-handed manner, made sure Kitty's last years were comfortable ones. Now her thoughts were focused on her father and the events that had caused her flight to London.

'It was dreadful when he died,' she whispered. 'We'd been so happy until then. Suddenly everything changed. Mother was heartbroken…' Her voice caught. She looked away, deliberately pushing the sad memories aside. She didn't want to make herself any more vulnerable to Gabriel than she already was.

'Why is there a flask hanging on that door?' she asked, trying to change the subject. 'It looks like the entrance to a palace, not an alehouse.'

'It is a nobleman's house,' said Gabriel. 'Flasks like that are common sight in Florence. All the nobility sell wine from their houses. In fact, only the upper ranks are permitted to sell wine retail here. Everyone else must sell wholesale. You see the little window and the knocker? If I knock, a servant will answer and sell me a bottle of wine.'

Athena looked at him in astonishment, which changed quickly to amusement. He grinned.

'Now I suppose you want me to demonstrate,' he said.

'Later,' she said. 'Otherwise you'll have to carry it.'

'You didn't object to me carrying chocolate in Venice,' Gabriel observed as they strolled onwards.

'That was different.' Athena tossed him a saucy smile.

Gabriel smiled, and unerringly guided Athena through the streets to the magnificent red-domed cathedral with Giotto's bell-tower standing beside it. Florence was not far from Livorno, and he was even more at home here than he had been in Venice. After Athena had admired the beautiful buildings they wandered back to the *Ponte Vecchio*.

'Another bridge.' Athena was fascinated by the similarities and differences between the *Ponte Vecchio* and the Rialto—and couldn't help comparing both to London Bridge.

The *Ponte Vecchio* was famous for its goldsmiths' shops, and Athena gasped at the gleaming display laid out before them at Gabriel's request. She listened as he spoke to the goldsmith, wishing she could understand what was being said. Was he really buying the glorious gold necklace? And if he was, who was he buying it for? Not for her, surely? She was standing right next to him and he hadn't asked her preferences. Besides, it was a gift for a princess—not a penniless widow with a dubious reputation.

In a moment of stomach-lurching horror, Athena remembered how Gabriel had claimed to be considering marriage to Lord Ashworth's daughter that day on the balcony in Venice. Was the necklace a betrothal gift for her? Athena fixed a serene expression on her face and pretended to have only polite interest in the incomprehensible transaction taking place before her, but her mind teemed with anxious questions.

'Is the necklace for Lord Ashworth's daughter?' she asked as casually as she could, as they walked off the bridge.

'No…*who?*' Gabriel frowned, apparently confused by the question. 'What? It's none of your business,' he said brusquely, but as she glanced up at him she saw a dull flush rising in his cheeks.

The sight of Gabriel blushing was unexpected and very intriguing.

'We're going for a drive on the Cascine,' he announced, before she could pursue the matter any further. 'You'll like it.'

'I will? Why?' Athena was absolutely convinced he was trying to distract her from the necklace he'd just bought.

'There are lots of flowers.' He gestured expansively with his free hand. 'All kinds of flowers. You like flowers.'

'Yes, I do,' she agreed demurely.

He looked down at her out of the corner of his eye and she thought she heard him utter a small 'humph' of embarrassment.

'Will you buy me some flowers?' she asked, hugging his arm with both hands and feeling unreasonably happy. Gabriel hadn't said outright the necklace was for her, but she couldn't help suspecting it was. He'd been so surprised at her suggestion he'd bought it for another woman. And his embarrassment at her questions reminded her of his similar embarrassment when he'd bought lace for her in St Mark's Square.

'A whole basketful of flowers if it will stop you bothering me with foolish questions,' he muttered.

Gabriel watched as Athena buried her face in an armful of orange blossom. She'd closed her eyes the better to appreciate the fragrant scent. She looked happy and relaxed. It was difficult to believe she was wilfully deceiving him, but she still hadn't mentioned Kilverdale.

Gabriel had thought of a possible connection between the Duke and Athena overnight, and he'd tried to draw her into talking about her family in an attempt to see if he'd guessed correctly. Gabriel knew Kilverdale was the only legitimate child of his parents—but that didn't mean the Duke had no siblings. It was highly likely his father had sired a few illegitimate children, and it was even possible that his mother had played her husband false. If Kilverdale was Athena's half-brother, it would account not only for why he impatiently talked about taking her 'home' and paying her expenses, but also for Athena's secretiveness about him. It wouldn't matter whether Athena's mother was the Duchess of Kilverdale—who had farmed out the daughter of an adulterous liaison to another couple to raise—or if her mother really was the former Lady Fairchild who'd had an affair with Kilverdale's father; in either case it would be her mother's shame Athena was hiding, rather than her own.

Unfortunately, Athena hadn't said anything about her family that either proved or disproved his hopeful theory. And instead of interrogating her more closely Gabriel had succumbed to impulse and bought the necklace—not that he'd been ready to admit it was for her. He'd have to find another way to provoke her into talking about Kilverdale.

In the meantime, the sun was setting over the poplar trees along the Cascine and it was time to return to the inn. Tomorrow they would complete their journey to Livorno.

'I like Florence,' said Athena, lifting her head to smile at him. 'You were lucky to spend so many years in Italy.'

'I always thought so,' Gabriel agreed.

'I would like to come back again one day,' she said.

Gabriel started to nod, then stopped himself just in time. There were still things to resolve before he made any more promises to her.

Chapter Eleven

'It's larger than I expected.' Athena looked around the great cabin with her usual curiosity.

'It may not seem so large after several weeks at sea,' Gabriel replied.

She threw him a quick glance, then returned her attention to her surroundings. Though she was doing her best to seem at ease, he knew she was nervous. He couldn't blame her. He still hadn't made it plain whether he would be sharing the cabin with her.

'Windows!' she exclaimed, immediately going to peer through one.

There were three windows across the after end of the cabin, glazed with small panes of glass. A built-in, upholstered seat stretched the full width of the windows and Athena knelt on it to look out at the harbour.

'I didn't expect windows,' she said, clearly delighted. 'I thought we would be in an airless little cupboard below decks.'

She'd said *we*, Gabriel noticed at once. Did that mean she took it for granted he would be staying with her? Then he saw the blush creep into her cheeks as she sent him another sideways glance.

'A table!' The utilitarian piece of furniture below the windows didn't warrant quite so much enthusiasm, in Gabriel's opinion. 'Oh, it's nailed down.' She pushed it experimentally. 'How clever. It won't slide across the floor when the ship rolls.'

She looked up and noticed the musket, pistols and cutlass hanging from the bulkhead. She frowned.

'Are you expecting us to be attacked?' she asked.

'No,' Gabriel replied.

'We are at war with the Dutch and the French,' Athena said. 'It was easy to forget in Venice. But now… Do you think we may meet trouble on the journey?' Her expression was serious, but not unduly alarmed.

'I don't think so,' said Gabriel. 'The English navy is patrolling the Mediterranean very effectively. But it is always sensible to take precautions.'

Athena looked at him for a few seconds, as if assessing how worried she ought to be.

'I would not have allowed you on board if I thought you were at serious risk from the enemy,' he said, an edge on his voice.

Her gaze intensified. He looked away, cursing himself for his hasty words, afraid he had revealed too much. To his relief, Athena continued with her exploration of the cabin. He sat down on the seat beneath the windows and watched her discover a cabinet full of plates and cutlery.

'The stools aren't nailed down,' she said, picking one up and putting it next to the table.

'No. I'll get the ship's carpenter to make a secure stand for your lace pillow,' Gabriel said. 'Can you make lace at sea?'

'I don't see why not,' said Athena. 'The flax prefers to be damp. They spin it in cellars for that very reason. And the pillow is stuffed with sea grass.'

'Will the pins rust?'

'They're made of brass. It will be an interesting experiment.'

She tried to open another cupboard door and belatedly discovered it was a sliding panel rather than hinged like the other cabinet door. She pulled it back, looked inside…and Gabriel heard her gasp.

'It's a bed!' Her gaze flew to his face, then slid away just as quickly.

Before Gabriel could reply, they were interrupted by two seamen carrying in his chest. Athena's gaze fell upon it.

'My lace!' Her eyes lit up. 'May I have it now?' She turned eagerly to him.

He tossed her the key and she found the lace and laid it on the table. Gabriel could see she was pleased to have it once more in her hands. She smoothed it beneath her fingertips, lingering for a moment over the small tear that had not been present when he'd taken it into his possession.

Gabriel's skin heated. He still wanted her to tell him the truth about Kilverdale, but he felt ashamed that his anger had nearly driven him to destroy her work. He tensed in anticipation of her questions but, though she glanced at him under her lashes, she didn't say anything.

'Are you going to sell it when we get back to England?' he asked, despite the fact that he was quite determined to keep possession of the lace.

'I meant to.' Athena touched a torn thread and frowned slightly.

'There are many wealthy men you could sell it to,' he said. 'The King himself would not despise work of such quality.'

With one slim finger Athena flicked the broken thread— and Gabriel's raw nerves—in a silent comment on *that* claim.

'Or one of his courtiers, perhaps,' Gabriel said in a gritty voice. He would not apologise when she still hadn't been completely honest with him. 'Rochester? Kilverdale…?'

Athena looked up the moment she heard the Duke's name.

Gabriel's body surged hot with satisfaction at finally getting a response from her—then cold in anticipation of what she might now say. He was a fool to have left it so late to challenge her, when they would be trapped aboard the ship with no escape for weeks. He could already hear the hails from on deck as the ship prepared to leave the harbour.

'Kilverdale?' Athena said. She'd looked surprised when she'd first heard the Duke's name, but now Gabriel could see growing amusement in her eyes.

The table did not span the full width of the seat. There was a clear space in front of Gabriel's legs and Athena walked around to stand before him, so close she was almost between his knees.

Dumbfounded, Gabriel saw the slight smile on her lips as she reached out to him. She picked up a lock of his hair and twisted it almost playfully around her index finger. She'd put her hand on his arm when they walked together, but it was the first time she had initiated such intimate contact since they'd met again in Venice.

Words lodged in Gabriel's throat. He could not speak as she continued to toy with his hair. One delicate fingertip traced his eyebrow and over the bridge of his nose. His heart hammered. His body began to pulse with arousal. He half-lifted his hands to pull her down on to his lap—then remembered he still had no idea how she knew Kilverdale. Was this just a trick to distract him?

'Kilverdale?' she mused. 'Well, he does admire my lace, it's true. He already wears it.'

'He wears your lace?' The question emerged hoarsely.

'Yes.' A teasing smile played on Athena's lips, though the expression in her eyes was soft and tender.

Her mood confused Gabriel. But he was snared by her seductive touch. By the fact that she was so dizzyingly close to him, standing willingly between his legs.

'If he was here, do you think I would caress him so?' Athena murmured. 'Run my fingers through his hair?'

Gabriel watched with baffled outrage as she actually laughed at the suggestion. In another instant he would put an end to her witch's game. Just as soon as he summoned the dignity and cold hauteur to put her in her place.

'Of course, if I tugged Kilverdale's hair, it would come off,' Athena observed. 'Not like yours.' She pulled gently to prove her point. 'Last time he visited me it was very hot and he *did* take off his periwig. His own hair is very short and just as black as his wig.'

The mere thought of Athena seeing Kilverdale without his periwig—and the circumstances that might have prompted the vain and foppish Duke to remove it—filled Gabriel with incoherent fury. His hands clamped on Athena's waist.

'He's my cousin,' she said quickly. 'Don't be angry, Gabriel. He's my cousin. His mother is my aunt Eleanor.'

'What?'

The Duchess of Kilverdale was Athena's aunt Eleanor! Gabriel couldn't believe it. He'd suspected Athena might be the Duke's illegitimate half-sister. Why on earth hadn't it occurred to him that they might be related in another way? He felt like a complete fool. He stared up at her, his hands still locked on her waist, while she continued to play gently with his hair.

'Why didn't you tell me about him before?' Gabriel said, damning himself because his voice emerged more like a frog's croak than the crisp demand he'd intended.

'I did.' Athena frowned briefly. 'Didn't I? I told you my cousins visited me and the last time one of them brought me chocolate,' she reminded him.

'I thought—' He broke off, clearing his throat. 'You spoke of your aunt and your cousins,' he said coldly. 'Naturally I assumed it would be your *female* cousins visiting you in the convent.'

'I am sure the Abbess would have preferred that too,'

Athena admitted. 'There were strict arrangements that, though I could meet Kilverdale, he was not to encounter any of the nuns.' She frowned again. 'Perhaps that's why I got into the habit of simply referring to him as my cousin, rather than by his name,' she said. 'It seemed to cause less offence. It was all very foolish. As if a simple glimpse of Jack could corrupt anyone!'

'That is his reputation,' said Gabriel, a dry note creeping into his voice.

'I don't know why. He is a kind and sweet-natured man.' Athena immediately rose to her cousin's defence.

'Sweet-natured?' Gabriel stared at Athena in disbelief and a resurgence of jealousy. She sounded so fond of the absent Duke.

'Well, he can be a little impatient and high-handed at times,' Athena conceded. 'But he knew how lonely and cut off from my family I felt in Flanders—though I did my best to be happy with my life. Don't you think it was kind of him to visit me, even though he had to travel from England and get the King's permission each time to leave the country?'

Gabriel didn't have a ready answer for her question. Somehow his back seemed to be against the wall in more than one sense. He leant against the upholstery and stared at her.

'This is what you've been worrying about since we left Venice, isn't it?' said Athena. 'Gabriel, if you'd only told me what was wrong, I could have reassured you at once.'

'I don't want reassurance,' he said, offended by both her words and the fond expression he saw in her eyes. As if he were a wayward child in need of comfort after grazing his knees. He would not allow any woman to patronise him, no matter how beautiful or desirable he found her.

He sat forward, meaning to push her away from him and stand.

'Who told you about Kilverdale?' she asked. 'Martha? Rachel Beresford never met him. I'm not sure I ever mentioned him to her. But Martha saw him several times. Unfortunately she'd been swayed by gossip and she was inclined to think the worst of him.'

Gabriel paused in the act of standing up. He suddenly realised the quagmire still ahead of him. If he showed Athena Kilverdale's letter, he would certainly provoke her anger. Even worse, he would reveal his weakness where she was concerned and she might start cooing reassurances at him as if he were a frightened baby.

Who the hell was Martha? If he was claiming even by default—because he didn't deny Athena's assumption—that Martha had told him about Kilverdale, he ought to know who she was.

'I hope she will be happy, married to Richard and staying in Venice,' Athena said.

Married? It was because her maid had wed that Athena was travelling without a servant.

'I see no reason why she won't be happy,' Gabriel said, relieved at having identified the woman. 'I don't imagine Rachel Beresford is a harsh mistress. How can you possibly be Kilverdale's cousin?' he exploded.

'His mother and my mother are sisters,' Athena said. 'You know my mother married Sir Edmund Fairchild. Aunt Eleanor married Lord Kilverdale. Jack's father was an Earl, but King Charles I made him a Duke as a reward for his loyalty and valour on the battle field—and I think because he gave him money,' she added.

'The Stuarts always need money,' Gabriel said, momentarily distracted by the comment.

'So I've heard. My father had royalist sympathies, but he managed to avoid direct involvement in the fighting. But Kilverdale Hall is in the heart of Sussex, and Sussex was controlled by Parliament from very early in the war,' Athena said. 'Aunt Eleanor went into exile in France in 1643 when Jack was only three years old. I'd never met her—I'm a year younger than Jack—but she and my mother used to write to each other whenever they could.'

Gabriel saw Athena's gaze turn inwards as she contemplated her family history. 'It was terrifying when I fled to her for help,' she said in a low voice. 'She was a stranger to me. I was afraid… But she took me in and comforted me just as if she were my mother. They both, Aunt Eleanor and Jack, know what it is like to be exiled from home. I think that's why Jack would visit me.' She focused her attention once more on Gabriel. 'He is like an older brother to me,' she said.

Triumph soared through Gabriel. He'd already come to the conclusion that Kilverdale was not a serious rival for Athena's affection, but it was still a relief to know the answer to the question that had been plaguing him since he'd read the Duke's letter. He pulled Athena down to sit on his thigh so suddenly she clutched his shoulders for balance.

'Gabriel!'

He covered her mouth with his, feeling her surprise and momentary hesitation. Then she melted into his embrace, heating his blood until he was aware only of her. He lifted his head a fraction.

'You will share my berth tonight,' he said against her lips.

By the time Athena had stood on deck to see the Italian coastline disappear over the horizon, eaten her first meal on board and watched the lamp being lit in the great cabin, her heart was beating in her throat. She sat in the seat beneath the windows, her hands clasped on her lap, and waited for Gabriel to return from speaking to the ship's Master. She'd already been introduced to the Master and Mate and seen the crew at work.

She had no thought of rejecting Gabriel when he came to her. She had waited a long time for her wedding night with him and, although she was not his wife and most likely never would be, she had no intention of denying either of them any longer. When she contemplated the coming night she was as full of excitement, anticipation and nervousness as she had been all those years ago. Tonight she would give herself to Gabriel, and he would give himself to her.

The lamp swung gently with the movement of the ship. She could smell the sea, hear the creak of the rigging and the lap of water against the hull. She remembered those three weeks she had waited each night for Samuel to come to bed. Her stomach clenched at the memory. She forced herself to relax. This was Gabriel. Despite his volatile temper she knew he would never hurt her, and he had given her such pleasure the morning they left Venice. Unexpected, astounding pleasure. If he did the same again tonight…

Her body began to tingle with anticipation. Her heart skipped a beat as the door opened. She swallowed, watching nervously as Gabriel stepped into the cabin. He closed the door carefully and turned to look at her, his hands on his hips, his feet braced against the easy motion of the ship. He had removed his splendid clothes and wore only breeches, a shirt, which revealed his broad shoulders, and a plain lawn cravat. His hair glowed a rich dark brown beneath the lantern. He gazed at her through narrowed eyes. She pressed her fingers even more tightly together. She ought to say something, but she couldn't think of a word.

'Do you feel ill?' he asked abruptly.

'Ill?' She stared at him in bewilderment. Of all the things she'd expected him to say, that hadn't been one of them.

'From the ship's movement,' he said impatiently.

'Oh. No. I feel very well.'

'Good. That is very good.' He continued to stare at her without coming any closer. The tension mounted until Athena couldn't stand the silence any longer.

'At least no one is making jokes or throwing stockings at us,' she said, with a nervous laugh, referring to the custom where the wedding guests followed the bridal couple into the bedchamber and stood at the foot of the bed to throw stockings at the newly-weds.

His expression darkened and her breath caught. She wished she hadn't mentioned marriage.

'You are to be my mistress,' he said.

'I know.' She lifted her chin. 'Since there is no need to stand on ceremony, perhaps you should get on with it,' she added, too agitated to pretend a serenity she didn't feel.

His eyebrows shot up. She saw she had startled him, but there was also a glimmer of reluctant respect in his eyes. He crossed to a cabinet and removed a bottle of wine and two plain mugs.

Athena sipped cautiously, watching Gabriel all the while. He watched her too with a gaze of lynx-like intensity. She tipped up her mug and recklessly drained it. He took it from her and she looked at him, her breath quick and shallow.

Gabriel put his hands on her waist and she stopped breathing completely. She was wearing one of her travelling gowns and he was able to slip his hands beneath the loose jacket. Only her chemise separated them and he pulled her closer. Athena let out her breath with a gasp and put her hands on his shoulders. Very slowly he lowered his head to hers—but when their lips touched passion ignited between them. His lips were firm and seductively thorough. His tongue claimed her and the kiss filled her senses. She did not even consider resisting. She buried her hands in his hair, stretched her body up to meet his, pressing her breasts against his chest. His large hand was splayed in the small of her back, holding her hard against him. Her limbs trembled and erotic fire pulsed through her veins, pooling between her legs.

Gabriel trailed devastating kisses down the side of her

neck and she let her head fall back with a sigh of pleasure. He kissed her throat, his lips and tongue branding her as his. He lifted his hand and began to unbutton her jacket, but his arousal made him clumsy and impatient. He gripped the fabric and ripped. Athena heard buttons land on the wooden boards and roll away and she didn't care. She was as eager to feel his hands on her body as he was to touch her.

He pushed the jacket from her shoulders and tossed it aside. Now the upper part of her body was covered only by her cambric chemise, trimmed by a narrow lace edging at the sleeves and neckline. Her nipples jutted against the material. She saw heat leap into his eyes as he put his hands on her sides and slowly raised them until his palms cupped the undersides of her breasts.

'O…ohh.' Athena was hardly aware she uttered a soft murmur of pleasure and need.

Gabriel began to circle her nipples with his thumbs, toying gently with the erect peaks. Breath exploded from her lungs at the exquisite sensation. She could feel the erotic tug deep inside her quivering body. She had waited years for him to touch her like this and her hands locked convulsively in his hair. Arching her back, she thrust herself forward into his caressing hands. He tugged at the narrow ribbon securing the neckline of her chemise and pulled the garment down to bare her breasts.

He bent his head and pressed a warm kiss upon the soft upper curve…then he froze, his whole body as still as a statue, every muscle rigid.

At first Athena's mind was too hazy with passion to notice the change in him. She pushed impatiently against him, wanting more of the wonderful sensations he created. But then he lifted his head and muttered a harsh curse.

Understanding hit her, jolting horribly through her arousal-sensitised body. Gabriel had remembered the moment he saw Samuel kiss her breast.

He pushed her away from him.

Frustration and anger burst through her in equal measure at his action. How dare he trifle with her feelings like this! Next he would no doubt shout abuse at her for events that were long in the past. She would not have it!

'Stop it!' She prodded him in the chest, already furious with him.

'Stop what?' His expression had closed as he pushed her away, but now he looked more shocked than angry at her sudden attack.

'Living in the past. You should be thinking about the way I am now—not when I was seventeen. Or was it only the seventeen-year-old girl who aroused your lust?' She advanced on him, incandescent with indignation and frustrated desire.

Gabriel took a step backwards. He looked thoroughly dumbfounded by her verbal assault, but she was too carried away by righteous indignation to notice.

'Look at me!' she ordered, hands on her hips, making no efforts to cover herself. 'Am I no longer beautiful to you? Am I not desirable to you any more? If all you want to do is claim what should have been yours eight years ago, then let us forgo this meaningless seduction.' She glared at him, her chest heaving with the force of her emotions.

Gabriel stared back at her, so aroused he could not form a single coherent word to answer her challenge. She was magnificent. From the fire that blazed in her blue eyes to the small breasts perfectly shaped to fit his palms, she was everything he could wish for.

The memory of Samuel touching her had risen unbidden into his mind when he'd kissed her breast, but her passionate response to his momentary hesitation burned away the unwelcome memory. He had never seen her like this before. She was no longer a girl but a woman, full of a woman's passion.

He took a step towards her, but then she spoke again. Her gaze had turned thoughtful. He paused, wondering what new challenge she was about to offer.

'You only have these disturbing memories when you kiss my breasts,' she said.

'Your breasts are beautiful,' he assured her, his voice thick with desire.

'Hmm.' She glanced down with a slight frown as if assessing the accuracy of his claim. Then shrugged slightly as if dismissing it.

The shrug had a potent effect upon Gabriel. He made another move towards her, intent on proving the truth of his words, but she held up a hand to stop him. He paused, torn between heavy arousal and dawning amusement.

'We must be practical,' she declared. 'If the sight of my breasts has an unfortunate effect upon you, you must not look at them any more.' She suited action to words by pulling on the ribbon to close the neckline of her chemise.

Gabriel swallowed an instinctive protest. Now he would simply have the pleasure of uncovering her a second time.

'You only suffer this…distraction…when I am in low cut dresses,' she reminded him. 'When I am in the high-necked jackets, or even the domino at the *casino,* you experience no such problem.'

'I am not…' Gabriel started to say that he didn't have a problem now. Then he changed his mind, curious to discover what Athena's solution would be.

She looked at him with thinly disguised concern in her eyes.

'I am sure you know best,' she said brightly. 'I have no experience in these matters. But isn't it the task of a mistress to…to…' She stumbled briefly over a suitable description. 'Er…to…er, stimulate the appropriate *mood* in her patron?'

Her expression was such an odd mixture of attempted nonchalance, anxiety and embarrassment that, despite his urgent arousal, Gabriel had to restrain the urge to laugh.

'If the patron is feeling particularly jaded with pleasure, that might be necessary,' he conceded. 'I must assure you, however, that I am not at all jaded—or in any way incapacitated in my pursuit of pleasure.'

'Of course not,' Athena assured him instantly. 'I know you are a man of utmost virility. In every way manly and exceptionally… er…vigorous.' Fiery colour burned in her cheeks and for a moment she couldn't meet his eyes.

Gabriel tightened his jaw. A few hours ago he wouldn't have believed he could find humour in this moment, but for the first time since he'd seen Athena on the Ambassador's balcony he was no longer at war with himself or the past. He felt carefree and happier than he had done for years.

'I am, yes,' he said, when he could trust himself to speak. His voice emerged more gruffly than he'd intended and Athena bit her lip.

'I know it is not modest of me to mention such things,' she said worriedly. 'I hope I haven't shocked you.'

'No. No,' he said. 'You have always been very practical. I believe we've discussed that before.'

'Oh, yes.' She sounded relieved. 'You seemed to approve of my practical nature.'

'Usually,' he agreed.

'Well, then…' she seemed to take fresh courage from his response '…I think what we must do is avoid any…any unfortunate stimulus for your thoughts,' she said.

'You're not going to let me look at your breasts,' Gabriel interpreted.

'No.' She bit her lip again.

'So we are to make love in all our clothes?' he asked, not liking her apparent solution.

Her gaze ran over his broad shoulders, down his chest and

legs and lifted once more to his eyes. He read her expression very clearly. She didn't want *him* to keep all his clothes on.

'I hardly think it is fair if I bare myself for you while you remain modestly covered,' he said.

'No. Very well, I will prepare myself.'

'Prepare yourself how?' He looked at her in fascination as she caught his shirt sleeve and began tow him towards the bunk.

'You must lie down and close your eyes,' she said breathlessly.

'Why?'

'You mustn't watch,' she said, sounding scandalised. 'Oh, wait.' She began to untie his cravat.

'Are you undressing me already? Am I to be naked for your pleasure while you prepare yourself?' he asked, struggling to resist the urge to haul her into his arms and forestall all her preparations. He was already feeling extremely vigorous.

'*No.*' She sounded even more shocked. 'It is to cover your eyes,' she told him. 'So you do not cheat.'

Gabriel smiled slightly. 'Do you think I would?' he asked softly.

'You mustn't,' she said, not answering directly. 'There.' She held the cravat in both hands. 'Sit down. I can't reach otherwise.'

He sat on the edge of the bunk and allowed her to tie the strip of soft lawn around his eyes.

'Now lie down,' she said.

He gauged his position carefully and did as he was bid. He did not like surrendering even one of his senses in this way, but his hearing was acute. He trusted that she would not be able to approach him without his hearing her and being forewarned. And he was eager to see how she meant to prepare herself to maintain him in—as she would no doubt put it herself—the utmost peak of vigorous virility.

He immediately discovered that unidentified sounds could be as arousing as things seen. He could hear the sound of the ship beyond the small cabin. Closer to hand he heard Athena's quickened breathing and the rustle of material. Instantly he imagined her stepping out of her clothes. Perhaps wriggling her hips to encourage her petticoats to fall at her feet. Was she standing naked only a few feet away from him? It took all his self-control not to tear off the blindfold and pull her into the berth with him.

He heard the soft pad of her feet on the boards. She'd taken her shoes off. She *was* naked! Then a sound which, after a moment of puzzlement, he recognised as the opening of his chest. A few moments later there was another sound like wood sliding against wood.

'Are you ready yet?' he demanded.

'Nearly,' she said, her voice muffled, as if she had something in her mouth. 'I must make a few…a few adjustments.'

Rrrrip!

He nearly leapt off the mattress at the sudden sound of tearing fabric.

'What are you doing?'

'Nothing. Lie back and relax.'

Relax? Was she mad? His whole body was in the grip of fierce arousal. Hard and heavy and urgent with need. All he had to do was remember her standing before him, confronting him in all her fiery temper with her breasts bare to his gaze and he could hardly control his rampant body.

'Can I open my eyes yet?'

'No! Only a little while longer. You mustn't look.'

'I am sure it would be excellent for my manly vigour if I watched your preparations.'

'I would be too embarrassed.'

'But you won't be embarrassed when you're ready?'

'I will try not to be,' she said. He heard the catch in her voice and suddenly he was flooded with tenderness for her, greater even than his physical desire for her. Whatever she was doing, she was taking great pains to make it easier for him. And he had not discouraged her because he was so curious about her intentions. He felt like a scoundrel. Taking advantage of her when she didn't even know that he did so. But it was too late to change things now. Besides, he wanted to know what seductive surprise awaited him when he removed the blindfold. Exactly how was Athena preparing herself?

'You can look now,' she said, her voice distinctly unsteady.

Gabriel ripped off the cravat and sat up in a single movement, his gaze unerringly finding her.

She stood in the middle of the cabin, only a few feet away from him. At the sight of her his heart thundered in his chest.

Her legs were bare, but she was covered from her shoulders to just below her hips by the lace she had made. He had never seen her legs before. He devoured them with his hungry gaze. They were as slim and shapely as they'd felt beneath his hand. His palms ached to stroke her silky thighs.

After the first rush of desire crashed over him, he had sufficient clarity of thought to wonder how the lace stayed in place. When she moved slightly he saw she had made a simple tunic. Her back was covered by a rectangle of cambric—she must have torn it from her discarded chemise. The lace was attached at the shoulders to the cambric and belted around her waist by a length of silk gauze she'd taken from his chest.

He could see one rosy nipple peeking from behind a lace flower. Lower down he caught glimpses of the triangle of blonde curls. His blood roared in his ears. Never could a woman have prepared herself so gloriously for a man.

Her hands hung by her sides as she stood at apparent ease before him. But then he saw how her fingers flexed and clenched and the hot colour in her cheeks, and knew how difficult she had found the past few moments. She had been very brave to set aside her modesty for his sake. He felt another rush of tenderness towards her. Wordlessly he held out his arms to her, determined to show her just how much he appreciated the effort she had made to please him.

Chapter Twelve

Athena's courage very nearly failed her a dozen times after she covered Gabriel's eyes. Her hands shook so much it was hard to thread the needle she'd taken from the drawer in her lace pillow. She tacked the lace and cambric together, standing naked only a few feet from Gabriel because, in the heat of the moment, she'd torn up the chemise she'd been wearing. She felt so exposed that, when she put on her makeshift tunic, even its limited protection was a welcome relief. As a respectable woman it had never occurred to her that she might one day brazenly cast aside her modesty for the sake of love. If it hadn't been for her determination to make up to Gabriel what he'd lost when he'd been denied their wedding night, she'd never have had the strength to go through with her plan. Even so, she was filled with trepidation as she told him to look.

When he sat up and pulled off the blindfold she fought the ridiculous urge to cover herself with her hands. She managed to hold her arms rigidly at her sides, but she'd never felt more vulnerable in her life. She saw how Gabriel looked her up and down, and how his gaze lingered longer in some places than others. Her toes curled on the smooth wooden planks. She clenched her fists. She felt so embarrassed. So scared. What would she do if he rejected her in scorn or disgust?

Then she saw the heat in his eyes. Undisguised arousal. He wanted her. He held out his hands and she went towards him. Putting his hands on her hips, he drew her between his legs. Her knees touched the drawers beneath the bunk and the polished wood was cool against her heated skin. She could feel Gabriel's palm directly against her hip in a gap between the lace and the cambric.

Her heart beat so hard and fast she didn't think she could speak.

'You mustn't take it off,' she said unsteadily.

'Your new shift?'

She nodded jerkily. 'Things look different—prettier—with lace trimmings.'

He smiled faintly, despite the fire in his eyes. 'You could not look more beautiful,' he murmured.

He stroked his hands gently down her naked arms, stimulating a delicious trembling throughout her entire body. He lifted her wrist and cupped her hand against his cheek. When he turned his hand to kiss her palm, warmth flowered low in her stomach. He trailed delicate kisses along her arm to the inside of her elbow. His tongue teased and excited the sensitive spot until she sighed with pleasure.

Gabriel laid both her hands on his shoulders and she could feel the flex of his muscles beneath her fingers. He stroked the outside of her thighs. She leant more heavily against the side of the bunk and he reached around to brush his fingers upwards from her knees to the firm curves of her buttocks. Then his hands slipped inside the loose cambric and he began to massage in sensuous circles.

'Gabriel!' she gasped, her fingers digging into his shoulders.

'Is that good?' he asked, his voice a deep rasp, his eyes never leaving her face.

'You have to take your clothes off, too,' she managed, before she lost all power of coherent thought or speech.

'Am I to dress only in lace?'

'N-no.' She tugged at his shirt, suddenly desperate for the feel of his naked body beneath her hands.

He was just as eager, and nearly as clumsy. Their hands collided and got in each other's way until, with a groan, he set her aside and stood up. He ripped off his clothes as speedily as possible and turned back to her.

Her eyes feasted on his naked body in the lamplight. From his broad, muscular shoulders to his deep chest and flat stomach, he was all hard planes and angles. His legs were so long, the muscles in his thighs clearly defined. He was utterly splendid. And his fierce arousal was breathtakingly obvious.

She had to touch him. He was irresistible. She laid her hands on his chest, and felt the hard thudding of his heart. She stroked her hands down and around his sides. His breath hitched, then he hooked one hand behind her head and pulled her up for a searing kiss. Her hands clutched his back, feeling the play of his muscles. She pressed herself closer to him, felt his erection hard against her stomach.

He groaned and set her away from him. In an instant he scooped her up with one arm behind her shoulders and the other under her knees, and laid her on the bunk. She expected him to join her on the firm mattress, but instead he knelt beside the bunk. She lifted herself on one elbow, confused.

'Be still,' he said.

'You should be up here.'

'Impatient.' He gave a strangled laugh. 'I will be soon. Are you so eager to have me inside you?'

His words heated her. She felt a little embarrassed at his directness. But when he spoke like that her body throbbed with a deep awareness of him. An urgent need that only he could satisfy.

He stroked her breasts through the lace, glided his hand down over her stomach and the sweep of her thighs. His fingers danced lightly upwards, following the bottom of the lace which rode scandalously high, only just preserving her modesty.

She uttered an incoherent question.

'What?' He traced circles on the outside of her leg with one fingertip. She ached for him to touch her more intimately.

'Are you going to do *that* again?' she whispered.

'Do you want me to do *that* again?' Through the sensual haze clouding her brain she thought she heard a thread of amusement in his voice.

She found his muscular shoulder, then grabbed a fistful of hair and tugged. 'You should be up here,' she insisted.

'Soon. I'm in charge now, sweetheart.'

She felt his hand on her stomach, then her thigh, and then he was indeed doing *that* again. The pleasure was just as stunningly exquisite as it had been the first time. She wanted to protest again. To say that she had covered herself in lace to please *him,* but her rebellious, greedy body didn't want him to stop.

But he did stop. She bit back a cry of frustration as she anticipated the greater delight of his body next to hers on the mattress. Above her. In her. Where she needed him.

He took her legs and drew her gently around until she was lying slewed across the bunk with her knees dangling over the side. She was short enough, and the bunk was wide enough, that the position, though awkward, was not uncomfortable.

'What…?' She pushed up on to her elbows, feeling confused and suddenly very vulnerable. She tugged ineffectually at the bottom of the lace, knowing that now it provided her with no protection at all from his gaze.

'Hush, sweet.' He caressed the outer sides of her thighs again. 'Lie down.'

'This is very strange,' she muttered.

'You talk too much.' He massaged her calves. 'Lie down. I am the captain of this berth and I will not tolerate mutiny.'

Athena let her head fall back on the mattress, but she was not at all sure she was comfortable with whatever Gabriel was doing. She tensed a little in anticipation of what he might do next. But for a while he just continued to stroke up and down her legs, occasionally circling her ankles with his large hands, but mostly soothing her with long, smooth caresses.

The tension ebbed from her muscles until she felt warm, malleable and very aroused. Her attention began to focus on that one place he had touched before and now wasn't touching. The place she urgently needed him to touch her.

He parted her legs so smoothly that at first she didn't realise what he had done. It was only when he hooked one of her knees over his shoulder and she felt his lips on the inner thigh of her other leg that she understood she was completely exposed to him.

She jerked her hips, trying to close her legs, but he held her firmly. She whimpered as he kissed her inner thigh once more. Then he parted her with his fingers and she felt the cool air against her hot, damp flesh. She whimpered again, turning her head from side to side, seeking escape even as she craved more of his devastating caresses.

Then she felt his warm breath and he kissed her where she had never expected to be kissed.

Air exploded from her lungs. She tried to sit up, saw the top of his dark head, and fell back, overwhelmed by what was happening. And, oh! It felt so good!

She closed her eyes, unable to resist the wondrous sensations flowing through her. His tongue destroyed the last vestiges of her self-control. She didn't hear her own moans of pleasure. The urgency building and spiralling within her until it rushed through her in a crescendo of ecstasy.

She lay panting, disorientated. Gabriel swung her legs back

on to the bed. He realigned her on the disordered bedclothes and lifted himself on to the bunk with her, positioning himself between her thighs.

She opened her eyes to see him poised above her, his face taut with passion. She raised her knees and felt the light dusting of hair on his legs against her inner thighs. The sensation was unbearably exciting. She rubbed her legs against him, thrilled by his hard masculinity. He growled deep in his chest. She felt the tip of his erection pressing against her, then he pushed steadily inside, stretching her, filling her with a whole new set of sensations.

He pulled out and pushed into her again with that same rigid self-control. But she didn't want him to be controlled. She wanted him to be as wildly overwhelmed as she had been. She lifted her hips against him, matching him stroke for stroke, increasing the tempo until he groaned, and thrust into her with unleashed passion.

She'd meant this to be for him, but the driving urgency of his powerful body created a new spiral of desire within her. She clutched at him, lifted her hips off the bed to meet every deep thrust, as wild as he was in her quest for ultimate fulfilment.

Her body clenched around him. Pleasure so intense it was almost painful radiated outwards from an inner surge of potent, soul-quaking sensation that blotted out all other awareness. Gabriel's thrusts became faster, wilder, until she felt him shudder with his own explosive release.

His movements slowed until at last he rested quietly on top of her, his chest heaving. Beneath her fingers his back was slick with perspiration.

She sighed and closed her eyes. Still breathless, her heart still beating fast, her body glowing with satiation. She had never felt so profoundly satisfied and contented.

At last Gabriel gently disengaged himself and lay beside

her, one hand resting on her thigh. Now and then he gave her an idle caress.

'That was…very unusual,' said Athena, when she was finally able to speak. She was so overwhelmed by what had happened she said the first coherent thought that came into her head.

'But you liked it?' He lifted himself up on one elbow to look down at her.

'Well, hmm,' she said. Still astounded by at least one of the things he had done.

'If you want me to perform with such vigorous virility again any time soon, you'll have to do better than that,' he said.

'You were wonderful!' Athena said hastily, suddenly afraid she might have damaged his fragile male pride. Then she saw the gleam of smug masculine satisfaction in his eyes and thumped his shoulder indignantly.

'I was talking about that…that *thing* you did with your mouth,' she spluttered. 'I'm sure it's indecent.'

'But you liked it.' He slid his hand beneath the lace. 'You can't deny it,' he added as she hesitated. 'I am a witness to your pleasure. I pleased you.'

'Yes, you pleasure me very much.' She drew his head down so that she could kiss him, too full of love for him to tease him any more. If Gabriel was happy with her then she was happy. And nothing that made them both happy in such a glorious way could be wrong. Just unexpected.

He smoothed the lace over her stomach. 'This was a very good use for your lace,' he said quietly. 'But we don't need it now. Take it off before I forget myself and tear it off.'

'Are you sure?'

'Yes, I am sure.' The look in his eyes was confident and untroubled. She let him help her lift it over her head. She laid it carefully aside and returned to his waiting arms.

'We will rest for a little while,' he murmured against her hair. A few minutes later she felt his breathing settle into the rhythm of sleep.

Athena lay with her head on his shoulder, lost in the wonder of what had just happened. In her mind they'd just enjoyed what would have been their wedding night, and it had been even more amazing and satisfying than she'd ever imagined.

She stroked his chest with a very delicate finger, simply because she loved the feel of his firm flesh. She loved him. Despite the strength of his passion he had been generous and so considerate. Athena's brief experience of the marital bed had involved no consideration for her feelings—emotional or physical. She had wondered whether some degree of pain might always be present at the consummation, no matter how passionately her senses were aroused beforehand. But she'd trusted Gabriel, and wanted him despite her secret fears of what that might ultimately entail. She slipped her hand around his side and hugged him possessively while he slept.

He had not hurt her, he had sent her soaring to unguessed heights of ecstasy. She didn't know what lay at the end of their journey, but tonight she was very content. She sighed and drifted into sleep.

Gabriel's dream was intensely erotic. Frances was in his arms, naked and responsive to his love-making. His hands moulded her entrancing curves, revelling in the soft silk of her skin. He tormented himself by kissing her shoulder and the soft warmth of her belly, though his body was hot and hard with the need to be inside her. He stroked his hand down her thigh and up between her legs. His blood pumped as he discovered she was just as hot and ready for him. She was swollen and slick with arousal. Unmistakable evidence that she wanted him.

Him. Gabriel. No other man.

He had never felt such all encompassing happiness, tinged with triumph and a measure of deep relief.

He woke suddenly, rising through the layers of the dream with growing understanding that it had been no more than that. Just a dream. He had dreamed of Frances so many times and woken to the pain and frustration of being alone. Without her.

But this dream was more potent than any previous dream. His erection was hot and insistent, demanding attention. He groaned, frustrated that a man had no defence against his unruly desires while he slept.

Then the fog of sleep cleared and he understood that the woman he held in his arms was not an illusion. Her head was on his shoulder. Her arm wrapped around him as if, even in sleep, she was determined not to let him go.

The happiness he'd felt in his dream was a pale imitation of the blinding joy that now cascaded through him. He tightened his arm around her waist, and she stirred and mumbled something in her sleep.

He let his thoughts roam easily, first over the glories of making love to Athena such a short time ago. Then his thoughts ranged back, into the painful past. He tensed a little as he allowed himself to remember what he'd seen on their intended wedding day, half-afraid he might feel a rush of familiar, scalding rage. The memory still hurt him. He doubted he would ever be able to think of it without the ache of regret, but the bitterness and the sense of betrayal no longer clawed at his gut at the mere thought of Athena with Samuel.

He caressed her arm as it lay across his chest. She was his. Completely his. He believed now that she'd loved him when he'd known her as Frances. Tonight she had given herself to him body and soul as Athena. Finally he understood deep in his heart that Athena and Frances were truly the same woman. She told him in Venice that she'd been christened Athena

Frances. Both names were hers by rights, and he was glad, because it meant his courtship of Frances eight years ago had been just as real as his love-making with Athena tonight. Athena had not come to him the untried virgin he had once fantasised about, but she had come to him with her innocence intact. As loving, open and sweetly unsure of herself as if he were her first.

And he was. He *was* the first man she had loved. And he was the first man to show her the exquisite pleasure of making love.

He thought of her covered in lace to tempt and distract him from his demons. He remembered how anxiously she had looked at him, so nervous of her reception, yet so determined to make it easy for him. Tenderness for her filled him, so intense he wanted to weep. He touched his eyes and found they were damp with tears.

To distract himself from his disturbing emotions, he stroked her arm again, gently chafing it to wake her so he could satisfy her and the fierce ache in his loins.

Livorno

'Lord Halross's ship sailed yesterday,' said Robert Selby, Lord Halross's factor in Livorno.

'Pour l'amour de Dieu!' Kilverdale couldn't believe he'd missed his cousin again. After spending one night in Venice, he had abandoned all notion of travelling in comfort. To Philpott's dismay the Duke had insisted on switching from carriage to horseback. Kilverdale had been born in the saddle. His Gentleman of the Privy Purse was less adept. After several frustrating delays, Kilverdale had left his servant to follow at his own speed and ridden on alone. But he was still too late.

'Did Halross have a lady with him?' Kilverdale demanded.

'It is not my place to reveal his business,' Selby replied, his expression guarded.

'Loyalty is an excellent quality,' said Kilverdale. 'But it is my cousin he has taken aboard that ship with him.'

The factor's eyes widened. 'Does he know that?' he asked unwarily.

'Possibly not.' Kilverdale had no idea whether Athena would have discussed her family with Halross. He recalled Athena telling him that she had called herself Frances Child when she had run from Samuel the first time. Kilverdale's primary consideration was for Athena's safety—but he acknowledged that Halross might have some grounds for dissatisfaction over her behaviour in London.

'Did he treat her kindly?' he asked abruptly.

'Yes, your grace. In so far as I had an opportunity to observe, I would say he treated her with great courtesy. He showed her around Livorno. She was very curious to see where he lived and worked when he was a permanent resident here.'

'He showed her around Livorno?' Kilverdale knew it was unlikely the factor would admit that Halross was treating Athena badly, but he was unlikely to volunteer a detail of such harmonious interaction between Athena and the Marquis if it wasn't true.

Kilverdale relaxed slightly. His worst fears were somewhat allayed, though he still had every intention of confronting Halross when he caught up with them.

'How long will it take them to reach London?' he asked.

'You've twisted the wrong threads. See?' Athena leant over Gabriel's shoulder to look at his work.

He grumbled under his breath and tried to undo his mistake.

'No, don't look at the bobbins, look at the threads,' she said. 'Then you can easily see where you've gone wrong and correct it.'

'This is ridiculous,' he said, checking to make sure all the bobbins were lying in the right order across the pillow. It was because one of them had somehow jumped across two of its fellows to lie in the wrong place that he'd twisted the wrong threads. 'There is absolutely no need for me to know how to make lace.'

Then he had to stop talking to concentrate on the next set of actions.

'Cross, twist,' he muttered, and pulled the two pairs of bobbins carefully apart. 'Pin.' He inserted a pin between the two pairs of threads. 'Cross, twist.'

He put down the right hand pair of bobbins, transferred the left pair into his right hand, and repeated all the movements with the next pair on the left.

'Very good,' Athena praised him.

'It is nonsense,' he complained, although he didn't stop.

'It was your idea,' she pointed out, smiling and overflowing with love for him as he bent over the pillow, scowling with concentration.

Every day they spent several hours walking and talking on deck. At night they made love and, when she was not doing anything else, Athena made lace.

Until Gabriel's curiosity had got the better of him and he demanded to know how it worked.

'It's making my wrists ache,' he said. 'It's easier for you. Your hands are smaller.'

'You get used to it.' But she silently acknowledged the bobbins did look exceptionally small and fragile in Gabriel's large hands.

'My elbows feel as if they are trying to dig holes in my sides,' he said.

'The position is a little awkward until you get used to it,' she conceded.

'And I'm getting a pain between my shoulder blades.'

'You poor sweetheart.' She moved behind him and began to rub his shoulders. In the cabin he wore only his shirt and breeches, an arrangement which met with Athena's strong approval. She liked to see his broad shoulders beneath the fine cambric. She was sadly afraid she touched him at every opportunity.

'Lower,' he grunted.

She began to circle her thumbs on either side of his spine, pressing firmly into the tense muscles. He uttered a small groan of pleasure.

'Why don't you stop?' she suggested. 'Since it is causing you so much discontent.'

'No, I will finish this section of the pattern,' he said stubbornly. 'It will not take much longer.'

'It shouldn't do.' She continued to rub his shoulders.

Then, unable to resist, she put her arms around his neck and slipped one hand inside the open neck of his shirt. His chest muscles flexed beneath her questing fingers. She delved lower, pressing her breasts against his back, and bent her head to kiss his cheek.

He breathed heavily. Athena heard the click of bobbins and looked up to see what he'd done.

'You've made another mistake.' She smiled against his cheek.

'Dammit, you should try to work under such conditions,' he exploded.

He caught her wrist and withdrew her hand from inside his shirt. Then he stood up, removed her loose jacket and sat her down in front of the pillow.

'Now we shall see,' he said, clearly relishing the opportunity to turn the tables on her. 'To work, madam. You must make another three inches before supper or you will go hungry.'

Her body already tightening in pleasurable anticipation, Athena corrected the mistake he had just made and began to work with only a little less than her usual fluency.

Gabriel stood behind her. Most of her attention focused on him. She moved bobbins automatically. With his two index fingers he traced the neckline of her chemise to the centre point between her breasts. Her breathing quickened and her hands slowed. He reversed the caress.

She wanted to close her eyes and surrender to the pleasure, but she was determined not to be an easy conquest. She put in a pin with only slightly trembling fingers and tried to concentrate on the lace.

He repeated that simple caress until her breasts were hot and aching for his touch and her nipples were clearly visible beneath the soft fabric. She could see them herself if she looked down, but she tried to look only at the pillow and the threads. She couldn't control her breathing, or the flush of arousal that warmed her skin. She knew Gabriel was entirely aware of the effect he was having on her. She crossed two bobbins that should not have been crossed and had to undo her mistake.

He untied the ribbon and pulled the neckline of her chemise wide, slipping it down her shoulders to fully bare her breasts. She swallowed a small moan. By sheer will-power she made another half stitch and put in a pin.

She could hear Gabriel's quickened breath. His lean stomach pressed against her naked shoulders and she was acutely aware of the insistent pressure of his erection against her back. His hands glided down her upper arms and he took the weight of her breasts in his palms. His thumbs began to tease her nipples. She let her head rest on his chest while the bobbins rattled forgotten on the pillow.

'It is full day,' she whispered in a half-hearted protest.

'You are as beautiful in sunlight as moonlight,' he said.

An inn near Milan

'I am sorry to say that your man's leg is broken,' said the physician.

'That I had guessed,' Kilverdale said. 'Can you mend it?'

'It is a relatively straightforward case,' said the doctor. 'Although complications can occur in the simplest of injuries. But with rest and proper care he should make a full recovery.'

'Good,' Kilverdale said. 'He will have both.'

He went it to see Philpott. The Gentleman of the Privy Purse looked pale, his features still drawn from the pain of the bone-setting. Kilverdale saw embarrassment and apology in Philpott's strained expression.

'I am so sorry, your Grace,' he said. 'I don't know how I came to fall.'

Kilverdale shook his head ruefully. 'It is my fault,' he said. 'We could have taken a carriage. I was too impatient.'

Despite his discomfort, Philpott smiled slightly. 'It is no one's fault but my own that I was clumsy,' he replied. 'But what will you do now?' He frowned with worry and an obvious belief that he had failed his master.

'It seems I must continue alone,' said Kilverdale.

'But, your Grace—'

Kilverdale held up a hand to halt Philpott's instinctive protest. 'I've travelled alone before,' he said. 'Despite abundant evidence to the contrary, I'm quite capable of taking care of myself.'

'I know, your Grace, but—'

'You will stay here,' Kilverdale said. 'I will make provision for you to be cared for until you are fit again. Then you may travel back to England by easy stages. You've already had most of the baggage sent home by carrier. I will leave most of what remains with you and take only necessities. I will do very well.'

Philpott's eyes flickered over Kilverdale's expensive clothes and came to rest on the huge signet ring the Duke wore on his finger. When Kilverdale had switched from travelling by coach to riding he had dressed far less flamboyantly than before. But even his plainest riding coat was still unquestionably that of a wealthy man.

Kilverdale smiled. 'You'll see,' he said.

* * *

The next morning Philpott did indeed see. His master stood beside the bed dressed not in his usual costly garments, but in a good plain coat very like Philpott's own. He'd removed the ostentatious ring and there was only a modest ruffle of lace at his cuffs and throat, no more than any gentleman of limited means might aspire to wear. His sword was at his side and there was a glow of anticipation in his dark eyes.

He swept his astonished servant a magnificent leg.

'Jack Bow, soldier of fortune, at your service,' he said.

'Jack Bow?' Philpott started to laugh from sheer surprise. 'And to think I would not believe Jean-Pierre when he told me stories about your adventures when you were still in exile,' he gasped, forgetting to speak with his usual deference.

Kilverdale grinned. 'I was much younger then. Now I am a man of maturity and discretion. All I want is an untroubled journey home.'

The days at sea rolled by bringing nothing but pleasure. Once a week Gabriel and Athena had dinner with the ship's Master. Gabriel spoke to his senior servants every day, though there was little new business to discuss on the lengthy voyage, and the rest of the time he spent with Athena.

He was happy, though every time the thought formed in his mind he pushed it aside in favour of teasing Athena, or temporarily satisfying his unquenchable desire for her. The joy he felt was too novel and fragile a phenomenon to dwell upon. He did not permit himself to think beyond the end of the journey.

'I have more than one cousin,' said Athena, lying beside him and tracing patterns on his chest with her finger.

'Really?' Gabriel roused himself from deep contentment to reply.

'Several of them, in fact. But the only one who visited me apart from Kilverdale was Jakob. Didn't Martha mention him?'

Gabriel felt a twinge of discomfort. He still had not revealed Kilverdale's letter to her. He would have to tell her before they reached England, but he knew she would be angry. There was nothing they could do about it while they were at sea, so he decided to wait until they were nearer home. By then she would be so content with him that she'd quickly forgive him for his doubts about Kilverdale. The fires of his suspicion had after all been stoked but that petty-minded jackal, Minshull, and Athena already knew what a troublesome fellow the Ambassador's secretary could be.

'Martha probably didn't mention Jakob because she approves of him more than Kilverdale,' Athenà mused.

'Why?'

'Well, Kilverdale, you know, is very dark. And his reputation is a little…'

'Devilish,' Gabriel supplied, when she hesitated.

'Hmm. Jakob, on the other hand, is as fair as me. Perhaps his hair is even a shade paler. And he is very handsome. Martha was much taken by him. He is one of my Swedish cousins.'

'Swedish? How do you come to have Swedish cousins?'

'My mother, Kilverdale's mother and Jakob's father are siblings,' she explained. 'There was another, older brother, but he was killed at the Battle of Edgehill, fighting for the King. Jakob's father was the younger son, and he went to make his future in Sweden. He married a Swedish lady. Jakob's father is dead now, but Jakob has promised me that one day he will take me to Stockholm to meet his mother and sisters and brother. I have three Swedish cousins I have never met. Birgitta, Gustaf and Lunetta.' She repeated the foreign names carefully, but with undoubted pleasure.

'Why was Jakob the one who visited you at Bruges?' Gabriel asked, coiling one of her blonde curls around his finger.

'He is a colonel in the Swedish army, and he has travelled more than his brother, Gustaf,' Athena said. 'Also he is Kilverdale's friend. Kilverdale used to wander when he was still in exile in France…'

It occurred to Gabriel that the Duke might still have a tendency to wander, since he had followed Athena so readily to Venice.

'He wandered to Sweden one time and met Jakob there,' Athena continued, unaware of the direction of Gabriel's thoughts. 'The first time Jakob came to see me it was with Kilverdale. Jakob is older, your age, I think.'

'That *is* old,' Gabriel exclaimed, with mock indignation.

'Thirty. Jakob has a little of the wanderer in him too. But his situation is difficult.'

'How?' Gabriel rubbed his hand idly up and down Athena's arm.

'He should have inherited his father's merchant business in Sweden. Gone into partnership with Gustaf. But Uncle Ralph died at Edgehill, and his son, cousin Andrew, died when he was living in exile in France. So now Jakob is Lord Swiftbourne's heir,' said Athena.

'*Swiftbourne?*' Gabriel was so startled he sat up, dislodging Athena.

'Ouch!' She rubbed her elbow where she'd banged it against the far side of the berth.

'I'm sorry.' Gabriel cupped her elbow in his warm palm. 'But you said Swiftbourne? Are you referring to the former Viscount Balston—one of the small group of men who did most to restore the King to his throne six years ago?' he added, to be absolutely certain they were talking about the same man.

'He's our grandfather,' said Athena.

'Good God!' Gabriel stared at her, then laughed with sheer surprise and lay down again. 'Do you mean to tell me that you are granddaughter to one of the most influential men in England?'

'I've only met him three times,' said Athena, as if that made a difference. 'Kilverdale hates him.'

'I know,' said Gabriel. The animosity between Swift-bourne, rewarded by an earldom for his part in the King's restoration, and the Duke was well known in London; but Gabriel hadn't realised Athena was related to Kilverdale because they were grandchildren of Swiftbourne.

'Jakob is not happy with the situation either,' said Athena.

'He is not happy that he will one day inherit an earldom?' Gabriel raised his eyebrows.

'He does not speak of it often, but I think he would rather stay in Sweden and be his brother's partner in their father's business. He…both Kilverdale and Jakob…they do seem to despise Lord Swiftbourne,' she said, speaking with some difficulty.

'Yes.' Gabriel didn't have to ask why. The cause of Kilverdale's hostility to his grandfather was rarely mentioned, but the secret was well known among the upper ranks of society.

As Viscount Balston, Swiftbourne had served Charles I as his ambassador to several countries, including Sweden. But when the Civil War began in 1642, the Viscount switched his allegiance to Parliament. Through all the political vicissitudes of the next two decades, Balston had preserved his own wealth and position, acting as a foreign ambassador to Cromwell's government, rather than the King's. After the death of Cromwell, Balston had bided his time until he had become one of the former Parliamentarians, like General Monck, to invite the King to return from exile. He had received the earldom from the grateful King.

It was easy to understand Kilverdale's hostility. In contrast to his grandfather's opportunism, Kilverdale's father had remained true to his first allegiance. As a boy Kilverdale had been forced in to exile with his mother. The family estates had been sequestered by Parliament, and his father had been hanged by Roundheads when he was caught escaping from the disastrous Battle of Worcester.

'I will visit my grandfather when we reach London,' said Athena. 'He came to see me in Bruges and I owe him that courtesy. I understand why Jack doesn't like him, and I owe far more to Jack than I do to Swiftbourne, but I would like to stay on good terms with my grandfather. I doubt he'll have much interest in me,' she added. 'As a poor relation I can hardly be of much use to him.'

A comment that Gabriel thought revealed a great deal about her expectations of her influential grandfather. He didn't like the man himself, though he had great respect for Swiftbourne's intelligence, and his ability to survive and prosper in the most hazardous of circumstances.

'Why did you not mention to the Ambassador in Venice that you are related to both Swiftbourne and Kilverdale?' he asked. 'Cracknell would have fawned all over you if he'd discovered you are Swiftbourne's granddaughter.'

'I considered it,' Athena admitted. 'But I thought Sir Walter might feel a Marquis in the hand was worth more than an Earl or a Duke in the bush—so to speak. There would have been delays getting a message to London and waiting for a response. Perhaps if the situation had been different—if you hadn't been there—I would have said something. He very likely wouldn't have believed me anyway.'

Gabriel drew in a deep breath, considering the implications of her remark. If she'd mentioned her connections to Swiftbourne and Kilverdale—and if she'd been able to convince the Ambassador she spoke the truth—events might have gone very differently in Venice. Did that mean that, even when she'd seemed to be resisting him with all her power, she had trusted and wanted him enough to risk everything to be with him?

Chapter Thirteen

Ostend, August 1666

'Would you like anything else, sir?'

Kilverdale looked at the serving girl and saw that she was offering more than another flagon of ale. She was young and pretty, with blue eyes, a trim waist and voluptuous curves. Kilverdale's eyes half-closed as he felt the stir of desire.

He had enjoyed his freedom from his retinue for the past few weeks. It amused him to play the pampered fop and, without shame, he acknowledged to himself that he missed his lace and fine scented velvets. But watching those around him do things with half the speed and efficiency he was capable of himself became tiresome for a man of his impatient temperament. The last few weeks alone had greatly improved his mood—if not the condition of his travel-stained clothes.

He tilted his head back, noting with appreciation the invitation in the girl's eyes. He was stuck in Ostend waiting for the packet boat to sail. He could be kicking his heels for days. Packets were often stopped and plundered by the Dutch, so it was usual for vessels to wait until they could cross the Channel in convoy. Here was a pretty distraction to entertain him while he waited.

But then he saw, not the girl's blue eyes, but a pair of brown eyes, as dark and arrogant as his own. The consequences of a fleeting pleasure could last a lifetime, and now that Athena had left the convent he had no reason to travel this way again.

'Nothing else, thank you,' he said.

The girl was disappointed. Her curtsy combined reproach and deliberate provocation in a carefully judged mixture.

Kilverdale thought he was probably a fool, but did not alter his decision. He picked up his lute case and walked out of the inn. When he travelled he carried the lute slung across his back. Besides his sword and his seal ring, the lute was the only one of his possessions he cared about.

He found a place in the shade overlooking the sandy beach and took the delicate instrument from its case. The calm blue sea glittered in the hazy August sunshine. It was a day for resting and making music. Kilverdale tuned his lute and began to sing.

He played to entertain himself, but ended up entertaining a small audience of fishermen, housewives and street urchins. A burgher in lace Kilverdale would have disdained to wear a few weeks ago threw him a coin. Kilverdale grinned his thanks and pocketed it. It wasn't the first time he'd played the troubadour, and his ready money was running low.

He caught a movement as another man joined the crowd and glanced in that direction. When he saw who the newcomer was, his eyes widened in surprise.

'Jakob!' Kilverdale sprang to his feet, delighted at the unexpected encounter with his cousin.

Jakob strolled forward, the crowd parting easily to allow him through. He was an inch or two taller than Kilverdale, and the sun shone on his fair hair as if it were spun gold.

He looked the Duke up and down and grinned, revealing good teeth in his handsome face. 'Jack Bow, as I live and breathe,' he said, his English tinged by a faint accent. 'Singing for your supper again? I dare say I can bear the cost of a meal for you.'

Kilverdale laughed and seized the hand that Jakob offered him. 'What are you doing here? Are you waiting for the packet too?' he demanded.

'For my sins.' Jakob's blue eyes crinkled at the corners as he looked quizzically at Kilverdale. 'I came via Flanders so that I could visit Athena. But when I reached Bruges I discovered she'd already left for Venice with you in pursuit. And now I find you here. You can pay for your dinner with the story.'

'Willingly.' Kilverdale put his lute back in its case to the vocal disappointment of some of his audience. One woman asked if he'd come to her house to play at a small party she was to hold.

Jakob grinned as Kilverdale gravely declined the invitation. 'A ragamuffin minstrel shouldn't turn down employment so heedlessly,' he said, as they strolled along the beach.

'I sing for whomever I please,' said Kilverdale, looking forward to the rest of his journey with renewed enthusiasm. Travelling alone had its attractions, but travelling with his cousin promised to be even more entertaining.

The days went by quickly. The ship's Master said it was the fastest passage he'd ever made. All too soon they'd sailed through the English Channel and were heading around the coastline of Kent towards London. Athena was grateful for the fair weather but, as they got closer to their destination, she felt increasingly unsettled. Gabriel had said nothing of what he intended for her when they reached London. The original bargain was that she would be his mistress for the duration of the journey and then he'd pay her off with her lace and additional compensation.

Was that still his intention? Or did he mean to keep her as

his mistress? Perhaps set her up with her own house and servants? Could she accept that? She desperately wanted to see her family again, and if she openly became Gabriel's mistress she was afraid her puritanical stepfather might forever deny her access to her mother, brother and sisters.

She was sitting in the cabin, working at her lace and worrying over her future when Gabriel appeared in the doorway. As soon as she saw his face tension began to flutter in her stomach. His mouth was set in a hard line and there was no humour in his eyes. He held his shoulders in a rigid brace, quite unlike his relaxed posture over the past few weeks.

Athena froze, the bobbins forgotten in her hands as she waited for him to speak. She knew instinctively that this was the moment when he would tell her his intentions towards her. He didn't say anything for several seconds. Her heart beat up into her throat, nearly choking her with apprehension. From his expression she knew he wasn't going to tell her anything good.

She dimly heard shouts from on deck, but all her attention was focused on Gabriel. He glanced downwards and she belatedly noticed he was holding something in his hand. He opened his mouth to speak—

Hasty footsteps sounded outside the cabin and a seaman suddenly appeared in the open doorway behind Gabriel. 'My lord, strange sail has been sighted. Cap'n thinks it might be Dutch!'

For a single second Gabriel didn't respond. Then he strode across the cabin to seize the musket and cutlass. 'Stay here,' he ordered Athena. 'Don't leave this cabin for anything until I return.'

An instant later Athena was alone. She sat quite still, too shocked by the unexpected turn of events to move a muscle.

Dutch? Yes, of course, she thought numbly. They were just as likely to encounter the enemy here as they had been in the Mediterranean. More likely, in fact. Kilverdale had told her the east-coast coal trade from Newcastle to London had been badly disrupted by Dutch raiders. Was she about to witness a sea battle? She strained to decipher the hails on deck. Any moment now she expected to hear shot whistling overhead through the canvas, or feel it crashing into the hull of the ship.

She waited, her muscles stiff with tension, but nothing threatening happened. At last she let out a long, shuddering breath and flexed her shoulders. She noticed she was still clutching the bobbins between her fingers and laid them down on the pillow. She took another deep breath and stood up. Her legs felt shaky as she walked across the cabin to kneel on the seat and peer out of the windows. She knew she ought to stay away from the glass, but she couldn't bear not knowing what was happening. For two pins she'd have gone on deck, but she knew it would be a mistake. At the best she'd be a distraction and at worst she'd get in the way. Neither Gabriel nor the crew needed anything more to worry about if they were about to engage an enemy ship.

She couldn't see anything. If they were fleeing a hostile vessel, it didn't appear to be behind them. After a few minutes she dropped down from her kneeling position to sit on the seat. She leant back against the upholstery and gazed blankly around the cabin, hating to feel so helpless in a potentially dangerous crisis. As she did so she caught sight of something lying on the floor. She frowned, her thought processes moving more slowly than usual as she tried to make sense of what she saw. Then she realised Gabriel must have dropped it when he seized the weapons. Glad of the distraction, she went to pick it up. She noticed at once it was a letter. Then she caught a glimpse of handwriting that was surely familiar. She looked at the direction and discovered it was addressed to her at the English Embassy in Venice. Her hands trembling, she opened it and started to read.

Athena, you are enough to try the patience of a saint...

* * *

She was sitting under the window, still clutching the badly creased letter, when Gabriel returned.

'It was a false alarm, thank God,' he said, crossing the cabin to hang up the weapons. 'But the crew know better than to relax their guard, even this close to home.'

Athena stared at him. So many emotions competed for dominance within her that for a few seconds she felt almost numb.

'I'm sorry you were given such a fright,' Gabriel said, turning towards her. 'But soon we'll be safely home.'

Anger suddenly overwhelmed her. Gabriel had concealed Kilverdale's letter to her. Not once in all their conversations had he mentioned it to her. He had deliberately deceived her.

'Do you want…?' he began. Then he saw what she was holding. He stiffened, his gaze leaping to her face. 'I was about to tell you—'

'Tell me? What?' she demanded furiously. 'That you spied on my correspondence? This letter is addressed to me. To me!' She sprang to her feet. 'How did you get it? How dare you keep it from me!'

Her rage was fuelled partly by the remnants of the fright she'd had when she'd believed they were about to be attacked—but mostly by the crushing pain she felt at this proof Gabriel still didn't trust her.

His expression closed. 'I was about to show it to you,' he said stiffly. 'There was no urgency while we were still at sea.'

'No urgency? How can you say that? My God! Jack was coming to get me. He must have arrived at the Embassy— found me gone… I owe him so much. Now he must think I'm the most ungrateful, selfish…' Her voice caught on a sob. She looked way, dashing a hand over her damp cheek.

'He won't think ill of you.' Gabriel came towards her. 'I will tell him you never received the letter. That you had no idea he was following you.'

'*You'll* tell him?' Athena gave a wild, disbelieving laugh. Even in the midst of her anger she was appalled at the possibility of the two men meeting. Duels were fought over far less serious offences.

'That doesn't make it right,' she said, pushing aside the horrific image of the two men crossing swords over her. 'For weeks Jack will have thought the worst of me. The whole Embassy believed I was your mistress even before we left. My God!' She pressed her hands against her face, horrified at all the ramifications of Kilverdale's presence in Italy.

'You are my mistress,' said Gabriel harshly. 'Did you intend to come back to England and pretend to be as respectable as the day you left the convent?'

'You didn't trust me. You thought he was my lover. I *told* you he is my cousin.'

'Only after we were already on the ship. And just because he's your cousin doesn't mean he cannot also be your lover.'

'He's like a brother to me. Does he write like a lover? You'll never trust me, will you? God, what a fool I was to hope.'

'Time and again I gave you opportunities to mention him—'

'Why didn't you just show me the letter and ask? Why did you open it at all?'

'I—' Gabriel flushed. A muscle twitched in his jaw.

'How did you even get it? Did you set your servants to spy on me?'

'No!' His eyes narrowed with anger. 'Dammit, I would not… Minshull gave it to me.'

'Minshull?' She threw her hands in the air. 'What a gift for you.'

'I wish I'd never seen the damn thing,' Gabriel snarled.

'I wish you'd given it to me.' Athena turned away and gripped the edge of the table for support. She was so overwhelmed with churning emotions she couldn't think clearly.

Gabriel put his hands on her shoulders.

She shook him off. 'Don't touch me! I thought you were a man of honour. Integrity. Not a thief and a liar.'

'I have never lied to you.'

'You allowed me to believe Martha told you about Kilverdale.' Athena turned on him, thrusting him away with all her strength. 'When you didn't tell me the truth you lied to me.'

'Just like you lied to me,' Gabriel said, his voice suddenly flat, uncompromising.

Athena went quite still. For several moments the only sound within the cabin came from their quickened breathing. She stared at a wooden panel straight in front of her, but she didn't see it.

'You let me believe you were an orphan,' he said harshly. 'I thought Kitty was your only family. You were going to marry me under a false name. My God, you were going to marry me under a false name! How can you ever defend that?'

'It wasn't false! I was christened Athena Frances. I told you.' She spun to look at him, but she couldn't control the trembling of her hands.

'Were you ever going to tell me the truth?' he demanded, ignoring her protest.

'Yes…yes…' She shook her head, struggling to bring order to her thoughts. 'I had good reasons—'

'So did I,' he cut in ruthlessly. 'After what I'd seen in London, and after you admitted to lying to me when I courted you, I had good reason to be suspicious when I saw Kilverdale's letter. And the only reason you know he wrote to you is because I brought the letter to you. I was going to tell you the truth. You cannot claim the high ground on this, Madam Deceiver.'

Madam Deceiver. The taunt wounded Athena to her very heart. She had suffered so much for Gabriel's sake, only to have him sit in judgement of her as if he'd never made a single mistake. But if his plan to assassinate Cromwell had been discovered after their marriage she would have gone from bride to the widow of a hanged traitor overnight. In the midst of his grand schemes, had he given any thought to what would have become of her then?

She lunged across the cabin to her lace pillow. She dragged out the drawer, scattering bobbins and pins in her haste.

'What are you doing?' Gabriel demanded.

Athena ignored him as she scrabbled at the inside of the drawer. After a few seconds she managed to pull up the thin wooden veneer, which acted as a false bottom. Beneath it was a small fragment of paper. She seized it and thrust it under his nose.

'One lie I told—and committed no crime!' She was almost panting with anger. 'But *you*—you were plotting to kill Cromwell! Treason and murder! When were you going to tell me *that?*'

'*What?*' He stared at her as if she'd gone mad.

She waved the paper furiously under his nose. 'But you didn't even have the constancy to carry out your plans!' she shouted. 'No loyalty to your political principles—such as they are. And none to me. You—'

'What the hell are you talking about?' Gabriel grabbed her wrist and pulled the letter fragment from her hand. 'What is this?'

'The evidence against you.' Athena put her hands on her hips, breathing heavily as she watched him study it. 'You could at least have had the sense not to put anything in writing. Impractical dreamer! How dare you accuse me—'

'I didn't write this!' Gabriel looked up at her, his eyes blazing with anger.

'What?' His denial made no sense to Athena. 'It's your handwriting,' she said. 'Your initial—'

'It is *not* my writing,' he said categorically. 'I did not write this.'

'It is yours,' she insisted. 'It is the same as the poem you wrote for me.'

'It looks like my writing,' he acknowledged, the hard edges of his voice softening slightly as he glanced down at it again. 'But it is a forgery. I would remember if I'd plotted to kill Cromwell.'

'You didn't write it?' Athena stared at him, as her world turned upside down around her. 'You didn't plot against Cromwell?'

'No and no. How could you possibly imagine I'd do something so stupid? Where did you get it?'

'Where…?' Athena put a hand to her head, then turned away from Gabriel and stumbled to the seat beneath the windows. She felt sick. Not sure whether to laugh or cry. Gabriel hadn't plotted against Cromwell. He'd been exactly what he'd seemed all through their courtship—an honourable, straightforward young man, more interested in advancing his career than getting involved in the treacherous world of politics. She didn't know how Samuel had done it, but he had forged the evidence against Gabriel. And she'd been such a gullible young fool she'd believed it.

'Where did you get it?' Gabriel sat down beside her and took her wrist in his hand.

She stared at him, stricken.

'Who gave it to you?' His hand tightened on her wrist and she knew he'd already guessed.

'Samuel,' she whispered. 'It was…' She looked away and swallowed.

'No more lies,' Gabriel said implacably.

'He said you would be safe if I went to him willingly,' she said, her voice cracking. 'Otherwise you would hang for treason.'

'Willingly?' Gabriel's grip tightened until it was almost painful, then abruptly he released her. She heard him swear, but she kept her head turned away, unable to look at him.

Water lapped against the hull of the ship. Wood and canvas creaked in the familiar background noises of their journey. Athena clasped her hands together in her lap and felt her vision blur with tears. She opened her eyes wide, trying not to let the tears fall.

'Is that what I saw?' Gabriel said, his voice raw. 'You… turning…willingly to Samuel…to save me from a traitor's death?'

She nodded once, not trusting her voice.

The strength leeched out of Gabriel's muscles. He stared at Athena's back, saw the tension in her shoulders and the proud lift of her head that she kept resolutely turned away from him. He didn't need to see her face to know she was crying.

The scene in the London bawdy house he'd replayed in his mind so many times over the past eight years rose before him once again. But this time he knew that when Athena smiled at Samuel and lifted her mouth to be kissed she was doing it to save his life. Now he understood that the reason she hadn't fought Samuel's embrace was because her smiling compliance was the price of Gabriel's safety. He heard a raw groan of pain and realised it had come from his own throat. Athena had sacrificed herself to protect him.

The realisation twisted and gouged in his gut like a knife until he could hardly breathe from the agony of it. One stray thought whirled through his mind and hovered just long enough for him to catch hold of it before it was swept away by the hurricane of emotions that battered him.

You saw and you didn't help me! How could you? Athena had cried in wild fury in the gondola. Now Gabriel understood the desperate intensity of her reaction when she'd learned he'd seen her with Samuel. She'd sacrificed everything to save him—but he'd failed to protect her.

He'd failed her.

Except…there had been no need for her sacrifice. He hadn't plotted against Cromwell. And if he'd known she was hiding from Samuel, he would have taken the necessary actions to protect her *before* the villain found and threatened her. Besides—

'How could you think I'd sell your virtue to save my life?' he exploded. 'Even if this evidence was real—even if I had been in danger of hanging—never…*never* would I have asked—'

'I know that!' Athena turned on him and snatched the fragment of paper from his hands. She began to rip it into tiny pieces with furious, shaking hands. 'I never meant to tell you. I *never* meant to tell you. It's past. Gone. If you hadn't made me so angry…keeping Jack's letter from me…'

'Why did you keep it all this time?' Gabriel asked, watching the torn shreds of paper scatter unheeded across her skirts and on to the dark boards.

She jerked a shoulder. 'It was all I had of you,' she said, pinching the words off as if she resented the admission. 'I didn't have your poem any more. I stole this from Samuel before I ran away—so he couldn't use it against you when I was gone. I meant to destroy it, but then…it was all I had of you. And now I find it wasn't you at all!' Her laughter was wild, almost hysterical. 'Everything was for nothing. *Nothing!*'

'Why didn't you have my poem?' Gabriel focused on the insignificant detail because the whole picture was too agonising to contemplate.

'I couldn't find it the night before the wedding.' She dashed the back of her hand across her eyes. 'I tried…Samuel and h-his friend were watching me…I couldn't find it.'

'Samuel had it,' said Gabriel. The scalding pain which had burned through his body only moments before was now giving way to cold, creeping numbness. 'He must have stolen it then used it as his model to forge the evidence against me.'

Athena twisted to look at him, her expression stark, her lips bloodless with shock. 'I never thought…I never guessed,' she whispered. 'What a fool I was.'

Gabriel wanted to reach out to her, but he couldn't. He didn't have any comfort to offer. Not now, when he was still struggling to come to terms with the devastating revelations of the past half-hour.

'Is that it?' he asked, his voice cracking. 'Is there anything *else* you haven't told me? Any other last secrets—?'

'No!'

Gabriel pushed himself to his feet. He felt as if he'd aged years since he'd returned to the cabin. A confrontation with the Dutch would have been easier to deal with than this. He looked once at Athena, then turned away and walked blindly out of the cabin. Somehow he found his way to the side of the ship. In a few hours they'd be back in the heart of London. He clutched the rail until his knuckles were white, watching without seeing as the familiar sights came into view. Eight years ago Athena had given herself to a man she'd hated and feared to save Gabriel's life. He couldn't doubt that she'd loved him. But how could he come to terms with the enormity of the sacrifice she'd made for him?

Athena mechanically brushed the pieces of paper from her lap, but the fibres of the torn edges clung to her skirts. She plucked irritably at one particularly stubborn piece. Who'd have thought a small bit of paper could cause so much trouble? Misery she could no longer control suddenly overwhelmed her. She covered her face with her hands and slumped sideways on to the seat. Tears scalded her eyes and swelled her throat. She tried to hold herself in check, but she couldn't stop the sobs that wracked her body.

She should never have told Gabriel about Samuel's accusation and threat. She should have remembered and trusted the instinct that warned her this would be harder for him to deal with than anything else. He was a proud man. If she'd given him a choice, he would never have accepted her sacrifice on his behalf. And she'd dishonoured him on the very day of their wedding. He'd forgiven her for being careless with the truth during their courtship, but this would be so much harder for him to bear.

'So Halross is the man Athena wanted to marry?' Jakob said.

'It seems likely,' Kilverdale replied. 'We've always known there was someone and I can't imagine her making that claim to her maid if it wasn't true.'

'Halross?' Jakob mused. 'I believe my brother may have mentioned him. Does he trade in silk?'

'As far as I can tell, he trades in damn near everything that will turn a profit,' Kilverdale growled. 'I had to endure a eulogy to his many talents in Livorno.'

'And you so lacking,' Jakob mocked.

Kilverdale studied his cousin in the early evening light. He had a good idea why Jakob might be visiting England now. Swiftbourne had been increasingly insistent that his heir should take his rightful place in English society. Was this to be another fleeting trip, such as Jakob had made a few years earlier? Or had he finally relinquished his commission in the Swedish army?

'You'll be visiting my mother,' said Kilverdale, approaching the matter obliquely. 'She'll be in Sussex at this season, and most disappointed if you don't make her your first priority.'

'I have been *summoned* to St Martin's Lane,' Jakob said, revealing his teeth in a smile that both recognised Kilverdale's ploy and gave an indication of his feelings on the subject.

'What are you going to do?' Kilverdale abandoned the subtle approach.

'I don't know.' Jakob began to toss an apple in the air, flipping it from hand to hand with rhythmic dexterity. 'I've resigned my commission,' he said. 'A man cannot serve two masters—'

'*Swiftbourne?*' Kilverdale could not believe Jakob regarded the Earl as his master.

'England or Sweden,' Jakob said, a bite in his voice. 'Not Swiftbourne. If I must cleave to England, so be it. But Swiftbourne is not my master. Perhaps I will follow in the footsteps of the infamous Jack Bow,' he said on a lighter note. He slanted a glance at his cousin. 'Live on my wits for a while.'

Kilverdale laughed. 'A man of nigh on thirty should be setting up his nursery and living a life of sober respectability.'

Jakob raised his eyebrows. 'I see you've allowed yourself another four years of irresponsibility,' he said drily.

Kilverdale grinned. 'When I reach your mature age I may reach a different conclusion,' he said.

'Your need is greater than mine,' Jakob pointed out. 'I have a younger brother and two stout nephews to step into Swiftbourne's unappealing shoes if anything happens to me. You are the last of your line—which is somewhat more honourable than mine.'

'Though hardly of greater vintage,' Kilverdale replied, deftly plucking Jakob's apple from the air. 'It is difficult to be pompous about your own lofty consequence when your great-grandfather was a grocer.' He bit into the filched apple, grinning irrepressibly as he did so.

'He was the Lord Mayor of London,' Jakob retorted. 'And no doubt just as much an opportunist as his descendant.'

Gabriel stayed on deck all night. The cool damp air was soothing against his face. The dark provided a measure of privacy for his thoughts. None of his servants or crew approached him. He would have preferred to be completely alone, but that wasn't possible on the ship. Tomorrow he would be back in the crowded streets of London.

He leant against the rail and traced everything that had happened between him and Athena from his first meeting with her in Lady Parfitt's shop to her shocking revelation in the cabin a few hours ago. At every stage he imagined how things could have taken a different turn—a turn which meant they would have been happily married these past eight years.

If Athena had told him the truth from the beginning, he'd never have let Samuel find and threaten her. If Athena had laughed in Samuel's face at the accusation Gabriel was involved in a plot to assassinate Cromwell and resisted his attempt to wed her—

Gabriel's grip tightened on the rail until his sinews cracked. If he'd seen Athena struggling in Samuel's arms, he'd never have rested until he'd rescued her. But if Athena had struggled, Samuel would have punished her, perhaps even killed her for resisting him.

Gabriel calmed himself with the recollection that Samuel was dead while Athena was alive and happy—or at least she had been, until she'd read Kilverdale's letter. If he'd told her about the Duke's letter earlier, she wouldn't have been provoked into showing him the 'proof' that he'd been involved in a traitorous plot. He rubbed his aching forehead. Ignorance was not bliss. He didn't regret knowing the truth. He just had to find a way to make his peace with the past and move forward.

Athena sat up all night, waiting for Gabriel. The longer he stayed away the closer her mood crept to despair. They'd reached the end of their journey. There was no more time to resolve the differences between them.

She heard his footsteps outside soon after dawn. A wave of apprehension washed over her. She straightened up, her hands instinctively lifting to pat her hair into place. As soon as she realised what she was doing she folded them in her lap. A second later he opened the door.

He glanced around the cabin and then his gaze came to rest on her. He seemed surprised to see her sitting beneath the windows. Athena's heart hammered behind her ribs as she waited for him to speak.

'I have business I must attend to,' he said, sounding as formal as if he were talking to a stranger. 'Then I'll take you to my house in Fleet Street.'

'I…' Athena began, but he'd already gone. A few minutes later she heard shouts on deck and realised he was leaving the ship.

It was midday by the time Gabriel climbed on board again. There were always many tasks to perform at the end of a voyage, but today he'd been impatient to conclude them. He had more important business with Athena. They had to make arrangements for their future. He took a deep breath, preparing himself for their discussion and opened the door.

The cabin was empty.

His gaze swept around the familiar space in disbelief. His first thought was that Athena must have gone on deck, though he hadn't seen her when he boarded. He knew how eager she was to experience once more the sights and sounds of London. Then he saw that her luggage was gone. Even her lace pillow in its travelling case.

Panic ripped through him. Terror that he'd lost her again. That this time he'd never find her. He turned and bolted back on deck, staring wildly around.

'Mrs Quenell left in a wherry,' said Hobb, in an expressionless voice.

Gabriel's hands fisted in the servant's coat, half-lifting his feet off the ground. 'Why the hell did you let her go?' he demanded.

'I was under no orders to prevent her departure,' Hobb replied with admirable composure, almost as if he'd been expecting

Gabriel's angry reaction. 'She gave orders for the wherry to take her to Lord Swiftbourne's house,' he added expressionlessly.

'Swiftbourne?' Gabriel released Hobb and stepped back. 'Summon me a wherry.'

Lord Swiftbourne had a house in St Martin's Lane. Gabriel hammered on the front door with no consideration for the consequence of the man who owned it.

'I want to see Mrs Athena Quenell.' He pushed past the porter without ceremony.

'Sir! I beg your pardon! But—'

Gabriel ignored the scandalised servant. Athena would *not* run away from him. He scanned the hallway, wondering which door she had taken refuge behind. One of them opened and Swiftbourne stepped out.

The Earl was thin and, even at the age of seventy-four, his back was poker-straight. His natural hair had once been light brown and his magnificently curled periwig was as close to the colour of his own hair as possible. One glance at the Earl's aquiline nose and high cheekbones and it was easy to see from whom the Duke of Kilverdale had inherited his distinctive features, but Gabriel was not interested in tracing family resemblances.

'Halross. You wish to see my granddaughter.'

'Is she here?' Gabriel brushed past the older man, but the room behind him was empty.

'Yes.' Swiftbourne's voice was as cold as his pale blue eyes.

'Summon her,' Gabriel ordered impatiently.

'She's asleep. I will not permit her to be disturbed.'

'Asleep? It's the middle of the afternoon!' Then Gabriel remembered how he'd discovered Athena sitting fully dressed in the cabin at dawn. She'd probably slept no more the previous night than he had.

Swiftbourne smiled thinly. 'She was tired and distressed

when she arrived here,' he said. 'She expressed relief at being under my protection.'

Gabriel bit back an angry retort. What had Athena told her grandfather? He knew enough of Swiftbourne's reputation to suspect that the Earl was more than capable of twisting the meaning of simple comments.

He had half a mind to search the house until he found Athena. He'd successfully snatched her from the embassy in Venice—but he doubted that Swiftbourne would be as complacent as the Ambassador if he made a similar attempt here. The Earl was one of the most powerful men in England.

Besides, Athena had come to her grandfather of her own free will. According to what she'd said on the journey, Swiftbourne had visited her in the convent and treated her kindly. She wasn't at any risk under her grandfather's roof. Perhaps their next meeting would proceed better if they were both feeling calmer and more rested.

'I will call upon her tomorrow,' he said. 'You may tell her to expect me at ten o'clock.' And if she refused him then, he would have to take more extreme measures to see her.

Swiftbourne bowed ironically. 'I will convey your charming entreaty,' he said, his tone leaving no doubt as to his unflattering opinion of Gabriel's person and manners.

Gabriel turned on his heel and left without another word.

Dover

'Sir, this is for you.' The tapman offered Jakob a sealed letter.

'Thank you.' Jakob turned the letter over in his hand, staring at it in mild puzzlement while he delved in his pocket for a tip.

'It is from Mr Bow,' the tapman volunteered.

'I see that.' Jakob recognised Kilverdale's impatient writ-

ing, even though he'd addressed the note with nothing more
than Jakob's initials.

'There was a horse and he took it,' said the tapman.

'He's left Dover?' Jakob glanced up quickly.

'Yes, sir.'

'The Devil he has!' Jakob swore softly in Swedish.

They had arrived in Dover only to discover there were no
sound riding horses for hire in any of the inns. They'd been
assured the situation would improve the following morning,
and since neither of them cared to travel on the public stage
they'd agreed to spend the night in the inn.

That had been three hours ago. Kilverdale had chosen to
spend the afternoon entertaining himself and earning a few
coins playing his lute. Jakob had gone for a walk through the
town. Now he'd returned for supper, only to discover his
cousin had already gone.

He broke open the wax. Kilverdale had not pressed his familiar seal into it. There was nothing to indicate he was anything other than he'd claimed to be—the lute-playing, rather
disreputable Jack Bow.

*Jakob, a horse has arrived so I'm taking it. You know I must
reach London as soon as I may to catch up with A and that
scoundrel H. Whereas you will be glad of an excuse to daw-
dle. By the way, I have taken your best suit. I really cannot
confront H dressed as a vagabond. Jack.*

Jakob reached the end of the message and swore again, this
time more forcefully than before.

'Is it bad news?' asked the tapman.

'The blackguard has stolen my clothes!' Jakob said, torn
between disbelieving laughter and anger.

His unwary exclamation caused immediate consternation.
The landlord overheard and, in his anxiety not to seem to be
in league with a thief, at once offered to raise a hue and cry
after the villainous Jack Bow.

For a few seconds Jakob imagined with relish the prospect of Kilverdale being hunted down as a common criminal, but Kilverdale would laugh off any scandal. It was those close to him, especially his mother, who would be most embarrassed if the incident became common gossip, so Jakob reassured the landlord.

'The villain is my cousin,' he said. 'When I catch up with him I'll make him sorry, but I would not want to see him hauled before a magistrate. Fetch me a tankard of ale and we'll say no more about it.'

'Yes, sir.' The landlord was clearly relieved no blame was to be attached to him.

'Family can be a terrible affliction,' said a man sitting a few feet away.

Jakob glanced at the stranger. 'They can be,' he agreed.

'I've a few problems of my own in that line,' said the stranger. 'Sit down and I'll stand you a drink and we can drown our sorrows together.'

Since Jakob had nothing better to do until he could hire a horse, he accepted the stranger's invitation. The man roused himself from his low spirits and for a good half-hour entertained Jakob with idle conversation. He had a talent for an amusing story. Jakob smiled and waited, completely at his ease, to discover why the stranger had accosted him. He did not for a second believe the fellow was simply passing the time of day.

'In my case it's my brother who has let me down,' the stranger revealed at last, with a long-suffering sigh.

'Brothers can be as unreliable as cousins,' Jakob said, looking at the stranger over the rim of his beer mug. He studied him with half-closed eyes as he swallowed a mouthful of ale.

'Stephen Potticary.' The man belatedly introduced himself.

'Jakob Smith,' Jakob responded, on impulse giving a false name. If Kilverdale could masquerade as Jack Bow, he could do something similar. He only wished that, on the spur of the moment, he'd come up with a more original alias.

'I heard your cousin describe you both as soldiers of fortune before he left the inn,' said Potticary, with an air of careful uninterest.

'I have been a soldier,' Jakob said. 'I fought in the Swedish army. Now I am looking for new ventures.' He stated the exact truth, but with the deliberate intention of providing Potticary with an opening.

Potticary took the bait. 'You'll be looking for a *rewarding* adventure, I dare say,' he said, looking intensely at Jakob. 'To pay for some new clothes.'

'Of course.' Jakob did not say his idea of rewarding might not be the same as Potticary's.

'I'd not normally deal with a stranger,' said Potticary. 'But my brother has let me down. Put me in a bit of a bind, as you might say.'

'Hmm,' Jakob responded with a non-committal hum, wondering how long it would be before Potticary was bold or desperate enough to provide solid information about his, almost certainly shady, business.

In Jakob's opinion a responsible man, particularly a responsible man in no hurry to get to London—perhaps even with a *reluctance* to reach his destination—had a duty to discover and, if necessary, thwart, whatever nefarious adventure Potticary had in mind. It would most likely prove a lot more entertaining than talking to Lord Swiftbourne.

'How did your brother let you down?' he asked.

'I wish to speak to Lord Halross.' Athena stood on the steps of Gabriel's new house in Fleet Street.

It was a very fine house, but she was too nervous to give it the appreciation it deserved. She resisted the urge to twist her fingers together as she waited for the porter to reply. She was afraid she'd made a mistake leaving the ship the previous day, though she'd made no attempt to conceal her destination from Gabriel. She'd even considered writing him a message, but couldn't think what to say. She'd decided it didn't matter because Hobb would tell him where she was going.

She'd been dependent on Gabriel ever since he'd seized her lace in Venice. Their arrival in London had given her the first opportunity in months to make her own decisions. She'd left the ship on impulse, driven by the need to reclaim her independence. The next time she talked to Gabriel she wanted them to be on more equal footing. She'd gone to her grandfather partly out of courtesy and partly because he was her only relative in London. She didn't intend to remain his guest for long.

She'd half-expected Gabriel to follow her, but she'd been so worn out with emotion when she first arrived at Swiftbourne's house that her grandfather had easily persuaded her to go to bed. She'd fallen almost immediately into a deep, but disturbed sleep. She'd woken late in the evening and not fallen asleep again. Anxiety gnawed at her. Now she'd had time to consider her hasty departure from the ship she wondered if she'd done the right thing. Perhaps she should have stayed with Gabriel, let him take her to his house. This house. She glanced up at the impressive façade. It would have been difficult, but they'd survived difficult conversations in the past. If she'd remained on the ship, at least she wouldn't be standing here, twisting her hands together as she waited to talk to him.

'I regret his lordship is not here,' the porter said.

'Not here?' Athena hadn't expected that. It was barely nine o'clock in the morning. Her stomach swooped with anxiety. Had he given orders to refuse her? 'Do you mean he is not receiving visitors?' she asked, trying to maintain at least an appearance of composure. 'Is Hobb here? I would like to speak to him.'

She knew Hobb's first loyalty was to his master, but perhaps she could at least persuade him to give a message to Gabriel.

At the mention of Hobb's name, which made it clear that Athena was familiar with the servants who had recently travelled with Gabriel, the porter immediately became more ingratiating. 'His lordship is not here,' he said. 'He went to the City.'

'Oh.' Athena felt a surge of relief that Gabriel had not intentionally denied her, followed by dismay that he had gone out. 'Will he be long?' she asked, glancing over her shoulder at the carriage in which Swiftbourne waited.

'I am sorry, my lady, I do not know,' the porter said.

Athena bit her lip, caught in the midst of a dilemma. Swiftbourne had offered to escort her on a visit to her family. She was desperately eager to see them, but she also wanted to see Gabriel. She hated to leave London without doing so.

But Swiftbourne had ministerial responsibilities and he'd made it clear that his time was limited. He insisted that they leave immediately. It had taken all Athena's efforts to persuade him to make even a brief stop at Gabriel's house on the way.

Athena's first instinct was to wait for Gabriel to come home, but she glanced around again and saw one of Swiftbourne's servants approaching her. The Earl was getting impatient.

Gabriel wasn't home. It rubbed against Athena's raw emotions that he was apparently so unperturbed by their last meeting that he'd gone to a *business* meeting rather than trying to see her! How could he think clearly about anything else when so much lay unresolved between them? Somewhere, deep inside, she'd harboured the small hope that when she saw him all their problems would vanish. She'd so longed for him to take her in his arms, kiss her, and tell her that *he* would take her to see her family instead of Swiftbourne.

Now that hope died, leaving her lonely and sad—and with a kick of rebellious pride in her heart. Since he was clearly in no hurry to talk to her, she wouldn't prostrate herself at his door like a lovesick fool. She would carry on with her own life, just as he was doing. But she couldn't simply leave London without telling him where she was going. There was, after all, the remotest chance he might follow her if he knew her destination. None at all if she disappeared without explanation.

Swiftbourne had tried to dissuade her from calling in person upon Gabriel. He'd said a brief note would suffice. Athena hadn't left a message for Gabriel yesterday. Today she would.

'May I write a letter to Lord Halross?' she said to the porter.

Chapter Fourteen

Athena's mother cried and clung to her daughter as if she never meant to let go. Athena cried too and held tight to her mother. She had prayed for this moment every day, so afraid that accident or unkind fate would not allow a reunion. She hadn't had the comfort of hugging her mother before she left. She'd been afraid that, if it was discovered her mother had known of her plans, Josiah might punish her as a disobedient wife.

'Let me look at you.' Her mother held Athena at arm's length, then gathered her close again. 'Oh, my baby, I was afraid for you.'

'I am sorry,' Athena whispered. 'I am so sorry. I never wanted to leave you like that.'

Her mother hugged her ever tighter. 'Child, you could not have stayed,' she said, her voice choked. 'I thank God he kept you safe and brought you back to me.'

At last she composed herself and looked at Athena again. 'You have hardly changed,' she said, gently touching Athena's hair. 'A very fine lady.'

Athena smiled, her lips trembling, her cheeks wet with tears. 'Kilverdale says the fashion is for dark hair,' she said, trying to strike a lighter note. Then she remembered that Kilverdale was not a favourite with her stepfather, and glanced nervously at Josiah.

Josiah Blundell had greeted his eminent father-in-law with reserved courtesy. During the years of civil conflict the two men had served on the side of Parliament, though they'd had little direct contact with each other. Swiftbourne had avoided becoming too deeply embroiled in domestic politics and rivalries by serving as Cromwell's foreign ambassador, while Josiah's influence had been—and still was—confined largely to his own county. What Josiah thought of Swiftbourne's very public change of allegiance to support the King, he had never said.

Now Athena noticed that Josiah and Swiftbourne were both watching her reunion with her mother. Perhaps it was easier than having to talk to each other. Neither man had a reputation for soft-heartedness, but both seemed untroubled by the mawkish scene before them. To her surprise, Athena thought she saw Josiah smile!

Before she could give any thought to the implications of her stepfather's unexpected reaction, her mother introduced her brother and sisters.

'You look just like Father!' she exclaimed, the moment she laid eyes on sixteen-year-old Luke. Both of their parents had been very fair and Luke, like Athena, had golden blond hair. 'You are so handsome. And so much taller than me!' she added, tilting her head back to look at him. Tears filled her eyes again at the memory of the eight-year-old boy she had last seen.

Luke flushed with embarrassment and hugged her awkwardly, which was more than she'd dare hope he would do. He was really a man. Nearly the same age she'd been when she fled from Samuel the first time.

Tabitha was next. She'd been eleven when Athena had last seen her. Now she was a very beautiful nineteen. She too was taller than Athena, and her hair was a shade darker than her siblings but, like Luke and Athena, she had their mother's blue eyes.

'I missed you,' she whispered, as she embraced Athena.

'I missed you, too. I missed you all.'

'And this is Hannah,' said her mother, 'the sister you haven't met yet.' She brought forward a shy seven year old.

Athena dropped down to sit on her heels so she could look directly at her half-sister. Unlike the Fairchild children, Hannah Blundell had her father's dark hair and dark eyes, but she also had much of her mother about her. She too was a pretty child.

'You sent me lace?' Hannah said in a very quiet voice. She was nervous, but she looked at Athena with alert eyes, obviously curious about the older half-sister she'd never met.

'Yes.' As soon as Athena had heard Samuel was dead she'd sent small gifts of lace to her mother and siblings—not in celebration, but because she was no longer afraid Samuel might do something terrible if he knew they were in contact with her.

'It is very pretty,' Hannah said.

'I will make you some more,' Athena promised. 'May I hug you?'

Hannah bit her lip dubiously, looking at the ground as she considered Athena's request. Then she looked up under her eyelashes and nodded.

Athena enfolded her in a warm embrace. She had missed seeing Tabitha and Luke grow up. Perhaps she would see the rest of Hannah's childhood.

Athena had expected her homecoming to be awkward and Josiah disapproving, but her stepfather seemed to have mellowed with the years. His expression was usually forbidding and he smiled infrequently, but she sensed immediately that no one in the household was afraid of him. In fact, she discovered, somewhat to her surprise, he seemed to be rather an indulgent father.

'I am not to be married unless the man pleases me,' Tabitha confided, when they walked together in the orchard the next day. 'Father has promised me.'

'Father?' Athena had never thought of Josiah Blundell as her father. That name and role belonged only to Sir Edmund.

Tabitha flushed slightly, but her gaze was steady. 'He has been a father to me,' she said quietly. 'I will always love and revere our father's memory, but I cannot remember him so very clearly.'

'No, you wouldn't.' Tabitha had been only ten when Sir Edmund died. 'I have always known Josiah is a good man,' said Athena. 'It was not him I ran from.'

'He was ashamed of Samuel,' Tabitha said. 'I overheard him once shouting at Sam. I was surprised. I didn't know Father ever shouted. But he said it then. Perhaps I shouldn't have said anything.' She looked uncomfortable with her revelation.

Athena realised her sister was torn between her loyalty to the man she now regarded as her father, and the sister she hadn't seen for years.

'It is over now. Oh, look at Luke and Hannah!' Hannah was sitting on her brother's shoulders so she could pick apples from the higher branches of the trees.

Tabitha laughed. 'He pretends he has no time for childish things now he is nearly a man, but he is very fond of Hannah.'

Tabitha's comment reminded Athena that the house and estate—even the orchard they walked in—belonged to Luke. His inheritance from his father, Sir Edmund. Josiah owned property of his own in the county, though the family had continued to live at Fairchild Manor after his marriage to Sir Edmund's widow. Athena wondered what would happen in the future, but she didn't say anything. Josiah had clearly managed Luke's inheritance well. She couldn't believe her stepfather intended to deny her brother his inheritance when he was of age to claim it.

* * *

'Where's Halross?'

Gabriel was sitting in his study nursing a glass of burgundy, the gold necklace he bought for Athena in Florence laid out on the table before him, when he heard the commotion. Before he had a chance to react Kilverdale burst through the door, pursued by Gabriel's servants. The next second the point of Kilverdale's sword was at Gabriel's throat.

'Where is she?'

Gabriel stayed quite still. He had always considered the Duke a fop, but Athena had presented a rather different image of her cousin. Gabriel noticed that, although Kilverdale's coat and breeches were reasonably respectable, his head was covered in a thatch of shaggy black hair that could only be his own. At some point in the past few months the Duke had abandoned his periwig and brocades.

'She has gone to see her mother and brother and sisters,' Gabriel replied. Athena's note hadn't mentioned her stepfather. He wondered if it was deliberate or a slip of the pen.

'On her own? You let her travel about the country unescorted?' The sword pressed against Gabriel's neck. He felt it pierce the skin, but it cut no deeper. He couldn't answer Kilverdale's questions if his throat was cut.

It wasn't the first time he had been in a dangerous situation. He felt little fear—the Duke wasn't about to kill him—but he saw that his servants were showing signs of recovering from their shock.

'Leave us,' he ordered them. The last thing he wanted was for an innocent individual to be hurt.

'But, my lord…'

'The Duke has a very direct way of making his point—but I believe we won't come to blows,' Gabriel said.

'You believe a great deal more than I do,' said Kilverdale, as the door closed on the reluctant servants.

'I don't suppose you plan to marry your cousin to a corpse,' Gabriel said sardonically.

Kilverdale's hawklike gaze intensified. 'Are you implying you'll marry her willingly?' he said.

'Yes,' said Gabriel. 'You may find it is your cousin who needs the persuasion of your sword,' he added, though it hurt to make the admission. 'She left my protection at the first opportunity and shows no eagerness to see me again.'

'Which is why you allowed her to jaunt about alone.'

'She isn't alone. Swiftbourne escorts her.'

'Swiftbourne?' Kilverdale's lips drew back in a silent snarl. 'Why did you permit that?'

'My permission wasn't sought. She fled to him from my ship.'

'Why haven't you followed her to Kent?'

'In her letter she said she would return to London in a few days. That she would meet me then if I wish to speak to her. She said she could think of nothing but seeing her family again.' Gabriel's throat constricted. He could think of nothing but Athena. She, apparently, was more eager for a reunion with her mother and siblings than to resolve the situation between them. It hurt, even though he knew he deserved no better. The morning of their arrival in London he'd still been fighting a battle with himself—knowing he had to accept Athena's sacrifice on his behalf, but finding it desperately hard to swallow. He should have said more to her before he left the ship, but words hadn't come easily. By the time he'd found the words he needed and had returned, she'd already gone to Swiftbourne.

'She said she hoped for a few happy, peaceful days in her childhood home,' Gabriel continued, talking more to himself than to Kilverdale. 'Then she would return to London. I haven't followed her. I don't want to spoil her peace or happiness. She has said she will return. I must trust her to do as she promises. So I am waiting.'

It had taken all of Gabriel's strength of will to remain in London. Every instinct demanded that he pursue Athena and confront her. No, not to confront her. To fall on his knees and beg her to forgive him for his accusations in Venice and his continuing unspoken suspicions on the journey. Surely she would accept that? She was the one who'd always insisted they couldn't change the past, that they had to go on from where they were now. He knew she was right. The weeks they'd spent together on the ship had been the happiest of his life. The past hadn't mattered an iota. Now all he wanted was the chance to tell her so.

But first he had to show he trusted her, and that he respected her wishes. She had told him she would come back to London. He had doubted her so many times in the past. Now he had to prove beyond all question his faith in her. So he stayed in London and waited. Driven nearly mad by guilt, frustration and need. Surely she would return soon?

After one last piercing look, Kilverdale sheathed his sword. 'In that case you can pour me some burgundy,' he said. 'I won't follow her either. Not if Swiftborne's with her. Is that for Athena?' he added, glancing at the necklace in front of Gabriel.

'Yes.' Gabriel's lips twisted as he remembered the day in Florence when Athena had tried to find out who he'd bought it for. He wished he'd given it to her without delay. Now it would be his betrothal gift to her.

'Nice piece,' said Kilverdale. 'Damn.' He shook his shaggy head. 'I'm in urgent need of a barber. Hardly dare show my face in London, despite this suit of Jakob's.'

'Your Swedish cousin?' Gabriel felt a flicker of curiosity. He was grateful for the distraction. 'Why are you wearing your cousin's clothes?' he asked, pouring Kilverdale some wine.

Athena's reunion with her family was a joyous occasion, but through it all she couldn't stop thinking about Gabriel. The longer she was away from London, the more agitated she became. She'd quickly discovered she missed Gabriel desperately. She had been in his company every day for months and his absence was an aching void she could never completely forget. She couldn't sleep properly without his hard body lying beside her. She dreamed about him. Woke in the night reaching for him, only to find he wasn't there. She didn't want miles of distance between them. She wanted him close. She wanted Gabriel within arm's reach so they could sort out their problems.

But what then? Could she be happy as Gabriel's mistress? She was fairly sure that the worldly-wise Swiftbourne would not suffer a single qualm if she accepted that role. But her mother would be devastated, and her fragile bonds with her brother and sisters might be severed before they'd had a chance to be re-established. She did not think Josiah would look on complacently if she lived openly as Gabriel's mistress.

She was sitting alone in the orchard one hazy afternoon, watching a wasp buzz drunkenly in a fallen apple in the grass near her feet while she worried about her future, when Josiah found her.

'May I?' he said with stiff courtesy.

'Of course.' She hastily pulled her spreading skirts close so he could sit beside her on the bench.

Josiah cleared his throat. 'Your mother is pleased to have you here,' he said.

'I am pleased to be here,' she replied quickly. 'You have all been very kind to me.'

'This is your home,' said Josiah. 'You may stay as long as you wish.'

'Thank you.' Athena was startled and touched by the gruff offer.

They sat in silence for several minutes. Athena sensed Josiah had more to say. Was he going to impose limits on her behaviour? Or demand some kind of restitution for the distress she'd caused? She pressed her fingers together and waited with increasing anxiety.

'I did not see you as a child,' Josiah said, making her jump when he suddenly started to speak. 'You looked like a woman grown when I married your mother. Hardly any different than you look now.'

'I was a woman grown,' Athena said quietly.

'Perhaps. Tabitha is two years older than you were when you married Samuel, yet I would be reluctant to let her marry so young. I would never expect her to wed a man she held in distaste.'

'I…that is very good, very generous of you,' Athena stumbled for words. This was the last thing she had expected her stepfather to say.

'I am sorry,' he said. 'Because I would not listen to you or your mother—she pleaded with me to keep Samuel away from you, but I wouldn't listen—I caused you both great unhappiness. I am sorry.'

'I…we have all survived.' Athena's throat constricted. She couldn't say no harm had been done, because great hurt had been done, not only to her and her mother, but also to Gabriel. But she was very touched by Josiah's apology. She understood now why Tabitha so readily accepted him as her father.

'Thank you.' Impulsively she turned on the seat and put her arms around him. Immediately she'd done so she stiffened, wondering if she'd made an embarrassing mistake. He surprised her again by hugging her back with remarkably little awkwardness.

'I've had more practice with daughters since you left,' he said, correctly interpreting her hesitation. 'Your mother has taught me a lot.' He drew back and patted her hand. 'I hope you will make your home here now. It will please your mother. And perhaps we may find you a husband who pleases you this time.'

Athena's lips trembled as she smiled at him. She'd said as little as possible about her journey back to England. She thought both her mother and Tabitha suspected it had been more eventful than she'd admitted, but apparently neither woman had confided their suspicions to Josiah.

'Thank you,' she said, wondering if she would indeed end up living back in her childhood home. Gabriel hadn't come to find her. She was slowly accepting that he was a lot less eager to see her than she was to see him. In her worst moments she imagined him occupied with business matters every day since she'd left, hardly even noticing her absence. Perhaps his sister had already chosen the perfect wife for him?

London, Sunday 2 September 1666

'More wine, my lord?' Sir Thomas Parfitt held the bottle poised over Gabriel's glass.

Gabriel grinned at his old master. 'No, thank you,' he said.

It was nearly three o'clock in the morning. They'd talked all evening and halfway into the night.

'I did teach you to keep a clear head,' Sir Thomas commented, setting the bottle back on the table.

'Most of the time,' Gabriel agreed, his smile fading. He hadn't been so clear-headed where Athena was concerned, but he would put that right as soon as she returned to London.

'You said your trip was successful?' Parfitt said, studying Gabriel with shrewd eyes.

'It was.' Gabriel shook off his momentary distraction. 'Your nephew has settled well in Livorno. He will be a credit to you—'

'Sir! My lord!' Without warning one of Sir Thomas's young apprentices burst through the door. His feet were bare and he wore only his nightshirt. 'There's a fire! We can see it from the attic.'

'Where? How far away?' Gabriel rose immediately.

Sir Thomas stood up more slowly. There was less spring in his muscles. 'After you, my lord,' he said. 'You remember the way to the attic, I'm sure.'

Gabriel had slept there in the two years before he'd gone to serve Parfitt in Livorno. He recalled the old wooden stairs very well as he followed in the wake of the apprentice. Fires were common and he wasn't greatly alarmed by the news, but the timber buildings of the City were always vulnerable to flames. It was sensible to assess the situation.

'There, my lord.'

Gabriel looked in the direction of the apprentice's pointing finger. The flare of orange was larger than he'd expected, but it was a fair distance from Sir Thomas's Cheapside home.

'Hmph. Can't really tell how far away it is in the dark,' said Sir Thomas, puffing a bit from his climb up the stairs. 'Which street is it, do you think?'

'I'm not sure.' Gabriel stared through narrowed eyes. The wind was blowing strongly and he could smell the smoke. 'I'll go and investigate,' he said, more because he welcomed the distraction than because he thought there was any danger from the distant blaze. He'd prolonged his visit with Sir Thomas because he didn't want to go home to an empty bed, but he couldn't keep his old master talking the whole night through.

'I'd come with you,' said Parfitt. 'But I doubt these old legs could keep pace with you.' He grimaced at the toll the years had taken on his body. 'Let me know what you find. And for God's sake take care!'

Kent, Monday 3 September 1666

'Ah, granddaughter,' Swiftbourne said. He'd found Athena alone in the parlour. She was sitting in the early evening twilight, thinking about Gabriel.

'Were you looking for me, my lord?' She rose politely. She didn't feel the same warmth towards her grandfather that she'd recently discovered for her stepfather, but she was grateful he'd put aside his own affairs so promptly to escort her home.

'Indeed.' He waved her back into the window seat and sat down himself. 'I recall I have a message for you, from Halross,' he said blandly.

'Gabriel?' Her heart leapt at the mention of his name. 'He has sent a message here?' A message was not as good as coming in person, but at least it indicated he was thinking about her.

'No, not here.' Swiftbourne glanced at his sleeve and fastidiously flicked a piece of fluff from the fine velvet. 'He gave it to me in London.'

'In London?' That didn't make any sense to Athena. Gabriel had not been at home when they stopped at his house on their way to Kent. When could he have given Swiftbourne a message?

'A few hours after you first arrived at my house, when you were asleep,' Swiftbourne clarified. 'I am afraid my memory is not what it used to be. In the turmoil of arranging our departure it completely slipped my mind he'd given me a message for you. But now I recall he mentioned something about coming to see you at ten o'clock the next morning.'

Athena gaped at her grandfather, hardly able to comprehend what he'd just said. His meaning slowly sank in.

'Gabriel was coming to see me the next morning at ten o'clock and you insisted we leave London before *nine!*' Her disbelief ballooned into anger.

'How could you?' She sprang to her feet. *'How could you?'*

All this time she had been wondering why Gabriel hadn't followed her. Now she knew why. He had been coming to call upon her and she'd snubbed him in the most insulting way. She hadn't known his intentions and hadn't referred to his planned visit in her letter. Fear mixed with her fury. Without knowing she'd done so, she had given Gabriel another reason to think badly of her.

'Why didn't you tell me? Why did you interfere? Does it give you pleasure to see other people unhappy?' she demanded wildly.

Swiftbourne's expression remained bland, but there was an icy glint in his eyes.

'Remember who you're talking to, girl.'

'I know who you are,' she said angrily. 'And I don't owe you anything. Safe escort here. Nothing else.'

'You may owe me a husband,' Swiftbourne replied. 'The man has the manners of a boar—' the Earl's lips thinned '—but he has wealth and influence. If you don't weaken your hand by throwing yourself into his arms the moment he lifts a finger, he may be sufficiently besotted to marry you.' He stood and strolled out of the parlour, before Athena could utter any of the bitter accusations seething on her tongue.

She had to go back to London. At once. She had to find Gabriel and explain she hadn't received his message. Hadn't known he meant to see her the very next morning. Oh, God, why had she listened to Swiftbourne? She sank her head into her hands, trying to compose herself before she went to tell her mother she was leaving.

'London is on fire!' Tabitha burst into the parlour a few moments later, her eyes round with alarm. 'Lord Swiftbourne has just had a message from Whitehall. The whole of the City is in flames!'

'Fire? The whole City?' Athena was still caught up in her own troubles. She could hardly comprehend this larger catastrophe. Then Swiftbourne came back into the room. There was a grim expression on his usually imperturbable face.

'We'll return to London first thing in the morning,' he said.

As a government minister, he had a duty to be in the capital during this disaster.

Athena wanted to protest. To insist they leave at once. Gabriel was in London. Now it was more urgent than ever that she find him. But she knew it would be foolish—and possibly dangerous—to travel through the night. Gabriel was a man, not a building. He would not stand still in the path of a fire. Besides, he didn't live in the City. His new house was in Fleet Street. Surely he would be safe there?

'At dawn,' she said, her voice so cramped with fear she didn't recognise it. 'At first light. We must leave at first light.'

Chapter Fifteen

Tuesday 4 September 1666

The black pall of smoke above London was visible from more than twenty miles distant. Athena couldn't believe the fire had been burning for two nights and two days before they'd received word of it, but Fairchild Manor was deep in the Kent countryside and it had taken a long time for the messenger to find Swiftbourne. She'd been sitting in the orchard on a perfect late summer's day, watching the wasps in the fallen apples, while in London the houses burned.

It was shocking. Unbelievable. At first she *couldn't* fully believe it. But as they got closer to London the roads grew busier and the rumours wilder. According to Swiftbourne's official message, the fire had started early on Sunday morning, most likely in a baker's shop in Pudding Lane. But the frightened people fleeing the inferno had other, most sinister explanations for the disaster. That it had been deliberately started by the French or the Dutch. Or that it was the work of Papists trying overthrow King and Parliament.

By the time they were close to London Bridge, the scale

of the catastrophe was terrifyingly obvious. Athena stared out of the carriage window, unable to tear her eyes from the approaching horror. The air stank with smoke. A fierce wind whipped up gusts of soot and ash.

Southwark was in chaos, the roads so clogged with traffic that Swiftbourne's carriage slowed to a standstill. London Bridge was impassable, though Athena later discovered it had been saved from destruction because of a break in the houses caused by a fire thirty years earlier. The rest of the City was not so lucky.

Swiftbourne sent his servants to hire a wherry from the river stairs on the west side of the bridge. Athena climbed out of the carriage after her grandfather. Without even the limited protection of the coach, all her senses were assaulted by the roar and stench of the fire raging on the other side of the river. The strong wind plastered her skirts against her legs. She tugged the hood of her cloak over her head for the minimal protection it provided. Swiftbourne's servants ruthlessly made a path for their master through the unruly mob of people while Athena held on to her grandfather's arm, for fear of losing him rather than support, and hurried to keep up. Within a few moments they made it down to wait on the river stairs.

Athena looked up from watching her footing on the slippery stones and had her first, unimpeded view of the fire. Shock momentarily paralysed her. She could see no western limit to the flames raging on the other side of the river. The whole world seemed to be ablaze. Dense black smoke blotted out the sky, hiding the early afternoon sun. Just occasionally a crimson disk would become visible between the roiling darkness, as fiery as the inferno below. A fierce gale drove the flames ever westward, but sometimes a wayward gust would cause glowing sparks to rain down upon the watchers. The fire droplets fell indiscriminately upon the river and the people. An angry ember landed just beneath Athena's collar bone. Trapped against her body it flared into brighter life…

She gasped and knocked it away with her gloved hand.

Dirty water slapped against the river stairs near her feet. Lighters and wherries crashed together on the crowded river. The boats were piled with possessions and people. Watermen cursed in harsh voices. Their passengers cried out with fear and grief at the disaster that had befallen them. People huddled on the piers of London Bridge, a few yards to the right. Most of them tried to keep beneath the arches where there was some protection from the heat and burning debris that swirled at the mercy of the savage winds.

An elbow jabbed Athena in the back and she stumbled and nearly fell on the slippery stones. Her grandfather seized her arm, holding her steady with a strength that belied his years.

'Stay close, girl!'

'My God! It's a scene from *hell!*' Athena inhaled unwarily and caught a lungful of acrid smoke. She coughed, rasping her raw throat. Tears flooded her fire-scalded eyes.

'Cover your face. Don't breathe so deep.' Lord Swiftbourne thrust his handkerchief into her hands. 'We'll be in the boat soon. The smoke is not so thick close to the water.'

Athena pressed the soft cambric to her mouth and nose. By sheer effort of will she resisted the urge to cough and thus drag more burning smoke deep into her body.

'Come.' Lord Swiftbourne hauled her forwards.

She saw the wherry her grandfather's servants had commandeered for their master and she accepted the aid of a footman to climb into it. The boat rocked alarmingly. She sat down, clinging to the edge of the seat with one hand for greater security. She looked up to see Lord Swiftbourne transfer into the boat. Though he was hale and strong, he was less agile than a younger man and he stumbled and collapsed on to the seat with uncharacteristic clumsiness.

A few moments later the oarsmen pushed away from the stairs and the boat bumped up and down on the choppy waters. The pointed stern grated sickeningly against the side of a lighter. The lighterman cursed them. A few minutes later the two-man wherry rowed free of the chaos of the waterside.

From the fragile safety of the boat the magnitude of horror was even more overwhelming. The flames towered above them. The water reflected both the vivid fire and the dark, sunlight-blocking smoke. The surface of the Thames had become a boiling confusion of crimson and black. A river of scorched blood flowing beside the stricken city.

It was only a few days since Athena had seen London basking beneath the haze of August sunshine. It was impossible to grasp the scale of the disaster that had occurred with such shocking suddenness. Almost impossible to believe she really was on the Thames and not being rowed straight into the mouth of hell.

She had been watching the column of smoke and fire for miles, but now they were not travelling towards the inferno but moving parallel to it. The heat was intense. Perspiration mixed with soot on her face. The roar of the flames was a deafening assault upon the ears. The fire seemed like a living beast—a monster—which devoured London in a demonic rage. Smoke and gritty soot swirled around them. Burning debris hissed into the Thames, and sometimes fell on to the occupants of the boats. Athena saw one of her grandfather's footmen knock a hot ember away from an oarsman so he need not interrupt his stroke.

The wherry pulled steadily upstream, tracking the extent of the fire. All the buildings along the entire northern water front were either in flames or crumbling in blackened ruins. Athena gasped when she realised the burnt-out shell on her right was all that remained of Baynard's Castle. She remembered the massive structure from when she'd lived in London. She'd never expected to see it so thoroughly destroyed. She tried to see beyond it, to pierce the flames and smoke to discover the fate of St Paul's—but the effort only hurt her eyes.

And what of the people? She couldn't forget the sight of the terrified souls huddled in the meagre shelter offered by the piers of the bridge. There had been a mother desperately hugging her children to her breasts. Babies crying. Men in despair because their homes and their livelihoods had been destroyed.

Athena blinked tears, which marginally soothed her scorching eyes, but didn't ease her shock and grief. Everyone had been going about their ordinary lives, preoccupied, like her, by their own personal joys and worries. The fire was a brutal reminder of how fragile and uncertain life could be. She wondered how many had died in the flames.

Where was Gabriel? Safe. He had to be safe. She had to find him. She had to tell him that she hadn't known he'd meant to call upon her. That she would never willingly leave him. That she couldn't live without him.

'Cut him down!' Gabriel's harsh command ripped his smoke-damaged throat, but his voice still possessed enough authority to gain the lynch mob's attention.

'He's a cursed papist!'

'Hanging's too good for him!' An angry man with a livid burn on his cheek blocked Gabriel's way. 'I *saw* him throwing fireballs into the tailor's house.' He shoved his soot and bloodstained face right into Gabriel's. *'Let him hang!'* he snarled.

Gabriel shouldered the vengeful man aside, repeating his order to the men of the trained bands who had been assigned to him.

For a few more seconds the man hanging by his neck from the projection of a house continued to jerk spasmodically, legs flailing in the smoke-filled air. Then the rope was cut and he was lowered to the ground.

'He fired the houses. I saw him. He should hang!' The man with the burned cheek continued to rage.

'He'll be questioned before the law. If he's guilty he *will* hang.' Gabriel held the angry man's wild eyes with his own unyielding gaze.

The mob stirred, muttering with dissatisfaction, though their words were lost in the thunder of the approaching fire. The nearest flames were only a few streets away. They wanted immediate revenge for the nightmare that had been visited upon them.

'You have two choices,' Gabriel rasped. 'Seek your own safety—or join in the fight against the fire.'

''Tis the Devil's work,' the man jeered, the expression on his blood and soot-blackened face ugly. 'No man can beat it.'

'Then save your own soul,' Gabriel snapped, stepping away from him.

The man's lips curled back with unreasoning fury, but already the lynching party had disintegrated, individuals putting personal safety above their search for savage justice.

Gabriel gave orders for the intended victim of the lynching to be taken to safety. Then he headed towards the fire, accompanied by two of his men. They stopped abruptly as they reached a position where they could look along Fleet Street. The timber houses at the far end were already alight. The gale swirled around Gabriel, seeming to come from all directions at once. It was so powerful it nearly sucked him towards the fire. He staggered and braced himself against the burning, roaring whirlwind. The militiaman beside him stumbled forward and fell to his knees. Gabriel seized his shoulder, hauling him back on to his feet.

Sulphurous smoke billowed into his face. Then an errant gust of air, like the blast from a furnace, cleared his vision and provided a brief opportunity to take a smoke-free breath. From where Gabriel stood he could see yellow and crimson tongues of flame insinuate themselves almost delicately into the cracks of the wood and plaster buildings.

Then gouts of fire burst from the windows like dragon's breath, destroying all in their path. The dark outline of a man suddenly appeared in front of the lurid flames. He ran before the fire. He was over a hundred yards from where Gabriel stood and far too distant to be given any aid. A thin ribbon of flame extended from the wall of fire, following him as he ran, as if the flames could sense his presence and would not let him escape. Gabriel watched in horror as the man fell—and the pursuing tongue of fire fell back into conformity with the leaping wall of flames.

'It is *alive!*' gasped the militiaman. 'The Devil has taken the form of fire and will eat us all!'

Gabriel jolted himself from his momentary paralysis.

'Not the Devil,' he grated. 'It is the work of man and Nature. But you are right. If we are to stop it we must deny it fodder. *Come!*'

The fire had not yet reached the Strand. Whitehall was safe and Lord Swiftbourne's house in St Martin's Lane quite undamaged. It should have been a relief to step out of the smoke and ash into the quiet normality of the entrance hall, but Athena was too desperate with worry to notice. All along the river she'd tried to track the extent of the fire. Had it reached Fleet Street? Where was Gabriel?

As soon as they entered his house, Swiftbourne was surrounded by lackeys. He was handed letters and several men spoke to him at once. His attention was entirely occupied.

Athena looked at him, stepping impatiently from one foot to another, but she couldn't wait for him to have a spare moment. She dashed back outside, too shocked by the horror all around, and too desperate to find Gabriel, even to think of taking a servant with her.

* * *

'My lord! You mean to blow up your *house!*'

'Yes, Hobb.' Gabriel glanced quickly around, checking that his orders were being obeyed.

'But you only just finished *building* it!' The usually imperturbable Hobb almost wept.

'If it's to be destroyed, then let it be in a good cause,' Gabriel said, raising his voice above the incessant noise of the wind and the fire. But he felt a sharp pang of regret. He'd wanted to show the house to Athena. Hear her comments on it. Ask her opinion on the furnishings. Now she would never see it. But it was a sacrifice that had to be made. It hardly compared to the sacrifice she had made for him.

'We must starve the flames of fuel,' he said. 'Good!' He saw the seamen carrying barrels of gunpowder up from a barge on the river. They were using large pieces of water-soaked canvas to protect their deadly burden from burning debris.

In nearby streets he could hear explosions as other houses were demolished. The King and the Duke of York had been indefatigable in their efforts to extinguish, or at least to contain, the conflagration. Now all efforts were being put forth to protect Westminster and Whitehall.

Barrels of gunpowder were placed in the ground-floor chambers of his new house and in the somewhat less magnificent houses of his neighbours. Gabriel gave orders for every one to move into positions of safety.

Athena had been driven into the ash-clogged streets by instinct, not logic. A frantic, uncontrollable need to find Gabriel. Huge flakes of ash whirled around her. Stinking smoke hurt her chest and temporarily blinded her. She paused on a street corner to make sure of her direction. She knew the way to Gabriel's house, but the streets looked so different in the swirling ash and gusting smoke. It would be easy to become disorientated. Although she was almost completely overwhelmed by the hell-on-earth around her, she still knew she couldn't afford to get lost.

The area around the houses had been cleared of people. Three houses were to be destroyed. Gabriel and two of the steadiest of the seamen had simultaneously lit the lengths of slow match, which had been thrust into the barrels of gunpowder. They'd all run for cover, spurred on by fear of the imminent explosions.

Then Gabriel saw a woman suddenly burst through the smoke, rushing along the street towards his house. He shouted at her to go back, but she didn't hear him. Her bent arm was raised to protect her face, and her head was covered with a protective hood.

But he recognised her. As she stumbled up the steps into his open front door he shouted her name.

'*Athena!*'

The strength of desperation surged through his body. He lunged forward. How many seconds before the burning slow match reached the gunpowder?

'Gabriel! *Gabriel!*' She was opening doors, frantically screaming his name. She didn't seem to notice that the house was empty of all furniture and people. Or, if she had, it only added to her panic.

'Athena!' Gabriel grabbed her.

She turned into his arms, but there was no time for talk or explanations. The house shook as an explosion roared through a neighbour. The tremor knocked Gabriel and Athena to the floor, large pieces of plaster falling from the ceiling. Dust choked the air.

Gabriel shoved to his feet, hauling Athena over his shoulder as he did so. His house would be next. With his head down, his muscles burning, he pounded out of the door and kept on running. Diving for the relative safety of a house corner further down the street that had not yet been planted with gunpowder.

A series of explosions shook the ground. Gabriel staggered forward and collapsed on to his knees. By exerting his last ounce of muscular control he managed to lay Athena down, rather than dropping her on the ash-covered cobbles. He braced himself over her on his hands and knees while gritty dust blew around him in violent eddies.

'Athena? *Athena?*' His voice was hoarse with desperation. Fear clutched his gut. She was covered in dust and grime. Her lips were cracked and dry. Her skin so ashy grey. She couldn't be hurt. Dear God, how would he live if she was dead?

She opened her eyes and stared up at him. For a moment she looked dazed, then she focused on his face.

'Gabriel?' she whispered. Then she burst out crying and threw her arms around him.

Tears of relief filled his own eyes and he held her close, overwhelmed with gratitude that she was safe in his arms. He had been so afraid she might never return to him. Then, after the fire started, he'd thanked God she wasn't in London. Now he sat on the dirty cobbles, buried his face in her hair and rocked her gently, oblivious to the pandemonium all around them.

'You weren't there.' Athena clung to Gabriel, still shaken by remnants of the utter despair that had consumed her when she'd discovered Gabriel's house was empty.

'I'm here now.' His arms tightened around her.

They were sitting in a boat on the bank of the Thames. The river was full of vessels of all types and sizes loaded with people and possessions. Angry shouts and the occasional wail of fear filled the air, but Athena noticed none of that.

She stared into Gabriel's smoke-grimed face, needing the assurance of being able to see him as well as feel his arms around her.

She touched his cheek. 'You're safe,' she whispered, and started to cry again.

He kissed her in a fierce confirmation that he was alive and that he wanted her. It was not a long or a sensual kiss. Athena's throat was raw from smoke and the uncontrollable paroxysms of coughing she couldn't suppress. Gabriel's voice was so hoarse she was sure his throat felt just as bad. But it was still the most wonderful kiss he'd ever given her.

He pulled her closer, her head on his shoulder.

'I'm sorry,' he said, against her hair. 'I'm sorry. You were right. The past is gone. It's the future that counts. The future… My God, I was so frightened you wouldn't come back to me… I'll never let you out of my sight again…'

The simple sound of Gabriel's voice—the fact that he was alive, unharmed and holding her—was more important to Athena than his actual words. Now that she was safely in his arms she began to realise she had been foolish to give way to such unthinking panic. Of course he had escaped the fire. He was too clever and resourceful to let it catch him. But things had gone so badly wrong for them before that it had been easy to fear the worst.

'Forgive me,' he said hoarsely. 'Please forgive me.'

'Forgive you?' Athena lifted her head.

'I should have saved you from Samuel,' Gabriel said. The self-recrimination in his voice was unmistakable, despite the smoke-inflicted rasp. 'I should have *known* as soon as I saw you, that you were with him under duress. Oh, God, sweetheart, how can you ever forgive me for blaming you and accusing you when you did it to save my life?'

'Gabriel.' Athena took his face between her hands and looked into his eyes. 'I love you,' she said softly. 'I did it because I loved you. I've never stopped loving you. I would do it again if I had to…'

He uttered a choke of denial. She saw tears in his eyes that owed nothing to the irritation of the fire.

'Wouldn't you have done the same for me?' she asked.

He stared at her, distracted by the question. 'I would protect you with my life,' he said fervently.

She smiled slightly and stroked his face tenderly. 'I know that, love,' she said softly. 'You just proved it. So you see—'

'I've done something harder than that,' he interrupted. 'I stayed in London, waiting for you to return. It took all my strength not to follow you and drag you back. But I had to show you I trusted you. You'd promised to come back, so I waited. I didn't expect you to run into my house just before it blew up,' he added. He tried to say the last comment lightly, but Athena heard the unsteadiness in his voice and felt the tremor in his arms before he tightened his hold on her.

'I'm sorry.' She stroked his cheek to soothe him. 'I don't think I was being very sensible. Swiftbourne didn't tell me until yesterday that you were going to call on me at ten o'clock. I was so angry with him. And so frightened you'd think I'd left London on purpose to slight you. I'd been hoping you'd follow me despite my letter. And then I realised why you hadn't. All I could think was that I *had* to find you.'

'I didn't stay here because I believed you'd slighted me,' Gabriel said with a shaken laugh. 'I thought you wanted me to prove I trusted you to come back. I nearly followed you a hundred times. And now you are here, I don't have a house to keep you in.'

'Oh, your beautiful house. I never had a chance to see it.' Athena started to cry again.

'Sweetheart, it was only a house. Bricks and mortar.'

'I know.' Athena tried to compose herself. 'I'm not really crying for the house,' she said. She hiccoughed and laughed a little at herself. 'Though I'm very sorry you've lost it. It looked so fine. But it is easier to cry for the house than to think of what we might have lost if we hadn't found each other again. I couldn't bear it if—'

'We haven't lost each other,' Gabriel interrupted. 'My love is deeper now than it was when I asked you to marry me the first time. We have overcome so many obstacles.' He kissed her, then added fervently. 'You're going to marry me as soon as I can arrange it. I will accept nothing else,'

Athena smiled at him through her tears. 'Of course I'll marry you,' she said.

'Where the hell did you go? I've got men out searching for you.' Swiftbourne sounded angry and more disturbed than Athena had ever believed possible.

'I'm sorry.' She felt a pang of guilt at his gaunt expression. He seemed to have aged years in the short time since she'd last seen him. 'I went—'

'I know where you went.' Swiftbourne threw a quick glance at Gabriel, as he stood behind her, his hands resting supportively on her waist. 'I know where you went. It was obvious. I sent men to Halross's house first. They came back with the news it was destroyed.'

'They must also have told you I pulled her out before the explosion,' Gabriel said, guiding Athena to a chair.

Swiftbourne poured two glasses of wine and gave them to Gabriel who, in turn, gave one to Athena. She sipped and immediately coughed as it caught in her throat.

'Perhaps water?' Gabriel suggested.

Swiftbourne strode to the door and gave a curt order to a footman standing in the hall.

'I assumed you'd have her safe,' he said, coming back into the room. 'I thought you'd get here sooner. You've no roof to keep her under any longer.'

'None of us may have a roof if the fire is not contained,' Gabriel said.

'You blew up your house to save others,' Swiftbourne said.

'If I hadn't, it would have burned anyway. It's not important. I have all that really matters.' Gabriel put his hand on Athena's shoulder.

Swiftbourne glanced between them. Just for a moment his grim expression lightened. 'We're to have a Marchioness in the family, I presume,' he said.

'Of course.' Gabriel's voice took on a haughty note. 'Did you think I'd offer anything less? Though it is she who has done me the honour of accepting,' he added in a softer tone.

Athena squeezed his hand as it rested on her shoulder, then lifted it to press against her cheek, but her eyes were on her grandfather.

'My lord, why are you so agitated?' she asked. She was sure Swiftbourne's perturbation was caused by more than her absence. She was back now, yet the deep lines of strain on his face had barely lifted.

'Jakob is missing,' he said brusquely.

'Jakob? I didn't even know he was in England,' she exclaimed.

'He came on the packet boat with Kilverdale,' Gabriel told her quickly. 'Kilverdale rode ahead and Jakob was to follow. What do you mean, he is missing, my lord?'

'Not missing, a prisoner,' said Swiftbourne. 'He was confined to Newgate on Saturday. He sent a message here, but I only received it when I arrived this afternoon.'

'He's been a prisoner for three days?' Athena said, stunned at the notion. She could not imagine any conceivable reason why Jakob, a man of honour and integrity, could have been thrown in goal. 'Why?' Then she felt the cold bite of fear in her stomach. 'What of Newgate?' she demanded urgently.

'It has already burned,' Gabriel replied, his grip on her shoulder tightening.

'But they can't have let the prisoners burn?' She looked at her grandfather in horror. 'Can they?'

Before Swiftbourne could answer there was a thunderous knocking at the front door. The next moment the parlour door crashed open and Kilverdale strode into the room.

'Jack!' Athena gasped. She jumped up and ran straight into his arms.

Gabriel's gut tightened. This was the image that had tortured him for so many weeks. Kilverdale's dark head bowed over Athena's fair one. He felt an instinctive urge to wrench Athena out of her cousin's arms, but then the impulse dissolved. His jealousy had been the direct result of Samuel's cruel meddling. Now he was sure of Athena's love, the doubts that had eaten him for so long had vanished. He watched, unperturbed, as Kilverdale hugged Athena.

After a few moments Kilverdale put his hands on her shoulders and held her away from him.

'Are you hurt?' he demanded. 'How the devil did you get covered with soot? Why are you crying?'

'I'm not hurt. Jakob—'

'Is he here?'

'No. Jack, he was in Newgate!'

'I know.' Kilverdale looked over her head at his grandfather.

'I see you have broken your vow never to step over my threshold,' Swiftbourne observed. 'I am gratified you hold my heir in such high esteem.'

Gabriel saw the expression in Kilverdale's eyes change from hard-edged concern to scornful hostility.

'I'm looking for Jakob,' the Duke said. 'I don't give a damn whose heir he is.'

'How do you know he was in Newgate?' Gabriel asked.

'He sent a message to my house in Putney. I wasn't there.' Kilverdale rubbed a hand across his brow. 'I only returned home this morning. I thought he might have sent a message here.'

'He did,' Swiftbourne said. 'But we only arrived a couple of hours ago.'

'If he's not here, and Newgate has already burned, then where the hell is he?' Kilverdale said, his impatience a poor disguise for his worry.

'I've sent to discover where the prisoners were taken,' said Swiftbourne. 'When I receive the answer we'll know more.'

Kilverdale acknowledged his grandfather's comment with a curt nod, but turned his attention once more to Athena.

'Has he asked you yet?' he demanded, with a hard glance at Gabriel. 'If he hasn't, I'll cut his liver out for you.'

'No!' Athena clutched Kilverdale's sword arm in alarm. 'You mustn't fight. I'm going to marry him.'

'Good.' Kilverdale looked her over again, taking in her torn clothes and the minor grazes on her face, as well as her soot and tearstained face. 'He's not doing a very good job of taking care of you,' he said, frowning. 'Perhaps we shouldn't be too hasty. I'm sure I can find someone else to ma—'

'No.' Gabriel stepped forward and reclaimed Athena, before Kilverdale could complete his offer to find her another husband. 'She will be my wife as soon as we can make it so.'

Kilverdale looked at Athena and she nodded, wrapping her arms possessively around Gabriel so that there could be no doubt about her sentiments.

'Good,' said the Duke. 'That's one cousin safely sorted out. Now, where the hell is Jakob? And how the Devil did he manage to get himself put in gaol?'

He spun on his heel as a messenger came into the room to tell Swiftbourne where the Newgate prisoners had been taken. Thirty seconds later Kilverdale was on his way to the front door.

It occurred to Gabriel, as he strode after the Duke, that Kilverdale was not a man who wasted much time on unnecessary thoughts or words.

'I'll come with you,' he said. He didn't know Jakob, but

he knew that Athena was deeply concerned about her cousin. He'd do anything to spare her worry.

Kilverdale stopped and looked at him, then glanced at Athena, standing with her hands tightly clasped together. For a moment his hawklike features softened.

'Stay with her,' he said. 'It doesn't require two of us to pursue this information. Athena is your first responsibility now. She'll worry if you're out of her sight.'

Without another word he walked out through the open door and disappeared into the smoke-filled street. The porter closed the door as Gabriel took Athena into his arms.

'I hope Jakob is safe,' she whispered.

'If he has anything in common with you and Kilverdale, I'm sure he will be,' Gabriel comforted her. 'You and your cousin both have a rare talent for surviving in difficult situations. Except when you run into a building seconds before it blows up,' he added, with a lurch of remembered horror.

'I only did it because I love you.' She hugged him tightly.

'I know. Is Jakob in love?'

'I don't believe so.' Athena looked up, puzzled by the question.

'Then I am sure he is quite safe,' Gabriel said confidently. 'His mind will be clear and cool. And he won't have any reason to put himself in unnecessary danger.'

'You're right.' Athena sighed with relief at Gabriel's sensible comment. She rested her head against his shoulder and relaxed into his embrace. She felt as if she had finally come home.

'Nothing and nobody will come between us now,' said Gabriel softly, echoing her thoughts. 'And together we can conquer any problem.'

* * * * *

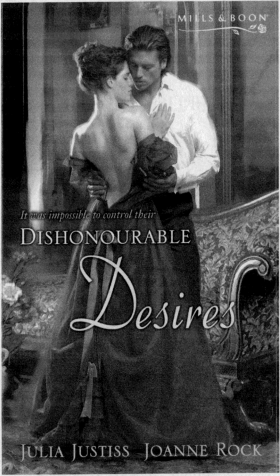

MILLS & BOON

It was impossible to control their

DISHONOURABLE

Desires

JULIA JUSTISS JOANNE ROCK

On sale 5th August 2005

Available at most branches of WHSmith, Tesco, ASDA, Martins,
Borders, Eason, Sainsbury's and all good paperback bookshops.

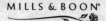

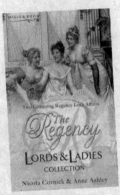

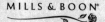

MILLS & BOON®

The *Regency*

LORDS & LADIES
COLLECTION

Two glittering Regency
love affairs in every book

Available at most branches of WH Smith, Tesco, ASDA, Martins, Borders,
Eason, Sainsbury's and all good paperback bookshops.

REG/L&L/LIST

2 FREE

BOOKS AND A SURPRISE GIFT!

We would like to take this opportunity to thank you for reading this Mills & Boon® book by offering you the chance to take TWO more specially selected titles from the Historical Romance™ series absolutely FREE! We're also making this offer to introduce you to the benefits of the Reader Service™—

- ★ FREE home delivery
- ★ FREE gifts and competitions
- ★ FREE monthly Newsletter
- ★ Exclusive Reader Service offers
- ★ Books available before they're in the shops

Accepting these FREE books and gift places you under no obligation to buy, you may cancel at any time, even after receiving your free shipment. Simply complete your details below and return the entire page to the address below. You don't even need a stamp!

YES! Please send me 2 free Historical Romance books and a surprise gift. I understand that unless you hear from me, I will receive 4 superb new titles every month for just £3.65 each, postage and packing free. I am under no obligation to purchase any books and may cancel my subscription at any time. The free books and gift will be mine to keep in any case.

H5ZED

Ms/Mrs/Miss/Mr ....Initials ....
BLOCK CAPITALS PLEASE

Surname ....

Address ....

....

....Postcode..

Send this whole page to:
UK: FREEPOST CN81, Croydon, CR9 3WZ